Ali McNamara attributes her overactive imagination to one thing – being an only child. Time spent dreaming up adventures when she was young has left her with a head bursting with stories waiting to be told. When stories she wrote for fun on Ronan Keating's website became so popular they were sold as a fundraising project for his cancer awareness charity, Ali realised that writing was not only something she enjoyed doing, but something others enjoyed reading too. Ali lives in Cambridgeshire with her family and beloved Labrador dogs.

To find out more about Ali visit her website at:
www.alimcnamara.co.uk

Follow her on Twitter and Instagram: @AliMcNamara
Or like her Facebook page: Ali McNamara

Kate and Clara's Curious Cornish Craft Shop

Ali McNamara

SPHERE

First published in Great Britain in 2020 by Sphere

5 7 9 10 8 6 4

A CIP catalogue record for this book
is available from the British Library.

ISBN 978-0-7515-7433-3

Typeset in Caslon by M Rules
Printed and bound in Great Britain by Clays Ltd, Elcograf S.p.A.

Papers used by Sphere are from well-managed forests
and other responsible sources.

MIX
Paper from
responsible sources
FSC® C104740

Sphere
An imprint of
Little, Brown Book Group
Carmelite House
50 Victoria Embankment
London EC4Y 0DZ

An Hachette UK Company
www.hachette.co.uk

www.littlebrown.co.uk

This is the first full novel I've written since my M.E. diagnosis, so I'd like to dedicate it to all my fellow 'Spoonie Warriors', their families and those who care for them.

Keep fighting and believing. We'll get there in the end.

One

'I don't get it?' my daughter says as she stares up at the huge, brightly coloured canvas on the wall in front of us. 'It's like something I did when I was little, and you stuck on the fridge for everyone to see.'

I have to agree with her but, wary of where we are, I choose my words carefully.

'It's called modern art,' I whisper, 'Not everyone gets it.'

'Do *you* get it?' Molly asks, still in a voice a little too loud for my liking. 'And more to the point, do you think it's any good?'

A few people standing nearby turn their intense gaze away from the artwork in front of them towards our direction.

'Molly, you need to keep your voice down,' I whisper again, not answering her question. 'Art galleries are a bit like libraries – people don't want to be disturbed while they study things.'

Molly folds her arms. 'In a library people actually want to take the books home. I can't see anyone wanting to take a series of blue blobs home again and again, can you, Mum?'

I open my mouth to agree with her, but a refined female

voice speaks first. 'As a matter of fact this painting is one of our most popular exhibits. Our shop sells more postcards, prints and bags reproduced from this one work of art than any other in the whole gallery.'

I look at the woman standing next to us. I've seen her around the town from time to time, flouncing about in brightly coloured scarves and layers of mismatched clothing.

'You obviously work here,' I reply politely. 'I thought I'd seen you around St Felix.'

'I'm one of the curators at the gallery,' she replies self-importantly. 'I'm in charge of the new Winston James exhibition. I assume you're here for the opening tonight?'

She looks us up and down as though she's wondering if we'd been wrongly invited.

'Yes, we are,' I say, pulling the invitation from my bag.

The woman takes it from me and examines it carefully. 'Ah,' she says knowingly. 'Local business, are you? That makes sense.'

'Yes,' I say, snatching back the invitation from her. 'I own Kate's Cornish Crafts on Harbour Street. We sell art and craft supplies,' I emphasise when she looks blankly at me.

'*Mmm*,' the woman says, quickly losing interest in us as some more people arrive through the main gallery doors. 'The party is through there.' She points vaguely in the direction of some heavy glass doors. 'Do enjoy your evening.' Then she scurries over towards a large man wearing a long black trench coat and a matching black trilby hat with a green feather. '*Julian!* How wonderful you could make it!' she gushes, air-kissing the man on both cheeks.

'Come on,' I tell Molly as she grins with amusement at the eccentric group of people following Julian through the

2

door. 'The sooner we get this party over with, the sooner we can go home.'

'Kate!' a young woman calls with delight a short while later, as Molly and I stand awkwardly with our complimentary drinks gazing at the people around us. Some of them we recognise as fellow St Felix residents, and some of them seem to be distinctly different from the usual out-of-town visitor yet seem to fit in extremely well with the art gallery surrounding.

'Poppy!' I call back, pleased to see one of my fellow Harbour Street shop owners. 'How are you? I haven't seen you in a while.'

'I haven't been in the flower shop much lately.' Poppy grimaces. 'Morning sickness,' she explains, patting her tummy.

'You're expecting again?' I ask with delight. 'How wonderful.'

'I certainly am!' Poppy replies looking pleased. 'Hopefully now I'm past twelve weeks I should start feeling a little better like last time. 'Hello Molly,' she says, spotting her. 'Having a good time?'

Molly shrugs. 'It's okay.'

Poppy grins. 'You remind me of my stepdaughter Bronte. She would have said something similar at your age, being dragged somewhere like this by one of her parents.'

Molly looks awkwardly at Poppy.

'It's wonderful news about the baby, Poppy,' I tell her. 'I didn't know you were expecting again.'

'Jake and I are only just telling people now it's safe to do so. Actually I think it's taken Jake all these weeks to get his head around the fact he's going to be a father again.'

'This will be his ... fourth child, won't it?'

'Yup, second by me. The first two are hardly children any more now. Bronte is twenty and Charlie is twenty-two.'

'Bronte is at art college, isn't she? I think she popped in to

3

buy a sketch-book from us once, but I don't think she was very impressed by our somewhat limited range.'

'You can't stock everything, can you?' Poppy says pragmatically. 'Most of the shops are pretty small in St Felix. You're lucky you have that extra basement to trade from. I'm sure Bronte found something in your shop that she could use – she never stops sketching.' Poppy leans in towards me. 'Her stuff is a lot better than most of the so-called art hanging on these walls. It's a bit ... *childish*, isn't it?'

'I guess, but it's better than some of the pieces in the other rooms. It looks like someone has just thrown paint at some of the canvases through there. At least you can tell what these paintings are.'

'That's true,' Poppy agrees. 'I'm only really here to show support for the gallery tonight, aren't you? It's great they've got it back up and running again after all the renovations. We always see an upsurge in visitors when this place is open. It seems there are a lot of people who appreciate modern art more than I do!'

I smile. Poppy never minces her words and I admire her honesty. 'It's good to know there will be more visitors soon then. I wouldn't really know – the gallery has been closed since I opened my shop.'

Poppy thinks about this. 'Yes, it must have been, I suppose. I'd forgotten it had been closed so long. You came here what ... twelve months ago?'

'Eighteen. They'd just closed the gallery for renovation when I first arrived.'

'Gosh, that long? How times flies.'

There's a clinking sound of someone tapping a wine glass with a spoon, and the room hushes as we all turn towards the noise.

4

'Ladies and gentlemen.' It's the woman from earlier. 'If I could have your attention for a few moments, please.' She waits for the entire room to quieten before she begins. 'Thank you. My name, as most of you will know, is Ophelia Fitzpatrick and I am Chief Curator here at the Lyle Gallery. As you know our magnificent gallery has only just opened again after our extensive, and if I may say, rather fabulous refurbishment, so I'm sure that this is the first time some of you have visited us since then. I'm certain you will all agree that the renovations have been more than worthwhile, and the gallery is now even more stunning than ever.' She gestures at our surroundings and there's a small ripple of applause. 'I'm sure you will also concur though that a gallery, however architecturally amazing, is only as good as the artwork it contains and, as many of you will have seen tonight, we have some incredible works of art on permanent display here.'

'Incredible isn't the word I'd use,' Poppy mutters next to me, and Molly grins approvingly across at her.

'But I am simply overjoyed,' Ophelia continues, 'that our very first *special* exhibition to be displayed here in the Lyle Gallery is by a local artist who lived and worked here in St Felix in the nineteen fifties. I'm certain you've all been appreciating and admiring his many works of art that we're proud to be displaying on our walls, but if you haven't because you've all been too busy enjoying yourselves, then I urge you to allow yourselves to be captivated and enthralled by them before you leave us tonight. But before you all rush off to do just that, it is my immense pleasure to introduce to you someone who can tell you much more about both these wonderful paintings and the artist himself. May I welcome to the stage someone who knew Winston James better than most – his son, Julian!'

Ophelia breaks out into enthusiastic applause, and the room joins in with a slightly more muted response as the same man we'd seen outside earlier wearing a hat and coat, now sporting a tailor-made navy-blue suit, pale blue shirt and a cravat with white polka dots, springs up on to the tiny temporary stage next to her. He kisses her extravagantly on both cheeks and then confidently takes the small microphone from her tight grip.

'Thank you, Ophelia!' he says, gesturing for her to step down from the stage, leaving no one in any doubt that it was now his turn in the spotlight.

'Greetings, friends!' Julian James calls out enthusiastically to the room.

I glance warily at Molly, but she's already grinning and holding her phone up that little bit higher so she can record this.

I put my hand over the camera lens.

'*Mum!*'

I shake my head at her. Scowling, she lowers her phone.

'May I call you friends?' Julian enquires, a concerned expression falling over his chiselled features. 'My father was so very much a part of life here in St Felix for so many years that I feel you are all his friends and family, and therefore mine too.'

Poppy snorts next to me and hurriedly takes another sip of her orange juice to conceal her amusement.

Julian seems to sense some dissent in the crowd and looks with concern in our direction. A disarming smile is immediately cast my way.

I smile politely back.

'You're in there,' Poppy mutters, nudging me.

'I hardly think so,' I say, pulling a face. 'I do have some standards.'

'He must be loaded though,' Poppy whispers with

6

amusement. 'Now the painter dad isn't around any more the dough must all be his. If you can get past the silly facial hair and the dodgy voice, it's all yours.'

'*Stop it!*' I hiss, trying not to laugh.

'St Felix was such a huge part of my father's life for so many years,' Julian continues, 'which is why he loved to paint it in his own unique way.' He gestures to one of the paintings behind him. 'So I know how utterly thrilled he would have been to know that all his St Felix paintings are being displayed here at the Lyle Gallery this summer for both you, the locals, and all of St Felix's many visitors to admire.' We raise our hands to applaud but Julian continues: 'In fact, I'm sure many of you small business owners will very soon be thanking my father that there will be even more visitors to the town this summer as a result of this exhibition, so I ask you to raise your glasses in appreciation of the genius that was, and still is, Mr Winston James!'

'He almost had me there,' Poppy says, as we half-heartedly raise our drinks, 'but then he told us how grateful we should be, and while I agree that the visitors are a bonus for all of us, he's a bit pretentious, isn't he?'

'He does seem very full of himself,' I say, looking around for Molly who seems to have slipped off somewhere.

'His pomposity is spilling out of the top of his head,' Poppy says in her usual direct way. 'Oh, do excuse me, Kate, I've just seen Rita over there. I need to speak to her about some flowers we're supplying for a wedding reception at The Merry Mermaid. Back in a bit.'

Poppy waves at Rita and then weaves her way through the crowd of attendees, many of whom now seem to be clambering to speak to Julian.

Where *has* Molly gone? I think again, looking around me. It wasn't like her to wander off.

Actually I have to admit to myself, it *was* more like her these days. Since Molly had become a teenager a few years ago she'd changed – not physically, she was still small and wiry, but in other ways. Now she dressed in jeans, heavy boots and T-shirts with bold emblems on them. However, it wasn't really her appearance that made the difference, it was that she was becoming ever more independent.

Feeling even more awkward standing on my own with no one to talk to I turn towards the painting nearest to me and pretend to examine it closely.

Poppy is right: the style is a bit childish at first glance. *St Felix Harbour at Dusk* it says on the little name tag underneath the picture.

Hmm ... I guess it is, I think, looking more closely at the canvas. It was easy to recognise the town's distinctive harbour with the small lighthouse at the end, and in front of that the whitewashed stone cottages that still line the edge of the harbour, now mostly shops, cafés and holiday accommodation rather than homes for fishing families as they were in the fifties. However, the perspective of the picture seemed off – a deliberate trait perhaps? Also, the artist had used really basic lines and brush-strokes to complete his work – making it look very much like a toddler's view of the fishing village I now called home.

'One of my father's favourites,' a deep rounded voice says over my shoulder.

I spin around and find Julian James standing a little closer to me than I feel comfortable with. He's holding a glass of red wine and he takes a long slow sip of it as he waits for my response.

'Really?' I enquire politely, turning back to the painting. 'Why was that?'

'Isn't it obvious?' Julian says, leaning closer to the painting and to me.

'Perhaps you could enlighten me?'

The smell of expensive aftershave and red wine fills my nostrils as I await what I expect will be a very long reply about the quality of the light, masterful brush-strokes, depth and feelings.

'It was one of his bestsellers!' Julian laughs, so I turn back towards him. 'There has been more merch made of this little beauty than any of his others.'

'Merch?'

'Merchandise!' He rubs his fingers together. 'And where there's merchandise there's money! Lots of money!'

'Ah, I see,' I reply, wondering if I could dislike Julian any more than I already do. 'I'm sure your father didn't ever think about his paintings being commercial when he created them though, did he?' I look at the picture again. Next to Julian's materialism it suddenly seems so pure and innocent. I couldn't imagine that anyone who had created a work of art as naive as this would have been so mercenary as to anticipate the money he might make from it.

'Are you kidding? My father was the most extravagant, reckless spendthrift I've ever known. He loved splashing his cash around. The more the better as far as he was concerned.'

'You paint a fine picture of him,' I say wryly.

'Ah . . .' Julian waves his finger at me. 'I see what you did there. You're quite the clever little birdie, aren't you?'

'I try,' I reply politely, wishing someone would come and whisk either myself or Julian away so I had to endure his

9

company no more. Why did no one want to speak to him suddenly? You couldn't get near him a few minutes ago.

'So what do you do here?' Julian asks. 'I believe some of the guests here tonight are local businessmen and, of course, women,' he adds, waving his hand graciously in my direction. 'Are you one of the aforementioned?'

'Yes, I own one of the shops on Harbour Street,' I tell him proudly. 'It's a craft shop. Kate's Cornish—'

'How nice,' Julian interrupts, not sounding the least bit interested. 'Your very own shop.'

'*I'm* very proud of it.'

'I'm sure. Here,' Julian says deftly, reaching into his pocket, 'why don't you take my card? Perhaps you'd like to give me a ring some time. We can chat business and *other* things …' He winks suggestively and I almost vomit. 'I'm often down in Cornwall. I have a holiday home here as well as a luxury villa in the South of France.' He continues listing his properties as if it goes without saying. 'Plus a flat in South London, but I doubt you get up to the Big Smoke too much, do you? It's quite the journey from here.'

'No,' I reply, taking his card. I want to say so much more but I bite my tongue, I don't want to create a scene. 'I don't get to the South of France much either. Taunton is usually my limit before I get jet lag.'

'Shame,' Julian carries on merrily, not realising what I'm saying. 'Travelling is what I love to do most, you see … Oh … very clever! Jet lag – I get it.'

'*Julian!*' Ophelia calls, hurrying over to us to my immense relief. 'There you are. You really must meet … Oh, you again,' she says, not even trying to hide the disdain in her voice as she sees me. 'Are you having a … pleasant evening?'

10

'I am indeed,' I say brightly, spying the perfect opportunity to get one up. 'I've seen some *wonderful* paintings, and I've just been invited to stay in a luxury villa in the South of France to talk *business* ...' I tap Julian's card casually against the palm of my hand so Ophelia can clearly see it, while I cast what I hope is a dazzling smile in his direction. 'I'd say that's pretty pleasant for a Tuesday evening, wouldn't you?'

'I'll be in touch,' I say to a smug-looking Julian as I take my chance to escape them both. 'Bye, Ophelia. Thanks for an utterly *unique* evening.' Astounded, she stares at me blankly. Then I turn and walk away from them as quickly as I can, knowing that if I ever see either of them again it will be far too soon, and that my being 'in touch' with Julian is about as likely as a seagull *not* stealing a tourist's Cornish pasty this summer.

Two

'I'm going to take Barney for a walk, Anita!' I call down the stairs of the shop. 'Could you or Sebastian come up for a while?'

I attach Barney's red leather lead to his collar, and he looks up at me appreciatively so I rub behind his blond ears just where he likes it and he nuzzles my hand.

'Don't get too excited,' I tell him, 'We're only going for a quick wander – I've got sewing to do later.'

Anita appears at the top of the stairs closely followed by her younger colleague Sebastian.

'You don't both need to come up,' I tell them. 'I won't be gone long.'

'Tea break!' Sebastian says, clutching theatrically at his throat. 'Gasping for a cuppa, aren't we, Anita?'

Anita nods her grey head in agreement. 'We've unpacked most of the delivery now. There are just a few fiddly bits left – crochet hooks, packets of embroidery needles … that kind of thing, but that won't take long.'

'You two got on with that quickly!' I say, amazed they've unpacked so many of the boxes we'd had delivered to the shop earlier in the day. It was a delivery of craft equipment so the majority of it was fiddly little things that took ages to hang on the wooden rails or stack on the glass shelves downstairs.

'We don't mess around when we get going, do we, Anita?' Sebastian says, putting his young arm around Anita's much older shoulders. 'We're a great team!'

'We are when you stop nattering for a minute or two,' Anita says good-naturedly, patting the hand on her shoulder affectionately.

Barney tugs a little at his lead. 'All right, I'm coming,' I tell him. 'I'll be back in a bit. Molly might be in from school before we get back. If she is, tell her she can have no more than fifteen minutes down here in the shop before she gets on with her homework upstairs. I know you'll be tempting her with some of your homemade cake, Anita.'

Anita smiles. 'Ah, but she deserves it. She's a good girl.'

'I know she is, but I also know she'd much rather spend her time down here with you two than upstairs doing schoolwork.'

'How did the pair of you get on at the gallery last night?' Anita asks. 'I heard it was a good turn-out.'

'Yes, it was packed – you could hardly move. Amazing what a couple of free drinks and a vol-au-vent can attract. The exhibition was okay, I suppose, if you like that sort of thing. The paintings weren't really my cup of tea. I should probably have given you the tickets, Sebastian.'

Sebastian is a student at an art college in London most of the year, but in the holidays he returns home to St Felix to live with his parents, and when he does he helps me out in the shop. We're so much busier in the summer months that I can just about afford to employ two part-time members of staff.

Sebastian shrugs. 'Nah, you're all right. I've been to the gallery plenty of times. I don't really know much about Winston James as it goes ... was his work any good?'

I wrinkle my nose. 'Good isn't a word I'd use to describe it ... childlike maybe?'

'Surely you mean *naive*, darling!' Sebastian says with a flourish of his hands. 'That's what the critics always say when something looks like it's been painted by a three-year-old.'

I loved that about Sebastian – even though he was an art student himself he never really behaved like one. He wasn't 'airy fairy' as Anita had suggested he might be when I told her I was hiring him last summer. He called a spade a spade and I admired his honesty. Yes, he was lively and a bit over the top at times, but he had a good heart, was a hard worker and the customers loved him.

'I'm sure that word would most definitely have been bandied about last night,' I say, winking at him. 'Okay, Barney!' I tell the golden Labrador nosing into my leg, 'I really am coming this time.'

'Before you go, Kate,' Anita says, 'I forgot to tell you – Noah called in earlier from the antiques shop. He says he might have something of interest to you.'

'Really?' I ask, wondering what on earth Noah could have that I might want. 'Right, thanks. I'll pop in after Barney's walk.'

Barney and I leave Anita and Sebastian to their tea and no doubt a good gossip, and we make our way quickly along the street down towards the harbour.

I'm very lucky to have found such good staff to help me out. Originally it had just been Anita and myself, and she had sort of come with the premises. Before I became the tenant it had

14

been an old-fashioned wool shop owned by a little old lady called Wendy, who had also lived above the store like Molly and I do now.

From what I'd heard, Wendy and Anita used to run the place like a gossip stop for the older ladies of the town and it had been very popular. However, I'm pretty sure they hadn't been making any profit for some time. When Wendy had sadly passed away there had been much talk about what was to become of Wendy's Wools, so much so that when I came along and said I wanted to open a craft shop the landlord had almost hugged me with joy and relief that the beloved place would be re-opening as something along the same lines. He even offered me a discount on my rent if I agreed to keep Anita on, which at the time I wasn't too sure about. Now, looking back, I don't know what I'd have done without her knowledge and advice on how to make my little shop work for both the locals and the holiday-makers who flocked to St Felix.

I say 'little shop', but we actually have two floors we trade from. To allow us to sell as broad a range of art and craft supplies as possible I'd renovated the basement to hold them all. Upstairs on the ground floor we stock my own textile designs, mostly handmade by me with a little help from some of the ladies of the town, who I'd hired when sales had really taken off last summer.

Having my own shop has been such a long-term ambition of mine that I occasionally have to pinch myself that I am not only 'living the dream' but making good money from it too.

In the summer when the tide is out, dogs are allowed on the vast harbour beach that's created by the expanse of sand the waves leave behind. Once Barney and I have weaved our way through the many grounded fishing boats the outgoing tide has abandoned at odd angles on the wet sand, I let him off his lead and he bounds across the beach until he finds his first interesting smell; then when he's stopped to sniff it a little too long I give him a whistle and he chases after me. When we've walked out far enough so we can see waves lapping against the sand Barney looks up hopefully at me.

'Oh no, you're not going swimming right now!' I tell him before he has time to bound off into the water. 'I haven't got time to wash and dry a wet sandy dog this afternoon. You can swim tomorrow if you're good.' I pull his ball from my pocket to distract him, and throw it across the sand well away from the lure of the sea.

When we've spent about fifteen minutes on the sand together with me throwing and him chasing the ball, all the while avoiding unsuspecting holiday-makers wandering haplessly across the makeshift beach, I call Barney to my side and we walk back towards the harbour again. The tide is already beginning to turn behind us, and I know all too well how quickly the waves will start rushing in to form a deep and dangerous sea once more.

Many an unsuspecting visitor has been caught on one of the high sand-banks in the middle of the harbour while the waves washed in around them. It's a St Felix tradition that someone has to be rescued at least once a week.

'Come on, you,' I say, attaching Barney's lead again. 'Let's head back the long way and we can call in on Noah on our way round.'

Barney, not minding at all that we are taking the long route to get back to the shop, sets off happily in front of me, and we wind our way along the cobbled streets until we come to Noah's

Ark, a charming little antique shop that's been a part of St Felix much longer than we have.

I open the door a little so the bell rings above me, and I see Noah pop up from the back room.

'Oh, it's you, Kate,' he says, coming into the shop properly. 'I hoped you'd pop by.'

'I've got Barney with me. He's a bit sandy so I didn't want to bring him in.'

'I run an antiques shop by the sea, Kate. I think I'm used to a little sand by now.' He grins at me. 'Bring Barney in. Clarice will be delighted to see him.'

Clarice is his little dog. A bit like me with Anita, Noah inherited her when he inherited this shop from his aunt.

I bring Barney into the shop and the two dogs sniff delightedly around each other at our feet.

'Anita said you wanted to see me about something?' I ask tentatively, still not sure what Noah could want. I knew Ana, his partner, well. She was infamous around town with her little red camper van, which she hired out for events. At anything from weddings to school proms Ana seemed to be in attendance driving Daisy-Rose as she called her, putting a smile on the face of everyone who saw them together.

'Yes, that's right. I got a job lot in from a house clearance the other day,' Noah explains, leading me towards the back room. 'The previous owner of the house was an elderly lady, and she must have been quite arty as the attic was filled with all sorts – paintings, art equipment, craft supplies and this,' he says, gesturing towards an old wooden box.

'It looks like a sewing machine,' I say, as he undoes two brass catches and lifts the lid. 'Oh, it is a sewing machine! And a pretty old one too.'

17

'I like to call it "vintage",' Noah says, winking at me. 'I reckon this one is from the early part of the twentieth century, or possibly before then.'

'Perhaps,' I say, looking at it. 'I doubt it works though.'

'No, I think this old girl sewed her last petticoat many a year ago! But I didn't think you'd want it to sew with. I thought you might be able to use it in your shop for display purposes. The machine would really set off your designs perfectly.'

'I suppose it could look quite cool in the window if I cleaned it up a bit. How much do you want for it?'

Noah shakes his head. 'Nothing. You'd be doing me a favour taking it off my hands to be honest. These machines don't make much money, especially in this state, and you did do Ana that favour last year with the interiors for Daisy-Rose. We owe you one.'

'Nonsense! I was happy to make those cushions for you.'

I look at the sewing machine again. 'I guess it *would* be quite a nice display piece ... but I have to give you something, Noah.'

'No, really, Kate, I've already made enough money selling all the old art equipment that came with it. A guy came in to browse yesterday and snapped it all up immediately. He's opening an art supplies shop and he said it would look great in there. That's when I thought of you and the machine.'

'Perfect timing! So where's his shop going to be – somewhere local?

'Yeah, just up the road from you, in the old butcher's.'

'*What?*' I exclaim. 'Here in St Felix? I thought you meant Penzance or Newlyn when you said local ...'

'Nope, he's just getting set up. I think he hopes to open in the next week or two. Nice guy. Just moved here apparently.'

18

'But *we* sell art equipment,' I say, my face darkening. 'In the basement of the shop.'

'Oh, so you do,' Noah says, suddenly realising why I'm so peeved. 'I hadn't thought of that. I'm sure it won't make too much difference to you though, will it? I mean, look at all the Cornish pasty shops here – they all seem to make a profit.'

'There's a lot more demand for pasties than art equipment though – it's more specialised. Look at it this way, if someone opened a vintage car hire shop in St Felix renting out retro cars and vehicles for events, would you and Ana be worried?'

'Sure,' Noah says, nodding pragmatically. 'I can see where you're coming from, Kate, but there's not really too much you can do about it if his shop is opening soon.'

'Oh, isn't there?' I say, folding my arms. 'We'll see about that ...'

Three

I leave Noah, thanking him again and promising I'll pop back for the machine. Then I walk Barney, my mind still buzzing, back to Harbour Street.

Noah was right, of course – I couldn't physically stop someone from opening an art shop here, but there was no doubt it would definitely put a dent in our profits if they did. Our forte was craft supplies. We didn't even attempt to stock as much art equipment as a specialist shop as we simply didn't have the room, but we were the only place in St Felix that supplied anything, so when one of the many amateur artists who flocked to the town every year ran short of ultramarine, cerulean or any number of shades of blue or green paint, as they so frequently seemed to, currently they only had us to turn to.

'I'm just popping out again,' I tell Anita as I let Barney through the door, and he heads immediately for his water bowl behind the shop counter. 'I won't be long. You and Sebastian are okay for a bit, aren't you?'

'Of course, dear,' Anita says, folding some swatches of quilting fabric into neat triangles. 'Off somewhere nice?'

'Not exactly,' I say quickly, not wanting to explain more right now. 'I won't be long. Did Molly get in yet?'

'She did. I've hurried her up the stairs to start on her homework just like you said.'

'You're a star, Anita!'

'She may have taken a little piece of cake with her to ease the burden,' Anita says, smiling serenely as she continues with her folding.

I leave the shop and walk quickly along Harbour Street. I wave to our local bakers Ant and Dec in the Blue Canary Bakery as I pass. Their window, as always, is looking pretty empty by now this late in the afternoon, and their shop much quieter than if I'd walked past earlier in the day, when queues usually stream out on to the cobbles as people wait patiently for their delicious cakes, sandwiches and, of course, traditional pasties.

The old butcher's shop that Noah had mentioned isn't on Harbour Street. It's just off the top, on a small cross-roads that holds more high-street-style shops – including a chemist, a bank, and a newsagent.

I'd noticed there had been some renovations going on when I'd passed by over the last few weeks, but because there had been shutters covering the windows I hadn't given any thought to what was going to open.

Now I was giving it a lot of thought.

'Hi,' I say to a few locals passing me on the pavement as I stare up at the building that had housed the old butcher. 'Lovely day, isn't it?'

One of the upstairs windows is open so I can hear the sound of a radio playing. Someone is definitely in there.

'*Hello!*' I call up to the open window. 'Is anyone home?'

21

Whoever is there obviously can't hear me over the music. I step forwards and rattle on the door, then I stand back again.

Nothing.

I bang even harder on the door, this time more aggressively.

'*Yo!*' I hear someone calling from the window. 'Can I help you? We're not open yet.'

'*Yes, I can see that!*' I call back as I step back again so I can see who I'm talking to. 'I wondered if I could have a word with the owner if he's in?'

'That would be me.' A man wearing a baseball cap looks down from the window. He smiles. 'What can I do for you?'

'Er, can't you come down and open the door?' I ask. 'It's a bit awkward me shouting up to you through an open window?'

'Not as awkward as it will be for me opening up the door to you.'

'Why?'

He looks away for a moment, then sighs. 'Trust me, it is. What do you want?' he asks, sounding a bit annoyed. 'I'm a bit busy right now.'

Charming. 'I wanted to talk to you about your shop.'

'Why? Do you want a job? I'm not really hiring yet.'

'No, I most certainly do not. I already own my own shop actually.'

'Congratulations!' he says grinning. 'That makes two of us. Aren't we the lucky ones?'

I can't tell if he's being sarcastic or not but he continues grinning down at me, and his dark brown eyes blink innocently as he awaits my reply.

'Look, I'm not prepared to have this conversation out in the open like this,' I tell him. 'There are ... things I would like to discuss with you.'

'Really?' I see his brows raise under the brim of his cap. 'Sounds intriguing. I'll be finished here in ...' He looks at his watch. 'Maybe an hour. Do you want to meet me in that pub on the harbour at say ... six? We can discuss all you like then when I've got a pint in my hand.'

'I assume you mean The Merry Mermaid?'

He nods.

I sigh. 'Well, if you're not prepared to come down and talk to me now ...' I wait hopefully in case he changes his mind.

'I'm not.'

'In that case then, yes, I guess I'll have to meet you at six.'

'Great.' His head disappears from the window. 'If that's all,' he adds, re-appearing again after a few seconds, '*some* of us shop owners have work to do.' His head disappears again and the window is shut.

I roll my eyes and shake my head in exasperation. Then I turn away smartly and walk back down the street.

Grrr, what a very irritating man, but if I wanted to find out more about his shop then I was going to have to do as he asked and meet him at the pub later.

There is nothing, other than Molly and Barney, that is more important to me than my little shop and its staff. I've worked incredibly hard to get it to where it is today, and I'm determined to discover whether this newcomer to St Felix is about to put our success under threat.

Four

'So who is this date with exactly?' Molly asks, as I sit at my bedroom dressing table in our flat above the shop attempting to pull a brush through my long thick hair.

'I keep telling you, it's not a date!' I insist, finally getting the brush through the stubborn knot I'd been pulling at for the last few seconds.

I stare at myself in the mirror. Even my critical gaze can see I look better now than half an hour ago when I'd finished up at the shop and grabbed a shower. It made a nice change to see my hair down. I usually wore it pulled up in a high ponytail, partly because it was easier in the shop, and partly because of the strong sea breeze that always seemed to gust around St Felix. 'I'm simply meeting up with the owner of the new art shop that Noah told me about.'

'To give him grief, right? Sebastian told me.'

'*No*,' I say, wondering if I should put some make-up on. I did look a little pale and heavy around the eyes this evening. 'I merely want to find out what sort of equipment he's going to be stocking, and whether it will affect our business in any way.

I don't know if his shop will *only* be selling art supplies or whether it might broaden its scope ...'

'Is he hot?' Molly asks.

'Who?'

'The guy that you met earlier. What's his name?'

'He didn't say.' I reach for some lip gloss. 'We never got around to exchanging names.'

'A blind date!' Molly squeals excitedly. 'Cool.'

'I think you'll find that a blind date is one where you know the name of the person but you haven't actually seen them before. This is the other way around.'

'So, I'll ask again then. Is he hot?'

I turn away from the mirror towards her. Molly is lying casually on her stomach on my bed, keeping one eye on the phone in her hand and the other on me getting ready.

'Not that it makes any difference but, no, I don't think so. I only saw him through an upstairs window, and he had a hat on.'

Molly thinks about this. 'What sort of hat?'

'Er ... a baseball cap, I think. Why?'

'Did it have a logo?'

'I don't know! Why does that matter?'

'Because we might be able to tell a bit more about him if we knew what sort of things he's into.'

I sigh and turn back to my mirror. 'None of this matters, Molly. Like I've already told you, this is *not* a date.'

'But you're putting on make-up. You never wear make-up.'

'I do sometimes.'

'Not unless you want to impress someone, you don't.'

'I want to feel confident tonight, that's all. You know how much the shop means to me. I want to make sure nothing is

25

going to ruin the success we've worked so hard to build up since we moved in.'

'Yeah, I know the story,' Molly says, pulling herself up and sitting crossed-legged now. 'How it was always your dream to own your own shop and sell your own designs. How you had to give up your career when I was born, and how it's taken until now to get yourself back to where you've always wanted to be.'

'Something like that.' I finish putting a light coat of mascara on. 'However, you make it sound like having you held me back.'

'Well, it did, didn't it?'

'Perhaps it did a little at the time.' I watch her reflection in the mirror. 'But you know I wouldn't have it any other way. Maybe waiting until now means it's much better than it would have been back then. The best things come to—'

'—those who wait. Yeah, you've said so before. You and your inspirational quotes, Mum. You should start an Instagram account.'

'I have enough trouble with the one we've got for the shop, thank you.'

'I've told you – let me do that.'

'You need to concentrate on your schoolwork.'

'I'm sure I could manage social media for the shop as well. You could pay me . . . '

I turn again and give her a rueful smile. 'I should have known!'

'You look great, Mum,' Molly says, looking at me with her head tipped to one side. 'Really good. You should make an effort more often.'

'Thank you, I think?' I stand up and glance at the bedroom clock. 'Golly, is that the time? I'd better head off. Come and give your mum a good luck hug.'

Molly rolls off the bed and we embrace for a moment.

26

'My mum, off on a date,' she says, standing back to look at me again. 'Whatever next?'

'For the last time, it's *not* a date!'

The Merry Mermaid pub is not far from the shop, and I can hear the church bells striking six o'clock as I walk towards the harbour. It's a gorgeous evening, and the town is still full of holiday-makers soaking up the evening sunshine.

I spot the man from the new shop sitting outside the pub at a wooden table with a pint of beer in his hand. He's not wearing a hat now so I can see he has a head of short wavy-brown hair. He's wearing aviator-style sunglasses and a white shirt, which is fitted tightly to his full chest and broad shoulders. He waves as I approach.

'Hullo, again!' he says, smiling at me but not getting up. 'Care to join me?'

'Thank you,' I say, about to sit down. 'Oh, I should really get a drink first. Would you care for another?'

'Oh, no, I'm fine, thanks.' Then for some reason I can't work out he looks a bit uncomfortable.

'I'll go and get mine then, shall I? Excuse me, back in a mo.'

I leave the man – I really must find out his name – and head into the pub. Rita, the landlady, is quick to serve me.

'What can I get you, love?' she asks. 'It's unusual to see you in here ... especially this early.'

'Just an orange juice with ice please, Rita. Yes, I'm meeting someone.'

'Ooh!' Rita exclaims, as she reaches for a bottle under the bar. 'How exciting!'

'No, it's not like that. It's business.'

'Oh,' she says, not hiding her disappointment as she scoops

27

ice into a glass and then pours my juice over the top. 'How very dull. I hoped it would be something much more thrilling, I love a bit of romance, I do.'

'Do you know anything about the shop that's opening where the old butcher's used to be?' I ask, purposefully dodging her comment as I pass her a five-pound note. Rita knows everything and everyone in St Felix, so she was bound to know something about this.

'It's going to be an art shop, isn't it?' she says as she reaches into the till for my change. 'The chap who's opening it is outside right now having a drink if you want to speak to him. Ah ... is *that* your business meeting?'

'It is indeed,' I say, taking the few coins Rita presses into my hand.

'Nice chap. I can't say I'd want to be running a shop in his position though.'

'How do you mean?' Suddenly, a large group enters the pub and Rita is forced to end our chat in favour of her own business interests.

The sun is so low in the sky as I head outside to the table with my drink that I have to shield my eyes from its glare. I take a seat opposite the man again.

I reach in my bag for my sunglasses.

'That's better,' I say. 'I couldn't really see properly before – the sunlight is so bright here on the harbour in the evenings.'

My companion smiles. 'It's going to be a stunning sunset. Please tell me the weather is like this all the time.'

'I wish. The only way to describe the St Felix weather is *changeable* – we have our own microclimate. It can be bucketing down a few miles up the coast yet sunny here, and vice versa.'

'I thought as much. Oh well, we'll need to appreciate this

glorious evening all the more then. You have to live for the moment, don't you?'

'Yes, I suppose you do. I haven't introduced myself properly yet – I'm Kate.'

'Jack,' the man says, holding out his hand. 'Pleased to meet you, Kate. Now, I hate to talk business, but you seemed pretty concerned about something earlier when you were outside my shop. What is it I can do for you?'

'I was just wondering what sort of shop you're going to be opening,' I say, taking a sip of my orange juice whilst trying to remain casual. 'I heard it's to be an art shop?'

'That's right, yes.'

'And will you *only* be selling art equipment?'

'Mostly, yes. I noticed there was a gap in the market here, and considering how many people come here to paint every year it seems a waste not to plug that gap, so to speak.'

'*We* sell art equipment in my shop,' I tell him, still keeping my tone light. 'We do quite well with it. You'd be surprised how many people run out of shades of blue when they're painting their seascapes.'

'Exactly my point!' Jack says, 'This place is crying out for a decent art supplier. Which shop are you again?'

My teeth grind together as my jaw tightens. Did he not realise he was being rude? *Decent* art shop indeed!

'I own Kate's Cornish Crafts on Harbour Street,' I say purposefully.

'Oh yes, I think I've seen it. You sell homemade bits and bobs, don't you – tea cosies, bags, that kind of thing.'

'They're a bit more than bits and bobs. I personally design and make all of the items – well, I have a little bit of help from some very talented ladies in the town – so our stock is

29

all handmade and one of a kind. I do all the machine embroidery myself.'

Jack looks at me with an amused expression. 'Steady! I wasn't having a go. That sounds very cool. And you do quite well with it?'

'Very well as a matter of fact.'

'I'm pleased. But you said you sell some art equipment as well? Where do you do that?'

'Our shop has a basement. We sell a wide range of art and craft materials from down there.'

'Ah, I see . . . a basement. No wonder I didn't notice it then.'

'It's very well signposted if you actually come *into* the shop, and we have notices in the window if you'd bothered to look.'

'Hey,' Jack says, holding his hand up. 'Why are you being so aggressive? I'm not here to diss your shop. Far from it. I got the feeling that the shop owners all support each other in this town.'

'We do.'

'Then what's the problem here?'

'You're stepping on my territory.'

A puzzled expression crosses Jack's face, and he takes off his sunglasses. 'I'm sorry . . . what?'

'You're stepping on my territory,' I repeat. 'By selling art equipment you'll take some of our sales.'

'Ah, I see.' Jack nods knowingly. 'You'll forgive me if I beg to differ? My shop will be selling professional equipment, not simply a few watercolour palettes and some children's painting books.'

My mouth drops open in surprise.

'We do not sell children's painting books,' I say, recovering from his insult.

'But you sell those watercolour palettes, don't you?' he says, grinning. 'Go on, I dare you to tell me you don't?'

I purse my lips together now.

'I thought so,' he adds, sitting back in his chair.

I'm so annoyed that I don't notice what he's leaning against.

'How dare you sit here and insult both my shop and me,' I say as calmly as I can. 'Do you even realise how rude you're being?'

'Aw, Kate, I'm only playing with you,' Jack says, looking sheepish. 'I'm sorry if I've offended you. It's my background. I'm used to banter, and I assume everyone else is too. I should probably rein it in a little when meeting new people.'

'Yes, you probably should,' I reply, still feeling aggrieved, but slightly calmer now.

'Look, I don't want to step on anyone's toes. Chance would be a fine thing, mind,' he says, rolling his eyes. I glance at him wondering what he means. 'I'm certain my shop won't sell anything that will interfere too much with your business. Promise. Not a knitting needle in sight!' He holds his hand up to his head in a smart salute. 'Scout's honour.'

I feel myself relax slightly, and I give him a half smile. 'I hope so.'

'There, that's better,' Jack says. 'Now we can be friends again. How about another drink?'

'I probably should be going soon,' I say, glancing at my watch. 'And I still have plenty, thank you.' I lift up my glass.

'Oh, that's a shame. You'll excuse me if I get another one though?'

'Of course.'

Suddenly, as he prepares to leave the table, I see it for the first time and I wonder, as he expertly begins to move towards the door of the pub, how I could ever have missed it.

Jack is in a wheelchair.

Five

Staring at the door Jack has just gone through I quickly try to run over a few things in my head.

How could I not have noticed he was in a wheelchair? Yes, it was incredibly bright out here this evening and I'd been temporarily blinded when I'd come out of the pub, but how had I been so caught up in my own drama that I hadn't noticed he was disabled?

I think about the first time we'd met and how he'd been incredibly reluctant to come downstairs to open the door of his shop. Was that because it would have taken him so long to get down to me?

And just now I'd thought how very unchivalrous he was being when he hadn't got up to greet me.

Damn it, Kate! You really need to open your eyes to the bigger picture, I scold myself. *There's you worrying about a few paintbrush sales while Jack is attempting to open a shop in his condition.*

'Hey, you're still here then,' Jack says as he emerges from the door of the pub. I watch as he expertly manoeuvres his chair through the narrow gap back to our table. 'I thought you might have left.'

'No, still here,' I say, feeling very uncomfortable. *Should I address the fact I hadn't noticed he was in a wheelchair or just ignore it?*

'You got served quickly,' I say instead, to make conversation.

'Always do,' Jack says, placing the pint of beer he'd been expertly balancing on his lap on the table. 'People tend to stand aside when they see you in this thing.'

'A-ha ...' I say, not knowing how to react to this.

Jack looks at me with a half-confused, half-amused expression. 'Anyway, I'm glad you're still here,' he says, settling himself at the table again. 'I don't know that many people here in St Felix yet. It's good I know you now ... even if you do think I'm going to ruin your business.'

'No,' I say, waving my hand dismissively at him. 'That's all sorted now. Don't worry about it.'

Jack's eyes narrow as he considers my sudden about-turn. 'You didn't know I was in a wheelchair, did you?' he asks suddenly.

'*Hmm?*' I ask innocently. 'What do you mean?' I lift my drink up and wish I hadn't drunk all my juice while he was gone. I place my empty glass awkwardly back on the wooden table.

'I mean you hadn't noticed until I went to get my pint that I was in a wheelchair?'

I shrug. 'I guess not.'

'And is that why you're suddenly being as nice as pie – because you feel sorry for me?'

'No.'

Jack raises his dark eyebrows at me. 'Oh, really?'

I sigh. 'Okay, so I didn't know you were disabled when I came banging on your door earlier and, no, I didn't notice you were in a wheelchair until just now. That isn't a crime, is it?'

Jack shakes his head. 'Nope. Neither is treating someone

33

differently because they're not able-bodied like you, but it doesn't mean I have to like it.'

He takes a long, slow, purposeful drink from his pint of beer.

'I'm sorry,' I say quietly. 'I didn't mean to offend you.'

'Still being nice?'

'Look, what do you want from me?' I snap in a loud voice. I look hastily at the other pub-goers sitting around us, but they're far too busy with their own conversations to notice my outburst. 'I've said I'm sorry, and I am. What else can I do?'

'Just treat me like you would any other awkward, obnoxious guy you meet,' Jack says, smiling now. 'That's all I ask. I admired your spirit up until a few moments ago, then you did exactly what ninety-nine per cent of people do on meeting me – you patronized me.'

'I did not!'

Jack simply shrugs.

'All right ... maybe I did a bit, but I was surprised that's all ... that I hadn't noticed it before – your chair, I mean.'

'I take that as a compliment,' Jack says, looking so directly into my eyes it unnerves me a little. 'People always see the chair before they see me. I'm always a second thought.'

'I'm sure that can't be true.'

'Ever been in one of these things?'

'No.'

'Then you can't possibly know.'

A silence hangs across the table, and I look at my empty glass again longingly.

'You want another?' Jack asks, nodding at it.

'Oh no, you're all right, I can get it.' I begin to stand up, and then I think better of it and sit purposefully back down

34

again. 'Yes, please, I would,' I say, sliding the glass across the table towards him. 'Make it a Diet Coke this time though.'

Jack looks at the glass, and then he nods approvingly at me. 'Diet Coke coming right up!'

'So,' I ask, as we sit at the table together again, this time on the same side so we can both watch the beautiful sunset that's beginning to form across the harbour in the evening sky. 'What made you want to open a shop here?'

Since Jack had come back with my drink we'd sat and chatted politely for the last ten minutes or so, mostly about St Felix and what it was like owning a business here, and I'd discovered that this was Jack's first time owning a shop.

'So why open one now?' I ask, even though the question *Why are you opening a shop when you're in a wheelchair?* wasn't too far from my lips, but I was far too polite (or is that cowardly?) to ask him that directly, even though that's what I really wanted to know.

'Why do I want to open a shop when I'm in a wheelchair, you mean?' Jack says, making me blush.

I nod.

'I guess I like a challenge.'

'There must be more to it than that?'

'Maybe there is.' Jack doesn't enlighten me as to what.

'Such as—?' I ask with sudden bravery. 'What?' I ask, when Jack turns to look at me. 'You can't have it both ways, you know? I'm simply being honest with you.'

'And I appreciate that, Kate, really I do. I'd just prefer not to talk about it right now if that's okay with you?'

'Sure. Of course.' I nod. I've pushed it too far.

'Don't look so worried,' Jack says, putting his hand over mine

35

where it rests on the table. 'I like the fact you're being direct with me. I wish more people were.'

I glance down at his hand and notice the beginning of a tattoo peeking out from under the rolled-up sleeve of his white shirt.

Jack stares with alarm at his hand over mine. 'Oh God, sorry!' he exclaims, pulling it away. 'Now I'm the one overstepping the mark!'

I'm about to tell him not to be silly and it doesn't matter when suddenly he slams down his almost empty pint glass on the table.

'Gotta go!' he says, looking at the place a watch should be on his wrist and then realising it's not there. 'Things to do, you know.' He begins to wheel himself backwards away from the table.

I hurriedly stand up to let him out.

'I'll send you an invite to the shop opening!'

'Sure ... ' I say, still standing as I watch him spin himself expertly around and then head off back in the direction of both our shops. 'That would be good ... '

'So how did it go?' Molly asks excitedly as soon as I arrive back at the flat.

'Yeah, all right, I think.' I try to sound as indifferent as I can.

'You think ... Don't you know?'

'He seems like a nice enough chap. He's not out to ruin us anyway – I've discovered that much.'

Molly sighs impatiently.

'So what's he like ... Did you at least find out his name?'

'Jack, his name is Jack, and he's ... confusing,' I say, realising this is how I actually feel after my drink with him at the pub. One minute he was stubborn, awkward and a little insensitive, and the next he was funny and, I'd even go so far to say, kind.

Jack is definitely a mystery, and I don't want to wait until his shop opens to discover more about him.

Six

'*Urgh!*' Sebastian groans as he dumps the box down on the shop counter. 'Next time you ask me to go and collect something for you, remind me to take my forklift truck!'

'Sorry,' I apologise. 'I probably should have warned you it might be a bit heavy.'

'*Ooh*, what have you got in there, dears?' Anita asks, appearing from the basement.

'This,' I say, lifting the old sewing machine from the cardboard box. I open up the latches on its case and reveal what's inside.

'My mother used to have a very similar one when I was young,' Anita says, examining the machine. 'Does it still work?'

'I don't think so. I got it from Noah – he thought I might like it for display in the shop. I doubt it's sewn anything for years.' I try to turn the rusty old handle, and the machine creaks as it tries to move its balance wheel and lift an imaginary needle.

'Painful.' Sebastian grimaces. 'Sounds like it needs a good oil to me.'

'I think it might need a bit more than that to begin sewing

again, but Noah's right – if I give it a bit of a clean we can make a very nice window display with this.'

'I hope you didn't pay much for it?' Sebastian says, still eyeing the machine. 'In that decrepit state it can't be worth much.'

'Freebie actually. Noah got it in a house clearance – it was with some other art equipment. Apparently Jack, the guy who is opening the art shop on the high street, has taken that.'

Sebastian nudges Anita. 'She means her date last night . . .'

'Oh, really?' Anita says, her pale blue eyes widening, 'I didn't know you had a date . . . Tell me more.'

'There's nothing *to* tell, Anita. It wasn't a date – it was simply a business meeting.' I turn to Sebastian. 'How did you know about that anyway?'

'I saw Molly on her way to school this morning—'

Of course he had.

'—she said you thought Jack was *confusing*. Is that your way of saying he's enigmatic and mysterious?' he asks, wafting his hands above his head.

'No. It's my way of saying he's *confusing*.'

'In what way, dear?' Anita asks.

'I don't know. He's a bit odd, that's all. I mean one minute he wants you to be all open with him, and then when you ask a question he doesn't like he closes up on you.'

'Heterosexual males *are* very confusing,' Sebastian says matter-of-factly. 'It's something to do with an overload of testosterone mixing up their emotional pathways. Either that or it's something to do with pheromones. I can never remember which.'

'Yes, thank you, Sebastian. Jack is nice enough, he's just . . .' I struggle for a new word to describe him. ' . . . complicated. He's got a lot going on. Did you know he's in a wheelchair?'

Anita and Sebastian both nod.

'Yes, I've seen him about town,' Anita says. 'Lou in the post office told me who he is.'

'Amber in the flower shop pointed him out to me,' Sebastian explains. You know what it's like here in St Felix – anyone new who's not a holiday-maker gets noticed immediately.'

'Great, so you both knew of him and I didn't. I could have got a heads-up.'

'Did you put your foot in it then?' Sebastian asks. 'About his disability?'

'A bit ... but it's fine. I do wonder how he's going to manage to run a shop in a wheelchair though. It's hard enough when you're able-bodied.'

'People do all sorts now,' Anita says, sounding a lot more open-minded than I just had. 'Having a disability isn't a barrier to doing anything these days ... not like when I was young. If you were in a wheelchair back then that was it – you were simply stuck in it until someone pushed you and moved you elsewhere.'

A customer comes into the shop putting paid to our conversation.

'Good morning! Can I help you?' I ask, as the lady looks around her.

'I'm looking for a particular colour of embroidery silk,' she says, smiling at me.

'Come this way,' I say, holding my hand out towards the stairs. 'Our silks are right down here.'

The rest of the day is a fairly typical one with a steady flow of customers. Then when Anita goes home after lunch it's just me and Sebastian looking after them, and later eventually only me as Sebastian leaves early for a dental appointment.

I spend the last quiet hour in the shop giving the old sewing machine a good clean – first with some soap and water, and then with a polishing cloth. When I've finished I stand back to admire my handiwork.

'You don't scrub up too badly,' I say to the machine, giving the ornate gold writing that twists and curls over the shiny black paintwork a final buff. 'Considering how old you are, you've survived extremely well. Someone must have looked after you.'

I try to get the machine to work by first inserting an appropriate needle from the various ones we stock downstairs, and then I use some oil to lubricate its parts in the hope they might begin to move again, but my efforts are to no avail – it seems to be completely seized up.

'Frozen in time, that's what you are,' I tell it kindly. 'Never mind, at least you still *look* pretty. We may not be able to give you much stitching to do any more, but I do hope you enjoy living in our shop.'

I cash up for the night, leaving the machine on the counter next to me, and then before I switch off the lights and lock up I glance at it one more time.

What a shame I couldn't get you to work, I think. *It seems wrong to leave you sitting there unused.* However, I knew I had what felt like miles of stitching to do on my own much more modern sewing machine tonight, and before that I also had to make dinner for Molly and me. Regretfully, I head upstairs.

The next morning, after I've washed, dressed and then taken Barney for a quick walk, I breakfast with Molly and see her off to school. Afterwards, I carry the till drawer complete with float downstairs and place it in the empty till. Then I switch

41

on the shop lights and unlock the front door to begin another day's trading.

Harbour Street is always so much quieter at this time of day. There are already a few early birds wandering around, but at the moment I can actually see the cobbles on the ground outside and not just a steady stream of flip flops, walking boots and trainers, as is so often the case in the height of the summer.

I take a couple of deep breaths of sea air and then I turn back inside.

'Looks like it's going to be a warm one,' I say to Barney as he settles himself down in the special basket we keep in the shop for him. 'Let's hope it's a busy one too.'

I'm about to head back over to the counter with the intention of doing some stock ordering before it gets busy, when I stop dead in my tracks and stare at the old sewing machine still sitting where I left it last night.

What is that underneath its presser foot? It looks like some sort of fabric ...

I hurry over to the desk to examine what's on the bed of the machine, and I'm astonished to see a swatch of pale-blue felt fabric with an intricate embroidered design stitched all over it.

'How on earth did you get there?' I ask, carefully lifting up the foot of the machine so I can see the design better.

I pull out the fabric gently, cutting the threads that are still attached to a reel on top of the machine and a bobbin underneath.

The piece of felt I now hold in my hand is quite amazing as the detail and work is simply exquisite. The stitching on the fabric has formed a picture, which looks very much like it could be a harbour filled with fishing boats. In fact, as I trace my finger over the embroidery silk, it could even be St Felix's I'm looking at. There seems to be part of a lighthouse, a harbour wall and the sea, depicted as large turquoise waves splashing up against the side of it.

When I'd left the shop last night, the workings of this machine wouldn't budge an inch, let alone stitch something as amazing as this. Where has it come from? And more to the point who has stitched it?

'Morning!' Sebastian calls as he enters the shop later. 'Gorgeous day out. Far too nice to be cooped up in here. Maybe we should shut up and have a staff day on the beach instead?' He looks hopefully at me, but I shake my head. Sebastian tried this at least twice a week when the weather was good.

'Worth a shot! Coffee?' he enquires.

'Yeah . . . ' I reply vaguely.

'Irish for you?' he asks.

'Yeah . . .'

'Okay, what's up?' Sebastian demands, putting his satchel down on the desk.

'What do you mean?'

'You just agreed to an Irish coffee at 11 o'clock in the morning? You barely drink alcohol at the best of times, let alone whiskey in your morning coffee!'

'Did I? Sorry, I'm a bit distracted this morning, that's all.'

'May I enquire as to why?'

'It's a bit strange actually. Look, put your bag upstairs, and I'll tell you all about it.'

'Sounds intriguing!'

Sebastian makes us both our usual coffees from the machine I have in the flat, and returns downstairs to where I'm still standing by the shop counter.

43

'So, boss, what's up?' he asks, sipping on his frothy cappuccino.

'This,' I say, lifting the blue embroidered felt from underneath the counter and sliding it across to him.

'That's pretty,' Sebastian says, lifting it up to look at it. 'Who did it?'

I nod towards the machine, which is now on a shelf behind us.

'I don't understand! Oh, did you get the machine to work in the end and you made this on it. That's fantastic!'

'No, *I* didn't do it.'

'But you said the machine did? Who was using it then?'

'That's the thing – I don't know! I wondered if it might be you, but by the look on your face it clearly wasn't.'

Sebastian's brow furrows. 'Er ... no, definitely not me. What's going on? You're making no sense at all!'

'Last night before I closed up the shop I spent a while cleaning the sewing machine. I tried to get it working but it was having none of it – completely jammed up, it was – so I left it on the counter thinking I might change the window display today to include it because it had scrubbed up so well.'

'*Uh-huh* ...' Sebastian says, keenly watching me while he sips his coffee.

'When I came down here this morning to open up everything was completely normal. The sewing machine was still on the desk where I had left it, *but* it had this in it!' I pick up the felt again. 'And it was still attached to the coloured thread on top on the spool.'

'How very odd! How did it get there?'

'That is exactly what I've been trying to figure out.'

'Maybe someone placed it there?' Sebastian suggests.

'That was my initial thought, but firstly, who would want

to do that and why? And secondly, how did they get in here to put it there? The shop was locked up overnight, there was only Molly and me upstairs, and this morning there was no sign of a break-in. And even if there had been, why would someone break in just to put some embroidery in an old sewing machine?'

'*Hmm.*' Sebastian puts his finger on his chin in a thoughtful manner. 'Have you checked with Molly? She's not playing a joke on you?'

'Yup, I texted her first thing. She knows nothing about it. I tried to play it down a bit as I don't want her thinking someone has been in here while we've been asleep upstairs.'

'Understandable. It has to be someone with a key then.'

'The only people who have keys to the shop are you, Anita and me. Why would Anita do it? It makes no sense.'

'Let's assume for a moment it's *not* Anita.'

'I very much doubt it is.'

'Exactly. So if it's not any of us three and you've not had a break-in, there's only one more person it could be.'

'Who?'

'Who's the only person you know who enters houses without breaking in and who leaves again without ever being seen. And most importantly, who always leaves a gift behind when he does?'

I think for moment. 'I have absolutely no idea, Sebastian, who?

'Santa Claus, of course!' Sebastian says with delight. 'It seems in all probability, and without any other sort of reasonable explanation, that you've had an early visit from Father Christmas this year!'

Seven

'*Hey!*' I hear called out behind me as I sit on a bench and watch Barney race around on the grass in front of me.

It's early in the morning, the tide is in and I can't face cleaning a lot of wet sand off Barney this morning before breakfast, so instead I've brought him up on to one of the grassy hills that overlooks St Felix Bay. It's a popular spot amongst morning dog walkers, and Barney is currently chasing after a brown Cockapoo whose owner is engrossed in something on their mobile phone.

'Hello! Earth to Kate?'

I turn around and see Jack wheeling himself up the very steep tarmac path that runs up the centre of the hill.

'Oh, hi!' I wave. 'Are you okay there? Sorry!' I say, clamping my hand over my mouth. *I'd said the wrong thing again, hadn't I?*

'Actually, no,' Jack says, sounding out of breath. 'I'm not all right. This hill is a killer ... but it's good for the old cardio!'

He wheels himself over to my bench and pulls up next to me still breathing heavily. 'Got to keep my hand in,' he says, smiling. He waves his gloved hands at me.

'Ah, yes,' I say, relieved I hadn't put my foot in it again. 'You have a different chair today?'

'It's my sporty model,' Jack says, lifting the small front wheel off the ground as if he's doing a wheelie. 'I use it for exercising. It goes much faster than my usual one, but it's not as comfortable.'

I look at the wheelchair. Jack's other chair, in which he'd been sitting the other day at the pub, had two big wheels at the sides balanced by two smaller wheels at the front. This one had a similar set-up except it looked much lighter and more pointed, and the large wheels were slightly angled in at the top.

'I've seen ones like that in the Paralympics.'

'Yeah, I didn't quite make it to that level sadly.'

'Really? You were good then?' I wonder what sport Jack had taken part in.

'So-so,' Jack says, shrugging. 'I competed at the Invictus Games.'

'The one involving Prince Harry?'

'Yeah, that one.'

'That's for ex-service personnel, isn't it?'

'Yup – army, before you ask. It's been a while since I competed properly, but I still like to keep my hand in.'

I smile.

'Good,' Jack says, grinning, 'You got my sad attempt at humour this time.'

'So how long were you in the army for?'

'Long enough,' Jack says abruptly, looking out towards the sea. 'So what are you doing up here this early in the morning? I had you down as a night owl, not a lark.'

Clearly Jack doesn't want to talk about his time in the army, but I'm surprised he's given *me* any thought whatsoever.

'I'm supposed to be walking *him*,' I say, nodding towards

Barney, who is now running around in a threesome with the Cockapoo and a small Jack Russell that's joined them. 'The crazy-looking Labrador is mine.'

'Nice,' Jack says, looking at Barney. 'Labs are always great dogs.'

'They know their own minds, that's for sure.'

'And their way around a dustbin!'

'You've had one then?'

'In the past,' Jack says quietly, and he looks wistful for a second.

Barney's two friends are called away by their owners, so I whistle Barney back over to me.

'Impressive whistle,' Jack says approvingly.

Barney comes bounding over. He immediately looks suspiciously at Jack before proceeding to sniff around his wheelchair.

'*Barney!*' I hiss. 'Stop that.'

'It's fine,' Jack says. 'He's only checking me out. Aren't you, boy?'

'I'm more concerned he might pee on you actually,' I say, looking nervously at Barney.

Jack just laughs. 'I've had worse.'

Barney behaves impeccably, however, and when he's finished sniffing Jack's chair, he lies his head on his lap.

'I think he likes me,' Jack says, stroking his head.

'He probably thinks you've got treats about your person.'

'Sorry, Barney, no can do, I'm afraid. My days of having dog treats in my pocket are long gone.'

'Here Barn!' I say, throwing him a small dog biscuit. 'And that's all you're getting.'

Barney deftly catches the biscuit in his mouth and chews it hungrily.

'Anyone would think I didn't feed him the way he carries on.'
Jack watches Barney affectionately.

'How's the shop coming along?' I ask, to make conversation.

'Great, thanks,' Jack says. 'We should be ready for our grand opening on Friday, all being well.'

'That's good. You said *we* – you have someone to help you then?'

'Because I can't manage in this, you mean?' Jack gestures to his chair.

'No, I meant like staff actually.' I fold my arms defensively across my chest. He wasn't getting me on that one again.

Jack looks at me and grins. 'Okay, I'll let you off then. Yeah, I have a part-time member of staff – Bronte.'

'Is Bronte Poppy's daughter? Poppy who owns the flower shop.'

'Yes, I believe she is. She's back from university for the summer, so it's only until October, but I guess it starts to quieten down around here then, am I right?'

I nod. 'Yeah, we get tourists all year round, but it's not anywhere near as hectic as the summer. It sounds like you're all ready to go.'

'I hope so. You'll come on Friday, won't you – to the opening? It's not going to be much, but I think it's important to mark the occasion.'

'Of course, yes. Will you have many there, do you think? Friends, family?'

'Just a few fellow shopkeepers probably – maybe some local press if I'm lucky. There's not much interest in someone opening an art shop, is there?'

'Probably not.' *So Jack didn't have a family then, or a partner . . .*

'I could pull the wheelchair card, I suppose, to get some press attention, but I don't really want to do that. As you've probably already deduced it's not really my way of doing things.'

'Really?' I smile at him. 'I'd never have guessed!'

Jack winks at me. 'How's your own business going? You looked deep in thought before I disturbed you a few moments ago. In fact, you looked like you had the worries of the world on your shoulders. I do hope I haven't chosen a bad time to start a business in St Felix? That would be about my luck!'

'Oh no, the business is fine. I'm sure your shop will do very well. As you know we get a lot of amateur and professional artists coming here to paint, and the Lyle Gallery attracts a lot of arty people too.'

'So why the long face then?'

'Got a few things I need to think about, that's all.' I didn't wish to share with Jack the fact that yesterday morning a vintage sewing machine had left a mystery piece of embroidery for me when I came down to open up the shop.

'I see. Should I leave you to it then?'

'No, it's fine. I'll get to the bottom of it. It's about time I headed back with Barney now anyway.'

'Mind if I tag along next to you?' Jack asks to my surprise. 'I think I've done enough for one morning too. It's my favourite part now – downhill!'

'Sure,' I reply, feeling happier about this idea than I would have expected to.

Barney and I walk alongside Jack back towards the shop.

I'm impressed at how skilful Jack is with his chair. He deftly manoeuvres round the tight St Felix bends and the infamous cobbled streets easily, just as though he was walking alongside us. In fact, as we chat I soon forget that he's in a wheelchair at all until we come to a set of narrow steps that wind their way down in-between some cottages towards the harbour. Automatically I turn to go down them and then I stop myself.

I turn back to Jack. I'm about to say 'Sorry' again, when I stop myself and instead say jokily, 'I don't suppose even you in your fancy contraption can get down there!'

Jack shakes his head. 'Nope, not easily anyway. I guess this is where we part ways.'

'Not necessarily – Barney and I can go another way back instead.'

'I don't want to put you out.'

'Don't be daft. The truth is I forgot you were even in a wheel-chair or I wouldn't have tried to go down there.'

'I'll take that as a compliment.'

'You should.'

We proceed a little way together in silence.

'Oh, I know what I was going to ask you,' I say, suddenly remembering as we pass the antiques shop. 'You bought some old art equipment from Noah, didn't you?'

'Yes, but how do you know about that?'

'I took the old sewing machine off him that came from the same house clearance.'

'Ah … right.' I sense Jack hesitating. 'What sort of sewing machine is it?'

I'm surprised by his question. 'It's an old Singer, probably from the early part of the last century.'

Jack nods. 'Where have you put it?'

'In my shop. Why?'

'No reason – I just wondered, that's all. Does it work, this sewing machine?'

I hesitate now. Technically, no, it didn't. I'd never seen it work with my own eyes anyway.

'No, it's all seized up. Display purposes only.'

'Oh, shame.'

Again, there's a short lull in our conversation, and I wonder why Jack is so interested in my sewing machine.

'Well, this is us,' I say as we arrive outside my shop. 'Barney and I live in the flat upstairs with my daughter Molly, who hopefully,' I add, looking up at the upstairs window, 'is up and getting dressed for school right now.'

'How old?' Jack asks.

'She's fifteen, going on fifty sometimes though. Much more sensible than me most of the time!'

Jack smiles. 'That's good to know you're not always so uptight.'

I stare at him.

'Ah, damn, I've put my non-existent foot in it again, haven't I?'

'I'm not uptight.'

'Sorry, I didn't mean uptight. I meant ... strait-laced.'

I glare at him again.

'Nope, I didn't mean that either. Er ... tense? Anxious? Guarded? Yes, that's what I mean – you're quite guarded, aren't you?'

'And you're not, I suppose?'

'How do you mean?'

'I mean, when I asked you the other day about why you were opening a shop here you went all silent on me, and earlier you clearly didn't want to talk about your time in the army.'

Jack thinks about this, then he nods matter-of-factly.

'Yes, you're probably right ... and, with that, I'll take my leave. Thanks for introducing me to your dog. See ya, Barney!' He gives Barney a friendly pat before setting off across the cobbles at speed.

I stand outside the shop, stunned for a moment that he's departed so abruptly, then I shake my head. *What is it with that man? I simply don't understand him at all.*

And why did his behaviour, and how he makes me feel, matter so much anyway?

Eight

The art shop looks busy as I approach on Friday evening, and I can hear a steady stream of chatter filtering through the open door out on to the street. There had been a poster in the window inviting people to the opening all week, and it seems the residents of St Felix have turned out in abundance to support this new local business.

Arty-Farty the sign above the door says, with a colourful little paint palette and brush illustrated below. I smile – the name is very Jack.

'Hi,' I say to a couple of people as I squeeze through the door into the shop. 'Bit crowded, isn't it?'

I spy Sebastian standing towards the back of the shop with a glass of bubbly, so I make my way over towards him. Luckily, there's quite a bit of space in between the shop's many shelves, which are all filled to the brim with tubes of paint, sketch-pads, watercolour paper, and it would seem anything you could want to paint the perfect picture with, so I manage to get through to him without too much fuss.

'You made it then?' he asks, looking me up and down. 'Take you a while to choose that outfit, did it?'

'No,' I lie. 'First thing I found when I opened my wardrobe.'

'Oh, really?' Sebastian says knowingly, taking a sip from his glass.

'Yes, really.'

The truth is I hadn't known what to wear tonight. I wanted to look casual because everyone in St Felix was relaxed about everything, including their dress, but I also wanted to look like I'd made a bit of an effort for Jack's special night.

'Prosecco?' I hear behind me, and I turn to see Bronte, Poppy's stepdaughter, carrying a tray with a number of glasses on it. 'Or we have orange juice?'

'Hello, Bronte,' I say, taking a glass of prosecco. 'How are you?'

Bronte looks at me for a moment in confusion.

'I'm Kate. I know your mum? I own the craft shop down the road.'

'Oh, of course. I'm sorry, Kate. Brain like a sieve, me. How are you?'

'Good, thanks, and you?'

'Yes, fab. I'm back for the holidays from uni, and I seem to have found myself a little job here for the summer.'

'Jack said he'd hired you. You'll enjoy working here amongst all the art equipment.'

'I'm afraid I might find it a bit too tempting and end up spending all my wages,' Bronte says with a grimace.

'All what wages?' a familiar voice says, and I see Jack feeding his way through the crowd towards us.

Of course. That's why there was plenty of space to get around in here compared to some of the overcrowded shops in St Felix. It was because Jack had made his shop completely accessible – not only for himself, but for any other disabled visitor who might want to have a browse. That's why there had been a small ramp outside, to the side of the two small steps needed to access the doorway.

'I'm not paying you enough to spend your wages in here, Bronte,' Jack teases. 'You must have me confused with a generous and kindly employer!'

Bronte, obviously already used to Jack's ways, just rolls her eyes at him and moves away with her drinks tray.

'Glad you could make it,' Jack says, looking up at me.

'Of course! I wouldn't have missed your opening.' I say, smiling down at him.

'She's only here to check that I'm not selling any craft equipment,' he says, winking at Sebastian. 'Isn't that right, Kate?'

'Hilarious,' I reply, rolling my eyes like Bronte. 'Have you met Sebastian?' I ask, putting my hand on Sebastian's shoulder. 'He helps me out in my shop.'

'No, I haven't. Pleased to meet you, sir.' Jack offers a hand up to Sebastian and they shake. 'I bet Kate had a few strong words to say about me when she heard I was opening this shop, didn't she?'

'Oh my goodness, she did!' Sebastian says without thinking. 'She was pacing and moaning about the shop like a cat on heat!'

'Oh really?' Jack says, lifting his eyebrows.

'I hardly think that's a fair or accurate comparison?' I protest, as Jack grins and Sebastian nods enthusiastically. 'I was simply concerned for my business, that's all.'

'And what about after she'd met me?' Jack asks innocently, looking at Sebastian.

'Purring like a kitten.' Sebastian smiles at me, and his smile rapidly drops as I glare back at him.

'Ignore my colleague,' I say, my cheeks feeling like they're the colour of the cadmium red paint I can see across Jack's

56

shoulder on the shelf. 'He tends to get a little carried away at times.'

'I like a man that tells it how it is,' Jack says, holding his knuckles out for Sebastian to bump, which Sebastian does with much glee. 'Now I must mingle! I'm glad you came, Kate,' he says, looking directly at me. 'Really glad.' Then he reverses in his chair and swings expertly around to chat to the next group of people keen to talk to him.

'Well,' Sebastian says, his eyebrows raised. 'He certainly has the hots for you!'

'*Shush!*' I say, turning my back to Jack, as if this will prevent Sebastian's words from reaching his ears. 'He has nothing of the sort. That's just his way – he's always trying to wind me up.'

'He can wind me up any day,' Sebastian says, gazing across my shoulder. 'You didn't tell me he was so *fit*.'

I shake my head. 'One, even if Jack were gay, which I'm pretty sure he's not, he's far too old for you!' I whisper to him sternly. 'And two, I hadn't even noticed he was ... well, hand-some,' I add, using a more appropriate term for me.

Sebastian grins and lifts his glass at me. 'You may be fooling yourself, Kate, but you're not for one moment fooling me!'

The opening continues to be well attended with even more people squeezing into the small shop, and it's good to see every-one from St Felix supporting a new business, like they had at the Lyle Gallery.

Jack makes a quick speech about halfway into the evening, which is well received. Then the guests, having had their nose around and their free drinks and nibbles, begin to thin out a little, allowing me to see more of the interior of the shop.

'Looks good, doesn't it?' Dec, from the Blue Canary Bakery, says to me as I gaze around.

'Yes, Jack seems to have squeezed a lot of stock into quite a small space, and yet it doesn't feel too crowded at all.'

'That's the problem with the buildings here,' Dec says, looking around him. 'They weren't built for shops that need to carry a lot of stock. The buildings were built for fishermen and their families, and have been reincarnated time and time again over the years to fit whatever business needs to inhabit them.'

'This wasn't always a butcher's before it was an art shop then?' I ask. I loved hearing about the history of St Felix and how it had changed over the years. There was always someone around who would chat to you about the 'good old days' if you wanted to hear about it.

'I don't really know,' Dec says, shrugging. 'It's been a butcher's since I came here. My uncle had my bakery before me.'

'Oh, that's right. I remember Ant telling me about it one day when I was in your shop and it was a bit quiet.'

'Must have been in the winter then,' Dec says ruefully. 'It's never quiet in the summer!'

'You shouldn't make such delicious cakes,' I tease.

'Ah, I can't take all the credit for that – family recipes passed down through the generations!'

'Evening,' Noah says, wandering over towards us. 'I can get over to speak to you now a few people have left. Kate, I wanted to tell you how great the old sewing machine looks in your window.'

We'd never solved the mystery of the sewing machine and where the embroidered picture had come from, so I'd popped the machine into the shop window yesterday with some of my designs, and as Noah had predicted it was showing them off beautifully.

'Thank you, yes, I'm very pleased with it.' I look around me. 'I would have thought Jack would have done something similar here with the art equipment he got from you?'

'Maybe he doesn't have the space right now?' Noah suggests. 'He's squeezed a lot of stock in here.'

'What equipment is this?' Dec asks.

'Noah did a house clearance recently and in it there was an old sewing machine that I now have, and some antique art equipment that Noah sold to Jack for the shop.'

'Ah, what house was this from?' Dec asks. 'Somewhere local?'

'Yes, actually. That large Victorian house just before you get to the coast road. The one with the blue door.'

Dec and I both nod.

'There was stuff in its attic that had been there for years, decades even. I don't think the elderly owner had any idea of the things that were hidden away up there. Her family simply seemed pleased I was prepared to take so much of it.'

'Is it empty now then?'

'Yes, but I think they want a fast sale. They seemed keen to get the place cleared as quickly as possible. I haven't really dealt with them all that much though. Unusually, the estate agent was my point of contact.'

'What a shame when your wealth is more important to your loved ones than your memories.'

'It is, Kate, but I see it all the time,' Noah says sadly.

'Why are you all looking so miserable?' Jack asks, approaching us. 'This is supposed to be a party!'

'Noah and I were just talking about the house clearance he did, and I was wondering what you'd done with the art equipment he sold you? We thought you might have had it on display tonight.'

59

Jack's face, which had been full of life and exuberance as he wheeled himself over to us, suddenly drains of its colour.

'Haven't really got room at the moment,' he says hurriedly. 'I will do something with it ... sometime. There's no rule that says I have to put it on display, is there, just because I bought it from you?' To my surprise he looks at Noah accusingly.

'Er ... no,' Noah says awkwardly. 'None at all.' He drains his glass and pops it down on a nearby counter. 'Well, I'd better be going.' He glances at his watch. 'Ana will probably be back by now with Daisy-Rose. Evening wedding,' he explains, 'down in Marazion.'

Dec and I both nod.

'Great shop you've got here, Jack,' Noah says, holding his hand out to him. 'I hope it does well for you.'

'Cheers, mate,' Jack says, shaking it. 'Sorry if I snapped at you before. It's been a long night, you know.'

Noah nods. 'See you guys around,' he says in parting to Dec and me.

'Bye, Noah.'

'Is Daisy-Rose his ... daughter?' Jack asks, looking at Dec and me.

'No.' I smile. 'Daisy-Rose is a little red camper van. Ana, his partner, rents it out for weddings and events.'

'Ah, I see. So much to learn about everyone here.'

'You'll get there,' Dec says. 'It takes everyone a while to get to know us, but then there's no turning back! Once you're in the St Felix gang, it's difficult to escape, isn't it, Kate?' He turns to me and offers me a high five, which I gladly return.

'He's right, but that's mainly because you don't want to leave,' I say happily. 'This place can be a little tight-knit, and odd things often happen here you can't always explain.' I think

60

of my sewing machine again. 'But we're a good bunch and St Felix is a lovely place to live.'

'It is that,' Dec agrees. 'Some folk even call it enchanted. There are a few tall tales that are regularly told in The Merry Mermaid about things that have happened here in the past.'

'Like what?' Jack asks with interest.

'Too many to tell you now,' Dec says. 'Pop in there sometime – you'll always find someone keen to talk to you about it all. Now it's my turn to depart. Where's that big lump of a partner of mine?'

'If you mean me,' Ant says, appearing behind him, 'I was just coming over to find you. Great event, Jack. *Lovely* food!'

'It should be – you made it,' Jack says, smiling at them.

'We did indeed!' Ant says beaming. 'That would be why then!'

Ant and Dec depart, and I'm left with Jack.

'I wonder where Sebastian has got to?' I say, gazing around vaguely. 'He was here a while ago. Everyone seems to be leaving all of a sudden.'

'That might have something to do with me,' Jack says, seeming a little uncomfortable. 'I think I get people's back up.'

'Don't be daft!' I reply, looking at him. 'Well, you can be a bit ... abrasive, shall we say, at times.'

'I don't mean to be. Sometimes I say things I think are amusing, but others don't seem to take it that way.'

'Is that your army background?' I ask kindly.

'Possibly. Perhaps I'm just an awkward bugger!'

'Maybe you are!' I say, grinning at him. 'But you were a bit odd with Noah when we mentioned the vintage art equipment. What was that about?'

'*Hmm* ...' Jack says, considering something. 'This is going to sound like a strange question, Kate, but has anything . . . *unusual* happened since you've had your old sewing machine?'

'How do you mean?' I ask as casually as I can when really I'm bursting with curiosity. Why was Jack asking? Had something happened to him too?

'I mean . . .' Jack looks incredibly uncomfortable. 'Has it *done* anything . . . something you can't quite explain?'

I look hard at Jack. This wasn't one of his jokes, was it? But he looks deadly serious.

'Actually . . .' I begin, but Sebastian suddenly reappears with Bronte in tow.

'Guess what, boss,' he says happily, his arm linked with Bronte's. 'We only go to the same art college in London!'

'I'm a year below Sebastian,' Bronte tells us. 'I never thought there would be another St Felixian studying there at the same time as me. What a small world.'

'Much as I hate to break up this school reunion,' Jack says to Bronte, 'I am paying you and we've got a lot of clearing up to do before we can go home tonight.'

'Soz, boss!' Bronte answers, saluting him. 'I'll get to it! See you around, Sebastian.'

'Of course, darling. Let's do coffee sometime?'

'Sure thing,' Bronte says. 'Okay, Jack, I'm going, I'm going.'

Bronte begins clearing up some glasses and discarded paper plates.

'Do you want some help?' I ask Jack. 'Clearing up?'

'Thank you, but we'll be fine. Maybe we can continue our conversation some other time though?'

I nod. 'Yes, of course. I'll pop back into the shop sometime, shall I?'

'I'll look forward to it,' Jack says smiling.

'Much as I hate to break up this gorgeous little tête-à-tête also,' Sebastian says, grinning at the two of us, 'do you want me to walk you home, Kate?'

I smile at his chivalry. 'That would be lovely, Sebastian, thank you.'

'Not a problem – it will be something new for me – walking a *woman* home. I feel the testosterone flooding through my body already!' He flexes his biceps.

I shake my head. 'Thank you for a lovely evening, Jack.'

'My pleasure. I hope it's the first of many that we share.'

I see Sebastian open his mouth to comment so I hurriedly put my arm through his where Bronte's has just been, and I guide him forcefully in the direction of the door.

As we're about to exit I turn back and quietly answer, 'I hope so too.'

Nine

'I'm just going to take Barney for a walk!' I call to Anita, as I grab Barney's lead and whistle for him to come to me. 'I won't be long.'

'Off to buy some art supplies, are you?' Anita asks, popping up from the back of the shop.

'No ... well, I might pass the art shop, I suppose, but why would I be going in there?'

'To see Jack, perhaps?' Anita asks with a twinkle in her eye.

'Has Sebastian been talking to you by any chance?' I answer. 'That boy can spread rumours quicker than I can spread Marmite!'

'I haven't seen Sebastian this morning,' Anita says in her usual demure way. 'He's not due in until this afternoon.'

'Then why would you say that?'

'We may have spoken on WhatsApp,' Anita says to my surprise. I didn't even think Anita knew what WhatsApp was, let alone how to use it.

'Gossiped on WhatsApp, more like!'

'Sebastian is simply keeping me updated. We often talk about the shop – what he's left for me to do and vice versa.'

'And the shop owner too by the sounds of it!'

Anita smiles demurely. 'We only want what's best for you, my dear. Besides, it might be pleasant for you to court a nice young man.'

I sigh. 'Firstly, I have no intention of *courting* anyone, Anita. And secondly, I'd hardly call Jack *a nice young man*. A difficult and often rude middle-aged man, perhaps?'

Anita just smiles again. 'If you say so, dear. If you say so.'

I deliberately walk Barney in the opposite direction to Jack's shop as I exit through my own shop door, even though I did have every intention of going to see him this morning.

It wasn't Jack's company I particularly sought. However, I did want to talk to him some more about what he had asked me last night before we were interrupted.

Because it had happened again.

When I'd been unlocking the shop this morning I'd glanced briefly into the window, as I always did, to check everything was all right and that nothing had fallen or slipped from our display overnight.

Nothing had been disturbed, but there *was* an addition to the window – another embroidered picture sitting under the foot of the sewing machine, like someone had just finished stitching it. This time it depicted a huge turquoise wave splashing over some grey-blue rocks. Again, it was exquisite work, but who had created it and how had it got in my shop window?

I hadn't said anything to Anita when she'd come in. I'd questioned her fairly intensively when the first picture had appeared, and it was clear she, like Sebastian, knew nothing about it, but now I had a feeling that Jack might.

After Barney has had a good run around I tether him to

his lead and walk back in the direction of the high street and the art shop.

I'm pleased to see quite a few people already browsing inside as I stare though the window hoping to spot Jack. I spy him talking to someone very intently about some pastel sticks. As if he senses me staring he turns to the window and raises his hand beckoning me to come in.

I point to Barney.

Jack nods and gestures for me to give him a minute.

While Barney and I wait outside I take part in one of my favourite pastimes – people-watching.

It's mid-morning and the majority of holiday-makers are just starting to appear from their holiday lets and the few hotel rooms that St Felix has to offer.

They're an odd mix: some have dressed appropriately for today's weather – slightly misty and damp with the promise of some light showers later – so a good few pairs of sturdy walking boots pass our way with sensible trousers and pack-a-macs at the ready, and some either haven't consulted any sort of forecast or they've stubbornly decided they're on holiday and are going to wear shorts, a T-shirt and flip flops, and consequences be damned!

I smile as I watch them amble by. I'd found it odd when I'd first moved here to be surrounded every day by people on holiday; they were rarely in a rush to go anywhere and it irritated me that they were always in my way, walking at what I felt was an incredibly slow pace. I'd spent a lot of my life living in big cities where people were always in a rush to get everywhere, but after I'd been in St Felix a few weeks I realised there was no point fighting against holiday-makers. It was like battling against the incoming tide – I was never going to win – so I'd allowed the much slower and more leisurely pace of life here by the sea to wash over me, and once I had I'd immediately noticed that I'd begun to feel much calmer and more relaxed too.

A couple of people exit from Jack's shop, and Jack follows them into the doorway.

'Hey, how are you?' he says. 'Do you want to come in?'

'What about Barney?' I ask. 'Do you mind?'

'Not at all. He's used to your shop, isn't he? He's not going to pee all over my easels?'

'I hope not!'

Jack reverses back in his chair and we follow him inside.

'I've got a dog bowl here that I was going to put outside the shop,' Jack says, reaching down behind the till, 'but I've been so busy this morning I haven't had a chance to fill it yet. Would you mind? Then Barney can have a drink.'

I'm touched he's thought not only of Barney but of all the other dogs that pass through the streets of St Felix, thirsty from long walks and playing in salty sea water.

'Sure,' I say, taking the bowl. 'Where should I . . . ?'

'There's a small basin by the loo at the back of the shop, but you'd be best filling it upstairs from the kitchen tap – it'll be cleaner water up there.'

'Okay, I'll be right back. Be a good boy, Barney!'

Barney is already sniffing around Jack to see if he has any treats for him.

I go through a side door that leads out to a small corridor and then up a set of newly carpeted stairs. I can't help wondering as I climb them how Jack copes with them.

When I get to the top I realise that Jack's flat is not too dissimilar to mine and Molly's. Through open doors I see a neat and tidy lounge area, two bedrooms, a bathroom and a kitchen, which is orderly and functional with newly fitted units, and as I run the water I think: *Why would Jack choose to live somewhere so difficult for him to get around?*

Yes, the flat obviously came with the shop, but surely he could have rented it out and lived somewhere more accessible? Perhaps he could only afford to do it like this? I mean it suited Molly and me to live above our shop, but Jack was different. How on earth did he cope?

I fill the dog bowl, realising for the first time that everything is much lower than I'm used to – the sink, the units, the cooker. Jack has had his kitchen designed to make it easier for him to access everything from his chair.

I carry the full bowl of water carefully to the top of the stairs, and notice for the first time a second wheelchair folded up next to the banister at the top.

Does Jack leave his other chair at the bottom and somehow make his way up here and use this one? I wonder, as I make my way slowly back down the stairs being careful not to spill the water.

'Here we go,' I announce brightly, carrying the bowl through the now empty shop towards Barney. I place it on the floor beside him and he laps thirstily from it.

'Thanks for doing that,' Jack says, watching Barney. 'As you can imagine it's quite the trek for me to get up there.'

'How *do* you get up and down the stairs?' I try to ask as casually as I can so as not to offend him again. 'It must be … difficult.'

'With these,' Jack lifts up his arms and flexes his well-defined biceps.

I must look puzzled because Jack continues, 'I sit on my behind and pull myself up and down.' He demonstrates in the chair by holding on to the sides and lifting his whole body up and down several times.

'You must be very strong.'

'In the upper body – yes. Not so much down below though.' He gazes regretfully at his legs. 'I haven't had the pleasure of either using or seeing them in years.'

I realise for the first time that the legs under Jack's loose trousers aren't real – they're prosthetics.

'Gosh, what happened?' I ask, my politeness evaporating. 'Oh sorry . . . I mean, you don't have to tell me. I don't mean to pry.'

Jack studies me for a moment; his chocolate brown eyes feel like they're scrutinising my every flaw. 'Landmine,' he eventually says matter-of-factly.

'You stepped on one?' I ask naively.

'You don't know much about landmines, do you?' Jack asks, quizzically tipping his head to one side. 'If I'd stepped on one I wouldn't be here now.'

'Yes, of course . . . sorry. So what did happen?'

'One of my mates caught a trip-wire. Two of them took the full brunt of the explosion. Blown to pieces, they were. Not to be too graphic but they found bits of them all over the place afterwards.'

'Oh God,' I shudder. This was terrible. Poor Jack.

'I was actually the lucky one,' he continues calmly. 'I was far enough away it only took my legs off. Most of this one' – he points to where his left leg should be – 'and this one just below the knee.'

'I'm so sorry, Jack.' I deliberately don't look at his legs but directly into his eyes. 'Really I am. It's just . . . ' I struggle to find the right word as they all seem pretty useless. ' . . . it's just awful,' I settle on eventually.

Jack shrugs, 'No need for you to be sorry. Used to it now, aren't I?'

'Couldn't you get prosthetic legs fitted to help you walk? Sorry,' I say again. 'That's none of my business.'

'Stop apologising, Kate! We went through all that the other day.'

'Sor—' I begin, and then I stop myself.

'The prosthetics thing is a fair question, and one I get asked quite a lot. What you see here' – he pokes at one of his legs – 'are cosmetic limbs. They don't work like functional prosthetics so I can't walk on them – they're simply for show. The nature of my injuries meant I wasn't suitable for functional ones. I'm not all that bothered about wearing these really, but people react better to me than when they see no legs at all. Plus functional prosthetics can be a right pain, or should I say *even more* of a pain than this thing.' He taps his wheelchair. 'It took a while to get used to my wheels, but I think I'm pretty damn slick in them now.'

I smile. 'I think you are too.'

A customer pops his head through the open shop door. 'Sorry to disturb, but do you have any Prussian blue? I thought I'd brought plenty with me but I've run out.'

'Of course,' Jack says, wheeling himself forwards. 'Oil or watercolour?'

'Oil, please. It's all the wonderful skies and seas here,' he explains to me. 'I can't stop painting them.'

The man pays Jack for the tube of paint. 'So glad I found you,' he says as he departs. 'I don't know what I'd have done if someone hadn't told me you were on the high street.'

'Call in any time!' Jack calls as the man departs.

'Will do!' He waves back. 'I'll be sure to run out of something else if I carry on being this productive while I'm here!'

'You might have found a gap in the market,' I tell Jack as he pops the money into his till.

'That's the idea!' Jack says. 'I know most people buy their art equipment online these days, but I'm here to cater to those who have run out or forgotten something, or those who are inspired to start painting while they're holidaying here. I've heard this place brings out the artistic side of people, sometimes when they don't even know they have one!'

'It's true. St Felix always attracted artists for the incredible light. It was in the fifties, I believe, when they first began to travel here in number. Do you paint yourself?'

'I dabble. I began during my rehabilitation and sort of carried on ever since. It's very relaxing. You said you sew a lot of what you sell?'

'Yes, with assistance.'

'Helps if you know something about what you're selling, eh?'

'Definitely. Talking of which,' I say, reminded of why I'm here, 'you were going to tell me something yesterday about the equipment you bought from Noah.'

'Ah, that.' Jack looks as uncomfortable as he had last night when we'd spoken about it. 'I wondered if you'd noticed any-thing *unusual* about your sewing machine?'

'What sort of *unusual*?' I ask, equally as guarded as Jack.

'I don't know . . . ' Jack looks down at the ground. 'Has it done anything *strange*?'

'Define "strange"?'

'Kate!' Jack says in exasperation. 'It's quite obvious to me it has, or you wouldn't be answering my questions with more questions of your own!'

'Well, you must have something to tell me too, or you wouldn't be asking in the first place!'

71

We stare defiantly at each other.

'Ladies first,' Jack says, holding out his hand in a gallant gesture.

I sigh. 'All right then ... So the first night I had the machine I gave it a really good clean. It brushed up really well, but however hard I tried to get it to work it still wouldn't sew.'

Jack nods. 'And?'

'And so I left it overnight in the shop, but the next morning ... ' I hesitate again. This was going to sound so daft and I could already hear Jack's mocking response to what I'm about to tell him.

'Go on, Kate.'

'The next morning I came downstairs into the shop, before it was unlocked or anything, and I found this piece of embroidery sitting in the machine, like someone had been stitching it and had left it there for me to find.'

I look at him, expecting to hear a smart comment or see amusement twinkling in his eyes, but he simply gazes back at me waiting for me to continue.

'What sort of embroidery?' Jack asks to my surprise.

'A picture. A very good one too – the embroidery is exquisite. It kind of looks like it's part of something bigger though.'

'How do you mean?'

'Like someone has taken a small sample of a larger picture and recreated it in embroidery thread.'

Jack nods. 'But you don't know who put it there?'

'Nope. I questioned everyone who might have been able to place something there overnight – only three of us have keys to the shop – but everyone denied it, said they knew nothing about it. It's still a complete mystery how it got there.'

'What was the picture of?' Jack asks quietly.

'Er, the first one was part of a harbour. It looked very much like the harbour here in St Felix, and the second—'

'Wait, there's been a second one?'

'Yes, last night. This time it's a—'

'—large wave crashing over some rocks?' Jack finishes to my amazement.

'Yes, how do you know?'

'Take a look out back,' Jack says, gesturing towards the back of the shop. 'There's a storage cupboard there.'

'Why?'

'Please, Kate, just take a look.'

Puzzled, I go to the back of the shop as he asks, and I open the cupboard he is pointing at. Inside I find lots of cardboard boxes, presumably filled with stock for the shop, but standing in front of the boxes is an old wooden artist's easel. It still has colourful splashes of paint on it from the previous owner, but the easel isn't the item I'm finding so astonishing, it's the painting that's perched on it and also the one below resting against its legs.

One is an oil painting of a harbour with a little white lighthouse at the end, and the other is of some large bluey grey rocks with huge turquoise waves splashing up over the top of them.

Ten

'Did you create these?' I demand, pulling the paintings from the cupboard and carrying them across the shop towards Jack. 'Is this your idea of a joke?'

'I wish,' Jack says, staring at them. 'I *wish* I was as good a painter as this artist is, and I *wish* I'd created them because then I'd know where the hell they came from!'

'What do you mean?' I ask, not following him. 'How can you not know where they came— Oh,' I say as the penny drops. 'Has the same thing happened to you too?'

Jack nods. 'Like you I put the old easel in pride of place in the shop window the evening before our opening, but when I came down the next morning the picture of the harbour was just *there*! I swear I'd left a blank canvas on it. Even fewer people have a key to this shop than yours, Kate. Bronte has a key now, but she didn't the other day. It was only me on my own.'

'And the second picture?' I ask, looking at the oil painting of the waves which is now leaning innocently against a shelf filled with sketch-books.

'It appeared this morning – out the back this time. I'd asked Bronte to take both the painting and the easel and put them in the store cupboard until I could figure out what was going on. I thought it might be some sort of St Felix initiation rite amongst the shop owners – you know, play a trick on the new boy in town – but when I asked a few questions at my opening night I realised no one knew anything about it. Then before I opened this morning the second painting had appeared on the easel just like the first . . . What the hell is going on, Kate?'

'I have no idea,' I say, shaking my head. 'It's so weird. It's definitely not the other shop owners. I mean, why would it be happening to me as well? I've been here for ages.'

'Exactly. Is it something to do with the equipment Noah sold us then?'

'Like what?' I ask. 'Do you think they're possessed?' I say jokily. 'A sewing machine that sews by itself, and an easel that produces paintings on its own! Are they haunted by their past owners?'

I grin at him, but Jack stares back at me with a haunted look of his own.

'No!' Jack says shaking his head. 'I don't believe in mumbo-jumbo like that. I was in the army for over fifteen years. Can you imagine the sort of ribbing you'd get if you said you believe in ghosts?'

'So what are we to think then?'

Jack shrugs. 'I really have no idea. It's a complete mystery.'

'Should we just wait and see if any more pictures appear?'

'What choice do we have?'

'Funny that both yours and mine are the same subjects though, isn't it?'

'Perhaps we should compare them?' Jack suggests. 'See

75

how similar they actually are – maybe that might give us some clue to why this is happening?'

'How about I pop over with the embroidery then later on tonight? It's a bit easier than yours to transport.' I look at my watch. 'I really should be getting back to the shop now. Anita will be wondering where I am.'

'That sounds like a plan,' Jack says, smiling at me. 'What time is good for you?'

'Er . . . ' I feel suddenly self-conscious, like we're arranging a date or something. 'About eight?' I suggest.

'Eight is good for me.' Jack's eyes lock with mine for a moment, and I'm the first to look away.

'Eight it is then!' I say overly brightly. 'Come along, Barney!' I call, waking my sleeping dog. 'Time to go!'

Barney yawns and slowly pulls himself to his feet. Jack smiles at him.

'He reminds me a lot of the sniffer dog we had in the last unit I was with,' he says wistfully. 'A springer spaniel that fella was, but he had a similar temperament to your Barney. Lovely dog, and bloody clever. He sniffed us out of many a dangerous situation. They're amazing animals, military working dogs. We're not supposed to get attached to them, but you can't help it when you're stationed so far away from home.'

I'm about to ask him more when an elderly couple walk into the shop.

'I'll see you later then?' Jack whispers.

I nod, and he goes over to greet his customers while Barney and I beat a hasty retreat from the shop.

As I stand outside inhaling deep breaths of fresh sea air I wonder whether the need to calm myself comes from discovering that strange things are happening not only in my shop but also here in Jack's, or whether I'm feeling ever so slightly giddy at the thought of spending more time in his company.

Eleven

'You're seeing him again?' Molly asks me later, when I'm hurriedly gathering our dinner things from the little table we share in the flat.

'Sort of,' I call from the kitchen as I load our plates into the sink. There are many, many things I love about our life here in St Felix, but the lack of space in our flat for a dishwasher isn't one of them.

'How is it only "sort of"?' Molly asks, following me with the condiments from the table. 'You're either going to his flat or you're not?'

'It's not a date, before you start with that one again. We've got some things to discuss, that's all.'

'What sort of *things*?' Molly replies, raising her eyebrows at me as she closes the fridge door. 'Leave them,' she says as I squirt washing-up liquid over our plates, 'I'll do it while you go glam yourself up!'

'I don't need to glam myself up!' I say, turning to Molly. 'Like I said it's not a date. However,' I add, pulling off my washing-up gloves and handing them to her, 'I'll still take you up on your very kind offer!'

Molly takes the gloves from me. 'Seriously, Mum,' she says, her pale green eyes blinking earnestly at me. 'It'll do you good to have some male company again. It's been ages since Joel.'

Joel, my last boyfriend, had been one of the main reasons I'd finally taken the plunge to give up my well-paid, secure job in a financial services company and move both Molly and myself down here to Cornwall to begin new lives as far away from him as possible.

He hadn't done anything that was too wrong – not to begin with anyway. It was his behaviour towards the end of our relationship that had caused the problems. We'd worked together in the same building, which was how we'd first met and why I'd had to leave – to get right away from him when he simply wouldn't accept that our relationship was over.

One of my friends had thought his behaviour way too controlling when we'd been together, and another had called it harassment when we'd broken up and had told me to get the police involved. Initially, though, I hadn't wanted to make too much of a fuss because of Molly. Joel wasn't violent to either Molly or me so contacting the police seemed a little harsh, but in the end it had become necessary as he just wouldn't leave me alone. As it turned out he did us a favour in forcing us to move away because both Molly and I were happier now than we'd been in a very long time. I'd therefore been surprised to hear her mention Joel's name, but they had been quite close in the time we were together so maybe it wasn't that strange.

'You're right,' I tell her, 'it has been a long time, but that doesn't mean I'm about to embark on a new relationship simply because I met a man a couple of times for a chat.'

'No, I know, but I think it would be nice for you, that's all. You work too hard, Mum. You need to play a little more.'

I reach out to hug Molly, and then I pause and hold her back a little in my arms. 'Wait, you're not just talking about me, are you?' I ask suspiciously. 'Where is it you want to go, and when and with whom?'

Molly grins. 'You're too good, Mum! Actually, there is a little party being held this weekend. One of my school friends' brother is having an eighteenth birthday party and he's said she can invite a few of her friends along too.'

'An eighteenth, Molly? You've only just turned fifteen!'

'*Purrlease*, Mum? I won't drink or anything like last time . . .'

I look at Molly's expectant face. The last time I'd let her go to a party had been against my better judgement when one of her former classmates had thrown a Halloween party. In my day Halloween meant trick-or-treating, and maybe a bit of innocent apple bobbing. It certainly didn't involve apples floating in a punch that had been laced with several varieties of alcohol. The end result had seen me spending most of the night at Molly's bedside while she threw up in a bucket, then scrubbing the hall carpet where she hadn't quite made it to the bathroom in time.

'I've learnt my lesson,' Molly adds, while I weigh all this up in my mind. 'I'll be super careful, I promise.'

'So who is having this party? Do I know their parents?'

'It's my friend Emily's brother, Sam.'

I think about this for a moment. 'Oh, Jenny's son – tall, red-dish hair? Works in the ice cream parlour sometimes?'

Molly nods.

Jenny and her husband are very sensible. They wouldn't allow anything bad to happen in their house, I was sure of it. 'Okay, then, you can go, but I'll be having a quick word with Jenny beforehand to see what's what.'

'*Yes!*' Molly exclaims, pumping the air. 'I mean, thanks,

Mum, you're the best!' She hugs me. 'I'll just text Emily, then I'll come back and do this washing up for you right away. The party is at the community centre, by the way,' she adds casually as she leaves the room.

I sigh. I should have known it wouldn't be in Jenny and Steve's newly renovated home, but I'd said yes now and I couldn't keep Molly wrapped up in cotton wool for ever, however much I'd like to. She was growing up fast, too fast, and I had to let her.

'I meant what I said before,' Molly says, popping her head back around the door. 'You deserve some fun too, Mum. Now Joel isn't in the picture perhaps this Jack might be the one?'

I head back to Jack's shop a little before eight o'clock, the embroidered pictures tucked away in my bag.

I press the buzzer next to the shop for the flat and wait.

'Hi Kate, come on up!' I hear over the intercom within seconds.

The door in front of me magically unlocks and I make my way inside, finding myself in the same hallway I'd been in earlier that runs parallel with the side of the shop.

I climb the stairs, following the sound of Jack's voice.

'I'm in the living room!' he calls, so I make my way across the landing towards the room I'd seen in passing earlier today.

'Sorry I couldn't come down to greet you properly,' Jack says apologetically, 'but you already know why.'

'Don't be silly, it's fine,' I say, wondering where I should sit. Jack is in what I now recognise to be his second, slightly smaller wheelchair by the open window. I notice immediately that he's not wearing his prosthetic legs; instead his cargo-style trousers are pinned up where his own legs end.

'You don't mind, do you?' Jack says, noticing me looking at them. 'I only wear the legs when I have to – they're not always that comfortable.'

'Of course not,' I say, wishing I hadn't stared. 'Why should I?'

'Ah, you know … people can be odd sometimes about disability.'

'Not me.'

'Good, have a seat,' Jack says, gesturing to the bright comfy-looking sofa. 'I saw you coming down the road. Perfect view from up here of all the comings and goings on the high street.'

'I bet you have,' I say, sitting down.

'I'd rather have a lovely view of the sea, mind, but those windows rent for a fair bit more than my busy view.'

'We're very lucky where we are because our shop backs on to the harbour – the flat has wonderful views out to sea.'

'Oh yes, so you do. You don't realise that when you're down in Harbour Street though. All the shops seem quite small and dark along there.'

'I prefer quaint and cosy,' I reply firmly.

'Yes, that's probably a better way to describe them. They're not as big as us up here on the high street, but you probably get a lot more of the tourist trade where you are, so I guess we're even.'

I look at Jack. Did he even know he was bordering on being rude again?

'Drink?' Jack asks brightly when I don't reply. 'I have various juices, some fizzy water … or maybe you'd prefer some wine?'

'An orange juice will be fine, thank you,' I say, still irked by his slight, unintentional or not, on my shop.

Jack puts his hands on his wheels.

'Would you like me to get—' I begin, about to stand up. 'No, of course you wouldn't. Go ahead.' I say, holding out my hand as I settle back on the sofa.

'At least you didn't say sorry this time,' Jack answers, grinning at me as he expertly wheels himself through the small doorway.

He returns a few moments later with two glasses of juice balanced on a small tray on his lap.

'Can I take that from you?' I ask, trying not to sound sarcastic. I was still getting used to Jack and his ways, and it was difficult to find the right balance between being too helpful and ill-mannered.

'You can indeed,' Jack says.

I lift the tray on to a little coffee table, take a glass of juice for myself and pass the other to him.

'So, these pictures . . .' Jack begins, resting his glass down on the table. 'You've brought yours, I assume?'

'I have indeed.' I reach into my bag and retrieve the embroidery, then I pass it to Jack.

'Wow, they're exactly like parts of my paintings,' he says, examining the two pieces. 'I mean *really* alike.'

'I know they are. I wish I knew why though. I thought about it so much this afternoon in between customers, and I still can't come up with any sort of sensible explanation.'

'Me either,' Jack says, passing the embroidery back to me.

'Are your pictures still downstairs? Shall I fetch them so we can take a look at them together?'

'They're still in the store cupboard at the back of the shop. The key is hanging on a hook at the top of the stairs. Oh, and you'll need to reset the alarm when you go in – it's just inside the interior door downstairs. The code is five, five, two, four.'

'Five, five, two, four. Got it! I'll be back in a bit.'

I head down the stairs again to the door that leads from the hallway into the side entrance of Jack's shop. I turn the key, open the door and then quickly silence the alarm by inputting the digits. I make two trips, carrying the pictures back up the stairs first and then the easel.

'Right,' I finally say as I stand the easel up in Jack's sitting room. 'First, the harbour pictures.'

I place the oil painting of the harbour up on the easel and hold my matching embroidery picture up next to it.

'Way too similar to be a coincidence,' Jack says, studying the two pieces of artwork.

'I know,' I reply, looking at them. 'But what does it mean? Who would do this and why? It makes no sense.'

'Do you think it's something to do with the fact that both of the items that seem to be – and I hesitate to use this term – *creating* these pictures come from the same house?'

'What do you mean?'

'I don't know really?' Jack says, shrugging. 'I'm grasping at straws, but the easel and the sewing machine came from the same house clearance, didn't they? Do you think they were owned by the same person?'

'They might have been, I guess. Perhaps it might help us if we found out more about the elderly lady who used to live there. It's that big old Victorian house with the blue door up on the coast road. Noah told me.'

'Has anyone new moved in there since the house clearance, do you know?'

'I don't. But we could probably find out easily enough. There's always someone who knows what's going on around here – you only have to speak to a few people before you find out the information you want.'

'Great, that's where we should start then.' Jack wheels himself closer to the easel to look at the two pictures. 'Let me have your embroidery again,' he says, holding his hand out.

I pass him the fabric.

'The scale is almost exactly the same,' he says, holding the fabric up next to the painting. 'Look – when I hold the embroidery up it's like a section that has been cut out of the painting.'

'Oh yes,' I say, standing behind him. 'It almost makes it three dimensional you holding it over the painting like that. The lighthouse comes to life. We could have created a whole new artistic genre here!'

I'm joking, but Jack doesn't laugh. Instead he simply stares at the fabric.

'What? What is it?' I ask, but Jack doesn't respond.

'You've gone a little pale, Jack,' I say, staring at him. 'What's wrong?'

'Er . . .' Jack rests the embroidery on his lap and rubs his eyes. 'I'm not really sure. Perhaps you should take a look, in case I'm seeing things.'

'What do you mean?' I ask, taking the fabric from him as he wheels himself backwards so I can stand in front of the easel. Was he playing a joke on me?

'Hold the fabric over the canvas,' he instructs, 'in exactly the right place so the two pictures match up.'

'Okay . . .' I say hesitantly, wondering what I'm supposed to be seeing.

'Look at it,' Jack says. 'I mean *really* look into it, and tell me what you see.'

I do as he says, first matching up the two pictures, then staring hard at them. 'I can't see anything unusual,' I say.

'Crouch down,' Jack says, 'so you're at eye level with them like I was.'

'Okay ...' I say again, bending down a little so my eye line is level with the little lighthouse on the harbour depicted in the embroidery.

'What do you see now?' Jack asks. 'Kate?' he asks again when I don't respond. 'Are you seeing what I did?'

'That depends,' I reply quietly, 'on whether you saw a moving picture?'

'I did,' Jack says equally as quietly. 'That's why I was rubbing my eyes. How are we both seeing a moving image in something as static as a painting?'

'I don't know,' I say, still observing what's going on, 'but I'm not going to stop watching now, are you?'

I make room for Jack to come in close beside me, and we peer intently at the pictures. Both of us let all our rational thoughts dissipate while we allow ourselves to become absorbed in the moving images in front of us.

St Felix ~ May 1957

'Please, Mummy, can we go a bit closer!' a young girl in a simple yet functional wheelchair pleads.

'All right, just for a little while,' her mother relents, and she pushes the wheelchair a little bit closer to the end of the harbour wall.

'Can I get out?' the girl asks. 'Just for a bit?'

'No, Maggie, you're not strong enough yet. Remember what Doctor Jenkins said – you need to rest and recuperate.'

'I'm fed up with recuperating,' Maggie says huffily, 'it's so dull.'

'I know, darling, but your convalescence is so important, otherwise you might never fully recover.'

Maggie sighs. 'Why did I ever have to catch silly polio anyway. None of my friends got it. Why me?'

Her mother sighs; 'Yes, you *were* very unlucky in that way, but so very lucky in others when you see how some of the other children who caught it have suffered. At least you will be able to walk and talk properly again. I've read some terrible stories in the newspaper about children being paralysed and only being able to breathe using one of those horrible iron-lung machines. At least you didn't have to use one of those when you were in hospital.'

'I saw those in another ward,' Maggie says, looking sad. 'They looked horrible.'

'Anyway,' her mother says brightly, 'let's not dwell on the past. We have a lovely new future to look forward to now we're here in St Felix. If you breathe in as much of the healing sea air as you can, you'll be back to your old self in no time.'

Maggie doesn't look so sure.

'Excuse me,' a man says, approaching them both. In contrast to the woman's neat, smart clothing of a pale pink cardigan, tweed skirt, pearls and a cream blouse, the man is wearing much more casual attire: a striped smock top, loose trousers and a red scarf tied jauntily at his neck, while on his feet he wears brown leather sandals. 'I hope you don't mind but I did a quick sketch of the two of you while you were at the end of the harbour just now, and I wondered if you might like it?'

The woman looks warily at the man, but Maggie eagerly pipes up, 'Ooh, yes, please!'

The man smiles at her and passes her a page from his sketch-book.

'Look, Mum, it's us!' Maggie cries excitedly.

The woman looks over Maggie's shoulder at the drawing. 'So it is.' She turns to the man. 'I can't afford to buy it off you, if that's what you're hoping for,' she tells him firmly.

'Not at all,' the man answers, smiling at her. 'It's a gift. I heard what you and your daughter were talking about – terrible disease.' He says this softly so Maggie, who is still happily examining the drawing, can't quite hear. 'I have friends who've been affected too. Hopefully the epidemic will be long gone now they've found a vaccine.'

'Yes, I hope so too,' the woman agrees. 'That's very kind of you to offer us your drawing. Thank you very much.'

'My pleasure,' the man says. 'You're new to St Felix?'

'We've been here a few weeks, but fairly new, yes.'

'Arthur,' the man says, holding out his hand, 'but my friends call me Arty.'

'Clara,' the woman says, taking it. 'Very nice to meet you, Arthur.'

Arty grins. 'So formal. St Felix will soon rub off some of that.'

Clara looks uncomfortable. 'I do hope not. Well, thank you again for the drawing. My daughter seems to like it very much.'

'See you around, Maggie!' Arty says, saluting as Clara begins to push her away.

'I hope so, Arty!' Maggie calls back, but Clara remains silent, her head down as she hurriedly pushes her daughter's wheelchair back along the harbour cobbles.

'Well,' Jack says as the moving pictures in front of us begin to swirl together and gradually fade away. 'That was ... unexpected.'

'You could say that,' I reply, still staring at the pictures in front of me. Everything has gone completely back to normal now, and in front of us resting on the easel are simply an oil painting and a piece of embroidered felt. 'Did we imagine what just happened?'

'How could we have? We both saw exactly the same thing, didn't we? A woman and a child in a wheelchair, talking to a man who'd drawn a picture of them.'

'Clara, Maggie and Arthur,' I say quietly as though clarifying it for myself.

'Arty,' Jack adds, smiling, 'He preferred to be called Arty.'

'So he did ...' I look at Jack; his mystified expression mirrors my own inner thoughts. 'When do you think that was supposed to be?' I ask. 'They were wearing old clothes – the fifties maybe?'

'Yes, I thought that too,' Jack agrees. 'Also, I think polio was around in the fifties. Didn't we have a huge epidemic in the UK back then?'

I nod. 'Yes, I think you're right, it was about then.'

'I felt sorry for the kid in the wheelchair. It's bad enough being in one when you're my age – at least in mine I can push myself around. Looks like she had to rely on her mother to push her everywhere.'

'Hopefully it wasn't for long though. It sounds like she was on her way to recovery from what they were saying. They sent people to the seaside to recuperate back then, didn't they? They thought the sea air was healing.'

'I think it still is,' Jack says. 'I've definitely felt better since I've been here ... but we're getting slightly off track. Back to these ... these pictures,' he says, for want of a better description of what we've just seen.

'Just why *are* we seeing a scene from the fifties played in front of us?' I ask. 'It's obviously something to do with our two works of art.' I look at them again. 'But what?'

Jack and I both stare at the easel.

Then we both turn to one another at exactly same time and say: 'The rock painting! The waves embroidery!'

I hurriedly take the harbour picture off the easel and replace it with the one of the rock and waves. Exactly as we'd done before, Jack holds my embroidery over the right spot on the painting so that the two of them match precisely and immediately, in the same magical way, the images begin to move and swirl together in front of us.

'Are you ready?' Jack asks, looking keenly at me.

'I am. Let's do this!'

Suddenly, there's a ringing sound that makes both of us jump.

'It's the shop alarm,' Jack says looking at me. 'Did you reset it properly?'

'Yes,' I reply, looking puzzled. 'I'm sure I did. Wait there. I'll go and check on it.'

I grab the key and hurry down the stairs. I unlock the door and immediately try to silence the alarm by putting in the same digits 5524, but it doesn't stop so I have to try again.

'It's not working!' I call up the stairs. 'I'm putting in the code but it's still ringing.'

'Try again!' Jack shouts back down. 'Five, five, two, four, yes?'

'Yes, that's what I'm doing.'

I hurry back to the shop and keep trying the code, but the painfully shrill noise just keeps going.

I dash back out to the hallway about to call up to Jack again, but to my surprise he's already heading down the stairs.

I watch in admiration and awe as he expertly propels himself down the stairs, his strong muscular arms swinging his body from step to step.

When he reaches the bottom I realise he's stretching for his wheelchair, so I hurriedly push it towards him.

'I can do it!' he snaps as he pulls himself up and on to the chair.

I stand aside as he now wheels himself towards the shop and through the door. Within a few seconds the alarm has stopped.

'You did it!' I say happily as I stand in the doorway watching him.

'Yes,' he says sourly. '*I* did.'

'What did you do?' I ask, wondering why he is being a bit off with me.

'What I asked *you* to do – merely press four numbers.'

'I did. I put in the numbers. Five, five, two, four, right?'

'Simple enough, one would have thought, but apparently not in your case.'

My eyes narrow as my hackles bristle. 'What's your problem, Jack? Why are you having a go at me, what have I done?'

Jack shakes his head and turns away. 'It doesn't matter. Perhaps you'd better go. I think I've had enough of your ... weirdness for one night.'

'*My* weirdness? I'm not the one who has an easel that brings pictures to life, am I? Or an alarm that only resets when it wants to.'

. . . alarm, but not at me.

. . . s first?'

I don't say goodbye. I simply walk past him, let myself out of the door and slam it behind me.

That man! I think, as I march back down the street. *His mood changes more often than the tides in the harbour. What the hell is wrong with him? And more to the point: Why do I care so much?*

Twelve

The next morning, I awake early and I lie in my bed still ruminating over what had happened in Jack's flat last night.

I'm annoyed, exasperated and saddened all at the same time, but the sound of the waves outside my bedroom window helps soothe my thoughts, and I begin trying to piece together the events in a calmer, more considered way.

Why had Jack suddenly flipped like that? If he was going to stress out, surely it should have been when we saw the moving images from the pictures, not when I couldn't silence his shop alarm?

I go over each moment in my mind in case I'd said or done something that might have upset him.

There was nothing. Everything had been going fine until the damn alarm had gone off and Jack had had to come down the stairs and sort it out.

I think about him descending the stairs, his strong arms lifting himself from step to step – it puts me in mind of an Olympic gymnast expertly swinging themselves around on one of those things we used to have to vault over in P.E. at school. What were they called? Ah, yes – a pommel horse.

Jack had carried himself with as much grace and muscle power as any of those athletes did. It had quite taken me aback, but why had he got the hump with me shortly after?

I sigh. I simply don't understand.

I decide the best thing, once it's time to get up, is to carry on as usual. Even though I'm dying to know what might happen if we match our second two pictures together there is no way I'm going to go back there after the way he behaved last night. I'll just have to wait and wonder.

Over the next few days everything goes back to normal. The amount of customers coming through the door of my shop as always starts to rise as we approach the end of the week and holiday-makers arrive for long weekends and for Friday bookings.

I don't see or hear from Jack at all. Although I deliberately avoid passing by his shop, I wonder why he hasn't popped by mine – if only to apologise for his strange outburst.

I've just finished serving a lady who is buying some new crochet needles when a large expensive-looking bunch of flowers appears through the door, hiding a familiar face behind it.

'Delivery for a Kate that owns the craft shop!' Poppy calls, peeking around the large bouquet.

'What?' I ask, staring at the flowers. 'You must be mistaken, Poppy.'

'Nope, no mistake. Says it on the card right here.' She lays them on the desk in front of me and points to a small white envelope on the front that simply reads *Kate*.

'But who would be sending me flowers? It's not my birthday.'

'Why don't you open it and see?'

I pull the small white envelope from the bouquet of flowers and tear it open. In typed black ink, it says:

> So sorry I've not been in touch.
> Speak very soon, I hope.
> J x

'Who sent these?' I ask Poppy.

Poppy shrugs. 'It was an internet order, I think. I'd have to ask Amber – she makes up all the bouquets.'

'Right.'

'How many people do you know whose name begins with J that might send you flowers though?' she points out. 'There can't be that many.'

I think about this. Could it be Jack apologising for the other night? It didn't seem his style, but then how well did I actually know him? Every encounter we had seemed to end awkwardly.

'No, there's not,' I reply, deliberately trying to dodge answering her question. 'It's a mystery.'

'*Ooh*, someone's popular!' Sebastian cries, appearing at the top of the stairs. 'Who's sending you flowers, Kate – a secret admirer perhaps?'

'I hardly think so,' I reply hurriedly, tucking the card in my jeans pocket.

'It's from someone with the initial J,' Poppy blurts out before I can stop her. 'But Kate doesn't know who?'

'Oh really?' Sebastian says, with one eyebrow raised. 'Now who might we know who has a name beginning with J ... *Hmm.*' He pretends to think. 'Could it be the local art-shop owner, perhaps?'

'Jack?' Poppy asks, her eyes wide. 'I didn't know you two were an item!'

'We're not,' I quickly retort. 'They're not from Jack.'

'How do you know?' Sebastian asks, looking at Poppy. 'There must have been a card.'

Poppy glances at me, but I shake my head with the tiniest of movements while glaring fiercely at her.

'Anonymous,' she says quickly. 'We get them sometimes.'

'Even more curious,' Sebastian says, looking at each of us, 'when you said just now they were from someone with the initial J.'

I sigh. 'Okay, there was a card,' I say, pulling it from my pocket. 'Here.'

Sebastian examines the card. 'Anita said you and Jack argued the other night. Why can't they be from him?'

I was beginning to regret telling anyone anything about Jack. They seemed to spend all their free time gossiping about me.

'Argued about what?' Poppy asks.

'It's nothing,' I reply. '*Really*,' I insist, when both of them open their mouths to ask more questions. 'These flowers won't be from Jack. I'll just have to wait and see whether my mystery admirer gets in touch another way,' I say to appease them. 'Now, Sebastian, we've got customers to attend to. Thanks for dropping these by, Poppy.'

'Sure,' Poppy says, taking the hint. 'I need to get back to my own shop anyway. Amber is going for a dress-fitting this afternoon. I can't believe that she and Woody are finally getting married – so exciting! Anyway, let me know if you figure the mystery out!'

Poppy leaves, and Sebastian and I spend the rest of a busy afternoon serving customers, but all the time at the back of my mind is the niggling little question: Who *had* sent me the flowers that now stand blossoming in a vase on the shop counter? If it is Jack then should I thank him for them? Or should I wait until he approaches me first?

And if it isn't Jack, then who is it? And why are they apologising to me?

Thirteen

'Barney!' I yell, as I watch him disappear around some rocks jutting out over the sand while the tide is out. 'Come back here at once!'

But Barney, usually so obedient, keeps going. I up my pace and hurry after him, jogging around the rocks.

'Oh!' I cry, startled by what I find. 'It's you.'

'It is indeed me,' Jack says, looking up at me while he pats Barney.

'How— How are you?' I ask, suddenly tongue-tied.

'Good actually. I'm trying out my new set of wheels.' He gestures to his wheelchair. 'They're made especially for sand. I've been waiting for them to arrive since I got here. Now I can travel across the beach at low tide like everyone else. I came down the slipway,' he adds, 'before you ask how I got over the soft sand.'

I look across to the slipway, which at high tide is fully covered with water, but now while the tide is out it's the perfect ramp for a wheelchair to travel down on to the hard compact sand.

'It's a bit like running on sand,' Jack explains. 'It's more difficult than on solid surfaces, so you work harder and gain more fitness as a result.'

'Ah ... I see,' I reply, not really knowing what to say. I feel a bit awkward, to be honest, as the last time we'd spoken it hadn't exactly been friendly. 'So now you have four wheelchairs?'

If I could have grabbed the words back before they floated across towards Jack I would have. I'm sure he didn't need reminding of that.

But Jack doesn't seem in the least bothered by my comment. 'I suppose I do. They all have their own purpose though.'

'You sound like me and bags,' I say, trying to recover. 'You can never have too many. Some women, it's shoes. But me, its bags.'

'Right,' Jack says, nodding.

'I mean, I'm not saying bags are like wheelchairs, obviously they're much more important. Wheelchairs, I mean, not bags.'

Oh Lord, I may as well dig myself a hole in the sand.

Jack just smiles, unlike me not seeming in the least bit uncomfortable. 'I think Barney spotted me across the sand just now,' he says. 'Sorry if he ran off.'

'It's fine. I wondered why he'd suddenly shot off like that – he's usually so well behaved on walks.'

'Yes ... ' Jack says, watching Barney run around on the sand. There's a slight pause in the conversation while we look at Barney, and I'm about to try to fill it but Jack gets there first:

'I'm sorry,' he says suddenly, 'about the other night.'

I turn to look at him.

'I shouldn't have snapped at you the way I did.'

I shrug. 'No harm done.'

'But I think there is,' Jack insists. 'I thought you might pop into the shop again if you were passing, but you didn't.'

'You could have come to see me,' I say. 'It's not like you don't know where I am.'

'I know,' Jack says, his head dropping towards his chest. 'I'm not very good at words. I'm much better at actions. They say actions speak louder than words, don't they?' He looks up again apologetically.

Was he talking about my flowers? He must be ...

'Thank you for the flowers,' I say without thinking. 'They are really lovely and very pretty. I have them on my shop counter.'

'Flowers?' Jack asks, looking mystified.

Oh no, it wasn't him. Me and my big mouth.

'Did you think *I'd* sent you flowers?'

'I ... I didn't know if it might be you?' I reply hurriedly, trying to dig myself out of the huge hole that has appeared beneath me. It feels like I'm standing on quicksand the depth of my embarrassment is so great. 'The card was signed *J*.'

'Sorry!' Jack says, holding up his hands. 'Not me. You must have another admirer.'

Did he just say *another* admirer?

'Obviously I have,' I reply lightly. 'Aren't I the lucky one.'

We stare at each other for a second.

'So, we, er ... we never got around to comparing that second picture, did we?' Jack says quickly, changing the subject. 'If you'd like to pop by sometime we could try it and see if the same thing happens again?'

'Promise you won't shout this time?' I reply teasingly, as I feel the atmosphere between us lightening by the second.

'Promise,' Jack says, saluting in return. 'It wasn't you I was cross with. I took my anger out on you, that's all, and again I'm truly sorry for that.'

'Who were you cross with then?'

'Myself,' Jack says so quietly I can barely hear him above the noise of the gulls and the sea breeze.

'I don't understand.'

'Look, come over to mine later and I'll explain properly,' Jack answers. 'If you're free of course – it is a Friday night.'

'It's a long time since I had regular plans on Friday nights. I leave that to my daughter now. She's off to an eighteenth birthday party later.'

'Good for her.'

'I know. I'm pleased she's being invited places, but she's fifteen and I worry about her, probably a little too much actually.'

'You'll always do that – that's a mother's job. And a father's too,' he adds.

'Do you have children?'

'Just the one – Ben. He lives with his mother now though. We split up a number of years ago.'

'Ah,' I nod with understanding. 'But you see him regularly?'

'School holidays, the odd weekend, that sort of thing. It's easier now he's a bit older as he can travel to see me – he recently turned eighteen.'

'Then we have something else in common – the joys of bringing up teenagers!'

Jack rolls his eyes. 'Yup! And ain't that fun and games!'

Barney is getting restless now; he's smelt all the interesting scents in the vicinity, played with the friendlier dogs on the beach and is heading back to see us.

'Right, we'd better head off. I'll pop round later then?'

'I'll look forward to it,' Jack says. 'Same sort of time as before?'

'Sure.'

I smile at him and give him an awkward sort of half wave as Barney and I depart across the sand together.

'Barney, I won't often tell you that you did the right thing by running off,' I whisper to him as I pat his damp fur, 'but today you were a star!'

'What time does the party finish again?' I ask Molly, as she looks at herself in my long mirror for what seems like the twentieth time in the last ten minutes.

'I told you – we have to be out of the community centre by eleven, so not late.'

'You'll be careful, won't you?' I say for at least the third time.

'Yes, Mum,' Molly says, turning towards me now. 'I won't drink alcohol.' She counts on her fingers. 'I won't take drugs. And I won't have unprotected sex.'

My eyes open wide.

'I'm joking!' she says, grinning at me. 'Lighten up, Mum!'

I breathe a sigh of relief.

'You have to promise me to do the same while you're over at Jack's,' she says, her eyes shining mischievously.

'Scout's honour!' I answer, playing along. 'Now, give your mum a hug.'

We embrace briefly and then the doorbell sounds downstairs.

'That will be Emily!' Molly says excitedly. 'Gotta go!'

She checks herself in the mirror one more time.

'You look lovely,' I tell her. 'Stop worrying.'

'Night, Mum. Have a good time with Jack. Don't do anything I wouldn't do!'

I shake my head as she departs down the stairs. When had someone replaced my little girl with this grown-up version? She might be eager to cut her ties and head off into the adult world, but it would be a long time before I was ready to let her go.

'Have a great time!' I call, just before I hear the door slam. 'And be good.' I whisper as the door closes behind her.

'So, you ready?' Jack asks a little later when we've set the easel up in his flat, ready to match the pictures together.

'As I'll ever be.'

I hold my embroidered felt over Jack's oil painting of the sea and rocks, exactly like we had the first time, so it matches the artwork of the canvas perfectly. Almost at once the images swirl and blend together and we're transported once again back to a vintage St Felix.

St Felix ~ June 1957

Clara pushes Maggie in her chair up a steep hill. It was difficult pushing her along this part of the coastal path, but it meant the two of them could venture further away from the town, which was becoming busy with visitors now summer was in full swing.

Hordes of excited holiday-makers arrived in their buses and on the coastal railroad by steam train, some just for the day and some staying in the many new B&B guest houses that were opening everywhere.

The town was alive with the sound of excited chatter as families from all over the country enjoyed, often for the first time, a traditional Cornish seaside holiday.

'Oh, Mummy, the air is so fresh up here!' Maggie calls, as Clara pushes her further up the hill. 'Thank you for bringing me – it's so beautiful.'

Clara remembered coming here with her aunt and uncle when she had stayed with them in 1945. It had been an easy walk at first, but as the months had passed the walk had become more and more difficult. However, it had been nowhere near as hard as pushing a wheelchair along this path today. Still, she would do anything for her only child, and if it meant she was the one who was a little uncomfortable today, then so be it.

'Oh look, Mummy,' Maggie calls. 'It's the painting man again.'

'Where?' Clara asks, looking around her.

'Arty!' Maggie calls before Clara can stop her. 'Arty, over here!'

Clara spies Arty sitting a little way below them in front of some rocks on a small stool. He has his easel set up in front of him and he's in the middle of a painting. He turns when he hears his name called and waves to them.

Maggie waves back. 'Push me over there, Mummy,' she insists.

'Please,' Clara reminds her. 'And I don't think I can – it's too steep for your chair.'

'Then I'll climb out,' Maggie says, already lifting herself out, but her weak legs begin to crumble underneath her after she's only taken a few steps and she tumbles on to the grass.

'*Maggie!*' Clara cries, trying to park the wheelchair so it doesn't roll down the hill after her.

Arty is already on his way over, so before Clara can get any-where near Maggie his long legs have carried him up the slope towards her. He scoops her up in his strong arms before Clara can get to them.

'Are you all right?' Clara asks, running barefoot towards them with her shoes in her hands.

'Yes, Mummy, I'm fine,' Maggie says, looking shyly up at Arty.

'I believe this young lady belongs to you?' Arty says, smiling at Clara.

'Yes, thank you for coming to her rescue. Your footwear is a lot more practical than mine for running up and down hills.'

Arty looks at Clara's neat black slip-on pumps. 'But nowhere near as pretty,' he says, smiling at her.

Clara's cheeks flush.

'Can you take me to see your painting?' Maggie asks, looking down the hill towards Arty's easel. 'Mummy says my chair won't go down there.'

'Of course!' Arty says. 'If that's okay with your mother?'

Clara looks uneasy. 'Well … if you have no objections, Mr—? I'm sorry I'm not sure I caught your full name the last time we met.'

'I'll repeat what I said then. Please call me Arty, and you are Clara if I remember correctly.'

'Yes, I am,' Clara says, a little flustered by his informality.

'Right then, I'll carry young Maggie down there first, and then I'll come back up for her chair. Will you be okay getting down there, Clara, or should I carry you too?'

'I will be just fine, thank you,' Clara says, choosing to ignore the twinkle in Arthur's blue eyes. 'But please be careful with Maggie, won't you – she's still convalescing and is quite delicate.'

Arty, competently, not only carries Maggie and her chair down the hill towards his easel but guides Clara too by holding on to her hand so she can make her way safely over the grass towards the edge of the cliff.

Now they all sit together looking out over the rocks that hug this part of the St Felix coastline and towards the sea that today delicately licks the edges of the granite but on a less calm afternoon would try to batter it into submission.

'I like your painting,' Maggie says, peering intently at Arty's easel.

'Thank you. Probably not one of my best, but it's a *work in progress* as us artists like to say when things aren't going too well.'

'Is this your full-time job?' Clara asks, in a tone that suggests it can't possibly be.

'It is.'

'And do you *sell* much?'

Arty grins. 'It may surprise you to know I do. It keeps the wolf from the door anyway. I teach a bit as well,' he adds.

'Would you teach me, Arty?' Maggie pipes up. 'I've always wanted to learn how to paint!'

'Maggie!' Clara admonishes. 'Don't be so presumptuous. I'm sure Arthur is far too busy to have you as a pupil.'

'Quite the contrary,' Arty says, eyeing Clara meaningfully. 'It would be my absolute pleasure teaching you how to paint, young Maggie.'

The pictures suddenly become blurry again and the colours, so sharp and vivid only a moment ago, spin around in a maelstrom, a bit like a child's kaleidoscope toy before the pattern takes shape. Our brief trip back to 1950s St Felix has ended once more.

'It's like reading a single chapter of a book a day at a time,' I say, still staring wistfully at the painting and the embroidery, 'except you're not allowed to read more – even though you desperately want to.'

'Or watching Netflix and only being allowed one episode when all you want to do is binge-watch the whole series,' Jack says, looking at me.

106

I turn towards him.

'I feel my slightly more ... poetic analogy is a little more appropriate to the situation and the time, don't you?'

Jack shrugs. 'Probably. It's still the same thing though, I want to know what happens next.'

'Me too. I wonder if any more works of art will magically create themselves now we've seen these first two – I've a feeling there's so much more to this story.'

'Yup, Arty obviously has the hots for Clara.'

My face screws up in distaste. '*Has the hots* for her? This isn't some lascivious made-for-television movie, you know. I sense a delicate love story is going to develop between these two star-crossed lovers.'

'One,' Jack says raising his eyebrows, 'how do you know they're going to be star-crossed? They could get it on in the next painting!' He grins at my horrified expression. 'And two, what the hell does "lascivious" mean?'

I shake my head. 'Lascivious means salacious, indecent or vulgar, even. And I hardly think they're going to *get it on* as you put it. Clara is obviously a very well-brought-up lady – you can tell by both her clothes and her manners.'

'That's always the worst sort.' Jack winks. 'Okay, okay!' he says, holding his hands up in surrender. 'I'll stop. They all seem like good people from what we've seen so far. Clara reminds me a lot of you actually.'

'She does?' I'm not sure whether to be pleased by his comparison or not. Jack's opinion of Clara so far seems to be as far away from mine as possible.

'Yeah, she's a classy lady, who holds herself in reserve, and yet I suspect there's a much more complex side to her.'

'Go on?' I ask, intrigued.

'She's obviously very protective of her daughter, as you are of Molly, and we don't know this for sure yet, but I suspect she might be a single mother too.'

'Why do you think that?' I'd wondered this too. We hadn't seen or heard any mention of Maggie's father thus far. 'It would be very unusual back then, unless she was widowed in the war, of course.'

Jack smiles at me, in a kindly way this time, instead of teasingly. 'Trust you to think of the honourable answer. What if she got pregnant accidentally, and the father abandoned her.'

Then she would be more like me than Jack knew.

'There's always that,' I say briskly. 'Who knows? We certainly won't unless we get another set of pictures of course.' I lift my embroidery off the easel. 'I guess I'd better get going.' I glance at my watch. It was only nine thirty so Molly wouldn't be ready for another hour and a half. 'Molly will be finished at her party soon.'

'What eighteenth birthday party finishes before ten o'clock?' Jack asks. 'Not any decent one anyway.'

'I have things to do before then,' I lie. The truth was I'd only go back to the flat and sit there worrying about what she might be getting up to. This evening with Jack had been a pleasant distraction.

'Stay,' Jack says solemnly, looking up at me. 'I don't know about you but these flats, so noisy in the day, get quite lonely at night when the streets outside are deserted. You'll be doing me a favour by keeping me company, and I might hazard a guess I'll be doing the same for you by distracting you from thinking about what Molly's doing?'

I'm surprised by the expressive nature of the first part of Jack's request. Unsure, I hesitate for a moment. 'All right then,'

I say. 'But no more talk about Arty having the hots for someone or getting it on, okay?'

I blush as I realise what I've said.

Jack grins. 'I'll do my best for you, Lady Kate, but I'm not promising anything . . .'

Fourteen

'Shall I walk you to the community centre to collect Molly from her party?' Jack asks as my watch strikes 10.45 and I make a move to leave his flat.

We've had a lovely evening together, in particular the last hour when we'd relaxed in Jack's comfortable living room and simply chatted about all sorts – St Felix, having teenagers, our shops. In fact, we'd covered a lot of topics since our last visit to 'vintage' St Felix, everything but ourselves.

'Er ... ' I'm hesitating for two reasons. Firstly, I don't want to put Jack out by forcing him to have to descend those stairs again for no reason other than me and, secondly, I'm not quite sure why he's offering in the first place.

'When I say *walk*,' Jack adds, grinning, 'obviously I mean *wheel*!'

'Well, yes,' I reply, still sounding doubtful.

'What's wrong, Kate? Will being seen with me cramp your style?' Jack is still smiling, but I sense that his swagger is fading somewhat. 'I'll put my legs on especially!'

'Don't be silly – it's not that.'

'What is it then?' Jack's smile has faded now.

'I don't want to put you out, that's all. I mean you've got to get yourself all the way downstairs and change your wheelchair. It's seems an awful faff.'

Jack looks down into his lap for a moment, then up at me. His face is solemn once more and his gaze is intense.

'My whole life is one big faff, as you put it, Kate. Everything I do is complicated, from the moment I get up in the morning to the moment I go to bed. I rarely do anything on the spur of the moment any more. I simply can't. Everything has to be planned so I can accommodate this thing.' He gestures to his wheelchair. 'So getting myself down the stairs to accompany you to the community centre, in the greater scheme of things, really isn't that big a deal. It might not mean that much to you whether I do or whether I don't, but perhaps you'd be kind enough to allow me that one moment of normality . . . allow me to at least pretend I'm being chivalrous.'

I stare at him.

I feel awful, I hadn't thought about it like that at all – what seemed like an enormous hassle to me was normality to him. He was simply asking me to allow him to be ordinary.

I'm about to say my usual 'sorry' but I stop myself, remembering how Jack usually reacts when I become apologetic. Instead I simply smile at him and say: 'No need for the sob story. If you want to come and watch a load of teenagers who've had too much to drink fall out of our local community centre, then this is your night!'

Jack and I make our way companionably towards the party together. He had insisted on attaching his legs before we left even though I had told him it wasn't necessary and no one would care.

111

'I will care, Kate,' had been his answer, and that had been enough.

'Thanks,' Jack says now as he wheels himself along next to me, 'for what you said before at the flat. I overreacted as usual. I often do.'

'Not at all. I hadn't thought about things in that way. What you said helped me understand your situation, and maybe you a little bit as well.'

'I'm not difficult to understand,' Jack says, his voice returning to its usual buoyant tone. 'As black and white as a chess-board me, most of the time.'

'You might think that, but I've already experienced many shades of grey since I met you – and before you say anything not *those* sorts of shades of grey.'

Jack grins. 'You already know me too well. But I still take offence at the term "grey". That suggests I'm a bit bland, and I try very hard to be anything but that.'

'No, I didn't mean grey as in wishy-washy, I meant grey as in you're not always as black and white as you think. Sometimes you give out mixed messages.'

'Such as?'

'Such as the other night when you virtually threw me out of your house for failing to turn off your shop alarm.'

'Ah, that.'

'You said when we were on the beach this morning you were going to explain.'

'I did.'

'So?'

'Is *that* the community centre?' Jack asks, expertly changing the subject as we approach a long dull-looking building that is currently vibrating with loud thumping music and excited voices.

'It is.'

'Seems like you're not the only parent on collection duty tonight.'

I recognise a few of the people leaning against the wall of the centre waiting for their offspring. I want to ignore them and continue talking as I get the feeling he's quite pleased to have a reason *not* to continue our previous conversation, but one of the dads waves and I feel obliged to go over with Jack and chat to him.

Eventually a few people begin to emerge from the community centre: groups of giggling girls and gangs of boisterous boys – all much older than Molly – pass us by, and then a few youngsters I recognise peer apprehensively about for their parents as they leave the booming hall and step out into the hazy lamp-lit street.

As I wait anxiously it takes all my resolve to stop myself from storming in, grabbing my precious daughter and wrapping her up until I get her to the safety of our home.

Where was she? Why wasn't she coming out yet?

'She'll be out in a minute,' Jack says, looking up at me as I fidget next to him. 'Stop looking so worried.'

I can't help it though. It only seems like minutes ago since I was waiting for her to come out from her first day at school. Now she'd spent the evening with all these ... well, they looked like adults to me as they spill out of the centre. Could they really only be a few years older than my Molly?

At long last she appears at the door, blinking into the night.

'Over here, Molly!' I call, waving.

She glances over at me, and to my dismay looks away again back into the hall.

'Molly!' I call again, moving towards her. 'I'm here.'

'Yes, Mum,' she sort of hisses under her breath. 'I see you. I'll be out in a moment. *Okay*?'

'Yes, of course ...' I mumble, stepping back a bit as she disappears back inside. 'Okay.'

'Embarrassing mum?' Jack enquires jokily as he wheels himself up next to me.

'Apparently,' I reply, my face hot. 'Was I that bad?'

'Nope, not at all. At that age you only have to breathe and you're a humiliation. Ben was the same. Now he's eighteen though it's beginning to wane a tad. I'm assured that by the time they're twenty-one you become a normal human being to them once more.'

'Twenty-one?' I exclaim, staring at him. 'I have six years of this to look forward to?'

'Them's the breaks, kid!' Jack says, winking. 'Oh, she's back again, and she has a friend.'

I turn expecting to see Emily, Molly's best friend, but instead I see a lanky-looking boy. He's wearing baggy blue jeans with a low-slung belt, a red T-shirt with some sort of band emblem on it, trainers, and he has too much product in his carefully coiffured (to look unkempt) hair.

Molly whispers something to him as they emerge from the hall and he looks in my direction. Then he kisses her quickly on the cheek and whispers something into her ear, making her giggle.

Then he holds his hand up in our direction, speaks quickly to Molly again and walks over to a group of lads who then all mooch off together down the street.

Molly watches them longingly before slowly making her way over to us.

'All right?' she asks, looking at me. 'You must be Jack,' she says, holding out her hand to him. 'Mum's told me a lot about you.'

'Guilty as charged!' Jack says, shaking her hand. 'And you are Molly! Your mum has told me a lot about you too.'

I stare at them both. Was no one going to say anything about what had just happened?

'What's up, Mum?' Molly asks. 'You look like you've been slapped a few times with a wet mackerel from one of the fishing boats on the harbour.'

'*Nice* evening?' I enquire as casually as I can.

'Yup, the best actually!'

'Good ... and who was that you were with just now?' I look back to where Molly and the boy had been a few moments ago. 'The boy you came out of the hall with?'

'Oh ... that's Chesney,' she says keenly, her eyes lighting up. 'I met him tonight.'

'Chesney,' I repeat, without quite as much enthusiasm. 'And how old is this Chesney?'

'Erm ... seventeen, I think.'

'Seventeen ...'

'Why are you repeating everything I say?' Molly asks. 'She's not normally like this, Jack. Please don't let it put you off.'

'Molly!' I scold, coming to my senses at last. 'Stop teasing Jack.' Jack just smiles. 'I didn't expect you to appear from the hall with a boy, that's all – especially not one that kisses you on the cheek.'

Molly grins. 'Good job you didn't see us earlier then!'

'Enough!' I say, holding up my hand. 'What is it you always say to me ... TMI. Yes, that's it. Too much information, Molly, I can't cope.'

'Should we head back now?' Jack suggests, 'Everyone seems to be leaving.'

'I'll just say goodbye to Emily!' Molly says, spying her friend talking to a man I recognise as Emily's father. 'Back in a mo!'

'I'm sorry,' I apologise to Jack as I watch her skip across the gravel. 'I left a little girl at this party earlier, and now suddenly a young woman is being returned to me – what on earth happened?'

Jack smiles kindly. 'Tell me about it. Although, it must be even worse with a girl, even more to worry about.'

I nod. 'It only seems moments ago since she would emerge shyly from a party with a gift bag and piece of cake wrapped in a napkin. Now she's coming out with a boy on her arm instead!'

Molly says her goodbyes and returns to us.

'Right, let's go,' she says happily. 'Now you've heard about my evening, I want to hear all about you guys on the way back. What did you get up to together – anything interesting?'

I glance at Jack and he smiles ruefully back at me.

'That good, eh.' Molly says with delight.

'Let's just say our evening was ... revealing.' Jack smiles knowingly at me. 'Wouldn't you say, Kate?'

'Informative and possibly even illuminating!' I reply beaming, as I remember our magical pictures coming together.

Molly looks at us. 'You two are weird!' she says good-naturedly, 'but it kind of suits you both, and if it makes you happy then I say the weirder the better!'

Fifteen

'Have you got another picture?' I whisper into my mobile phone while I'm downstairs in the basement sorting out some new stock. Anita is upstairs minding the shop, and I've taken this moment to call Jack because overnight a new embroidery has magically appeared in my sewing machine again, and I'm hoping that he too might have a new painting to share with me.

'I have, yes,' Jack replies. 'Is yours of a beach?'

'It is! Do you think it might be one of the beaches here?'

'Well, mine looks very much like St Felix Bay. Does yours?'

'Difficult to say . . . mine's all sand and shells. I imagine your painting is, as usual, on a much larger scale.'

'When shall we compare them? Tonight?'

'Ah, I can't tonight. I have a parents' meeting at Molly's school.'

'How's Molly getting on?' Jack asks. 'Is Chesney still in the picture?'

It was a little over two weeks since the party, and since Jack and I had last taken a trip back in time to yesteryear St Felix. We'd seen each other a couple of times in passing over that time and had waved or had a few words in the street, but nothing more than that. Now we had the excuse of some new magical pictures I was keen to see him again.

'Yes, Chesney is still hanging around,' I reply, sighing. 'I can't say I'm too happy about that, but he could be a lot worse, I suppose. He's polite enough to me on the rare occasions Molly allows me a moment to speak with him.'

'That's good,' Jack says encouragingly, 'isn't it?'

'Yes, but I'm worried about how Molly's schoolwork might suffer – she seems to spend every spare minute with him.'

'Ah, young love!' Jack says. 'We've all been there.'

'Yes, that's why I'm worried! Anyway, about these pictures – I should be finished by eight at the latest. Shall I come round then?'

'That would be great!' Jack says, sounding pleased. 'I'll get the easel prepared!'

The parents' evening finishes earlier than I expect, with Molly receiving high praise from all her teachers and the promise of amazing GCSE results if she continues to 'apply herself diligently' to her studies. It seems the 'Chesney effect' hasn't affected her schoolwork too much after all, not for the time being anyway.

I therefore make my way towards Jack's shop a little earlier than we'd agreed, and walking along Harbour Street towards the high street I bump into a friend of Anita walking her dog, Rosie.

'Hi, Lou! Hi Rosie!' I say as Lou pauses to let Rosie sniff the ground. 'How are you both?' Lou would often bring her dog into the shop when she popped in to see Anita. Rosie was a slightly odd-looking dog – a cross between a Basset Hound and a Springer Spaniel. Lou had once explained to me how that had come about – her friend's Basset Hound, Basil, had got a bit too friendly with her own dog, Suzy, and the result had been a litter of slightly odd-looking but very cute puppies. Lou had kept one of them and my friend Poppy had given a home to another. My dog Barney was as fond of Rosie as Lou was of Anita, and so they both always received a warm welcome when they came in to visit.

'Oh, hello, Kate,' Lou says, her gaze turning from Rosie to me. 'We're good, thank you. How are you?'

'Yes, very well.'

'Barney not with you tonight?'

'No, I've just come from Molly's parents' evening.'

'All good?'

'Luckily, yes it is, very good. She's predicted As and A stars in all her subjects.'

'Bright girl. You must be very proud.'

'I am, yes.'

I'm about to say goodbye and continue up the road when a thought occurs to me. 'Lou, you've lived in St Felix most of your life, haven't you?'

'Yes, for most of it I have.'

'Do you remember the fifties very well?'

Lou looks surprised. 'The nineteen fifties? A little, yes. I was quite young back then though. I'm not that old!'

'Sorry, no, I didn't think you were, but I was wondering if you happened to remember a young girl called Maggie, and her mother who was called Clara? Maggie was in a wheelchair back then if it helps jog your memory?'

The wrinkles on Lou's forehead deepen as she attempts to remember. 'Yes, as it happens I think I might recall them.

Didn't they come to St Felix in the late fifties – maybe around fifty-seven or fifty-eight?'

'I'm not sure,' I reply, stunned that the people we'd been seeing in the pictures might actually be real.

'The reason I say that is I remember her mother took a shop around then – dressmaker's it was, and she began selling all the fashions of the day from there – you know: full skirts, bright fabrics etc. I badgered my own mother to buy me a skirt like that because all the older girls were wearing them that year. All summer I went on and on until eventually she asked Clara to make one for me – it was the best thing I'd ever owned. I remember me and my best friend Rose – that's who Rosie here is named after – sitting on the harbour wall swinging our legs listening to Lonnie Donegan, Little Richard and Elvis Presley on her portable transistor radio.' She smiles wistfully. 'What good times they were.'

'Clara had a shop?' I ask intrigued. 'Where?'

'Er ... ' Lou looks down the street, trying to place it. 'You know something – I think it might have been where your shop is now. Yes, in fact I'm sure of it. A few doors down from the baker's, on the opposite side. Back then the baker's was owned by Dec's uncle, I think. "Mr Bumbles" it was called back then.'

'Clara ran a dressmaker's from the same shop as mine?' I repeat slowly, trying to get a grasp on this extraordinary coincidence.

'Yes, that was until ... *hmm*, perhaps the mid- to late sixties? It's difficult for me to remember because I moved away for a few years with my husband's job around then. I was a young bride,' she says wistfully, thinking back. 'Anyway when we returned to live here it was already the wool shop, and it stayed that way until you opened your craft shop. Why all the questions, dear?'

'Lou, would you mind if I pop round to your house one day and ask you some more about this?'

'No dear, not at all. I quite enjoy a trip down memory lane. I'm not sure how much more help I can be to you though.'

'Oh, you'd be surprised, Lou. Your little snippets of information have already helped me out no end. One more question for now though – do you remember an artist back then called Arty?'

Lou thinks. 'It doesn't ring any bells, but you have to remember if we're talking about the late fifties I would only have been thirteen or fourteen. A lot has happened in my life since. Also, like now, there were a lot of artists painting here back then. That's one thing that doesn't change.'

'Oh, talking of painting, I'd better go.'

'Off to see our local art-shop owner are you?' Lou asks, her eyes twinkling.

'How did you know …?' I begin, and then I simply say. 'Don't tell me – *Anita*!'

'I bumped into Lou on the way here,' I tell Jack as I prepare for our two pieces of artwork to come together.

'Lou?' Jack asks. 'Who's that?'

'Lou's lived in St Felix for ages on and off. She's the aunt of Jake, who owns the nursery up on the hill, so I guess that makes her aunt-in-law to Poppy at the flower shop, and Bronte's great-aunt.'

'Wow!' Jack says, raising his eyebrows. 'Is everyone here related?'

'It seems that way sometimes. A number of St Felix's older residents have lived here all their lives. If you chat to any of them for long enough they'll tell you their stories.'

'I bet. So what did this Lou tell you?'

'You won't believe this but she thinks that Clara ran a dress-maker's from the same shop that I have now.'

'Really? That's incredible.'

'Yes, she remembers Clara and Maggie, but not Arty. There were a lot of artists here in the fifties apparently, like there are now.'

'It must mean something,' Jack says, his eyes narrowing, 'but what though?'

'Let's put the pictures together again, and see what happens today,' I say keenly, sitting down next to him on the chair opposite the easel. 'Maybe that will tell us more . . .'

St Felix ~ June 1957

'It's an amazing view you have here,' Clara says, as she stands at the window of Arty's ground-floor studio that looks out over the sands of St Felix Bay. 'I'm amazed you don't sit and paint this vista all the time.'

'It's tempting,' Arty says, watching her from across the studio, 'but I think my clients would get a bit bored with the same scene all the time. It's the light that's truly amazing here – it floods into the room making everything I do seem better.'

Clara turns towards Maggie, who is frantically trying to finish her own piece of artwork for the day. This was the first time Clara had actually been inside Arty's studio. Before she'd always collected her daughter at the door, even though Arty had always invited her to come in. 'Maggie, are you nearly finished? We really must be going. You're already over your allotted hour with Arthur.'

Arty grins at Clara's continued insistence on calling him by his full name, but he kind of admired her for sticking to her formality. It was one of the *many* things he liked about Maggie's mother, and the list seemed to grow longer every time they met.

'It's fine,' Arty says kindly. 'You can't rush art – can you, young Maggie?'

Maggie grins up happily at him from her easel.

'But even so,' Clara says, 'we don't want to outstay our welcome.'

'You could never do that,' Arty says softly, 'Either of you.'

Clara, pretending she hasn't heard, bustles towards Maggie's easel. 'No, Mummy!' Maggie says, leaping up as she tries to hide her work. 'It's not finished yet.'

'Maggie,' Clara says, stopping in her tracks. 'You're standing – on your own.'

'I know,' Maggie says proudly. 'We've been practising while I've been here, haven't we, Arty? Look I can even walk a few steps on my own now without falling over.'

Clara watches in shock as Maggie walks slowly but confidently away from her easel. She takes each step precisely and carefully, but the look of delight on her face as she accomplishes this simple act is a joy to behold.

'See!' she cries elatedly as she reaches her mother's arms. 'I told you I could do it if you'd only let me try.'

Clara hugs her daughter to her. 'Amazing, darling,' she says. 'How long have you been doing that?'

'Since Arty said I should try and walk a bit more often.' Maggie looks happily over her shoulder at him. 'He said if I didn't try occasionally I might never walk properly again.'

'He did, did he?' Clara asks, looking sternly at Arthur. 'Are you a doctor now as well as an artist?'

'No ... but I felt she was ready. If she sits in that thing too

123

long her leg muscles will atrophy, and she'll be weak for ever. Atrophy means—'

'Yes, I know what it means, thank you very much,' Clara says sharply. 'When you've lived with this as long as we have you know all the terminology, and if you'll pardon my frankness, I think you'll find I also know what's best for my daughter too.'

Clara looks around for Maggie's wheelchair. 'Come along, Maggie, it's time to go,' she says, grabbing the chair and wheeling it over to her. 'I don't think you're quite ready to walk all the way back home just yet.' She eyes Arty meaningfully. 'Perhaps you think otherwise?'

Arty shakes his head, and silently watches them as they prepare to leave.

'Same time next week, Maggie?' he calls, before they reach the door.

'I'm not sure that's a good idea any more,' Clara says frostily, turning back for a moment.

'No, Mummy! I want to come back and see Arty,' Maggie cries from her chair.

'Clara,' Arty says, walking quickly over to them. He places himself in front of the door and grabs the handle. 'I'm sorry if I've done wrong by Maggie. I think she's a great girl, and quite the promising artist.' He smiles down at her. 'Please don't let your anger with me prevent your daughter from doing something she enjoys.'

Clara's face softens a little, but her lips remain firmly pursed together as she looks coldly at Arty.

'I'll think about it,' is all she says. 'Now kindly open the door so we can be on our way, please.'

Arty relents and stands back, holding the door open for them.

He waves gloomily to Maggie, who waves equally forlornly back at him.

Clara purposefully pushes the chair out of the studio and down the street, striding as far away from Arty as she can.

'Oh …' I say despondently, turning to Jack as the moving images swirl before us. 'That wasn't so much fun tonight.'

'No. Poor Maggie and poor Arty.'

'Clara is only trying to do what's best for her daughter,' I add, feeling the need to defend her. 'She probably felt Arty was overstepping the mark.'

'He was right,' Jack says, 'About the atrophy. If she doesn't use her legs, the muscles will weaken and deteriorate. Believe me I know *all* about this sort of thing.'

'I'm sure that's quite true, but I know what it's like to be a single mother. You get very defensive when people try to tell you what's best for your child.'

Jack looks at me. 'Yes I can imagine that. I don't see Ben all that often, but at least I share parenting with my ex. We don't exactly get on well, but she's always rung me if there's anything important I need to know about him, or anything we need to discuss. I guess when you're on your own it's all up to you. Molly doesn't see her dad then?'

I feel myself tighten, as I always did when people started to delve into my past.

'No,' I reply brusquely. 'She doesn't.'

'That's a shame,' Jack continues. 'I'd be gutted if I didn't see Ben at all.'

'Yes, well, things aren't always as simple as that.'

Jack watches me, assuming I'll continue.

'I wonder what will happen next?' I say, deliberately

changing the subject. 'To Clara and Arty? We know she starts her dressmaker business, but I wonder what will happen to the two of them, and to Maggie?'

'Let's hope we get a new set of pictures soon so we can find out,' Jack says, taking the hint. 'I set the easel up every night in case. I wondered if I should leave a fresh canvas out at first, but now I leave it empty and a new painting appears like magic. Do you leave supplies out for your sewing fairy?'

'No, I don't. The fabric and the embroidery magically appear under the machine plate in the morning, which makes it all the weirder. Do you still wonder who's doing this?'

Jack shrugs. 'I've given up thinking about that to be honest. The whole thing is so unbelievable I've suspended my natural scepticism. The story of Clara and Arty has taken over any thought I might have about *how* this is happening – I'm simply enjoying the fact that it is.'

I smile at him, 'That's exactly how I feel about it. Strange, isn't it? If you'd told me a couple of months ago that I'd be sitting here with a perfect stranger waiting for pictures to come to life I'd have laughed in your face.'

'I'm not such a stranger now though, am I?' Jack asks quietly. 'I'd say we were getting to know each other quite well as the days go by. I quite enjoy our little get-togethers.'

I'm surprised to hear him say this: not about enjoying our painting reveals – I do too – but it's rare that he's so candid. His usual chat is so flippant that it always comes as a shock when he says something with genuine sincerity.

'Yes, I do too,' I tell him shyly. 'It's been quite nice to have a new friend to talk to.'

'There's not really anyone else we could talk to about this,' Jack adds, gesturing to the paintings, 'is there?'

I shake my head. 'I wonder why us though?'

'What do you mean?'

'I mean, I wonder why *we're* seeing these—' I hesitate, trying to find the right word '—these images. Do you think this would have happened if Noah had passed on the sewing machine and the easel to some other customers?'

Jack shrugs. 'Would the artwork have appeared for them? Who knows? And would they have matched them together to make them come alive like we have? It's highly doubtful.'

'Why?'

'The sewing machine and the easel could have gone anywhere, couldn't they? We have visitors from all over the world here.'

'Yes, but it would be unlikely they'd buy such bulky items – they'd have a job transporting them home.'

'True, so if they had been bought by someone local and they did start producing ... let's say *unusual* pictures, what are the chances they'd have been brave enough to tell someone about it, or for the person they confided in to be the exact same person who was also experiencing it!'

'You know, you're right – it's just as incredible we ever put the two pictures together as them actually appearing in the first place.'

'Maybe it's fate?' Jack says quietly.

'I thought you didn't believe in all that sort of stuff?' I reply smiling, but my insides are a lot less calm. Jack was being very ... pleasant tonight. Things I hadn't expected to hear him say were coming from his lips and it was throwing me off guard.

'I don't usually, but it's this place – St Felix. There are so

127

many stories about strange events happening here – unexplainable events – that I'm starting to believe we're experiencing one of them.'

'Who've you been talking to?' I ask, still trying to keep my tone light. 'Someone down the pub?'

'Yes. Noah said I should ask down there if I was interested, so I did one night when it was quiet and there weren't too many people about, and I was quite staggered by some of the tales the locals told.'

'I've heard some of them myself. Even my friend Poppy will tell you a tale about how her flower shop became successful and how she met her husband, Jake.'

'Yes, I heard that one too.'

'Maybe it's our turn now,' I say, still smiling. 'To experience a little St Felix magic, I mean?'

'Maybe it is . . .' Jack says, watching me closely. 'And I'd say the magic is working *very* well so far – wouldn't you?'

Sixteen

'Who are they for this time?' I ask hesitantly as I walk back into the shop with Barney after our afternoon walk.

'It says Kate on the card.' Anita gazes at the huge bunch of flowers taking up most of the shop counter. 'Secret admirer?'

'Definitely not! When did they arrive?' I pull the card off the flowers and tear open the envelope.

'Amber brought them in about ten minutes ago. She asked about her wedding invitation while she was here – have you replied yet?'

'Gosh, no, I haven't. I'll have to get an acceptance card for Molly and me. Are you going, Anita?'

'Yes, it sounds like it's going to be a lovely do on all accounts. Sebastian is going too ... What's wrong, dear? You don't look very happy.'

I stare at the card I've pulled from the envelope.

I hope you enjoyed my last 'apologetic' offering?
This time my bouquet is sent in the spirit of friendship.

I will be in St Felix very soon and I would very
much enjoy the pleasure of your company once more.
   J x

'Yes, I'm fine, Anita, I'm just not sure who's sending me these
flowers. The last one was only signed *J* too.' I pass her the card.

'Do you know anyone with the initial J?' Anita asks. 'I
mean anyone who might send you flowers. They obviously
know you.'

I think for a moment. 'Only Jack, and he made it very clear
the last bunch wasn't from him. And, anyway, this isn't his style
at all. Jack is much more direct. He'd never do anything ...' I
search for the right word. 'Anything as *clandestine* as this.'

'Good word,' Anita says approvingly. 'Well, they say they
want the pleasure of your company *once more*, so you must
know them?'

I shake my head. 'I really can't think of anyone, Anita.'

'Hey, Mum,' Molly says, coming into the shop. 'Ooh, who are
they from – not your secret admirer again?'

I look at my watch. 'What are you doing here? It's not time
for school to finish yet.'

'Study period. I told you I'd be getting them occasionally
from now on.'

'Oh, yes, so you did.'

'So, these flowers then,' Molly says, smelling them. 'Was
there a card again?'

Anita passes Molly the card. 'Your mum can't think of anyone
with the initial J who would send her flowers.'

'Definitely not Jack,' Molly says with certainty. 'Not his style.'

'Exactly,' I agree. 'But why does everyone seem to think that
Jack would be sending me flowers? He has no reason to.'

Molly and Anita exchange knowing looks.

'And you can stop looking at each other like that!'

'So, who is it then?' Molly asks. 'Hang on a minute, you don't think . . . '

'I don't think what?'

'It couldn't be *Joel*, could it?'

I stare at Molly for a moment. *Why hadn't I thought of Joel?*

'*No,*' I say, shaking my head. 'Why would Joel be sending me flowers now? I haven't seen or heard from him in nearly two years.'

'Maybe he's going to be passing and he wants to pop in to see you?' Molly suggests, sounding almost hopeful. 'He might be trying to say sorry?'

Although it had affected us both, I'd never told Molly the full story about Joel. Naturally I'd wanted to protect her, so I'd kept her out of it as much as possible, which is why I hadn't ever mentioned the sewing machine's rather curious behaviour either. I didn't want Molly to spend her time worrying about me – I wanted her to concentrate on herself and, most importantly right now, her studies.

'No one passes through St Felix,' I say lightly. 'You have to make a purposeful trip here. It's completely out of anyone's way otherwise.'

'Maybe he's holidaying nearby then?'

'It's not Joel,' I insist.

'How do you know?' Molly demands. She'd always liked Joel, and I think she had secretly hoped he might become the father figure in her life she'd always lacked and that I'd always felt guilty about not providing. 'This person obviously knows you and wants to see you again, Mum.'

'But why would he send me flowers?' I say, desperately trying to make her understand without telling her the truth. 'Why not simply get in touch over the phone?'

I'd had to change my number after Joel and I had split up, and when we'd moved here to St Felix I'd only given my new number to a select few people so the chance of him being able to contact us in that way was in reality pretty slim.

Molly shrugs. 'Maybe he's trying to be romantic?'

'After all this time? I hope not.'

Molly's keen expression drops.

'I'm sorry to interrupt, dears,' Anita says quietly, 'but who is this Joel you're talking about?'

'My ex,' I explain. 'We were together before we moved here. It didn't work out.' I give Anita a meaningful glance and I see in her eyes she understands immediately.

'It happens,' she says knowingly. 'Right then, Molly, dear, since you're home early from school to *study*, perhaps you'd like one of my fresh fruit scones to help you along. There should be some jam and clotted cream in your mum's fridge to go with them.'

'That sounds sick, Anita!'

Anita looks perplexed by her comment.

'"Sick" means good in her language,' I explain.

'Oh ...' Anita says, looking relieved. 'It meant something else when I was young.'

Molly hungrily heads upstairs to the flat.

'I sense there's something more to your story with Joel,' Anita asks quietly, when we can hear Molly moving around in the kitchen. 'It's none of my business, of course, if you'd rather not talk about it.'

'It's fine, Anita. I don't mind telling you anything. I like to think by now we're friends, aren't we? Not simply colleagues.'

'Of course, dear,' Anita says warmly. 'I feel exactly the same way about you.'

I return her smile with just as much affection. 'I'll try to keep this as simple as I can,' I say in a low voice. 'Joel is my ex. We were together for over a year, but he became ... *demanding*.'

'How so?' Anita asks.

'It started with small things ... like we didn't even live together but he always wanted to know where I was and what I was doing. I didn't think anything of it at first – it just seemed like he was taking an interest in my life – but then if I wasn't at home when he popped round or he phoned, or I was out late on a night out with friends he'd get ... *funny*.'

'Funny?' Anita repeats.

'Annoyed. Really sulky and difficult. When he started calling my friends to find out where I was and attempting to check up on my diary at work, it all got a bit too much. The final straw was when he started following me around – *stalking* my friends said it was – so I had to finish it. It was then the real problems began.'

I think back to those times a couple of years ago. For the first time in my life I had understood how a celebrity might feel when one of their fans got a bit too close for comfort. It wasn't nice, in fact it was downright scary. Yet whereas a celebrity stalker will usually be someone the famous person doesn't know, in my case this had been my ex-boyfriend calling my friends at all hours of the day and night, constantly contacting me over social media and standing outside my house every evening.

'He just wouldn't accept that we'd split up,' I tell a concerned-looking Anita. 'He pestered everyone who knew me and he'd hang around my house. The last straw was when he tried to meet Molly after school one day. He waited outside her school gates, for heaven's sake! So it was then I had to get the police involved.'

'Restraining order?' Anita asks, sounding like she's watched one too many American cop shows.

'No, it didn't get that far. They simply warned him off, and he seemed to listen then, but he still lived quite close to us and so did his family and friends. There were too many reminders and I always felt like we might bump into each other, so I made the decision to move away with Molly. I didn't know at the time it would be quite so far away as here, but when the opportunity of the shop came up I took it. As you know it had always been my dream to have a shop selling my own designs.'

'So, do you think this is him trying to get in touch again?' Anita asks, gesturing to the flowers.

'I don't know. I hope not, not now. I hoped that part of my life was over with. I don't want to go back and have to start dealing with him again.' I'm on the verge of crying, so Anita puts a soothing arm around my shoulder.

'I'm sure you won't, my dear, and if he does turn up here, Sebastian and I will see him off for you. Sebastian can be quite fierce at times if he wants to be.'

'Oh, I know!' I say, blinking back my tears. 'And I bet you can be too if pushed.'

'Anita!' Molly says, coming back into the shop again carrying a half-empty plate. 'Your baking, it's just too good! You could easily rival The Blue Canary if you wanted to open your own bakery.'

'That's kind of you, my dear,' Anita says, dropping her arm from my shoulders, 'but I prefer to keep my baking small and personal so only my friends and family can enjoy it.'

'Then I for one am glad we're a part of your family,' Molly says, hugging her.

'And so am I,' I say, smiling at Anita over Molly's shoulder. 'Very glad indeed.'

Seventeen

'Did you get another one?' I ask breathlessly into my phone, as I stand in the corner of the basement of the shop trying to be as quiet as possible.

'Sure did!' Jack replies. 'Does it look like Harbour Street to you?'

'Mine looks like a shop, but I guess it could be in Harbour Street.'

'When shall we compare them?'

'I'm supposed to be going to see Lou later this afternoon, but I could pop in afterwards. Are you working today?'

'I work every day. I don't have quite as many staff as you!'

'I have one more than you, that's all. You'll need to take on someone else!'

'My son Ben is coming soon,' Jack says, and I can hear the delight in his voice as he tells me. 'Maybe I can take an odd day off then. He's going to work in the shop in his summer holidays before he goes back to uni in October.'

'That's wonderful news,' I tell him. 'It will be good for you to spend some time together.'

'I hope so. It's the longest he'll have stayed with me. I guess the lure of a summer by the sea has swayed him a fair bit. Anyway, back to these pictures – what time are you going to see Lou?'

'Four thirty. I could probably be with you around five thirty depending on how it goes?'

'Five thirty is fine. If you get here earlier Bronte can close up the shop. Then you can have me all to yourself.'

'Great …' I suddenly feel embarrassed at Jack's choice of words.

'Could you sound any less enthusiastic?' Jack says lightly, and I know I've probably dented his pride.

'Sorry, I wasn't talking to you,' I pretend. 'I was talking to Sebastian. He popped his head around the door to ask me something about a product. Yes, Sebastian that's fine,' I say, taking my phone away from my mouth a little as though I'm talking to someone across the room. 'Now, Jack, what were you saying?'

'It doesn't matter,' Jack says quickly. 'You're obviously busy. I'll see you later then?'

'Yes, see you later.'

'Do I have a ghost?' Sebastian says, making me jump as he appears at the entrance to the basement. 'Only I could have sworn I heard you talking to me as I came down the stairs.'

'What are you doing down here?' I ask briskly. 'Who's minding the shop upstairs?'

'Calm down, I'm just getting something for a customer.' He pulls a packet of knitting needles off the wall. 'They're elderly and can't manage the stairs so I've not abandoned your empire for long! Anyway, we have cameras, don't we?'

He dashes back up the stairs again while I stand staring after him.

Of course – the security cameras! Why had I not thought of this before? In fact, why had none of us thought of this when the first embroidery appeared? To be fair the cameras were pretty small. I'd only been able to afford a cheap system when we'd opened the shop, and they didn't record for long. Quite often I forgot to change the memory card when it filled up as we thought about them so little. I'd always figured the cameras worked more as a deterrent than anything else, so none of us gave them much thought, but now I was giving them *a lot* of thought. We had one stationed down here so we could keep an eye on things when customers came down here on their own, and we had one upstairs in the shop that not only recorded everything going on during the day but also what happened at night too . . .

While Sebastian is on his lunch break, I collect the memory card on which our CCTV footage is stored, wishing that I'd invested more money in a better system that recorded for longer than twenty-four hours at a time. At least I should have last night's footage – that *had* to show something of the strange goings-on in my shop overnight.

When Sebastian returns from lunch, I head upstairs to take my break. 'I might be a little longer than usual,' I tell him before I go. 'I want to do some . . . paperwork while I'm upstairs.'

'Okay, boss,' Sebastian says, not seeming at all bothered. 'See you later.'

'Give me a shout if it gets busy.'

'Will do!'

I head upstairs quickly and find my laptop, then I insert the memory card and wait for it to load.

'Right, my mysterious visitor,' I say to the computer as I tap play, 'let's see who you really are.'

After a minute or two of watching an empty shop, I begin to fast-forward slowly through the footage. Six o'clock passes, seven, eight, nine and on past midnight. I don't have a full view of the shop, just the shop counter where the till is, but access to the inside of our small window is directly to the side of this, so if anyone is going to come past and insert embroidered fabric into my window display, I'm going to see them.

Yet, as the early hours of the morning dawn on the footage, I haven't seen a mouse scuttle across the floor, let alone a person, and I begin to wonder whether I'm going to see anything at all.

'This is impossible,' I mutter to myself as I watch the time tick on to 5am. 'Why haven't I seen anything?'

6am, 7am, 8am, and then the first movement is a little before nine when I see myself carrying the till drawer across the shop floor and placing it into the till. I then go to unlock the door and I see myself jump as I realise there's something new in the window.

'That's impossible,' I say out loud. 'How did I miss it?'

Not only had I been watching the screen as I forwarded through the footage, I'd been watching the clock too. I'd seen enough TV detectives solve crimes by discovering there was a jump in CCTV footage where a few seconds had been deleted by the perpetrator of the crime or their accomplice. Yet every second of last night's recording had been there on the screen – I'm sure of it.

'I should have known better than thinking something so modern as CCTV would be able to solve this mystery,' I tell myself as I remove the memory card and close the computer. 'I've a feeling we're going to have to take a few more trips back in time to St Felix if we're ever going to get to the bottom of this.'

*

139

Later that afternoon I knock on the door of Snowdrop Cottage and wait for Lou, but to my surprise Poppy answers. 'Hello, Kate,' she says, holding open the door. 'Come in. Lou said you were dropping by.'

I follow Poppy through Lou's hall into the sitting room of her cottage. Lou is sitting in an armchair with a small toddler on her lap, and next to her on the sofa sipping on a cup of tea is Jake, her nephew, who is Poppy's husband.

'Hi Kate,' Jake says. 'Don't worry, we're leaving in a moment. We just popped in with Daisy to see Lou. Here, sit down,' he says, shuffling along the seat a little.

'Please don't go on my account,' I say, sitting down on the edge of the sofa.

'Daisy needs to take a nap anyway,' Poppy says, gathering up her daughter's toys. 'And probably Jake too for that matter.'

'Hey, it's not easy having a toddler running around when you're my age!' Jake says, putting his tea down, and then standing up and stretching.

'Wait until you have two running around,' Lou adds, passing Daisy to Poppy.

'Tell me about it,' Jake says, 'I've been there before, remember?'

'You shouldn't have married such a young wife then,' Poppy says, winking at me.

'I wouldn't have it any other way.' Jake kisses her on the cheek. 'Right, Aunt Lou,' he continues, kissing his aunt on the cheek now. 'We'll see you on Thursday for Daisy's birthday tea.'

'You will indeed. Bye-bye, Daisy,' she says, waving at her great-niece.

Daisy waves back from Poppy's arms.

'We'll let ourselves out,' Poppy says. 'You see to your next guest. See you soon, Kate.'

They head out into the hall and we hear the door shut behind them, and Lou's little dog Rosie comes poddling through.

'Rosie avoids Daisy,' Lou says, bending down to stroke her. 'She's that little bit too small and too grabby for her right now. Would you like a cup of tea, Kate?' She points to a large china tea-pot standing on a tray on the table. 'There's still some in there if you do.'

'No, thank you, I'm fine. I had a cuppa before I came out.'

'So you want to talk to me about the fifties?' Lou asks, sitting back in her chair.

'That's right.'

'Any particular reason why?'

I had thought Lou might ask this so I'd already prepared my answer. 'I found a few old diaries up in the attic of the shop. Nothing that interesting, but it got me wondering about the history of St Felix around that time.'

Lou nods, but I'm not sure if she entirely believes me.

'So what do you want to know? Like I said the other day I can't remember too much as it was a long time ago.'

'I was wondering if you remembered any more about Clara's shop?' I begin. 'You said it used to be where mine is now.'

'Yes, that's right. I thought about that a little bit more after I saw you. I remember the shop well – quite successful it was. As you can imagine we were a bit remote here in the fifties. The railway opened things up a lot, bringing holiday-makers and the like, but it was difficult for us teenagers to access all the latest fashions, magazines and records. We could order things from catalogues but they took so long to get here, not like today when you can order something over the internet one day and it's delivered the next. To suddenly have a shop that was making and selling fashionable clothes was quite unique, and very popular amongst us girls.'

'I can imagine – and you say Clara made everything herself?'

'I think she did to begin with, but as the demand grew I believe she hired a few local ladies to sew for her.'

A bit like me, I think to myself, but instead I say, 'Goodness, she must have been doing well.'

'I think she was. You know, I thought a bit more about her daughter too – she would have been about my age back then.'

'Really? So you did know her.'

'Well, not really. When she moved here because she'd been ill – polio, I think it was – she was held back a year at school, so when she became well enough to start at our local grammar school she was a year below me.'

'Did she recover from polio?' I try to ask as casually as I can. 'Did she walk again?'

'I think she was on crutches for a long while. I seem to remember her around the school on them – big wooden things they were, but she wasn't in a wheelchair then like you said.'

'That's good to know,' I say, thinking about Maggie. Perhaps Arty pushing her to walk had helped after all. 'Do you remember anything else? What about the artist I mentioned – Arty or Arthur, you might have known him as?'

Lou shakes her head. 'No, but like I said there were a lot of artists coming to St Felix back then. That's when it all began really, in the fifties. We didn't have the big art gallery like we have now, or all the smaller galleries dotted about the streets, so people used to display their paintings in the windows of their homes and people would buy them direct.'

'That's lovely,' I say, totally able to imagine this.

'I do remember this one old man – lovely fellow, he was. Quiet, unassuming. He used to paint on all sorts of things, usually bits of old wood – you know, scrap bits when they'd broken up one of the fishing boats. I don't think he could afford proper canvases and I'm surprised he could even afford paint. He was very kind to us children though. If you asked him nicely he'd let you have a go with some of his paints.' Lou screws her forehead up trying to remember something. 'Oh, what was his name ... on the tip of my tongue, it is.'

'It doesn't matter now,' I say in a kindly way. 'So you don't remember an Arty then?'

Lou shakes her head. 'No, the only other painter I remember was another Lou, strangely enough – except this one was male. He used to travel around in a red camper van – the same one Ana uses now, I believe. Now that's a story and a half ... Poppy told me all about it if you'd like to hear?'

'That's kind of you, Lou,' I say, smiling at her, 'but it's really the late fifties I'm interested in right now – only because the diaries I found date from then.'

'It's a shame Stan isn't still around,' Lou says. 'He would have been able to tell you more. Stan was wonderful for old stories about St Felix. He would have been in his early twenties back then. Sadly, he passed away a couple of years ago.'

'Oh, that's a shame.'

'Yes, Poppy, Jake and myself were very close to him.'

'Well, thank you for your time, Lou,' I say, standing up. 'You've been very helpful. It's good to join up the dots. The diaries are a bit vague, you see.'

Lou nods. 'If there's anything else you want to know you only have to ask,' she says. 'I'll do my best to help.'

'Just one more thing,' I say, suddenly thinking of it. 'Do you know who used to own the house up on the hill as you enter St Felix? The one with the blue door. I've heard it's up for sale – Noah from the antiques shop did a house clearance for them.'

'I think it may have had a few owners over the years. I'm not sure who the last ones were though, sorry. You should ask Anita – that wool shop was home to all the local gossip at one time or another. I bet she'd know.'

'Great, I will. Thank you again, Lou, you've really been most helpful.'

'Any time, dear, any time.'

I leave Lou's and head eagerly back down into the town towards Jack's shop. It was time to take a trip back to fifties' St Felix again.

Eighteen

Clara stands proudly outside the building in Harbour Street. She still couldn't really believe this was her own shop.

It had all happened so quickly. One minute she had been sewing dresses for herself and a few other ladies in the town who had come to her with fabric and asked her to make up their patterns for them, and then the next the elderly man who had run his rather old-fashioned tailor's from this building had died unexpectedly and she had discovered through some local gossip that the landlord wanted someone to fill the premises as soon as possible. When Clara had gone to him and suggested she should take on the lease he had laughed at her to begin with, but as she had been expecting that she had presented him with a very detailed plan of how she would run the shop and, more importantly for him, how she was going to make a profit to enable her to pay her rent every week.

After a lot of persuading, and a month's rent up front, which had used up all her savings, he'd finally agreed and she'd opened her own dressmaker's, which after a slow start was now starting to attract more work than she could cope with and she was considering taking on more staff.

'Nice dress,' Arty says, appearing in the reflection next to Clara as she gazes at her newest window display. She'd dressed one of the old tailor's dummies in her very newest design – a red and white gingham dress with small yellow primroses scattered over the bodice, and a full skirt with a huge petticoat underneath. To finish off the display she'd added a small bouquet of yellow flowers she had bought from the florist's down the street, its vase of water disguised by a big straw hat.

'Thank you,' Clara says, feeling herself stiffen. Even though it had been over a month now since she'd angrily pushed Maggie in her chair away from Arty's studio, she still hadn't properly forgiven him.

'How's it all going?' Arty asks, keen to keep the conversation flowing. He'd missed seeing Clara and Maggie since Maggie's painting lessons had been suddenly cut short.

'Very well, thank you,' Clara answers brusquely.

'Good. Good. You've certainly made quite the impact here in St Felix. I've seen quite a number of ladies wearing your creations already.'

'Have you?' Clara says, wondering how he knew they were her designs. Had he been keeping an eye on her window displays? Every time she showed a new design she would get at least five ladies and now young girls too wanting it in their size. She could barely keep up with the demand.

'Yes, and very pretty they look too. Is that one of your own you're wearing today?'

'Of course.'

'Very nice,' Arty says approvingly, looking her up and down. 'I like the colour scheme.'

The dress Clara is wearing today is white with a bright blue and green sea print scattered over it. It looked a little like the painting she'd seen Arty doing on the cliffs the day he'd carried Maggie down to his easel. It was something a bit new for her. She'd experimented with embroidering over parts of the print to give the dress a unique texture and she was extremely pleased with the finished result, but as she'd created it on her little Singer sewing machine she'd tried hard not to think about Arty, even though the fabric made her do exactly the opposite.

'It looks a bit like one of your paintings,' Clara says.

'It looks a bit like one of my paintings,' Arty says at exactly the same time.

Arty smiles. 'How's Maggie?' he asks, sensing perhaps Clara might have softened a little.

'She's fine. Doing well actually.'

'Good. Good. Is she still painting?'

Clara turns away from him back to the dress in the window. 'Yes,' she says quietly. 'You seem to have given her a taste for it.'

'I'm glad,' Arty says. He looks through the glass into the shop. 'Is she around? I'd love to see how she's getting on.'

'No, she's not right now. Since I've been working here I've been paying one of the local girls to look after her in the afternoons, until she starts school, that is. It's better than her being stuck in the shop with me all day.'

Arty nods. 'Good, I'm pleased she's getting out and about in the fresh air.'

'I wouldn't keep her cooped up in here all day if that's what you're suggesting?' Clara says, bristling again.

'No, not at all. I know she liked being out and about, that's all. She told me.'

147

He wasn't wrong, Maggie did prefer to be out in the fresh air rather than indoors, but Clara wasn't going to admit he was right.

'Well, she's not here at the moment, so if there's nothing else I have work to be getting on with.'

'Sure,' Arty says in his usual relaxed way. 'So do I. I'm about to do some preliminary sketches for a commission I've been asked to paint.'

'That's good, what is it of?'

'The town council have asked me to paint some canvases of St Felix, not only the usual pictures of the harbour and the sea but some of the other areas of the town too, including Harbour Street. So I guess you might be seeing quite a bit of me over the next few days ...'

'How lovely,' Clara says brightly. 'For you, that is,' she adds as a sting in the tail.

'I think so,' Arty says, batting her insult away with ease. 'I'll look forward to sketching your little shop and you in due course.'

'No, you're not putting me in the picture,' Clara protests. 'Paint the shop all you like but I'm not to be in it, do you understand?'

Arty shrugs. 'I was only joking. It's the buildings they're interested in anyway.'

'Oh ... good,' Clara says, feeling a tad embarrassed that she's overreacted. 'That's all right then.'

'But you'd make a lovely subject if you did want to sit for a portrait,' Arty offers. 'Just let me know – any time. No charge. Although I'm not sure even I could do justice to your beautiful face.'

'I'll bear it in mind,' Clara says, her face, to her annoyance, blushing furiously.

'You do that,' Arty says. 'Right, gotta go. See you around!' He waves casually as he sets off down the street with his canvas bag slung across his shoulder carrying, Clara assumes, his sketching equipment.

'Goodbye, Arthur,' she says, and she gazes after his disappearing figure slightly longer than is absolutely necessary.

'Mummy! Was that Arty?' Clara hears Maggie call, and she turns around to see a young girl wearing one of her own pansy-patterned skirts with a matching bright purple tight-fitting blouse pushing her daughter along the cobbles in her wheelchair. 'Did he come to see me?'

'Hello, Babs,' Clara says to the young girl. 'Yes, darling,' she says to Maggie. 'He did ask after you.'

'And what did you say?' Maggie asks.

'I told him you were doing very well with your painting. Is that another one?'

Maggie proudly holds a piece of what looks like wood in her hand. She passes it to Clara.

'It's very good,' Clara says admiring it. 'One of the fishing boats in the harbour, yes?'

Maggie nods. 'Freddie helped me do it.'

'Freddie?' Clara asks, looking at Babs.

'The old man that does the paintings from his cottage on the harbour,' Babs explains. 'Maggie loves going down there and watching him paint. Today he gave her some paint and let her join in. That is all right, isn't it?' Babs asks, looking a bit worried.

Clara nods. 'Of course it is. I'm just happy you're enjoying yourself, Maggie.'

'I'd rather paint with Arty,' Maggie grumbles. 'Freddie is very kind, but Arty was much more fun.'

'Well, thank you, Babs,' Clara says, taking the handles of the wheelchair from her. 'Same time tomorrow okay? Or would you prefer the afternoon?'

Babs shrugs. 'I don't mind. My fella Bertie is doing his national service at the moment so I don't have much else to do. Would you like to see a photo of him in his uniform?' She rifles through her handbag and produces a photo of a young man in a Royal Air Force uniform.

'Very handsome,' Clara says, looking at the photo.

'Yes,' Babs says proudly. 'I've always liked a man in uniform, haven't you?'

Clara pauses before she answers. 'Yes, Babs. As it happens I do – very much.'

The images all blur and whirl together, and as Babs' bright purple blouse disappears along with everything else, Jack and I turn to each other.

'Good to see that Maggie is still painting,' Jack says, as we lean back from the pictures lined up in front of us. 'That Clara can be a frosty one though. Poor Arty always seems to get it in the neck.'

'She's a bit proper, that's all,' I say, still thinking about what we've just seen. Could the man Maggie was painting with be the same one Lou had spoken to me about? 'She does like Arty really – you can see it in her face.'

'Can you?' Jack asks. 'If that was me I think I'd be avoiding her by now, rather than trying again and again like our boy Arty does, but then I guess some women are harder to crack than others.' He gives me a sly glance which I choose to ignore.

'*Harder to crack*?' I question instead. 'What's that supposed to mean?'

'You have to try a bit harder with some women than others, that's all.'

'The ones you don't have to try with aren't usually worth it anyway,' I counter. 'Not in my experience.'

'I really don't know what you mean, Kate,' Jack grins mischievously. 'Can you explain further, please?'

'You know exactly what I mean, Jack. You weren't in the army for as long as you were without knowing that, I'm sure.'

'I know. I'm only teasing you.' Jack winks now. 'Forgive me, it's *too* easy sometimes.'

'Do you miss it?' I venture, taking my chance now we're on the subject, but knowing he's likely to shut me down immediately. 'The army, I mean, before you start twisting my words!'

'Yes, I do,' Jack says reflectively. 'Not necessarily the months spent abroad living in the middle of a desert somewhere, but more the structure of it. The daily routine. You always knew what you were doing, and where you were supposed to be. Each day was a challenge. I miss that.'

'Is that one of the reasons you took a shop here?' I ask, while he seems in the mood to talk. 'St Felix is a wonderful place to live, of course, but the shops – they were built so long ago and not really designed for ... well, for wheelchairs to get around.'

Jack looks at me with that unwavering gaze he often has.

'And then there's the cobbled streets – they must be difficult for you to navigate. That's a challenge, isn't it?' I continue when he doesn't answer. 'You could have rented a shop anywhere – somewhere much easier for you to manage – but you chose here. I think you did it so you could challenge yourself again.'

Jack carries on staring at me. 'You might be right,' he eventually admits. 'It's not the easiest place to be in a chair, that's for sure, but I knew I had to test myself and see if I could not only manage my own business but manage it in a place that was going to be demanding for me too.'

'And how are you finding the challenge? Difficult enough for you?'

'The shop actually hasn't been as bad as I thought it might be. Bronte's been a star in that department. I don't know what I'd have done without her help. St Felix has been fine too, once I got the hang of the cobbles, and I'm loving the beach now I've got my new chair, but do you know what the hardest thing has been?'

I shake my head.

'Meeting you.'

'Me?' I ask, totally thrown by this answer. 'Why me – what have I done?'

'Blown my mind,' Jack says to my surprise. 'I really like you, Kate – you must know that by now. I like you *very* much. This . . . ' he waves his hand towards the easel ' . . . this has been the best excuse to spend time with you I could have been given. I'd never have got you up here all these evenings otherwise.'

'That's not true. How do you know that?'

'I just know.'

'But how?' I demand.

Jack eyes flicker towards his legs.

'Oh, I get it! Are you saying that because you're in a wheelchair I wouldn't have looked twice at you? How shallow do you think I am? That's lovely, that is.'

'Kate, I've seen it too many times before, I'm afraid.'

'You're judging me by the standards of others – that's not fair.'

'I'm simply judging you by what I'm used to.'

I glare at him. We're still sitting next to each other in front of the easel, and as we stare challengingly into each other's eyes, something strange happens. I suddenly feel something shoot

152

through me, not a bolt of lightning or anything dramatic like that, more a sense of daring.

So, Jack thinks I'm prim and proper, does he, like Clara? I'll show him!

Before I change my mind I lean forwards and kiss Jack firmly on the lips, pausing just long enough there so he's in no doubt whatsoever of my intentions. When I sit back in my chair again Jack is still staring at me like he was before, but his expression is much more shock now than defiance.

'Didn't expect that, did you?' I ask, not feeling in the least bit regretful of my actions.

'No, I certainly didn't.'

'Never judge me by the standards of others,' I tell him. 'I'm my own person. I make my own choices in life.'

Jack smiles at me. 'I'd say that was one of your better choices. Want to try it again?'

'I might ... one day.' I tease, loving the sense of liberation I suddenly feel.

'Then I'll look forward to that day,' Jack says. 'With *great* anticipation.'

Nineteen

'You seem happy this morning, Mum?' Molly says as she helps me unpack a box of my own creations for the shop. They're a new line of fabric phone cases that I've designed and that Jenny, one of the ladies who sews for me, has recently made up.

It's Saturday, and Molly is covering for Sebastian who has an emergency dental appointment. 'What's happened?' she asks knowingly. 'I can tell by your face something has.'

'Nothing has happened,' I fib. Something has happened, of course – I've kissed Jack – and even now I can still feel the very pleasant sensation on my lips when I think about last night.

After we'd kissed the atmosphere had definitely shifted between us. There was a new frisson of excitement simply being in each other's presence, which we'd both strangely ignored, talking about anything other than what had just happened. We'd discussed Clara and Arty, the pictures and what Lou had told me about St Felix.

At the end of the evening, when it had been time to leave, I'd simply leant down and kissed Jack on the cheek this time, and told him I'd see him soon.

'*Hmm* ...' Molly says, bringing me back to the present. 'I do know you, Mum. I know when you're hiding something.'

'I'm not hiding anything ... honestly. When is Chesney calling for you?' I ask, changing the subject.

'In about ten minutes,' Molly says, looking at her watch.

'How's it going?' I ask casually, knowing Molly will likely be as keen to talk to me about her romantic life as I am to her about mine.

'Okay, thanks,' she says, rummaging about in the box again.

'You seem to be getting on very well,' I say cautiously. 'You're always texting him.'

'He texts me a lot,' Molly answers, neatening the pile she's placed on the shelf. 'I'm just replying.'

'Oh, I see. That's nice though – it shows he's keen.'

'Yeah, I guess,' she says, lifting another packet of colourful fabric from the box. 'I'm not going to moan about a boyfriend that's keen. Most of my friends say I'm lucky. The only boyfriends they've ever had can barely be bothered to text – they usually have to make all the effort.'

I definitely wouldn't use the word 'lucky' to describe her friendship with Chesney. He was far too cocky and sure of himself for my liking, but sensibly I don't say anything.

'It might be nice to see Chesney for a little longer than the few seconds when he collects you,' I try. 'Would he like to come for tea one day?'

Molly grimaces. '*Mum!* That would be so uncool. Chesney doesn't do tea!'

What does he do other than hang around street corners trying to look intimidating? I wonder. *Because that's the only thing I've seen him do so far.* 'Okay, I only asked. If you change your mind though, let me know. I'd like to get to know the boy my daughter is so smitten with.'

'Do you think Sebastian will be back by the time I leave?' Molly asks, deliberately ending this line of questioning. 'I don't want to keep Chesney waiting.'

'Probably, but he won't be long even if he's not. He's only getting a filling after his check-up the other day.'

'Ony ge-ing a fewilling?' a woeful voice says at the door. 'I cawn aqu-ally spea!'

I smile at Molly. 'A bit numb, are you?' I ask Sebastian as he comes through the door looking wretched.

Sebastian nods, and cups his cheek in his hand.

'I be alwry tho,' he tries to insist.

'Perhaps you'd better spend some time out back until your numbness wears off,' I suggest. 'Have you taken some painkillers for when it does?'

Sebastian nods. 'Eh den-ist sa I shou be too ba tho.'

'Good. I'd tell you to go home but Anita has her daughter staying this weekend, and Molly and Chesney are going to some festival?'

'It's not a festival,' Molly says, 'It's a few local bands playing in Penzance, that's all.'

'That sounds like a festival to me,' I begin, but someone comes through the door carrying a huge bunch of flowers disguising their face. It's definitely not Poppy or Amber this time as the bouquet is clearly being carried by a man.

'Uh-oh,' Sebastian says. 'Es yo sequet amirer aguain.'

Molly watches eagerly as the man reveals himself.

'Good afternoon, ladies,' he says to Molly and me, as we both look equally as appalled at what the flowers have revealed. The man nods at Sebastian. 'I'm not quite sure what you just said, young man, but I am equally as pleased to make your acquaintance too.' He turns back towards me. 'It is I, Julian James at your service again, my dearest Kate.'

He thrusts the flowers towards me.

'Er . . . thank you, Julian,' I say, stepping forward to take them from him. 'What are you doing here?'

'I told you I'd be back in St Felix soon,' he explains, looking puzzled that I seem surprised he's here, 'in my last bouquet?'

'*You* sent Mum the flowers?' Molly asks with dismay. 'But I thought—'

'I did indeed, my dear child. Did you not get a card with them?' he asks, looking at me.

'I did, but it was only signed *J*. I had no idea it was you.'

Julian seems perplexed by this, as though it could never have been possible that I might know someone else with this initial.

'Ah, a quandary for you indeed . . . but I am here now!'

'Woo isth thi?' Sebastian asks Molly.

'This is Julian James. His father's paintings are being exhibited at the Lyle Gallery at the moment. We met him at the opening of the exhibition.'

'You did indeed!' Julian says, as though it was an honour for us. 'A fine evening was had by all, I imagine.'

'I still don't understand what you're doing here, Julian?' I say. 'Or why you have been sending me flowers?'

Again, Julian looks surprised by this. 'I don't believe you've managed to get in touch with me since that night, have you?'

I must be the one who looks confused now, because Julian continues to explain: 'You took my card with my number on . . . said you'd be in touch so we could talk *business*?'

Ah, that.

'I assumed when you didn't call that you preferred the man to do all the running. You know, the old-fashioned way, so I sent you flowers. I find most women respond well to flowers.' He directs this comment to Sebastian.

'I woo-ant reary no,' Sebastian tries to respond.

'What did he say?' Julian asks me.

'He said he wouldn't really know.'

'Ah, not found the delights of the female form yet, young man? Don't worry, your time will come.'

Both Sebastian and Molly pull equally repulsed faces, but Julian is already looking at me.

'So, when can I take you out to talk this *business*?' he asks. 'I'm free tonight? I'll book us a table at The Lobster Pot – I gather that's the best restaurant here.'

'Ah . . . ' I desperately try to think of a reason why I can't go, and I'm about to say I have other plans when I stop myself. 'Yes!' I say, much to Sebastian and Molly's utter shock. 'That would be lovely. What time?'

'Is eight acceptable to you?' Julian asks, looking like the cat who's got the cream.

'Yes, perfect. I'll meet you at the restaurant, as long as you can get us a table?'

'I never have a problem getting a table,' Julian says confidently. 'I shall very much look forward to spending the evening with you, Kate.' He gives a tiny bow. 'Enjoy the rest of your day, everyone!' He waves his hand in a sort of flourish and exits smartly through the door.

'Mum, what are you thinking?' Molly demands. 'He's awful.'

'Yeh, wafful,' Sebastian agrees.

'He might not be too bad if you get to know him,' I lie. 'Maybe there's more to him than there first appears.'

158

Molly shakes her head in disgust, and Sebastian does his best to tut, but it sounds more like a sucking sort of noise.

What they don't know and what I can't tell them is that, for all his pomposity and pretension, Julian's father was Winston James, and as Winston James painted here in St Felix in the fifties he might have known Arty. If so, Julian might be able to help me put another piece in my sewing-machine puzzle – a piece that might lead me to discover who Clara and Arty really were, and why Jack and I seem to be so involved in their story.

Twenty

While I sit at my dressing table and run the straighteners over my hair, Molly sighs behind me.

'I still don't know why you're going out with this Julian,' she says, looking sulkily at my reflection. 'He's a horrible man.'

'That's a bit strong, Molly. He's not horrible, he's a bit pompous and full of himself, that's all. I'm sure underneath all his bluster he's perfectly nice.'

Molly grimaces and shakes her head. 'Jack's much nicer than him.'

'Quite possibly, but as I seem to be explaining a lot to you lately, just because I'm meeting a man doesn't automatically make it a date.'

Molly's phone beeps. She glances at the screen. 'It's only Chesney,' she says. 'I really thought it was Joel sending you those bunches of flowers, you know,' she continues with a hint of sadness.

'We've been through this before, Molly,' I say gently. 'It was never going to be Joel. He doesn't know where I am and he won't be contacting me. I don't know why you would think he would after all this time.'

Molly looks sheepishly down at the bed.

'Molly?' I ask, turning around to look at her properly. 'What's going on?'

'Nothing,' she says as her phone beeps again. She looks at the screen and then drops it. 'Oh, for goodness' sake, you've only just texted,' she adds impatiently.

I glance at the phone but my mind is elsewhere. 'Molly, why would you think that Joel was the one sending me flowers?'

'Because I rang him, that's why!' Molly says, looking accusingly at me.

'You did what? But why . . . why would you do that?'

'Because I felt sorry for you. I thought you might be lonely. It was before Jack came on the scene, and this Julian too. I know it was difficult before, Mum, but Joel really liked you.'

I'd often heard people use the phrase 'their blood was boiling' and now I know why. My insides are on fire as I stare back at Molly.

'And you told Joel where we are living now?' I ask, as calmly as I can.

Molly nods silently, sensing this calm exterior might only be a cover for my true feelings.

'And what did he say?'

'Not much really. He asked how I was and how you were, and did we like living here?'

'And?' I demand.

'And what?' Molly asks. 'I don't know why you're so mad, Mum. It was only a phone call.'

Molly's phone beeps again, so she picks it up. 'I'm going

to have to reply to Chesney,' she says, 'or he'll never stop texting me. Back in a minute, Mum.'

While Molly steps out of the bedroom to call Chesney, I turn back to my mirror and take a few deep breaths. I have to remain calm or Molly will begin to question why I am so angry.

Right, think sensibly about this, Kate, I tell myself. *Molly said she'd rung Joel before the bouquets had started arriving and before I met Jack. That was weeks ago now, and nothing has happened so far. We haven't heard anything from him and we haven't seen him. Perhaps I really don't have anything to worry about. Surely Joel would have appeared by now if he was going to. Maybe he had got the message when we moved away, and everything will be fine.*

'Sorry about that,' Molly says, returning. 'He gets annoyed if I don't reply quickly.'

I nod, then I look at Molly again. 'What do you mean *annoyed*?'

Molly shrugs. 'Annoyed – cross, sulky, I guess you might call it. It's fine though – it's just his way. Like you said, at least it shows he's keen on me.'

Molly comes over to the dressing table before I have time to consider this. 'I'm sorry I phoned Joel,' she says hugging me. 'If I'd known you were going to have all these men fighting over you I wouldn't have contacted him.'

'It's fine,' I tell her, hugging her back. 'You were only doing what you thought was right. Promise me one thing though. If Joel contacts you again in any way, don't reply, just tell me immediately, yes?'

'Sure, Mum,' Molly says, looking a bit puzzled. 'Of course I will.'

'But I've booked a table!' I hear a loud voice remonstrate, as later that evening I walk down towards the harbour along a

162

small side street. I'm still thinking about Joel and Molly, but as I get nearer to the voice I realise it's Julian.

As I turn the corner on to the harbour, standing in front of me on the cobbles are Julian – wearing a very smart navy suit, blue shirt and paisley-patterned tie – and Patrick, the owner of The Lobster Pot restaurant, in his chef's whites.

'I'm very sorry, sir, but as I just explained we've got a problem with our wiring, and we won't be able to open up until an electrician can come in tomorrow to fix it. I can recommend a number of other very good restaurants in the town for dinner tonight though, if you'd like me to.'

'Is there a problem?' I ask, approaching them.

'Kate! Hello,' a flustered-looking Patrick says. 'Yes, my fuse box has completely blown in the restaurant. I've had to close for the night.'

'Oh, no, how awful.'

'I'm trying to explain to this *gentleman* that I can recommend several other perfectly good eateries for him to try.'

'But you are supposed to be *the* best in town,' Julian says, looking aggrieved. 'I always eat at the best restaurants.'

'I thank you for the praise, sir, but you won't be tonight, I'm afraid. Perhaps you'd like to try us another evening? Complimentary wine on the house, of course. Excuse me,' Patrick says to me, 'I spy more about-to-be disappointed customers.' He heads off to greet a couple heading towards him.

'I'm so very sorry, Kate,' Julian says with a wounded expression. 'It seems we are without sustenance this evening.'

'Don't be silly, it's not your fault. Besides, there are lots of restaurants here we can try, and if for some reason we can't get a table we can always have fish and chips outside on the harbour.'

Julian looks horrified by this suggestion, but I simply smile at him. 'Come on, let's have a wander.'

Sadly, I'd underestimated just how busy the restaurants are in St Felix on a Saturday evening and we are turned away apologetically at every door.

'Let's try The Merry Mermaid,' I say. 'If they can't fit us in then it really will be chips on a bench, I'm afraid. They don't reserve tables so we might get lucky if someone is just leaving.'

We are lucky. As we push our way through the busy bar I spy a couple standing up about to leave. 'Would you mind getting us a drink, and I'll grab that table,' I tell a bemused-looking Julian. 'A Diet Coke with ice would be great, thanks.'

Julian, clearly feeling incredibly awkward, politely pushes his way nearer to the throng at the bar while I grab the small table by the window.

A young waiter comes over to clear the dirty plates and glasses.

'Busy in here this evening,' I say, making conversation.

'Manic,' he says. 'I've not stopped all evening. Have you eaten here before?'

'Yes, I have.'

'Good, then you know you need to order your food at the bar and we'll bring it over to you.'

'I do, thank you. It's Leo, isn't it?' I ask, recognising the young man as one of Molly's school friends.

'Yes.' He looks hesitantly back at me. 'Oh, you're Molly's mum, aren't you?'

'I am. I didn't know you worked here, Leo.'

'Yeah, summer job, innit. I'm starting to regret it already though if it's going to be like this every weekend.'

'At least your evening won't drag.'

164

'Barely time for my feet to touch the ground, let alone drag!' he says grimacing. 'Here's a new menu,' he says, popping one on the table. 'Like I said, order at the bar and I'll be back later with your food.' He gives the table one last wipe, then carries the empty plates and glasses away to the kitchen.

I wait for Julian to bring our drinks over, feeling slightly guilty I'd abandoned him at the bar. Julian didn't strike me as the type to frequent pubs. I'm sure he was much more used to having his order taken at his table and then being brought a vintage bottle of wine to sample, before deciding whether to accept it.

Eventually he finds his way back to me, carrying a glass of Diet Coke and what looks like a gin and tonic.

'What an ordeal,' he says, putting the drinks on the table. 'Having to fight your way through a crowd to purchase a beverage, and then fight your way to a table to drink it. I feel like I've gone back in time to a bawdy sixteenth-century tavern.'

I smile as he pulls back the chair and sits down. 'You don't go to many pubs then?'

'Can you tell?' he says, pulling a wry expression.

'Just a tad!'

We smile at each other. Julian obviously has a sense of humour hidden under all his pomposity.

'Always good to experience new things though,' Julian says, lifting his glass. 'Especially in such very pretty company. Here's to a pleasant evening.'

'And new experiences,' I say, lifting my own glass.

'Oh, I do hope so,' Julian adds, lifting his eyebrows suggestively at me as he takes a sip from his glass.

I hurriedly take a sip from my own. I could see this being a very long evening indeed.

*

Julian, surprisingly, is actually quite pleasant company. He's witty and amusing. He listens when I talk. He's more courteous than anyone I've ever met.

It takes him a while to get over the fact that we're going to eat in a pub – on a table without a cloth – and that we have to get up to order our food at the bar. When Leo brings our cutlery wrapped in paper napkins, in a basket with packets of ketchup, mustard, vinegar, pepper and salt, his eyes widen for a few seconds but he chooses not to say anything.

I find myself watching him with interest after Leo departs.

'Something amusing you?' he asks, returning my gaze. 'Obviously my handsome face is rather hard to resist!' He turns his head to and fro playfully.

'You're very well mannered,' I tell him.

'I like to think so. Is there something wrong with that?'

'No, nothing at all. I appreciate good manners.'

'I'm glad to hear it. Sadly, not everyone does these days. Ah, our food is here!'

'Chicken?' Leo asks.

'That's me,' I say, and he puts a plate of southern fried chicken, chips and salad down in front of me on the table. 'And the steak and kidney pie?'

'That would be mine, young sir. And what a fine, hearty-looking pie it is!'

Leo gives him an odd glance. 'Anything else I can get for you?'

'I think we're fine, Leo, thank you,' I say.

'A napkin, perhaps?' Julian says, looking hopefully at him.

'The serviettes are wrapped around the cutlery,' Leo replies, looking pointedly at the basket in the centre of the table.

'This?' Julian says, lifting a bundle of cutlery from the basket.

'Er, yeah.'

'Well, well, paper napkins!' Julian unwraps his cutlery, and with much amusement lays the thin white napkin in his lap. 'Thank you, young man, for another new experience tonight.'

Leo looks at me with a *Who's this guy?* expression, but I just smile at him and he leaves us to tend to another table.

'Steak and kidney pie,' I say, taking my own cutlery from the basket. 'I wouldn't have chosen that for you.'

'One of my favourites,' Julian says, cutting hungrily into it. 'My grandmother used to make it for me when I was a small boy.'

'Really, were you close to her?'

'I was,' Julian says, lifting up his fork. 'I spent a lot of time with her when I was young.' He tastes the pie. 'Not as good as Nanny's, but still pretty good.'

'Why did you spend a lot of time with your grandmother?' I ask, hoping this line of conversation might eventually lead us on to his father.

'My parents weren't around much,' he explains. 'Always travelling. I went to a boarding school in term time, and the holidays I spent mostly with my grandmother.'

'Oh, that must have been hard on you?'

Julian shrugs. 'Not really. I liked being with Nanny.'

'But you must have missed your parents?'

Julian looks puzzled, as though no one had ever asked him this question before. Perhaps no one ever had. Maybe in his circles going to boarding school and being away from your parents was the norm.

'A little, I guess. We usually spent Christmas together – when they were in the country, that is.' He eagerly tucks into his pie again while I help myself to a little bit of my chicken. I was keen to talk more about his father.

167

'Why were your parents away so much?'

Julian chews and swallows his latest mouthful. 'Why all the interest in my family?'

'No reason.' I shrug. 'Just making conversation. Plus your dad was a famous artist, wasn't he? I'm sure everyone is interested in him.'

'Usually that's all they want to talk about – my father. Never me.'

Oh Lord, now I feel bad.

But that's why you're here, Kate, I tell myself. *To find out more about Winston James and the painters he might have spent time with* . . .

'I guess that's what comes of having a famous father,' I say sympathetically. 'It's always hard on the children.'

Julian looks at me. 'I think you might be the first person ever to acknowledge that,' he says quietly, and he puts down his knife and fork. 'I've spent my whole life trying to live up to his name . . . and usually failing miserably.'

'I'm sure that can't be true,' I say, thrown a little. I hadn't expected Julian to reply in that way at all. He always seemed so full of himself, and now he seems to be deflating visibly in front of me. 'You . . . you seem so successful.'

'Do I?' Julian asks. 'Tell me, Kate. What do I do? I mean for a living – what's my job?'

'Er . . . ' I struggle.

'You see? You have no idea, do you?'

'No, it's not that . . . We haven't discussed it, have we? I assumed you promoted your father's work.'

'I do. That is it exactly. I work for the business he built. My life is all about his success. I've never had a chance to try and build my own.'

'I'm sure that can't be true.'

'It is true, Kate. I've done nothing with my life but try to live up to my father's name, while at the same time living off the fruits of it.'

Now I'm completely confused. I'd come out tonight thinking I knew exactly what sort of person Julian was. I was prepared to bypass all his arrogance and pretension in the hope I could find out more about Winston James and St Felix in the fifties, and now instead I find myself sitting opposite a lost and unhappy man, who instead of annoying me is making me feel incredibly sorry for him.

'Then why don't you?' I ask. 'Start building your own achievements instead of living off your father's? We all make our own choices in this world. Why don't you start by doing what you *want* to do?'

'I'm too old,' Julian says woefully. 'I've done this for so long I wouldn't know where to begin.'

'Nonsense. You're what . . . ?' I look at Julian closely. *Don't get this wrong, Kate.* ' . . . thirty-nine?' I say, knocking a few years off, in case.

'You're very kind. I'm forty-five.'

'That's not old – you're a little stuck in your ways, that's all. I made a huge change in my life only a couple of years ago. I gave up a good solid job with a financial firm and made the move here to St Felix to open up my own shop – something I'd always wanted to do but had never been brave enough to try.'

'Really? What changed to make you do it?' Julian sounds like he's genuinely interested, and not simply asking to be polite.

'I was pushed into it, I guess. Let's just say an ex made it easier for me to take the leap.'

'Maybe I too need a push? Sadly, I don't have anyone to give me that shove right now.' He gives me a wry smile. 'I don't suppose . . . ?'

' . . . I'd be your ex?' I smile too. 'That would mean we'd need to have a relationship first, and to be honest, Julian, I'm not really looking for that right now.'

'Shame,' Julian says. 'I think you could be just what I need, Kate. Someone who tells me how it is, and who doesn't pander to me. I think I could do with a bit of straight talking, and you're very good at that.'

'Thank you, I think?' I beam at him. 'Any time you need someone to give you a shove, you give me a shout. Now, we really need to eat some of this delicious food in front of us or it will get cold!'

But before I've a chance to take hold of my knife and fork I feel a hand placed firmly over mine.

'Thank you, Kate,' Julian says, looking earnestly at me across the table. 'Your wise words this evening have really touched me.'

'Don't be silly,' I say, tapping his hand reassuringly, hoping he will remove it if I do. 'I haven't done anything except speak the truth. You need to find some new people to hang around with if no one has ever told you that before. Perhaps you should spend less time in all the cosmopolitan places you frequent and more in places like St Felix if it's new friends you want? The people around here are usually quite sociable. I've always found them to be so.'

As I say this I gently remove my hand from under his, and smile with relief that I've extracted myself from a tricky situation, but as I glance over his shoulder out into the pub, I realise that I've immediately walked slap bang into another. My relieved smile disappears from my face as my gaze falls on to another man, and he's not looking at me with anything like the affection that Julian is.

I've been so busy listening to Julian's woes that I haven't noticed Jack has made an appearance in the pub this evening. As I stare back at him I'm in no doubt that he has definitely noticed that I'm here, and also that I'm not alone.

Twenty-one

Jack very deliberately turns away from me in his chair and takes up conversation with the person next to him, who happens to be PC Woods or 'Woody' as he's known to everybody, our local policeman.

Oh god, had Jack seen Julian's hand over mine? Of course he had. That's why he stared at me like that.

I wasn't doing anything wrong though. I was simply talking to a . . . well, I'd have to call Julian a friend now, I suppose. That was definitely something I hadn't expected to call him before tonight, but he'd turned out to be nowhere near as awful as I'd originally thought him to be, and anyway, it wasn't like Jack and I were a couple or anything, was it?

As I, slightly less enthusiastically, tuck into the rest of my dinner while Julian does the same, I can't help but worry what Jack must be thinking of me.

'Are you all right?' Julian asks, when I've been lost in my thoughts for a while. 'Is your meal not to your liking?'

'Oh, no, it's perfectly fine. How is yours?'

'Best steak and kidney pie I've had in years.' He puts down

his knife and fork on his empty plate, while I glance over his shoulder again at Jack. He's talking to Amber who's joined him as well now – Woody's fiancée.

Julian turns around to see who's capturing my attention. 'Someone you know?'

'No one special. Everyone knows each other here – it's like that.'

'Yet again this place reminds me of my grandmother's. Everyone knew each other down her street too. I'm liking it more by the minute. I've been to St Felix a number of times, Kate, but this is the first time I've felt any affinity to it at all. This is due to your influence, I feel.'

'Where was she from, your grandmother?' I ask, eager to move the subject away from me. Julian had already made his feelings pretty clear and I didn't want to encourage him.

'Liverpool – a Scouser through and through.'

'Gosh, when you talked about her before I didn't imagine you were staying in a city as a child. I thought it was the countryside you were talking about.'

'You imagined a fancy country house somewhere, no doubt? An idyllic childhood spent running through sun-kissed fields of straw – 'fraid not. This privately educated young boy had to stay in inner-city Liverpool when he was on his school holidays, in a two-up two-down terraced house. You can imagine the ribbing I got from the other children in the street when they heard my accent.'

Everything about Julian was becoming more understandable now I knew more about him.

'The way you are,' I suddenly say, 'that's all a front, isn't it?'

Julian stares at me. 'How do you mean?'

'I mean your demeanour. You've developed that over the

173

years more as a coping mechanism rather than show anyone your real personality. You're not actually pompous and full of yourself at all. You're much nicer than that.'

Julian appears shocked at first that I dare to describe him this way. Then when I say he's nicer than he seems his head drops and he shakes it disbelievingly. 'Were you some sort of psychologist before you came to St Felix, Kate?' he says, looking up at me again in total wonder. 'You're far too perceptive about people to simply run a shop.'

'Hardly. I think I'm good at seeing the person behind the mask, that's all.' I glance towards Jack again, but I can't see him now. 'And most of what people see of Julian James *is* a mask, isn't it? You keep the real you hidden.'

'Wasted in a craft shop,' Julian says, deliberately deflecting my observation. 'Totally wasted.'

'Kate is never wasted,' I hear Jack say, and I turn around to find him about to pass our table. He must have been to the disabled toilet behind us. 'Not in my experience anyway.' He raises his eyebrows at me. 'She barely drinks.'

'Jack ...' I say, finding myself extremely surprised yet pleased to see him.

'Jack Edwards,' Jack offers, holding out his hand to Julian. 'Good to meet you.'

Julian shakes his outstretched hand. 'Julian James. The pleasure is mine!'

Jack looks expectantly at me, waiting for an explanation. I'm about to tell him that Julian is the son of Winston James and connected to the exhibition, but then I realise I will be doing what everyone else does to Julian – introducing him via his father – so instead I say: 'Julian is a friend of mine. He's ... visiting St Felix.'

'Very nice,' Jack says in an overly friendly tone. 'And will you be staying long?'

Julian's gaze pauses on me. 'Possibly longer than I first thought ...'

'Great,' Jack says with what I know is a forced smile.

'Julian is in the art business,' I say diplomatically. 'So you two have something in common. Jack owns a shop in St Felix selling art equipment,' I explain to Julian.

'Ah,' they both say, and nod politely at each other.

'Do you paint?' Jack asks Julian.

Julian grins. 'No, not me. My father did though.' He gives me another conspiratorial glance, which Jack can't help but notice.

'What *do* you do then?' Jack asks bluntly.

'I *promote* art,' Julian replies carefully, 'but after tonight I could be changing my career path.' Again, he looks knowingly at me.

I wish he wouldn't keep doing that. I know it's annoying Jack, and I don't want him to think there's anything going on.

'Well, you two obviously have a lot to talk about that doesn't involve me,' Jack says, wheeling himself back from the table. 'I'll leave you to it. Nice to meet you, Julian. See you around, Kate.'

He looks deliberately at me, before pushing himself away.

'Nice chap,' Julian says, apparently not noticing anything is wrong. 'You said the people were friendly here.'

'Yes,' I say, watching Jack push himself out of the pub. 'They are.'

'I think I *will* stay on a while,' Julian adds, gazing at me while I gaze at the door Jack's just exited through. 'I'd like to make some *new* friends, and get to know a few others much, much better ...'

Twenty-two

Do you have another?

Jack's text gets directly to the point.
I respond in an equally blunt manner:

Yes.
When should we compare them?
Are you free tonight?
I am.
7 OK?
Yes.
See you later then.

Nothing ...
'So, it's like that now, is it, Jack?' I murmur sighing.
'What's like what?' Molly asks, wandering into the shop.
'Oh, nothing,' I say, looking up from my phone.
'Someone giving you grief, Mum?'

'No, don't be silly.'

'Which one of your many beaus is it this time? The rugged ex-soldier or the suave sophisticated man about town? Or is there a third I don't even know about yet? And before you say anything, I don't mean Joel!'

'Very funny. Shouldn't you be at school by now?' I ask, looking at my watch. 'Wait, don't tell me – a free period?'

'Yep, plus there's not much going on now it's the last week of term. Hardly worth going in at all . . .'

'Nice try. You're going. You're as bad as Sebastian always trying to get a day off.'

'Did someone say "day off"?' Sebastian asks, springing into the shop.

'No, no one is having a day off!' I snap.

'Ooh, did someone get out of the wrong side of the bed this morning?' Sebastian asks, looking at Molly.

'Men trouble,' Molly says, nodding.

'I do not have *men* trouble!'

'Which one is it?' Sebastian asks Molly as if I'm not here. 'The soldier or the suit?'

I shake my head and carry on pricing up some of my own work with the tiny white card tags we attach with cotton. This is a particularly lovely line I've created of small zipped bags that can be used as make-up bags, pencil cases or however the purchaser wishes.

'She won't say,' Molly whispers.

'Maybe it's both?' Sebastian whispers back.

'I can hear you, you know?' I tell them.

'So which is it then?' Sebastian asks. 'I'm kind of hoping it's the soldier. I like Jack.'

'*Both* of the gentlemen you are referring to are my friends,

177

and *only* my friends,' I reply adamantly. 'And neither of them are giving me grief, as you put it.'

'Are they giving each other grief then?' Sebastian asks hopefully. '*Ooh*, duelling at dawn over the fair maiden?'

I sigh. 'And why would they do that when we're just *friends*?'

'I think the lady doth protest too much,' Sebastian says, with a knowing look towards Molly, who nods her head in agreement. 'Though why you'd want to be only friends with Jack is beyond me. Julian – yes, I'm surprised you even went out with him again after the first time. I would have thought an evening with him would have been one too many in anyone's lifetime.'

'Now, stop right there,' I say seriously, putting down the pricing labels on the counter. 'I told you, Julian is misunderstood. Once you get to know him he's actually quite nice.'

Sebastian nods slowly in a disbelieving fashion.

'You'll have to take my word for it then. He is. The only reason I went out with him again – platonically, I might add! – is that he's trying to change and make some new friends, and possibly even a new life for himself. I know how hard it is to do that, so I think we should support him, not make a joke of him.'

'Mum's right,' Molly says. 'It was really hard for us when we moved here not knowing anyone. If Mum says he's not as bad as he seems then I trust her judgement.'

'Thank you, Molly,' I say appreciatively.

'Yeah, I'm sorry too,' Sebastian says, 'but you can't blame us for taking an interest in your love life. I wish I even *had* a love life for someone to joke about.'

'I wouldn't mind if I had a love life either,' I tell them. 'When I say these two men are only friends I genuinely mean it.'

'Really?' Sebastian asks. 'Nothing with either of them?'

'Nope.'

'Would you like there to be, Mum?'

I look at Molly. She deserves an honest answer.

'Julian – definitely not. He really is only an acquaintance. I like to call him "friend" because I don't think he has many of his own, and that's why I'm seeing him – to help him make some around here.'

'What about Jack?' Molly asks now. 'You like him, don't you?'

I nod. 'Jack is … complicated.' I hesitate. 'There are … *things* going on between us I can't explain that are bringing us closer, but then there are other things that seem to be pushing us apart.'

That thing was Julian. I hadn't seen or heard from Jack since the night in the pub nearly a week ago, apart from his text this morning after we'd both discovered new pieces of art in our shops.

However, I wasn't going to stop trying to help Julian because Jack might be … it seemed daft even thinking it … but it felt like Jack might be jealous.

'Relationships are hard,' Molly says knowingly.

I look at her. Really, she knew this already at fifteen?

'Everything all right with Chesney and you?' Sebastian enquires.

Molly shrugs. 'Yeah, I guess.'

Sebastian looks at me, but I shrug too.

'Do you want to talk about it?' he adds.

'Nah,' Molly says. 'Not really. I'll sort it out.'

'Right then, I think a group hug is in order!' Sebastian announces. 'Come, come,' he says, beckoning us towards him.

Reluctantly, I follow Molly into Sebastian's long, skinny arms, and I put my own arms around Molly and him.

'Here's to relationships,' he announces.

'I don't think group hugs usually have toasts,' I suggest.

'Well, this one does. Here's to relationships!' Sebastian tries again. 'Healing for those who are in difficulties.' He pats Molly and me on the back. 'And hope for those of us who are not in one right now.'

We both pat Sebastian.

'May we all find the right man for us in the very near future . . .' He pauses dramatically. 'But for now, let us all have fun trying!'

St Felix ~ August 1957

Clara glances out of her shop window.

Arthur is still there, painting away behind his canvas. How long did he need to be sat outside her shop – it felt like he'd been there days already.

'It must be very exciting to be the subject of a painting,' Mrs Harrington says, as she pulls her purse from her handbag to pay Clara for the dress she's collecting. 'I'd want to be out there all the time looking over his shoulder.'

'Oh, it's not me he's painting,' Clara says, taking the note from her customer and finding her some change in the little wooden drawer she kept all her takings in. 'It's the shop. Actually, it's all the street really. The town council has commissioned several paintings of St Felix.'

'Yes, I know. Jonathan, my husband, is on the council so he was at the meeting when it was decided. I think it's a wonderful idea to commemorate the town as it is today. It's changed such a lot over the last few years. We've grown from a small fishing community to a vibrant holiday destination. With the war years firmly behind us and rationing now finally over we should celebrate in any way we can.'

'Of course. I'd forgotten your husband is on the council.'

'Yes, he has been for some time now. Very proud he is of this community.'

'He has every right to be. St Felix is a wonderful place to live in and to visit.'

'Forgive me if I'm prying . . . ' Mrs Harrington says in a low voice, leaning over the glass cabinet towards Clara, 'but was it the war that took your husband from you?' She glances down at the narrow gold band on the third finger of Clara's left hand.

Clara hesitates. She always hated it when someone asked this for, as much as she detested telling lies, the thought of telling someone the truth petrified her even more.

She looks down at her ring. The truth is the ring had been her grandmother's. Her mother had given it to her when she'd come to St Felix for the first time to stay with her aunt and uncle. 'So people don't ask questions,' her mother had said.

'Yes, it did,' Clara says with the obligatory sadness in her voice. 'I prefer not to talk about it though if you don't mind.'

Mrs Harrington pats Clara's hand. 'I totally understand. The war left very few of us untouched by tragedy. I can't believe it's thirteen years since I lost my darling brother during the Normandy landings.'

'Oh, I had no idea. I'm so sorry.' Now she felt bad – this was someone with a genuine reason to grieve.

'He died a hero . . . like so many before and after him. I'm sorry for your loss, Clara. Maggie must miss having a father.'

'We manage,' Clara says, with an air of well-practised bravado that usually did the trick.

'Well done, you.' Mrs Harrington gives Clara's hand one last pat, and lifts her brown paper package from the glass cabinet between them. 'Thank you so much for this. It's truly beautiful. I don't know how you do it on that little machine of yours.' She glances across to where Clara's black Singer sewing machine sits on a table in the corner of the shop with another of her creations waiting patiently to be completed.

'Ah, it's the machine, not me.' Clara smiles. 'I should be getting back to it – lots to do. I'm so pleased you like your dress, Mrs Harrington.'

'Please, call me Annabel.'

'Annabel it is.'

'Thank you again. Good day, Clara.'

Clara walks Annabel to the shop door and bids her farewell.

She pauses to watch Annabel cross the street to have a quick word with Arthur. Her customer smiles as she looks over his shoulder at the painting. Then she bids him farewell too and heads off down the street, happily carrying her new dress.

When Clara glances back to Arthur again he's beaming up at her from his easel. Before she realises what she's doing she finds herself smiling back at him.

'Would you care for a cup of tea?' Clara asks, not knowing what else to say now.

'I would love one,' Arthur says. 'Milk and two sugars please.'

I find myself smiling as I pull back from the canvas, and I turn to Jack. He's smiling too.

'They've made up,' I say happily.

'Let's hope so,' Jack says. 'It's about time.'

'Can we make up?' I ask quietly. 'I don't like it when we fall out.'

182

'Have we fallen out?' Jack asks innocently.

'Considering you've hardly spoken to me since the night in the pub, I think we have.'

'Been a bit busy, that's all.'

'Really?' I ask a little sarcastically. 'Busier than usual?'

'Yes, actually. I've been getting ready for Ben coming.'

'Oh, yes, I'd forgotten about that. Is he arriving soon?'

'Yes, his mother is going away with her new fella – a cruise or something – so when Ben said he wanted to come and stay with me for the summer she was more than happy. I don't think she trusts him in the house on his own.'

'And you're sure that's the only thing that's been keeping you *busy*?'

'Yes. Why? Should it be something else?' Jack asks, wide-eyed.

I shake my head. 'No, not at all.' I turn back to the picture.

'Clara was acting a little odd when she spoke about Maggie's father,' Jack says, changing the subject for both of us. 'He must have died in the war, like you suggested before when we were wondering about him.'

'Possibly,' I say, not so sure. 'Or maybe she was covering herself. Judging by how she reacted to Annabel I think it might be more likely your guess was correct.'

'That she got pregnant and the father abandoned her?' Jack says. 'Really, why?'

'Don't know. I just get a feeling.'

The truth is I've spent years trying to do exactly the same thing as Clara – pretend about the father of my child to strangers. I know the signs all too well.

Molly had been born about sixty years after Maggie, but a one-night stand resulting in a baby was not uncommon these days. That's what had happened to me. I'd never seen Molly's father again after I'd spent the night with him following a post-graduation party. What must it have been like for Clara as a single mother in the 1940s when those things were much more taboo than they are now?

Molly knew the situation with her father. I'd never tried to hide it from her once she'd started asking questions. I wonder if Clara had been quite as honest with Maggie.

'Did you see Clara's sewing machine?' I ask, deciding that changing the subject again is the best idea. I really don't want to get into why I think I know Clara's story with Jack right now. 'It looks a lot like mine, doesn't it?'

'Yes, I thought that about Arty's easel too, but surely there were a lot of black Singer sewing machines around at that time, and big dark-wood easels too. I don't think we can read anything into it.'

'Probably not ... but what if they *are* the same ones as ours. What if I have Clara's machine and you have Arty's easel? It might help explain why we're seeing their story in the pictures.'

'Well, they came from the same house clearance, didn't they? I guess they could be ... but it would be a huge coincidence.'

'Not if Clara and Arty did eventually get together, and stayed together. They might have continued living in St Felix for the rest of their lives.'

'Until Noah came along and did a house clearance for them?' Jack says, raising his eyebrows. 'Now, I know I've had to suspend disbelief to accept what we see in these pictures, but even you must agree that *is* getting a bit far-fetched.'

'Not really. Noah said it was an old lady's family who were

selling everything off. It could have been Clara, couldn't it? She might have outlived Arty? Women usually do.'

Jack stares at me. 'Kate, even if they did eventually get together in your fairy-tale version of their lives, Clara would have to be what – a hundred years old by now?'

'No, not that old. She seems to be in her thirties.'

'Older than that, surely?'

'No, they dressed older then. I bet she's not even my age.' I pause to do the maths in my head. 'Annabel said her brother died on the Normandy beaches thirteen years ago, so that's D-Day, and that was in nineteen forty-four, so we're definitely in nineteen fifty-seven. So if Clara is in her thirties there, then she'd be in her ... nineties now.'

'So it could have been her who died then, leading to the house sale?'

'We don't know that she died.'

'What other reason do families have for clearing elderly relatives' houses?'

'She might have gone into a home or something?'

Jack smiles. 'You always see the bright side, don't you?'

'Not always. But it's true, whether it's Clara or not, the old lady could still be alive. *Hmm ...*'

'What's the *hmm* for?' Jack asks, obviously still amused.

'Well, I've lived here in St Felix for nearly two years and I've never met a Clara, or heard anyone talk about one, and surely Lou would have mentioned that Clara was still alive if she knew she owned my shop previously.'

'True. So if it wasn't Clara then who was it? They must have had something to do with Arty and Clara if the sewing machine and the easel they owned were in their house.'

'So you do think they might have been theirs now?'

185

'I don't know what to think, but if they weren't Clara and Arty's why are we seeing their lives played out in works of art made with them?'

I sigh and look at the easel again.

'The house!' I suddenly say. 'The one with the blue door. It's still up for sale, isn't it?'

'I suppose so.'

'So the estate agent must know who's selling it? All we need to do is ask them and we'll have our answer.'

'It can't be that simple, can it, surely?'

'Nothing is *ever* that simple, Jack, but we have to start somewhere and it's as good a place as any.'

Twenty-three

However, as Jack had correctly pointed out, nothing is ever that simple.

'I'm sorry, miss, but I'm afraid I can't tell you who the vendor is,' Jackson of Parkes & Parker estate agent in Penzance tells me over the telephone the next day. 'That's confidential information.'

'I know that, Jackson, but I don't want you to divulge it for any other reason than I'm simply interested to know who the previous inhabitant of the house was. I'm superstitious, see,' I add suddenly, having an idea. 'I can't possibly even think of *buying* a house if the previous owner's name begins with a C or an A?'

'You're superstitious?' Jackson asks, clearly thinking *This is a new one*.

'Yes, very.'

'But you *are* considering purchasing this property?'

'Very much so,' I fib. 'I live locally, and I've had my eye on that house for a long time. I said to my husband if that house ever comes up for sale, Trevor, then I want to live in it!'

'I can arrange a viewing if you'd like me to?' Jackson says keenly. 'Would that help calm your fears?'

'Er ... yes, I think it might.' *Actually seeing inside the house couldn't do any harm, could it? We might find something ...*

'How about this evening?' Jackson suggests. 'I have another viewing in St Felix at six. Could you and your husband make it for seven?'

'Seven would be perfect. Thank you.'

'So your husband is Trevor, and your name is ... ?'

'Fiona,' I grab from nowhere.

'Excellent. Fiona and Trevor.' Jackson is obviously writing this down. 'Right, I'll meet you at the house tonight at seven. Have a good day, Fiona.'

'And you too, Jackson,' I say, ending the call.

Right, I think, as I look at the phone in my hand, *that wasn't quite how I saw that going.*

Now I have the difficult task of calling Jack to tell him that not only are we to pose as a married couple tonight so we can see inside the house, but that his name temporarily is Trevor ...

'I can't believe we're doing this,' Jack says, as we wait outside the blue door of the house that evening for Jackson to arrive. 'And why did you pick the name *Trevor* for me?'

'First one I could think of. Plus, I didn't know at that point you were actually going to have to use the name or I'd have thought of something better.'

Jack looks up at the house behind us. 'I hope this is worth it. What do you expect to find in there anyway?'

'I don't know. Nothing probably ... but it's worth a try. I got nothing from Noah when I popped into his shop earlier. He said the house clearance was arranged by some American lady called Susan. He wasn't sure if they were a relative, and it was mostly arranged by email, I believe.'

'There must be someone in St Felix who knows the person who lived here. You're all in each other's pockets enough – I can't believe someone doesn't know the old lady's name?'

'We are not *in each other's pockets*. It's a friendly place to live, that's all. *Some* people like that – I thought you did too.'

'Yes, I do, but when you're new somewhere everyone seems to know each other already. I feel like an outsider.'

'I thought you were getting along fine? You're always down the pub. I assumed you'd met people there.'

'I am not always down the pub!' Jack says, looking aghast. 'Just because you saw me down there the other night when you were on your date doesn't mean I'm always there.'

'I was *not* on a date,' I insist. I'm aware our voices are rising, but as we both try to match each other's accusations it seems somehow necessary. 'I was simply having dinner with a friend, you know that. We weren't even supposed to be in The Merry Mermaid – we were going to The Lobster Pot, but they lost their power that night and had to close.'

'*Ooh*, The Lobster Pot – fancy! I should have known the local hostelry wouldn't have been good enough for Julian James.'

I stare at Jack. Why was he being like this?

'Do you know anything about Julian? You can't know enough to make comments like that.'

'I know,' Jack says firmly. 'I've asked around.'

'You've asked around! Why would you do that?'

'It doesn't matter now,' Jack says, turning away from me.

'Oh, I think it does matter—' I begin.

Jack shushes me. 'Is this the estate agent guy?' he whispers, as a young man in a blue suit comes through the gate.

'Probably,' I reply sulkily.

'You keep up that tone,' Jack says, ignoring my scowl, 'and he'll definitely believe we're a married couple.'

'Jackson Goldsmith,' the agent says, holding his hand out as he approaches us. 'Pleased to meet you both.'

'Hi,' I say, holding my hand out first. 'I'm Fiona, and this is my husband *Trevor*,' I say, gesturing to Jack.

'*Hello*, Trevor,' Jackson says, and I notice his voice changes as he speaks to Jack. 'I didn't know you were in a wheelchair?'

Jack picks up his change of tone immediately.

'Oh!' Jack says, looking down at his chair in surprise. 'So I am. I hadn't realised. Thanks for pointing that out for me.'

Jackson looks uneasily back at him.

'Don't worry, mate. Just my idea of a joke.'

'Ah, yes,' Jackson says, recovering his estate agent patter. 'Good to see you still have a sense of humour.'

'Why wouldn't I have a sense of humour?' Jack can't help himself, and I can't say I blame him. 'Do you think it got taken away with my legs?'

'No, no, of course not. I mean it must be very . . . challenging for you being in a wheelchair. Easy to lose sight of the lighter side of life.'

'*Hmm*,' Jack says, in a kind of growl.

'Shall we go in?' I suggest brightly.

'Yes,' Jackson agrees with relief. 'A wonderful idea. Let's do that.'

As Jackson moves forwards to unlock the door I flash my eyes warningly at Jack.

'What?' he mouths silently. 'It's him.' He points to Jackson.

'All ready?' Jackson asks, turning around.

I beam at him. 'Yes, please.'

Luckily, the doorstep is a low one so Jack manages to get his chair up and over it with very little assistance, and we enter into a large elegant hallway with black and white tiles covering the floor.

'Now, would you like me to give you a guided tour, or just leave you to have a wander? Oh, no offence,' he says to Jack.

'None taken,' Jack says, grinning a little too vehemently.

'Is it all right if we look around ourselves?' I suggest. 'Then if we have any questions we can give you a shout.'

'Of course,' Jackson says. He glances nervously at the large mahogany staircase rising gracefully up to the second floor in a beautiful curve.

'Don't worry, Jackson,' Jack says, watching him. 'I won't be asking you to carry me up there.'

'Ha ha.' Jackson forces a smile. 'Yes, very good.' A look of deep concern crosses his face. 'I'm sure though, if you did purchase the house, the necessary adaptations could be made. Stairlifts are very good these days and not only for the elderly and infirm.'

Could he dig himself any deeper, I wonder?

'Right . . . ' he says as Jack glares at him. 'I'll wait outside in the garden, shall I? I have a few phone calls to make. Just shout if you need anything.'

'We will,' I say hurriedly. 'Thank you, Jackson.'

'Idiot,' Jack grumbles before Jackson is barely out of earshot.

'He can't help it,' I say, waiting until he's left the building at least. 'Some people panic, don't they, when they meet someone with a disability. They don't know what to say.'

'Tell me about it. From the moment he began talking down to me I knew he was a fool.'

191

'Yes, I did notice that. Do you get that a lot?'

'Being spoken to like I'm five? Yes, you'd be surprised. It's like I'm a toddler in a pushchair, not an ex-soldier in a wheelchair. I fought for my country. That guy couldn't fight his way out of a paper bag.'

'I didn't do that when I met you, did I?' I ask, pretty sure I hadn't. 'Talk down to you, I mean.'

Jack shakes his head. 'No, you were okay. If I remember rightly you had a right strop because I wouldn't come downstairs and let you into my shop.'

'I didn't have a strop. I was simply a bit annoyed, but I didn't know then that—'

'I had no legs?' Jack states bluntly, finishing my sentence.

'No. Actually I was going to say you were an awkward bugger, but the legs thing will do . . .' I wink at him, and he grins back at me.

'Come on then,' Jack says, still smiling. 'Let's explore this house as best we can and see if we can find anything. Although what exactly we're looking for I'm yet to discover.'

We make our way as best we can around the old house, but all we find are empty rooms, often with old paper peeling off the walls, and occasional dirty lines betraying where pictures had once hung. There is no furniture left at all – everything has been removed, presumably by Noah and his house clearance team.

When we've explored all of the ground floor we arrive back in the hallway, and I gaze up the stairs.

'It's all right, you go,' Jack says. 'If it's anything like down here one person will be more than enough to check it out.'

I nod. 'I'll be as quick as I can.'

I hurry up the long winding staircase that curves upwards to

192

the top floor. I've always wanted to live in a house with a grand staircase like this, so I can't help running my hand over the smooth wood of the handrail as I go.

I scoot through a few of the empty rooms, not seeing anything different than downstairs – only more faded wallpaper, this time more appropriate to bedroom living.

It's only when I come to the last room that I pause.

This room is much bigger than the others, and whereas the other bedrooms all have carpets this one has bare boards. It's not so much the sight of floor-boards that is fascinating me but what's on top of them. All over the wood are splashes of colour – more specifically splashes of oil paint – as though someone did a lot of painting in this room and simply didn't care about the mess, because it was their room – their own room for creating works of art.

'Jack!' I call downstairs. 'Guess what I've found! Jack!' I call again, when he doesn't reply. I hurry back down the stairs. *Where is he?*

'I'm here!' he suddenly calls, and I turn around at the bottom of the stairs to try to place his voice.

'In here,' Jack says, opening a small door under the stairs and wheeling himself out.

'What are you doing under there?' I ask. 'Guess what I've found upstairs – a room where someone definitely did oil painting! There are splashes of paint all over the floor.'

'Great,' Jack says, still holding the door of the cupboard open. 'That definitely backs up what I've found too. Look!'

I hurry over to the under-stairs cupboard and look at what he's pointing at. On the back of the wooden door are a number of carved doodles where someone has deliberately defaced the wood with a knife.

193

The one that Jack is pointing to very clearly spells out *MAGGIE*.

'It can't just be a coincidence, can it?' I ask breathlessly. 'Are we simply looking for proof that isn't really there?'

'I don't think so. If you go into the cupboard there are even more doodles – some of them quite arty – and we know Maggie liked her art.'

I look at Jack. 'So they did live here ... Clara, Maggie and Arty, in this very house.'

'Did someone call?' A voice comes from the open front door and we see Jackson popping his head in.

'Er, no, I don't think so,' I say, hurriedly moving towards him as Jack closes the door behind us.

'I'm sure I distinctly heard my name called in a women's voice,' he says, looking at me. 'You called "Jack" a couple of times, didn't you?'

'Oh! Oh that, yes, I did ... '

'She sometimes calls me "Jack",' Jack says, swiftly pulling up next to me. 'It's like a pet name.' He takes hold of my hand. 'And I call her ... ' He pauses, and I see a wicked glint appear in his eye. 'Gertrude,' he says, looking lovingly up at me. 'Don't I, Gerty?'

'Yes,' I say, staring back at him, not quite as fondly. 'Yes, you do.'

'Ah ... I see,' Jackson says, seeming slightly bewildered. 'So, what did you think of the house then?'

'It's very nice,' I say, 'But I'm not sure it's for us after all, is it, *Trevor*?'

Jack shakes his head. 'No, Gerty here can be a bit superstitious, and she's not getting the right vibes about this house, are you, Gert?'

194

I shake my head.

'Or the previous owners,' Jack continues. 'Do you know much about the previous occupants, Jackson?'

Jackson shakes his head. 'No, I'm afraid I don't. It's such a shame you don't like the house. It's been on the market for a bit and we've been instructed to put it up for auction if it doesn't sell by the end of the summer. Someone could get a real bargain if that happens. It's a lovely place and in very good structural order for its age. A quick lick of paint and some new fixtures and fittings and it would make someone a beautiful home.'

'I'm sure it would,' I agree, looking around me. 'Well, we don't want to take up any more of your time, do we, Trevor?'

Jack shakes his head. 'No, thanks for letting us have a nose around, Jackson. Good luck with finding a buyer.'

'Thank you,' Jackson says, holding the door open for us. 'And good luck to you with . . . ' He looks at Jack as he pushes himself outside. 'Well, with everything really.'

Jack stares at him. 'Luck doesn't come into it, Jackson. Tenacity, perseverance, and dogged determination to be as normal as possible is what gets me through the day, and *that* will never change.'

Twenty-four

'So, what do we do now?' Jack says, as we make our way back down the hill into town.

'That's no clearer than it was before Trevor and Gerty visited the house,' I reply. 'Thanks for that name by the way.'

'You're very welcome! We do know a little more though. Someone called Maggie and someone who painted lived there, and the house provided both the easel and the sewing machine to us. Could it be anyone other than Clara and Arty?'

'I guess. It would be a huge coincidence if it wasn't them.'

'Exactly.'

'We need to ask around to find out who lived there before it went up for sale. Someone will know – they have to.'

'I agree. Now, are you hungry?' Jack asks. 'Would you like to go for some food?'

'Oh ... that's a lovely thought, but I can't, I'm afraid. I'm meeting Julian for dinner.'

'Ah,' Jack says, looking straight ahead. 'I see.' He begins pushing his wheels that little bit harder.

I have to walk faster to keep up.

'Sorry,' I apologise, 'I really would have liked to, but I'm trying to help Julian change his life and—'

'Change his life?' Jack scoffs, interrupting me. 'Why does he need to change his life? That guy has everything, doesn't he? Money, success, homes all over the world. What does he need to change about that?'

'He's lonely,' I say, and I stop walking so Jack has to pause and turn himself around to see me. 'Money doesn't buy you friends, Jack.'

Jack stares at me.

'I misunderstood Julian, as I'm sure a lot of people do,' I say pointedly. 'I only saw the brash, showy side of him, but that's not the real him – that's the person he's had to become to try and shake off his father's name. I'm trying to help him change.'

Jack suddenly smiles, but it's not a friendly sort of smile – it's a smug, knowing sort. 'If you believe that, you'll believe anything,' he says. 'He's using your natural compassion and incredible ability to see good everywhere, to … well … how can I put it politely?'

'Just say it, Jack,' I say quietly. 'You might as well get it off your chest.'

'Okay. To get in your knickers. There, I've said it.'

I simply stare at him, then I shake my head. 'You need to get your mind out of the gutter,' I tell him. 'Not everyone thinks like you. Julian is my friend, and if you don't like that then it's a real shame because I thought you were my friend too, Jack. Perhaps I got that very wrong.'

Without saying anything more I push past him and stomp off down the rest of the hill so Jack can only watch me go.

*

197

'Are you all right?' Julian asks later that evening, as we sit in The Lobster Pot waiting for our first course to be brought to the table. 'You're very quiet.'

'Yes, sorry. I'm fine. Had a bit of a weird day, that's all.'

'How so?'

Where do I start? I wonder. With a visit to an old house pretending to be someone's wife so we could see whether some mystery people used to reside there who we've been watching come alive via embroidery and paintings? Or the part when I left my pretend husband on a pavement after we'd argued about you?

'Ah, it's nothing,' I say tactfully. 'You know, life.'

'Bit of a weird one for me too actually,' Julian says, and I'm pleased he seems able to share his day with me more easily than I can with him. 'Someone went into the gallery and started kicking off about my father's pictures.'

'Kicking off? What do you mean?'

'Saying they weren't painted by him of all things.' He shakes his head. 'As if! Some nutter, no doubt. I wouldn't have known anything about it if I hadn't seen Ophelia from the gallery in the bakery earlier. She was pretty shocked to see me here, and somewhat embarrassed by what had happened, but she thought she'd better tell me in case someone was gossiping about it.'

I haven't the heart to tell him the people of St Felix have better things to gossip about than what goes on at the Lyle Gallery. Most of the locals have never set foot in the building – they see it only as a place for the many day trippers and holiday-makers to visit while they are here.

'That was good of her.'

Julian nods. 'I know, I thought so too. Of course I could only reassure her that of course my father had painted them – who else would have? He loved this place.'

'When did your father first come here?' I ask, seeing the perfect opportunity to delve deeper into Winston James' experiences of St Felix.

'The mid-fifties, I think,' Julian says thoughtfully. 'He came here as a young struggling artist, I believe. I wasn't around then, of course. He didn't meet my mother until the early seventies in New York, and they were married a short time after. I spent the first few years of my life in the States, but Mother wanted me to be educated in England, which is how I found myself at boarding school for so many years. She was much younger than him, but it seemed to work for them both. Do you have a problem with age gaps in relationships?' Julian asks casually, lifting his glass of wine and taking a sip.

'Er, no, not really. So,' I ask, keen to continue with the previous subject. 'Do you know much about your father's time here? In the fifties, I mean? I hear that's when a lot of artists started coming to St Felix.'

'Not too much. Only that he did some of his best work here. The funny thing is he didn't show anybody the paintings initially. I think he was embarrassed by them because they appeared so simple. Little did he know they would go on to become some of his best-known work.'

'So he didn't have any friends here back then – you know, like other artists?'

Julian shrugs. 'Not that I know of, but why would I, I wasn't even alive then. Now enough about my father or I will think you've become *one of them*!'

I stare at Julian for a second. 'Oh, I'm only talking about your father again, aren't I? I'm sorry. Let's talk about you instead. How have the last few days been?'

'Good, thank you. You were right, the people are quite

friendly if you try a little harder to get to know them. I've become quite the expert in making small talk!'

I laugh. 'That's good to hear. I'm pleased for you – perhaps you can carry this experience into your usual life once you return to it.'

'But that's the great thing. Since I've been here I'm wanting less and less to go back to my usual life. In fact, I'm thinking of staying on here permanently.'

He waits for my reaction.

'How very ... unexpected!' I reply carefully, wondering how he wants me to react. 'But is it practical for you? I mean we're so remote here. We're hardly handy for commuting or transatlantic flights.'

'I'll manage,' Julian says with a wave of his hand. 'I've got my eye on some interesting properties that will make much more impressive permanent homes than the place I'm staying in now. That was once my father's too, you know. He bought it as a little bolt-hole so he could come back here from time to time. When he died he left it to me. It's only small, but it's very quaint and cosy if you like that sort of thing.'

'It's great you're thinking of staying on, Julian,' I say, still wary. 'I have to say I'm a little surprised though. I can't imagine you living here permanently. It seems so ... rural, I suppose, and you always strike me as much more cosmopolitan.'

'Things change,' Julian says, holding my gaze across the table. 'And so do people. Meeting you has changed me, Kate, and I hope to show you just how much influence you've had over me in the coming weeks and months, as we get to know each other a *whole lot* better.'

I open my mouth to say something, and then I close it again in relief as a waiter appears at the table with our first course, preventing me from having to respond.

As we begin to tuck into our tiny yet delicious appetisers, however, I can't stop my mind from wandering back to Jack earlier today and what he'd so crudely told me.

I glance at Julian, and he smiles at me and lifts his glass in a toast.

'To the two of us,' he says, his eyes shining, 'and to St Felix. May the three of us have many, *many* good times together.'

Twenty-five

I stand outside my shop and stare into the window at the latest artwork to appear underneath the sewing machine's footplate. Although it's upside down, I can just about see what looks like a face staring up at me.

Usually when a new piece of embroidery appears I can't wait to retrieve it from the window and see what it's of, but this time the sight of this fresh creation is doing nothing but make me sigh. Now I'll have to go and see Jack again. No doubt he too will have received something very similar this morning in his own shop.

'Couldn't you have waited?' I murmur, looking into the window. 'At least a few days until the heat dies down a bit.'

'It is a warm one, isn't it?' a voice behind me says, and I turn to see Anita arriving for work wearing a flowery sundress and carrying a parasol. 'Goodness knows what it will be like later if it's this hot now. Good morning, Kate.'

'Morning, Anita,' I say, greeting her, but not revealing that the heat of the sun wasn't the type of heat I'd been thinking about. 'Yep, we'll have to get the fans out and that air-con unit we bought last summer,' I reply, turning away from the window and following her into the shop. 'I think they're in the back room somewhere. If you hold the fort when you've put your things away I'll have a search.'

Once Anita is settled in the main shop I head out back. I find the fans without too much bother and, eventually, the small air-conditioning appliance we'd purchased in the record-breaking heat St Felix had bathed in last year. I ferry them back one by one and place them in various positions that will allow a cool breeze to flow through the shop.

'There, that's better,' I say when I'm done. 'At least we won't die of heat exhaustion now, and we might get a few extra customers venturing in if it's cooler in here than outside.'

'I was going to make a cup of tea,' Anita says, handing me a glass. 'But I thought you might prefer an iced lemonade instead? I gave Eve a wave across the road and she brought us two over.'

Eve runs the fresh coffee and juice shop a few doors across from us. Whatever weather St Felix throws at our visitors Evie is prepared with either a hot cup of something to warm them up or a refreshing juice to cool them down.

'Fabulous! Thanks, Anita.' I take the cold glass from her. '*Mmm*, that's lovely.'

'That's a pretty little piece of embroidery you've got in the window there,' Anita says. 'It sets off the old machine beautifully. Did you do it? If you did you should make some more and sell them in the shop. They'd sell like hot cakes.'

'No, it's not mine,' I have to admit.

'Oh, where did you get it from then?' Anita looks through the back entrance into the window again. 'It looks familiar – is it from someone local?'

'I'm not sure ...' I reply, not really knowing how to answer this.

Anita looks at me with a puzzled expression. 'How do you mean, dear?'

I sigh. I'd known Anita a long time now, and Anita had known St Felix a long time too. She had been one of the people who had told me the most tales about some of the many 'unexplained' things that often went on here. If I was going to confide in anyone, Anita would be one of the best people to share with.

I take a deep breath and confess all, from the first embroidery to the last and all the others in between. I tell her all about Jack's paintings and what happens when we put the two types of artwork together. Then I tell her about the house with the blue door and who we think might have lived there in the past.

Then I pause and wait for her reaction.

'Well,' she says, when I've told her my highly improbable and very strange tale, 'I did wonder whether it might happen to you at some point.'

I'm surprised by her calm reaction. If someone had told me all this, I'd have been looking at them with very different eyes now. 'What might happen to me, Anita? Paintings and embroideries bizarrely coming to life?'

Anita shakes her head. 'No, dear, the magic of St Felix. I told you before it often strikes in the most unlikely of places. This time it seems to be your turn.'

'My turn? My turn for what?'

'To help someone, or be helped yourself. It's often both at the same time in my experience – that's how it usually works. I think I told you the story of the Cornish sorceress Zethar, and of how the townsfolk of St Felix helped her shelter from her persecutors when she was on trial for witchcraft?'

'Yes, you did, and how she cast an enchantment on not only the building where she hid and the ground below it – where Poppy's flower shop now stands – but over the whole town too. That's right, isn't it?'

'Yes, that's the one. It's a story embedded in St Felix's history. Anyone who comes here and stays is always subject to Zethar's magical spell. When it strikes it's always something different, but it always involves helping others in some way ... like the villagers helped her.'

I shake my head a little. Seeing moving images in static pictures was one thing, but believing it was all to do with some ancient Cornish sorceress's spell hundreds of years ago was another. 'So you're saying *I'm* being helped, is that right? But helped to do what?'

Anita shrugs. 'Like I say, it's always different. You might be being helped along a little, but most likely if you are, it will involve you helping someone else too.'

I immediately think about Jack and his struggles, and then I think about Julian. Was it one of them I was supposed to be helping?'

'How will I know who it is?' I ask, hoping Anita will have all the answers.

'I don't know, dear,' she says gently. 'I don't think it works the same way every time. I guess you'll just know when it happens.'

'Have you ever been helped, Anita? You seem to know a lot about it.'

'Everyone who comes to St Felix likes to think they've been helped by the magic in some way. That's part of the charm of the place, when you discover all these stories you have immediate hope, and hope is a very powerful emotion, but whether your fortune comes from the magic, or simply from the belief that something good will happen, no one truly knows. My good fortune came after Wendy passed on and I thought this shop would be closed for ever. I'd have lost not only my job but a part of my life too. You know how much I love being here. So when you came along and said you'd keep me on, I have to admit, I did wonder if it was the magic of St Felix that had helped me.'

I smile at Anita. 'It was never in doubt you were to stay,' I tell her. 'I think I'd have had a riot on my hands if I'd ever tried to let you go.'

'You're a good girl, Kate, which is why I think the magic has struck in such a big way for you. Some of us can only wonder whether it might have been Zethar's enchantment helping us along in times of need, but you and Jack seem to have been granted something much bigger, and likely more important, to do. Don't think of this as something to worry about, think of it as your chance to do something special, something that will truly make a difference to someone.'

'Oh Anita, you're the one who's amazing!' I say, giving her a huge hug. 'Only you could have made it seem like that, and not like I was going mad! So you think we should keep pushing to find out more about Clara and Arty?'

'Oh definitely. I'm sad I can't really help you any more, I only know that the lady who lived in the house you're talking about was called Peggy. She was a bit of a recluse by all accounts. I remember Wendy trying to be friendly and going up there once to see if she wanted to be a part of the community a little more, but she didn't get very far. The lady was polite enough to Wendy, but she really wasn't interested in us. She preferred to be on her own, I think. Probably why she chose that house – it is a bit isolated, isn't it? Up on the hill in its own grounds.'

'A little bit, I suppose, but it has some amazing views of the town and the coast. I wouldn't mind living there if I had the money. It's a fair bit bigger than my little flat upstairs.'

'Who knows, maybe one day you will,' Anita says kindly.

'I'd better start buying a lottery ticket then!' I grin. 'Because that's the only way I'll ever find myself able to afford to live there.'

St Felix ~ August 1957

Clara glances out of the window of her shop. The morning had started quite busily, but now, as the heat of the afternoon penetrates Harbour Street, people are much preferring the cool breeze of the beach and the cliffs than the stuffy little seaside shops.

She fans herself with one of her dress patterns to try to cool down but it's not helping at all, so she goes to the door to see if there's any more air on her door-step.

'Oh,' she says, surprised to see Arty standing not far from the shop. 'I didn't know you were here again, Arthur?'

Clara hadn't seen Arty for a few days, and although she hated to admit it, she was missing seeing him outside with his easel set up along the street somewhere. She had assumed that he'd moved on to another part of the town now.

'Yes,' Arty says, walking over to her. He holds up a box camera in front of him. 'I'm taking some detail shots on my Brownie so that I can go back home and work in the comfort of my studio when I've got them developed. I've already got the basics, but I'm missing something I can't quite put my finger on.'

'Very good,' Clara says politely. 'I didn't know you had a camera.'

'I've not had it all that long, I picked it up in a junk shop. To me this seems brand new, but to someone else it's old-fashioned now. Strange, eh?'

'Yes, it's a little like that with clothes now. For years we were told to make do and mend, but now everyone wants the latest styles as soon as they come off the catwalk. I can barely keep up.'

Arty holds his camera up as though to take a photo of Clara.

'No!' she puts her hand out to block the shot. 'Not of me, you don't!'

'But why?' Arty asks, lowering his camera, 'You'd make the perfect subject. In fact, that might be exactly what I need – someone to put life into the street. My paintings are too static at the moment.'

'Well, it won't be me giving you life,' Clara says adamantly, folding her arms. 'Take your camera away from me.'

'What if I said please?' Arty says, his kind brown eyes suddenly turning doleful as he blinks back at her. 'You're by far the prettiest shopkeeper down this street.'

Clara, to her intense annoyance, feels herself blush.

'You'd be doing me a *huge* favour.'

Clara thinks about this for a moment. 'All right then,' she concedes. 'But I may want a small favour from you in return . . .'

Arty attempts to take several photos of Clara in different poses in front of her shop, then he sighs and puts his camera down.

'Relax,' he says gently. 'You're being far too formal.'

'I can't relax when you're pointing that thing at me. It's not natural.'

'It will be if you loosen up a bit.'

Clara sighs now. 'I told you this wasn't a good idea.'

208

'I know ... what if we try taking one with you looking into your shop window instead of at the camera? That might help.'

Clara nods and turns towards her shop.

'Just turn a little to the side so I can still see your face,' Arty instructs. 'That's it, now think of what this little shop means to you.'

Clara's tight face and taut body immediately relax as she thinks about the shop and how proud she is of it.

'Fantastic!' Arty calls, pressing the shutter and hurriedly winding on the film to the next exposure. 'Now turn your body towards me a tad, but still keep looking into the shop window.' Another click of the shutter and a wind of the film as Arty takes another two exposures with Clara in the same position.

A movement behind Arty makes Clara turn and she sees Maggie and Babs coming up the street. Her natural instinct takes over and she beams warmly at her daughter.

'That's it!' Arty calls, pressing the shutter for the final time. 'Now you're smiling!'

'Yes, that is it,' Clara says, hurriedly straightening her blouse and skirt. 'Hello, Maggie. How was your afternoon?'

'Arty!' Maggie says happily on seeing him. 'How are you?'

'Very good, young Maggie. Very good. And *you* are looking very well, I must say!'

Arty looks behind Maggie's chair at Babs. 'I'm sorry, miss, I don't believe we've had the pleasure,' he says holding his hand out. 'Arty Jenkins.'

'Barbara Smith,' Babs says, shaking it. 'You're one of them artist fellas, aren't you, who hang around here? I've seen you painting.'

'I am indeed.'

'If you ever need a model,' Babs says, flicking her blonde

hair and puffing out her ample chest, 'I am available to have me portrait done. I've been told I have a look of Jayne Mansfield about me.'

Clara visibly bristles at Babs' overfamiliarity with Arty, but he just smiles in a kindly way. 'Yes, I can see that, Barbara. You very much have the look of a Hollywood film star. What a wonderful model you would make someone. Sadly, I mainly paint landscapes, but if that ever changes I'll be sure to give you a shout.'

'Worth a try,' Babs says, shrugging. She turns to Clara. 'Same time tomorrow, Clara?'

'Yes, if that's all right? What have you two been up to today anyway?'

'We went to see Freddie again,' Maggie says, holding up a piece of wood. 'He let me paint with him.'

'Ah, I see.' Maggie glances at Arty for a reaction, but his face gives nothing away. 'That's very good,' Clara says, taking the wood from Maggie. 'What do you think, Arty?'

Arty takes the wood from Clara. 'Yes, indeed it is. Where are you doing this?'

'With Freddie,' Maggie says again. 'He's very kind to me.'

'Freddie?' Arty repeats. 'I don't think I know a Freddie?'

'He's that old geezer who paints in his cottage in down-along.' Babs explains. 'I don't think he's got two ha'pennies to rub together. He certainly don't look like he has, but he manages to paint still. He uses bits of wood and stuff instead of canvases.'

Arty nods thoughtfully. 'And what do you do, Babs, while Maggie goes to paint with Freddie?'

Babs shrugs. 'I sit outside mainly, topping up me tan.'

'Babs!' Clara says sharply. 'You're supposed to be looking after Maggie. That's what I pay you for.'

'That's all she wants to do!' Babs protests. 'I've tried doing other things with her, but she just wants me to take her to the old fella's to paint.'

Clara looks at Maggie. 'Is this true, Maggie?'

Maggie nods. 'Don't be cross with Babs, Mummy. I ask her to take me to Freddie's. It's not her fault.' She hesitates. 'If it's anyone's fault, it's yours, Mummy. You stopped me painting with Arty.'

Clara glances at Arty, but to his credit he doesn't look smug. Instead he simply looks with concern at Maggie. 'And that's all you do when you're at Freddie's, Maggie,' he asks, 'painting?'

'Yeah,' Maggie says, 'Freddie, doesn't say much. He's very quiet, but I kind of like that. He doesn't make a fuss of me like everyone else does. He accepts me for me and we paint together.'

Clara and Arty both breathe a sigh of relief at the same time.

'Could you take me to see this Freddie sometime?' Arty asks. 'Perhaps tomorrow, instead of Babs taking you, I could? If it's all right with your mother, of course?'

Clara nods.

'Great!' Maggie says excitedly, 'I'd like that, and I'm sure Freddie would too. I don't think he knows any other proper artists like him.'

'Don't worry, Babs, you won't be out of pocket,' Arty reassures a worried-looking Babs. 'Will she, Clara?'

Clara shakes her head. 'No. Just see it as a day off.'

'All right,' Babs says, shrugging. 'Sounds good to me! I'll be off now then, shall I? See you on Monday. Unless you need me Saturday?'

'No, Monday will be fine, thank you, Babs.'

Babs heads off down the street, and Clara turns to Maggie.

211

'Why don't you go and get yourself an ice cream from the shop across the road?' she says, pulling half a crown from the pocket of her full skirt.

'On my own?' Maggie asks, staring in amazement at Clara.

Clara nods. 'Take it slowly though. There's no rush.'

Maggie beams at her mother. She pulls herself up from her chair and then begins to walk very slowly, leaning heavily on a wooden walking stick, across to the shop, while Clara and Arty watch her.

'Thank you,' Clara says, smiling gratefully at Arty, 'for offering to take Maggie tomorrow. I'm sure everything is fine with this Freddie, but you never know, do you? You hear things . . .'

'No need to explain,' Arty says hurriedly, still watching Maggie until she is safely in the shop. 'It's not a problem at all. I'm sure we have nothing to worry about, but I'd still like to check it out. Now,' he says, turning his gaze fully to Clara, 'I've got my photographs, which I hope will turn out to be as wonderful as their subject when I have them developed.'

Clara blushes again.

'But I believe I still owe you a favour?'

Clara shakes her head. 'No need,' she says, smiling at him. 'What I was going to ask of you, you've already offered to do tomorrow with Maggie, and I'm very grateful.'

Arty looks puzzled for a moment, and then he grins. 'Great minds, eh?' he says.

'Indeed,' Clara replies. 'We're obviously more alike than I realised, Arthur.'

I sit back from the painting of Clara standing outside her shop.

'Arty obviously did paint Clara then,' I say casually, not

212

really looking Jack in the eye. 'It's clear that this painting you have must have been done from one of the photos we saw him taking.'

'Yes, that's what I was thinking. Do you think all the paintings have been Arty's? There's no signature on them – I've checked.'

'Yes, I do. This easel must have belonged to him, and I bet the sewing machine was Clara's too. It all fits in with the house now, doesn't it?'

At the mention of our visit to the house, Jack's lips purse together.

In the end I'd bitten the bullet and texted Jack about my newest finding. After a long wait he'd texted back and con-firmed, as I suspected, he too had received another painting overnight, and we'd very formally (for us) agreed to meet that evening to compare them.

So far we'd been polite towards each other, but nothing had been said about our visit to the house with the blue door, or about what had happened afterwards.

'Yes, I suppose it does.' Jack says. He glances at me, and for the first time since I arrived tonight, looks properly into my eyes.

'I'm sorry about the other day,' he says.

'I'm sorry about how I spoke to you,' I say at the same time.

'Go ahead,' Jack says, holding out his hand.

'I was going to add, I'm sorry about walking off and leaving you, but you made me really cross.'

'I know I did, and I'm sorry. I shouldn't have said what I did about Julian.'

I nod. 'He *is* just a friend,' I tell him. 'Whatever you might think, I'm not interested in him like that, even if he is in me.'

Jack raises an eyebrow as if he's going to say something, but then he thinks better of it. 'That's good to know,' he says instead.

'Is it?'

Jack nods slowly, and we hold each other's gaze for a few seconds longer this time. Then Jack sighs and looks down at his chair. He shakes his head angrily.

'What's wrong?' I ask.

'It's this thing. All I want to do right now is let you know how much what you said means to me, but as usual this stupid thing is preventing me from doing what I really want to.'

'What is it you really want to do?' I ask quietly.

Jack looks at me. 'Wrap you in my arms and kiss you so hard you've no doubt how I feel about you.'

I feel a shiver of pleasure run through me at the thought of him doing just that.

'How strong is your chair?' I ask.

Jack looks puzzled for a moment, then he smiles.

'Strong enough for two if that's what you mean?'

'I won't hurt you if I sit on you?'

Jack shakes his head. 'No, you won't hurt me, but I must warn you I do still have some feelings down there. I'm not completely immobile ...'

He grins at me, and I smile as I stand up in front of the easel and move from my chair to Jack's. I'm about to sit on his lap when I pause. 'Did you hear something?'

'No, definitely not ...' Jack says, still gazing at me.

I go to sit down again but footsteps make me stop.

'There's someone downstairs in the shop,' I say, looking with horror at him.

'There can't be. I left the inside door to the shop unlocked

214

so you could bring the easel up, but the street door is secured for the night. There can't be anyone down there.'

But again I hear something. 'Wait there.' I tell him.

'Kate, no!' Jack protests, spinning himself around as fast as he can in his chair and following me as I head for the stairs. 'Kate, wait! I need to tell you something . . .'

I look around for something to grab and see a pair of rarely used crutches. I grab one and I'm already thundering down the stairs before Jack can reach me. No one was going to break into Jack's shop and get away with it!

I burst through the inside door, kicking it open like I'm in some sort of cop show. 'Stand back, I'm armed!' I shout, as I bound in brandishing the crutch.

A tall young man wearing a black hoody spins around, looking at first surprised and then amused by what he sees in front of him.

'Hey,' he says, holding up his hands in mock surrender. 'Don't beat me with your crutch, lady! I'm innocent!'

'H . . . how are you innocent?' I ask suddenly, wondering what I'd hoped to gain by this. It was now me against the intruder. What was I going to do? Hopefully Jack had called the police from upstairs already.

'I didn't break in, did I?' he says, stepping forwards, but I hold the crutch out like a bayonet in front of him to keep him back. 'I let myself in with a key,' he continues, stepping back again, 'via the front door in the corridor over there. I thought I'd have a look around the new shop on the way in.'

'How do you have a key?' I begin, but then I notice the intruder looking over my shoulder.

'All right, Dad,' he says grinning. 'Quite some security guard you've got yourself here!'

215

Twenty-six

I look back at Jack, who's managed to get himself down the stairs now and into his second chair, then I turn and stare at the boy in the hoody, and slowly I lower the crutch.

'Hi, I'm Ben,' he says, stepping forwards again smiling at me. He holds out his hand. 'Dad obviously didn't tell you I was coming?'

'Er ... no, he didn't,' I say, shaking his hand. 'I'm Kate, pleased to meet you.'

I turn and glare at Jack.

'Sorry,' he says, 'I did try to warn you, but you set off at such a speed down those stairs I couldn't stop you.'

'It's good to know someone's watching out for the old fella,' Ben says. He heads over to Jack and leans down to hug him. 'Good to see you again, Dad.'

'And you,' Jack says, hugging him extra tightly. 'It's been too long, son.'

Suddenly, I feel a little awkward standing here, still holding Jack's crutch.

'I . . . I'll just take this back upstairs,' I say, 'and then I'll let the two of you be. You must have a lot to catch up on.'

'Kate, you don't have to go,' Jack says. 'The truth is I wasn't expecting Ben until later tonight. I sent him a key so he could let himself in easily when he got here.'

'I got an earlier train,' Ben says, shrugging. 'I thought I'd surprise you, and it appears I have! Sorry, I didn't know the old man would have company.' He winks.

'Oh no,' I hurriedly protest. 'It's not like that. We're just friends, aren't we, Jack?'

Jack doesn't look quite as keen to use this excuse. Instead he just nods.

'What do you want me to do about the *things* upstairs?' I ask. 'Shall I move them before I go?'

'Yes, if you could.'

'Do you have much luggage?' I ask Ben. 'Do you need a hand?'

'Nah, you're all right,' Ben says. 'I can manage. Look, don't leave on my account. I can make myself scarce for a while.' He raises his eyebrows suggestively at Jack, and immediately I can see Jack in him. They have the same dark eyes and the same dimples in their cheeks when they grin mischievously.

'I have to go anyway,' I tell him firmly. 'I have things to do. I'll just pop upstairs and get my things, and then I'll be gone.'

Without giving them the chance to object, I hurry past Jack and head back up the stairs. I grab the embroidery from the easel, and then quickly lift the painting of Clara and place it behind Jack's sofa. I fold the easel and pop it in the hall in a prominent enough place for Jack to see it but hopefully tidily enough to avoid questions from Ben.

Then I grab my bag with the embroidery tucked safely away and head quickly back to the top of the stairs just in time to witness Jack hauling himself back up the steps, while Ben, looking impressed, watches him from below.

I stand aside when Jack reaches the top so he can access his wheelchair, then I wait again while Ben bounds up the stairs carrying a rucksack on his back and a large holdall in his hand.

'Please don't go on my account,' Ben says again. 'It's good to see that Dad has made a friend here. Be nice to get to know you a bit more.'

I smile. Ben has obviously been heavily drilled in manners from his mother. His overt politeness didn't sound like Jack at all.

'That would be lovely,' I say, 'Perhaps we could all have dinner together one night?'

'Sounds like a plan,' Jack says. 'Why don't you bring Molly along too. Ben and your daughter might have a bit more in common than us oldies!'

'Sure, sounds like fun. Right, I really must be going. I've folded the easel and popped it over there,' I tell Jack. 'I'm sure Ben can carry it downstairs again for you.'

Jack nods.

'See you both soon,' I say, giving a casual wave in their direction. Then I hurry back down the stairs and outside into the balmy evening air.

Once outside, I take stock of what has just happened. It isn't the surprise appearance of Jack's son that's making me feel on edge as I walk back towards my own flat, more the things that Jack had said to me before he'd arrived.

And what might have happened if he hadn't.

'What?' Molly says a couple of days later when I tell her that I've arranged for us to go out for dinner with Jack and Ben. 'Why?'

'Because Ben is new here, and it might be nice for him to know someone younger than Jack and me.'

Molly rolls her eyes. 'What's he like, this Ben?'

'He seems perfectly nice. He looks like Jack, but other than that I don't know much about him. He's a bit older than you, so I don't think you need worry about him wanting to hang around with you.' I look at her imploringly. '*Please*, Molly, I've said you will now. Are you supposed to be seeing Chesney tonight, is that it?'

Molly looks awkwardly down at her Converse trainers. 'Nah, not tonight.'

Did I sense some reticence on Molly's part again? This was new. The last time we'd spoken about Chesney Molly's eyes had lit up at the very mention of him. Her opinion of him seemed to change as often as the tide.

'So you're free then?'

'Yeah, I suppose so. Where are we going?'

'Just to The Merry Mermaid. It's nothing fancy – a quick bite to eat, that's all.'

'Sure, I'll do it, but you owe me one, Mum!'

'When don't I? How about I start making that list I keep talking about – the one where I write down every favour we've done each other, and we'll see if we've equalled out yet?'

Molly rolls her eyes again. 'All right, you win. What time?'

'Eight.'

'Okay, I'll be ready for eight o'clock.'

'Thank you!'

Later that afternoon I'm alone in the shop when Julian pops his head around the door.

'Busy?' he asks.

'Not particularly. The warm weather may be filling St Felix with holiday-makers but they're spending their time on the beaches not in the shops.'

'Ah,' Julian says, not knowing how to react to this. 'How do you fancy dinner tonight – my treat! I have something to celebrate!'

When wasn't it Julian's treat? He never let me pay when we went out. As chivalrous as that was, it was also very frustrating.

'Oh, I'm sorry I can't ... I already have other plans.'

Julian looks disappointed. 'Ah, too late as usual. I should have known a beautiful lady such as yourself would be a popular dinner companion. I will form an orderly queue.'

'No need for that. I'm only going to the pub with my daughter, my friend Jack and his son.'

Julian looks relieved.

'So, what's your big news?' I ask. 'Can you tell me now?'

'I have found a property at last!' Julian says excitedly. 'Here in St Felix,' he adds, in case I don't know.

'You have? Where?'

'Up on the hill as you go out of town. There's a huge house up there, bit derelict, needs a fair amount of modernising, but I can get some people in. It'll be as good as new in no time.'

'Do you mean the house with the blue door?' I ask, feeling a little dismayed by this news.

'Er ... I think it has a blue door, yes. But it won't be there long – that will have to go too. The door to your home says a lot about you, and that peeling old wreck does not say what I want it to about me at all!'

I just nod.

'Aren't you pleased for me, Kate?' he asks, looking a little aggrieved. 'I thought you would be?'

'Of course I am. If you really do want to put down some roots here then why not buy that house? It's one of the biggest in St Felix after Tregarlan Castle.'

'Yes, I looked into the castle, but it seems it's part of National Heritage now so it's very definitely not for sale.'

I smile at him. Julian really was from a different world.

'So when do you exchange contracts?' I ask. 'I assume you've put in an offer on the house?'

'*Hmm*, that's a slight bone of contention right now. I wanted to but the estate agent says it's possible it might be going up for auction. He said he'll consult with the vendors though and see what they say.'

'Auction – really? When I was there they seemed pretty desperate for an offer . . .' My voice fades out. Now I was going to have to explain why I'd been to the house.

'You were at the house?' Julian asks. 'Why?'

'I wanted to see what it was like. I've always loved the look of it, so when it came up for sale I thought I'd take a peek.'

'And what did you think?' I can tell by the tone of his voice that this is anything but a casual question.

'Very nice. It will make *you* a lovely home.'

'A little sizable for only one perhaps?' Julian suggests.

'Maybe, but I'm sure you can make it work.'

'I have every intention of doing just that,' Julian says meaningfully. 'In *all* aspects of my life.'

'Hi,' I say to Jack, as Molly and I arrive at the pub and find Jack already sitting at a table. 'How are you?'

'Good thanks,' Jack says. 'Hi, Molly, thanks for coming. Ben is just getting some drinks in. What would you like?'

'Er, Diet Coke please,' Molly says warily, pulling out a chair.

'Make that two,' I say, sitting down next to her.

'Would you mind adding two Diet Cokes to that order, Ben?' Jack asks as his son comes over to the table with two pints of beer in his hands.

'Sure,' he says, beaming at us. 'You must be Molly?' he says, inclining his head towards her.

Molly nods feverishly.

'Great,' he says. 'See you in a mo,' and he heads back up to the bar.

I look at Molly. 'You all right?'

Molly nods again. 'Excuse me, I'll be right back,' she says. 'Bathroom!'

I watch mystified as she rushes over to the Ladies loo.

'Kids, eh?' I say, shrugging. 'Although Ben is hardly that now, is he? He's very tall.'

'Gets that from me,' Jack says. 'Not that you'd know it now though.'

'He seems like a good lad,' I say, smiling as Ben turns to look at us. 'I don't know what he thought of me the other night though, brandishing a crutch at him like some sort of lunatic!'

Jack laughs. 'I think he was just pleased someone was looking out for me. For some reason my family worry about me.'

'I'm not surprised. You're far too independent for your own good. I've only known you a while and I've learnt that the hard way.'

'Am I that bad?'

'A nightmare! But you do have some redeeming qualities, I suppose.'

'Like?' Jack asks, grinning.

'Like a handsome helpful son!' I say, grinning back at him as Ben brings our drinks over.

'Where's Molly?' he asks, looking around for her.

'Popped to the loo,' I say. 'She'll be back in a minute. I'm really sorry, Ben, for the other night,' I begin.

'Nah, don't be daft. You were only looking out for Dad. I tell you what though, I wouldn't fancy my chances as a burglar with you in the building!'

'So, what are you going to study at university?' I ask to change the subject. 'Jack said you were off there in October.'

'Medicine,' Ben says. 'I want to be a doctor.'

Jack looks proudly at his son.

'That's wonderful,' I say. 'Any particular field?'

'I'd like to be a surgeon, if I'm good enough – trauma and orthopaedics. I saw how they saved Dad's life and I want to be able to do that for someone else's father one day.'

Jack and Ben exchange a tender look, and I feel my heart leap into my throat.

'Ah, Molly, you're back,' I say as she arrives at the table again, and I notice she's brushed her hair while she's been gone and applied some lip gloss.

'Hi,' Molly says, looking shyly at Ben.

'Hey,' Ben says, giving her a quick look. 'How's it going?'

'Good, thank you,' Molly says in a high-pitched girly tone I'm not used to hearing from her.

'Ben was just telling us how he wants to be a surgeon,' I say. 'He's going to study medicine at university.'

'That's so cool,' Molly says. 'That might be something I'd like to do in the future too.'

This is the first I've heard of it!

'Aren't you a bit squeamish for that?' I ask. 'You almost fainted when you had to dissect that frog in biology.'

Molly glares at me.

223

'What? You did!'

Molly glances hurriedly at Ben to see his reaction, but Ben just looks back at us with a slightly amused expression.

Suddenly it clicks. Molly likes Ben!

'Shall we order some food?' Jack asks, diffusing the moment.

'Yes, let's.'

We order our food at the bar, and then we sit back to talk again while we wait. Ben is a lovely boy, and chats happily about himself and his dad, telling us some hilarious stories about Jack's time in the army, much to his embarrassment.

'I knew I should never have introduced you to some of my army mates,' Jack says, rolling his eyes. 'It was never going to end well for me.'

'They miss you, you know?' Ben says, serious for a moment. 'I bumped into Dave Bryant the other day at the cinema. He was asking how and *where* you were?'

'And what did you tell him?' Jack asks uneasily.

'I told him you were well, and you'd moved to Cornwall, but I didn't tell him anything else. He was pretty surprised to hear you'd moved down here though.'

Jack just nods.

'I don't know why you don't just tell everyone,' Ben says. 'People are asking after you all the time. It's not like you're hiding out or anything. You're running a legitimate business down here. It is all legit, isn't it?' He glances at me.

'Of course it is!' Jack says. 'Why would you think otherwise?'

Ben shrugs. 'I dunno. You and Kate were in a mighty hurry to cover up something the other day when I arrived . . . and you've been a bit shifty around the shop, Dad.'

Jack glances quickly at me.

'I am never shifty!' he protests. 'You're imagining things.

That's your mother's influence. She was always seeing things that weren't there – usually things that put me in a bad light!'

Ben holds up his hands in surrender. 'Easy, man! I'm not Mum. Let's not start a fight about nothing.'

'Sorry,' Jack says, patting Ben on the shoulder. 'One mention of Georgia and the touch paper is lit! Ah, is this our food coming now … great!'

As we tuck into our pub meals the atmosphere returns to its previous jovial level. I notice Molly doesn't eat much, and keeps stealing glances in Ben's direction when she thinks no one is looking.

'So what will you do now school is out?' Ben asks Molly when we've finished eating. 'Same as me, work in your parent's shop?'

Molly's cheeks immediately redden. 'Er … yes, probably. Mum lets me do some shifts in the school holidays.'

'I think it's important that Molly concentrates on her school-work during term time,' I reply, 'especially now she wants to go into *medicine*.'

I smile at Jack, and he grins knowingly back at me.

'If it's really what you want to do I can give you some help if you like?' Ben offers. 'You know, what subjects to concentrate on and stuff.'

'That would be wonderful, Ben, thank you,' Molly gushes.

'But I'd want something in return.'

'Anything.'

'Could you show me around St Felix? You know, introduce me to a few people? Much as I love Dad, I don't want to spend my whole summer in his shop. Where are the best places to hang out? I wouldn't mind learning to surf while I'm here.'

'My friend's brother teaches surfing,' Molly says excitedly. 'I'm sure I could introduce you.'

'Cool, thanks.'

'Well, it looks like *everyone* is happy with their summer plans,' Jack says, raising his glass. 'Here's to the rest of the summer in St Felix. May it bring much sunshine, good friendships and new experiences for all!'

He taps his glass with mine.

'Including for you and me,' he mouths quickly while Ben and Molly are clinking their own glasses.

'Especially you and me,' I whisper back.

Twenty-seven

St Felix ~ August 1957

'Which way again?' Arty asks Maggie as he pushes her chair down towards the beach.

'Down here,' Maggie says, pointing to a row of fisherman's cottages. 'It's the one with the black stable door. That's it, this one right here.'

Arty looks at the narrow whitewashed cottage in front of them. Both the windows and doors are painted black, and the upper half of the door is already open waiting for them.

Maggie climbs out of her chair eagerly.

'Careful, Maggie,' Arty warns.

'Stop worrying, Arty. I'm much stronger now. Even stronger than Mummy knows.' Maggie knocks hard on the bottom of the door. 'Is it okay if we come in, Freddie?' she calls. 'I've brought a friend to meet you today.'

'In ye come, young Maggie,' a gentle voice calls back. 'I'm just through here.'

Arty follows Maggie into the tiny cottage, where they immediately find themselves in what is supposed to be a kitchen but what looks to Arty more like a painting studio. There are pots of paint and clean and dirty paintbrushes in jars on the worktops, with both finished pictures, random bits of wood and also metal stacked up against the walls. In the middle of all this sits an old man with white hair. He's wearing rough trousers and a simple collarless white shirt, and is currently hunched over a table painting on a small piece of broken wood that looks like it's come from a boat's hull.

The man looks up as they enter.

'Afternoon,' he says amiably.

'Freddie, this is Arty,' Maggie says excitedly, pulling up a chair and sitting down next to him. 'Remember I told you all about him?'

'Pleased ta meet ye,' Freddie says, nodding at Arty. 'Take a pew, won't ye?'

Arty pulls up a wooden stool and sits down opposite Maggie and Freddie.

'So where's the other gal then?' Freddie asks Maggie. 'Got the day off, has she?'

'Yes, Arty is looking after me this afternoon,' Maggie says. 'He's a painter too. I thought you might like to meet him.'

Freddie gives Arty the once-over. 'I dare say you're a professional by the look of ye,' he says, continuing with his work. 'I just dabble meself. Grab yeself a piece of wood and a brush if yer staying, young Maggie.'

'May I take a look at your paintings?' Arty asks, while Maggie does what Freddie has suggested.

'Be my guest,' Freddie says. 'I'd hardly call them paintings though, more me own scribblings.'

Arty goes over to the stack of pictures on the floor and looks through them.

'Some of these are rather good, you know?' Arty says, pausing to gaze at a simple picture of some boats in a harbour. 'You have a very unique style.'

'Thank ye kindly,' Freddie says. 'I just paint what I sees, in my own way.'

'Why all the wood and bits of metal though?' Arty asks. 'I mean, I quite like it – it's different – but isn't it difficult to get the paint to adhere?'

Freddie looks at Arty kindly. 'Probably, but the proper stuff is expensive, ain't it. I get all my canvases for free, and some of me paints too. Make them meself, I do.'

'How wonderful,' Arty says, with genuine appreciation. 'That's truly amazing.'

Freddie simply shrugs. 'Needs must.'

'So when did you start painting, Freddie?' Arty says, moving around the room to examine more of Freddie's work hung on the walls.

'When me wife died,' Freddie says steadily. 'To fill the time, ye know?'

Arty nods. 'I'm sorry to hear that. Art can be such wonderful therapy.'

'I don't know about that, but once me fishing career ended, I had too much time on me hands without Irene. It was something to while away the hours. That's why I like having the little uns in to paint with me – they keeps me company.'

He smiles warmly at Maggie, and she grins back happily as she sits down next to him again ready to paint her own picture.

'Yes, I bet they do,' Arty says, feeling ashamed that he had thought anything less about Freddie. 'I can see that now.'

*

The images begin to swirl into a kaleidoscope of colours, and I lean back from the painting of Freddie's cottage with Jack by my side.

We're sitting closer than we usually do because we're currently squeezed into Jack's stock-room at the back of the shop. It was too difficult to arrange an evening meeting in Jack's flat now Ben was around, and too difficult for Jack to transport his newest painting to my shop. We've had to squeeze into Jack's stock-room while Ben has gone for his lunch-break, praying that we'll have enough time to watch our latest instalment of vintage St Felix before he returns.

'Looks like the old guy was genuine after all,' Jack says. 'Both Arty and Clara obviously had their suspicions about him spending time with Maggie.'

'Yes . . . ' I say absent-mindedly.

'What's up?' Jack asks. 'It's unusual for you not to have a view.'

'I'm thinking,' I reply vaguely, 'about Freddie's pictures. We couldn't see them all that well. Annoyingly, Arty either had them turned towards him or he was blocking them when he was standing in front.'

'So?'

'So, from the little I could see, they seem familiar, but I'm not sure why?'

'How do you mean – like you've seen them before somewhere?'

I nod.

'That's very odd.'

'I know. *Arrgh*, I wish I could have seen them a little better.'

'Perhaps we will next time? I wonder how long before we get another pair of matching pictures?'

'Hopefully not too long. I do love spending time with Clara, Maggie and Arty – I feel like I'm addicted to a soap opera that no one else knows about.'

'Yes, indeed.' Jack hesitates. 'I also love spending time with you too. It seems a shame viewing these pictures are the only time we meet up.'

'Oh ... Well, they don't have to be, I suppose.' I feel a little taken aback. 'We could go for a drink sometime if you like?'

'I'd like that,' Jack says. 'I'd like it very much.'

We gaze at each other for a moment, and then as we're both leaning towards each other the door next to us flies open.

'What the—?' Ben says, staring at us sitting in front of the easel. 'Oops, what am I disturbing here then?'

'Nothing!' I snap, leaping to my feet. 'Nothing at all.'

'What are you two *doing* in here?' Ben continues. 'I came back from my lunch to find the shop shut and no one about. Then as I was about to go upstairs and see if Dad was okay I heard voices coming from the stock cupboard.' He looks between the two of us and then at the painting on the easel and the felt embroidery sitting in front of it. 'What's that?'

'It's a project we're working on together,' Jack says quickly. 'Nothing you need to worry about.'

'A *project*?' Ben says, a knowing smile spreading across his lips. 'Is that what they call it here?'

'Yes, a project,' Jack insists. 'Why are you back from lunch already anyway? I thought you were going to eat by the harbour today?'

'It's now raining in case you hadn't noticed. Oh, that's right, you were cosying up together in here – you wouldn't have seen or heard it. It's hammering down out there.'

'Look, I'd better go,' I say grabbing my felt – this time

231

embroidered to look like a black door – from the easel. 'I'll see you soon, Jack. Then we can talk some more about our project.'

Jack nods, and Ben stands back to let me pass.

'Nice to see you again, Ben,' I say, feeling embarrassed once more in his presence.

'And you, Kate, and you,' he says, still grinning. 'Say hi to Molly for me.'

'Will do.'

Ben is right – it is raining and pretty heavily, and since I haven't brought a brolly out with me I have to run back through the suddenly empty streets as people take cover inside the shops or head back to their holiday accommodation.

As I'm about to turn towards Harbour Street, I suddenly think better of it. *Now, which way would it be?* I wonder. I think back to watching Arty push Maggie through the streets of St Felix. They had gone past the church and then turned left towards the sea-front . . .

I walk quickly in the direction I think Arty and Maggie took, and then I slow down when I get to a row of fisherman's cottages, which are now mostly holiday homes.

Nope, not this one, or this one . . . Bingo! This must be it, I think, as I pause outside a neat-looking, whitewashed cottage. The black stable door is no longer there, of course. It's been replaced by a pretty pale-blue door, and the window frames are painted the same colour to match. This is definitely it – Freddie's cottage.

I stare at the building lost in the memory of what I've just seen in the moving pictures, but then jump suddenly as someone calls my name.

'Kate, what are you doing standing out there in the rain?'

232

I look up and to my enormous surprise see Julian staring down at me from the upstairs window.

'Wait a moment, I'll be right down!'

I blink a couple of times, partly in shock and partly to bat away the huge raindrops that are still tumbling down my face.

'Come in! Come in!' Julian says, flinging open the door in front of me. 'You must be soaked through.'

Slightly confused, I step into the warm and dry of the cottage. It looks nothing like it had in Freddie's time. The front room that had been the kitchen-cum-art studio was now a cosy sitting room, and the wall that Freddie's paintings had been hanging on has been knocked through so the whole space makes a large open-plan kitchen and sitting room, perfect for the needs of today's modern holiday-maker. Where Freddie's huge black stove had been stands a widescreen TV, and where Maggie and Freddie had sat painting together an L-shaped sofa now fills the space.

'Let me get you a towel,' Julian says, looking around. 'I think there are some fresh ones upstairs in the linen cupboard.'

He dashes up a narrow staircase while I stand looking around me. Why was Julian here in this house? I'd only come here hoping to find Freddie's cottage – to see if it was still here. I hadn't expected to find anyone I knew in it, let alone Julian!

Julian returns with a couple of fluffy white towels.

'Thanks,' I say, taking one from him and squeezing my hair into it. 'I didn't realise the rain would be quite so heavy when I set out.'

'But why were you standing outside my cottage?' Julian asks, watching me as I dry off my bare arms and dab at my shirt and jeans. 'I had no idea you knew I was here.'

'I didn't. I . . . I was looking at the paintwork outside, think-ing it was very pretty.'

'In the rain?' Julian asks suspiciously.

I shrug.

'Do you want me to fetch you some dry clothes?' Julian asks. 'Or a dressing gown? I can soon get your wet clothes sorted out. I do believe there's a tumble-drier somewhere ...' He looks around at the kitchen as if the whereabouts of this particular appliance is a huge mystery yet to be solved.

'You're staying *here*?' I ask, not answering him. The last thing I wanted was to be sitting in Julian's presence in nothing but a dressing gown. He hadn't said as much, but he'd suggested enough times that his feelings towards me were a little more than simple friendship. 'I know you said you were staying in your dad's old property while you were here, but I didn't think an old fisherman's cottage was your sort of place?'

'It wouldn't be usually. Normally I prefer to stay in one of the luxury apartments overlooking the bay, but because they were fully booked when I extended my visit I came here. I rent it out, you see. It's usually taken for most of the season, but luckily we had a cancellation so it was free. It's a little bit pokey and there's no view, of course, but it will do for now.'

'Your father bought *this* cottage? I ask. Something wasn't adding up.

'Yes, funny little place, isn't it? Not my father's usual style at all. Most of his properties were luxury villas and Georgian townhouses, but this one always seemed special to him for some reason.'

'How long has your family owned this place?' I ask. Something is bugging me but I can't quite work out what it is.

'Oh, for ever,' Julian says. 'I can't remember a time when we didn't have it. Kate, I really think you should get out of those wet clothes. As my grandmother used to say, you'll catch your death of cold. The robes upstairs are rather lovely – we provide them for the guests.'

'Okay, then,' I agree, but only because I need to ask some more questions about this cottage.

'Good,' Julian says, nodding. 'Upstairs on the left. Big closet on the landing. It's locked most of the time as it's where we keep all the clean supplies for changeovers, but I've just opened it to get the towels. You'll find a stack of white robes up there waiting for you.'

'Great.'

'Would you like a warming hot chocolate when you come back down? The little café down the road does some rather lovely ones. I could pop out and get us a couple.'

'But then you'll get wet as well!'

'I'll take a brolly.'

'Sure,' I relent. 'That would be lovely, thank you, Julian.'

'My pleasure.'

I head upstairs, and as Julian had promised find a pile of newly laundered white fluffy dressing gowns in a cupboard. I grab one, and another towel, and then I quickly find the bathroom, peel off my wet clothes and pop the robe around me. Then I towel dry my hair a little more and am about to head back downstairs when I pause.

At the top of the landing are a series of prints hung together in an artistic group. They look familiar ... where have I seen them before? *Oh, that's right*, I remember as I look a little more closely at them and see two initials at the bottom right of each. These are reproductions of Winston James originals – copies of the paintings I'd seen in the Lyle Gallery exhibition. It made sense that Winston would have wanted prints of his work hung here in the house he originally owned.

Thinking no more of it I head back downstairs with my wet clothes, quickly find the mysterious tumble-drier, switch it on and then settle down on the sofa to wait for Julian. He seems to have been gone a while. I hope he hasn't gone to too much trouble getting us hot chocolate.

While I'm waiting I text Anita at the shop.

Going to be a bit longer than first expected. Don't think you'll be busy in this weather. But if you are call me. Kate x

As I'm putting my phone back in my bag, Anita texts back.

Everything fine here lovey. You take as long as you need. Everything just fine. Don't worry about anything. x

I stare at the phone for a moment. Why does that text from Anita seem odd? I'm just reading it through again when I see Julian through the window. He has our hot chocolates in a cardboard carrier in one hand and a big black umbrella in the other.

I hurry to the door to let him in. He passes me the drinks and then he shakes his umbrella outside. 'It's still torrential out there,' he says. 'I don't know why you were out in it in the first place.'

'Just got caught in it,' I say. 'Thanks for going and getting these – they smell delicious. Where did you go? You were gone a while.'

'Oh, one of the little cafés along the harbour,' Julian says, leaning his damp umbrella against the back of the door. He turns around and his eyes almost pop out of his head when he sees I'm only wearing a white fluffy dressing gown. 'You found them then – the robes, I mean.'

'Yes,' I say, pulling the robe a little tighter around me, 'and the tumble-drier, thanks. My clothes should be dry in about half an hour, I hope.' I sit back down on one end of the sofa, praying that Julian will sit at the other.

He doesn't quite do that, but sits far enough away that I feel comfortable.

'So,' I begin casually, after taking a warming sip of my hot chocolate. 'You said your father bought this cottage a long time ago?'

'Yes, I think not that long after he left St Felix. I guess he must have wanted a little bolt-hole to come back to from time to time.'

'But you've no idea when that was?'

'Er ... I think he left St Felix in the late fifties, so possibly around then. Perhaps the early sixties?'

I nod. I had to be careful or Julian might get suspicious. To be fair, I didn't really know why I was asking all these questions. I just knew I might learn something important.

'Most of these little cottages would have been owned by fishermen back then, wouldn't they? They wouldn't have been holiday homes like they are today.'

'No, I suppose not, but even back then the fishing industry was beginning to die out. The smaller fishermen couldn't compete with the big boys with the big boats. It's a shame, but that's progress for you.'

'Yes, I suppose so. Do you think your father got a bargain with this place? I mean if a fisherman had been living here who couldn't afford to any more, he might have been able to buy it for next to nothing.'

'I doubt any fisherman living here owned this house. He probably rented it, so my father would have had to buy it from his landlord.'

'Oh yes, I hadn't thought about that … but still, that would have been expensive, wouldn't it? Your father must have been doing well with his painting to afford to buy a cottage here and still continue to live somewhere else.'

Julian looks suspiciously at me. 'Why all the questions, Kate?'

I shrug. 'No reason. I'm interested that's all.' As Julian doesn't look all that satisfied with my answer, I continue, 'I've always been interested in the history of St Felix. I love to talk about its past. Someone has always got a story or two to tell.'

'That is very true. Most of it is nonsense, of course. You don't want to be listening to all the tittle-tattle, only the true stories with historical significance.'

'Well, I don't know about that—' I begin.

'Really, Kate, there are some dreadful tales. I've heard them.'

'From who?' I ask, wondering who Julian had been gossiping with. Usually most of the tales were told in The Merry Mermaid of an evening, and I didn't think he'd spent much time in there.

'A few people,' he says carefully. 'Apparently my father isn't all that popular here, despite the gallery putting on a special exhibition of his work.'

'Really?' This was the first I'd heard of this. 'Who told you that?'

'A couple of folk. Not that I'd treat what they say with any seriousness. They were propping up the bar in one of the local hostelries at the time.'

'Which one?'

'Er, the one on the high street, a little way down from your friend's art shop.'

'The Feathers?' I say, surprised Julian has even set foot in there, let alone engaged with the locals.

238

'Yes, that's the one.'

'Why did you go in there?'

'You said I should try to make some new friends, so I thought I'd make a foray to the local pub. Turns out they weren't all that friendly though.'

'You should have gone to The Merry Mermaid – they're much friendlier in there. The Feathers is mainly full of locals who play darts and pool. It's not a family pub at all.'

'Yes, there were some rather portly-looking gentlemen in there throwing sharp objects at a numbered board.'

'That would be the darts team. You didn't try to make friends with them, did you?' The thought of Julian trying to bond with the local darts team was highly amusing to me.

'No, I did not. I sat at the bar and tried to converse with the barman ... but when he found out who I was he became very unfriendly indeed.'

'Why?'

'I don't know. Something to do with his relatives. He was a little vague, to be honest. Apparently my father had had some dealings with them which hadn't gone all that well.'

'Oh.'

'So I drank my gin and tonic and left. There was another reason I didn't go to The Merry Mermaid though.'

'What's that?'

'I was concerned I might see you in there with your ... *friend*.'

'My friend?' I ask, trying to think who he might mean. 'Do you mean Jack?'

Julian nods.

'But why would that matter?'

'Oh, Kate, do you really not see it?' Julian says dramatically, moving closer to me along the sofa. 'I'm in love with you, and seeing you with another man – even if you claim he's only a friend – it's too much for me to bear.'

'Ah.' I wish I hadn't sat right at the end of the sofa now, because then I could have slid further along it myself. 'That's very lovely of you, Julian,' I say, again pulling my robe a little tighter around me. 'And I'm incredibly flattered . . . but the thing is, I only see you as a friend. A very good friend,' I add, hoping this will help. 'But friends it has to be, I'm afraid.'

'I see,' Julian says, his head drooping. 'Your heart is with another.'

'No, it's not that.'

'Ah, Kate, even if you don't see it yet, I do. You've given your heart to another man, and it is no longer mine to claim.'

'Perhaps.' I wonder if it will be easier to agree with his reasoning than argue against it.

'If only we had met earlier.'

Julian to my horror slides further along the sofa now so he's right next to me. I'm about to leap up and make a break for it when he grabs my hand and kisses the back of it.

'Yes,' I say, attempting to gently remove my hand from his. 'If we'd met earlier then who knows?'

'I shall do the gentlemanly thing and relinquish my adoration for you . . . for now,' Julian adds, letting go of my hand. 'But if anything should change?' He stares at me longingly.

'You'll be the first to know!' I finish, leaping up. 'Right, I think it's time to see if my clothes are dry.' I hurry through to the kitchen.

Even if my clothes are still soaking, escaping in wet attire is much preferable right now to staying here with St Felix's answer to Casanova!

Twenty-eight

'Everything all right?' I ask Anita, as I arrive back at the shop. 'You've coped without me?'

'We've had exactly four customers since you left, Kate,' Anita says calmly, 'and that was before it started raining so, yes, I've coped just fine.'

'Your text seemed a bit strange though? Are you sure everything has been okay?'

'Where did you get the umbrella?' Anita asks, changing the subject. 'You didn't go out with one.'

'It's Julian's.'

'Julian? But I thought you went to see Jack?'

'I did. Look, my clothes are a bit damp, Anita. I'll pop upstairs and change, and then I'll tell you all about it.'

After I've put on some dry clothes and come back downstairs I tell Anita about everything that's happened over a cup of tea.

She raises her eyebrows when I tell her about Julian's declaration but doesn't comment.

'And that's when I came back here,' I finish.

'Well, you've certainly had a productive afternoon,' Anita

says diplomatically. 'Before you ask, I know nothing about this Freddie or even a Winston James buying his cottage. I didn't live here back then, and even if I had I would only have been a child.'

'Yes, I know. There are very few people still here who did live in St Felix at that time. Even Jake's Aunt Lou probably wouldn't remember anything about Freddie selling his house – she was a teenager then.'

'Why all the interest anyway?' Anita asks. 'I mean, I know why you're interested in what happens to Clara, Maggie and Arty, but why Freddie?'

'I don't really know. I just get a feeling it's all relevant in some way.'

'Gut instinct is a much neglected tool,' Anita says knowingly.

'Do you know if Julian is right? Is Winston James disliked here?' I ask. 'Did you ever hear anything in the wool shop? I hear it was a hotbed of gossip!'

'Hardly! We were like a hairdresser's – we couldn't help it if people told us all their news.'

'Yeah, right!' I grin. 'So did anyone ever mention any *news* regarding Winston James?'

'Not that I can remember. The first I knew of him was the exhibition at the Lyle Gallery you went to with Molly.'

'*Hmm*, there has to be something. Why have Jack and I been shown all this stuff if there isn't a reason for it?'

'You'll find out soon enough, dear, I'm sure. Just give it time.'

Luckily, we don't have to wait long for a new instalment because the next morning another embroidery appears. This time it seems to show two silhouettes surrounded by a blood red sky. Excited, I text Jack straightaway.

Another one! When can we meet?

A reply comes back promptly.

**Difficult at mine with Ben here now. Do you fancy that
drink later? Maybe I can hide my painting in my chair
and we can look at it at yours first?**

I think about this before I send my reply:

Will it work without the easel?
Damn, I hadn't thought about that. We could try?
Wait, I might have a better idea ... I'll text you later x

'Morning,' I say a bit later as Molly comes sleepily down into
the shop. 'What are you up to today?'

'Not much,' she shrugs.

'Not seeing Chesney?'

'Nah, not today.'

I raise my eyebrows. As far as I'm aware Molly hasn't seen
Chesney in well over a week now and I can't say I'm too
unhappy about it.

'Is everything okay with you and Chesney?' I ask.

Molly shrugs again.

'It's only I've noticed you've not seen that much of him lately?'

'Nah, I'm trying to distance myself a bit.'

'Oh, really?' This was news to me.

'Yeah,' Molly says. 'He got a bit ... clingy.'

My ears prick up. 'What do you mean?'

'He's just a bit too full on.'

'In what way?' I ask, suddenly worried Chesney had been

243

pressuring Molly to do things she hadn't wanted to. 'Is he pressuring you to have sex with him?'

'Mum!' Molly says, her cheeks bright red.

'I'm sorry but I have to ask.'

'No, it's not that.'

'Then what is it?'

Molly wrinkles up her nose, 'It's difficult to describe really. He's always texting me, wanting to know what I'm doing or where I am, and if I don't text or phone him back he immediately gets really angry.'

My blood doesn't boil this time, it simply turns ice cold.

'He hasn't got physical with you, has he? I mean he hasn't hit you when he's been angry?'

'No, nothing like that. When I'm with him I feel ... what's the word?'

'Claustrophobic?' I suggest.

'Yeah, that's exactly it. Like he wants to control me all the time. I feel ...'

'Smothered?'

'Yes! How do you know all this, Mum?'

I swallow hard. I had to talk to her about it. It was happening to my daughter now too, and it would only get worse if we didn't discuss it properly.

'Because that's what Joel was like, Molly,' I say quietly. 'That's why we broke up.'

Molly stares at me. 'Joel texted you all the time as well?'

'He did a bit more than that, which is why there was that incident at your school. You didn't think there was anything wrong in him trying to meet you, but it was just the tip of the iceberg. How Chesney is behaving towards you is how it starts, Molly. Boys ... or maybe I should say *men* who want to control your life aren't the

244

sort you should be having a relationship with. It will never end well. Joel wanted to control me . . . well, us really, and I had to put a stop to it. I didn't tell you everything at the time because you were so young . . . and it was my problem to deal with.'

Molly, still staring at me, eventually nods, and her expression is filled with so much understanding and sympathy that in that split second I think I actually see her grow up.

'I get it, Mum,' she says hugging me. 'Really, I get it. I'm so sorry I contacted Joel. I wasn't thinking properly – I thought you might be lonely. I had no idea it was as bad as that.'

'That's because I didn't tell you the whole story,' I say, holding her back from my embrace. 'I wanted to protect you. You're my little girl, and I didn't want to expose you to any of it. Little did I know you'd experience something so similar.'

'Joel didn't hurt you though, did he?'

I shake my head. 'No, I was lucky in that way, but no one has the right to try and control our lives, Molly. We're the only ones who should be in the driver's seat. We, and only we, are in charge of what happens to us.'

Molly nods. 'You're right. I guess I should end it with Chesney, shouldn't I?'

I nod. 'As soon as you can.'

'It's just . . . he's my first boyfriend. What if no one else wants me?'

'Are you kidding? A bright, funny, pretty girl like you? The boys will be lining up!'

'I hardly think so.'

I think for a moment as an idea strikes. 'Have you seen Ben since the meal we had at the pub?' I ask casually.

'No.'

'Only Jack said he was asking after you.'

245

Molly's face brightens immediately. 'Really?'

'Yeah, something about how he hoped to start surfing soon and he was keen for you to introduce him to your friend's brother.'

'It's beginner surf school tonight on the beach,' Molly says eagerly, as all thoughts of Chesney quickly vanish. 'Do you think I should ask him if he'd like to go?'

'Oh,' I say, trying to sound surprised. 'Is it? What a good idea. Why don't you do that?'

Molly's cheeks pink a little. 'I don't know if I can.'

'Why ever not?'

'Because he's well fit, Mum! You can't just ask boys like that out, especially boys who are much older than you.'

'I'm not suggesting you ask him out – you're simply offering to accompany him to the surf school.'

Molly still looks unsure.

'What if I contact Jack and ask him to see if Ben wants to go with you?'

'No way! I can't have my mum asking for me. The humiliation.'

'Ah, well,' I say, turning away. 'It was only an idea. I thought it might cheer you up . . . ' I wait, hoping what I think will happen does . . .

'Maybe you could just *find out* whether he's interested,' Molly says softly. 'You know, without saying it's me asking?'

I smile quickly to myself before turning back again with a straight face. 'I'm sure I could do that for you.'

'He mustn't know it's me asking though, Mum. Promise?'

'I promise. I'll be very discreet. Now, why don't you head back upstairs. I'm sure you have some studying to do. I can't have all this talk of boys distracting you from that, can I?'

Molly rolls her eyes and grins. 'All right, I guess one good turn deserves another. I really am sorry, you know ... about Joel. If I'd known—'

I wave my hand dismissively at her. 'It's all forgotten now. You go on back upstairs. I'll let you know what Jack says later.'

When I have a break between customers I text Jack again:

Can you delicately suggest to Ben he could ask Molly
to take him to the surf school tonight? PLEASE don't let
him think Molly is asking though or she'll never speak
to me again!

Jack replies:

Great idea! I'm on it now.

A few minutes later another text arrives from Jack:

Ben is on his way over to the shop – act natural!

I reply quickly:

Fast worker!

'Hello, Ben,' I say casually a few minutes later, when Ben arrives at the shop. 'How are you?'

'Good, thanks, Kate. Is Molly about by any chance?'

'Yes, she's upstairs. I'll call her. Molly!' I call up the stairs. 'You have a visitor.'

Molly comes bounding down the stairs and looks both horrified and elated at the same time to see Ben standing in the shop.

247

'Hey, Molly,' he says calmly. 'How are you?'

'Great, thanks.' Molly replies, running her hand casually through her hair.

'I was wondering if you might introduce me to your friend's brother. Dad says the surf school is on tonight.'

Molly quickly glances at me, but I'm already pretending to be busy with pricing some new stock. 'Is it?' she asks innocently. 'Yes, of course, if you'd like me to.'

'It would be cool if you could.'

'I think it starts at six o'clock. What if I meet you here and we can walk down together?'

'Great. Guess I'll see you later then.'

'I guess you will.'

'Bye, Kate,' Ben says as he's leaving.

'Bye, Ben!' I say, smiling at him. 'Say hi to your dad for me.'

Ben winks at me and then he leaves.

'Oh my god! Oh my god!' Molly says, flapping her arms. 'What am I going to wear? I have nothing!'

'You're going down to the beach. Wear what you'd normally put on.'

Molly looks at me with a horrified expression, as if I've suggested she should wear a ball gown and silver slippers to walk on the sand. 'I hardly think so, Mum. I'll phone Emily and ask her opinion. Oh no, she's on holiday. *Sebastian!*' she cries, as Sebastian comes through the door to start his shift. 'What should I wear for a date on the beach?'

'Molly, it's not a date—' I begin.

'It's as good as,' Molly says, dismissing me.

'You've got a date on the beach?' Sebastian asks, looking surprised. 'With Chesney? Not usually his style.'

'No, forget him. He's history. With Ben.'

248

Sebastian looks confused. 'Ben is Jack's son,' I explain. 'And it's *not* a date. He's far too old for you, Molly. I'm certain he only sees you as a friend.'

'Whatever, Mum!' Molly says, already heading for the stairs. 'Date or not, I'm going to the beach with a hot older guy. My friends might see me so I have to look good!' She disappears up the stairs to her bedroom.

I shake my head as I watch her go. Talk about one extreme to another.

'Have I met this Ben yet?' Sebastian asks, still looking confused.

'Not properly, no, but you probably passed him if you came in via your usual way. He'd be heading back to Jack's shop. Tall guy, dark hair, looks a bit like a younger Jack.'

'Was he wearing a red T-shirt and denim shorts by any chance?' Sebastian asks.

'Yes, that's him.'

Sebastian nods slowly.

'What's wrong?'

'Well, I may be mistaken, but I rarely am these days. If Ben *is* the guy that I passed in the street just now, you'll have nothing to worry about if Molly goes anywhere with him.'

'What do you mean?'

'I mean that Ben is more likely to fancy me than your Molly any day!'

Twenty-nine

'Sorry, I'm a bit late,' I say, as I arrive up in Jack's flat that night, carrying his newest painting and the easel I'd collected from his stock-room. 'We had a sudden rush of last-minute customers. As soon as the weather brightened up everyone came out again.'

'That's okay. Ben should be a good while yet. Great idea by the way – the surf school.'

'Thanks. Yes, I hoped that might work.' I hesitate as I erect the easel and pop the painting on it. *Should I bring the subject of Ben up now? Was it the best time?* 'Molly was so pleased when Ben popped into the shop,' I try. 'She really seems to like him.'

'That's good,' Jack says, while I grab my usual chair. 'Be great if our kids got along too.'

'Yes.' I sit down next to Jack in front of the easel. He looks expectantly at my bag, waiting for me to pull out my embroidery. 'The only thing is, Ben is a few years older than Molly . . .' I pause, hoping Jack will fill in the blanks for me, but he doesn't.

'Yes, he is,' is all he says.

'And Molly is at quite an impressionable age,' I continue, eager to get this sorted out.

'Are you asking if my son will lead your daughter astray?' Jack asks in his usual straightforward way.

'Well ... yes, I am.'

Jack smiles. 'Molly will be quite safe with Ben, Kate. He's gay.'

So Sebastian was right!

'You know?' I say, forgetting I'm not supposed to.

'Of course I know. I'm his father. How did you know?'

'Sebastian,' I say. 'He told me.'

Jack nods. 'The old gaydar, eh. I'm assured by Ben that it does actually exist!'

'Yes, apparently it does. Oh, I'm pleased you know,' I say, without thinking. 'That makes things easier.' I go to pull the embroidery from my bag.

'Hang on a minute,' Jack says, 'Why wouldn't I know?'

'No reason,' I say, extracting the felt from my bag and laying it on the easel.

'Did you think he wouldn't tell me because of my background, is that it? We do have gay soldiers in the army, you know?'

'No, that's not it at all. Sometimes parents are the last to know in my quite limited experience of these things.'

Jack still doesn't look convinced. 'Did you think I wouldn't accept a gay son, is that it? I know I can be a bit stubborn sometimes and set in my ways, but—'

'Jack,' I interrupt him. 'Please stop putting words in my mouth. I thought none of those things. I'm pleased you have such a great relationship with Ben. We're both very lucky with our children. Now, shall we get on with the reason I'm really here?' I gesture towards the easel.

Jack still looks at me suspiciously, but he nods.

'Good.'

'Ben can talk to me, you know?' Jack says, still not happy he's convinced me. 'When he told me I didn't go off on one, or make a scene. I was quite relaxed about it. Just pleased he'd confided in me.'

'Wonderful,' I say, turning towards the easel.

However, Jack's not finished: 'You seem to be under the impression that I'm some sort of Neanderthal who can't accept anything new or unusual?'

'Where is all this coming from?' I ask, turning towards him. 'I never thought any of those things. Yes, you're stubborn and you've got a bit of a quick temper on you, but—'

'I haven't got a temper!'

'What about the alarm incident?'

Jack looks puzzled.

'Don't you remember the first night I was here with you looking at the pictures and your shop alarm went off? You had a right go at me, and you never did explain why?'

'Ah, that.'

'Yes, that.'

'It wasn't you I was cross with that night. It was myself.'

'Explain.'

'I was cross because I had to come down the stairs and you had to see me like that. I didn't want you to see me compromised – I hardly knew you then.'

'But I didn't see you as compromised at all. If anything the complete opposite. I saw a strong, capable man, who was using his strength and ingenuity in the best way he could. You might not think it, but traversing those stairs like that is pretty impressive. It had *quite* the effect on me.'

'Really?' Jack asks, suddenly much more chipper.

'Yes, now if you've quite finished fishing for compliments, shall we continue with our pictures? Or do you want to throw your line out a bit further?'

'All right, let's get to the pictures. You haven't got the felt lined up quite right though,' he tells me. 'It needs to go a tad to the left.'

I sigh and shake my head, but I move the felt a little and suddenly we're ushered back to the enthralling story of Clara and Arty once more ...

St Felix ~ Summer 1958

Clara sighs as she stares at the beautiful sunset in front of her.

'Isn't this simply gorgeous?' she says to Arty, as they sit next to each other on the clifftop overlooking St Felix Bay.

'Nature at its finest,' Arty says, and he squeezes Clara's hand. 'I don't know whether I want to paint it or photograph it, it's so beautiful.'

'You and that camera of yours,' Clara says, smiling at him. 'It was bad enough when you wanted to paint everything, including me, but now you have a need to photograph everything too.'

'You know how much I love documenting our lives together, Clara. These photos will be our memories in the future.'

'No, our memories will always be up here,' Clara says, tapping her head, 'and in here,' she adds, touching her heart.

'You're right, of course,' Arty says, looking adoringly at her. 'You usually are.' He winks.

Clara beams back. 'I'm so happy, Arty,' she says. 'This past year has been one of the happiest of my life.'

'Mine too. I'm so pleased I bumped into you and Maggie

that day at the harbour … although I don't think you thought all that much of me back then, did you?'

Clara smiles. 'I was different a year ago. Much warier of people. Life up until that point had let me down, but St Felix, my shop and you have changed all that, Arty. You've been so good for me, and for Maggie.'

'She's doing so well now, isn't she?' Arty says. 'You wouldn't know a year ago she was in a wheelchair – she's so strong, both in body and in character. I do love her as if she were my own.'

'Oh, Arty,' Clara says. 'I know you do. You're a better father to her than anyone could ever be. She thinks the world of you.'

They gaze at each other, and then Arty looks down at Clara's hand. He lifts it up and clears his throat.

'Clara, I love you more than anyone I've ever met. I love everything about you, from your kind and generous personality to the way you never put up with my nonsense. I never thought I'd find a soulmate on this earth, but I have, and it's you. For some strange reason I know not, you seem to feel a similar way about me too, so now, my darling, I would like to ask one more thing of you?'

Clara nods, utterly spellbound by Arty's words.

'Clara, would you do me the greatest honour of becoming my wife?'

The colours begin to swirl and mix together, and frustratingly the images in front of us disappear.

'No!' I cry out. 'Not now. I want to hear what she says!'

'She'll say "yes". Of course she will,' Jack says in a quiet voice next to me.

'How do you know though?' I say, still staring at the silhouettes of Clara and Arty on the canvas in front of me.

254

'You can see they're totally in love with each other, that's why.'

'But they hated each other to start with – well, Clara didn't like Arty. When did it all change?' I turn to Jack and to my surprise notice his eyes are a little misty. 'Are you all right?' I ask.

'Yes, of course I am,' Jack says gruffly, rubbing at his eyes. 'Hay-fever, that's all. Things change, don't they?' he says, hurriedly changing the subject. 'You could see in the previous couple of paintings they were getting on better, and Clara was softening towards him at last, poor guy.'

'So why the sudden leap forwards in time?' I ask, choosing not to mention Jack's sudden 'hay-fever' any further. 'They said they'd known each other a year, so we must be in nineteen fifty-eight now.'

Jack shrugs. 'You're asking me to explain why the magical pictures we've been watching for the last few weeks have suddenly missed a few chapters? It's hardly the strangest thing going on here, is it?'

'That's true, I suppose. It's lovely though, isn't it?' I say, clasping my hands together delightedly, 'that they're going to have a happy ending.'

'If this is the ending?'

'How do you mean?'

'Come on, Kate! You can't think we've watched all this only to see Arty propose to Clara? There has to be something more to it.'

'You're probably right,' I say, my hands dropping back down into my lap. 'It would seem odd for it just to be this. In my experience life is never that straightforward.'

'Ain't that the truth. I'm glad we know Maggie didn't end up in a wheelchair for the rest of her life. Believe me, no one would want that, especially not back then. It would have been a lot harder to be in a wheelchair in the fifties and sixties than it is now. Things aren't great these days, but they're a hell of a lot easier than they would have been sixty years ago.'

'Yes, it's good to hear she recovered. I wonder what she went on to do. She'd be what, mid- to late seventies now – I wonder if she's still alive?'

'She might be. It could have been her who had been living in the house we went to visit, not Clara.'

I shake my head. 'No. According to Anita, the woman who used to live there was called Peggy, so it wasn't her.'

'So what *do* you think all this is about then?' Jack asks. 'Do you think like me there's a reason to it?' He gestures to the painting.

'Anita says St Felix is like that. Things happen here that can't always be explained, but usually only to people who need help or who can help someone else.'

'Anita is a very wise woman,' Jack says knowingly.

'Yes, she is,' I reply. 'I didn't think you knew her all that well though?'

'We've bumped into each other a few times. Which of her categories do you think we fall into?'

'*Hmm?*' I ask, still wondering when Jack and Anita might have come across each other. 'Oh, I see. Er, I'm not sure,' I reply honestly. 'But I bet it's not long before we find out.'

'I hope so,' Jack says. 'All this strange mystery stuff doesn't sit well with me at all. Right, fancy that drink now?' he asks suddenly, while I continue to stare wistfully at the painting of Clara and Arty.

'Oh, yes, why not?' I reply turning to him. 'Let's hide this stuff first and then we'll go.'

We head down to The Merry Mermaid. Even though we've

been here a couple of times together already, I suddenly feel very conscious this is our first proper date.

We go inside the pub as all the seats outside are taken, and while I let Jack go to the bar (I know better than to try to take that role by now) I try to find us a table where I know Jack will be able to get his wheelchair in with a minimal amount of fuss.

Eventually, Jack arrives with our drinks – pint for him and a glass of white wine for me – and we settle down together.

'How's the shop going?' I ask, suddenly aware that all we seem to talk about when we're together these days are the pictures.

'Good thanks, and yours?'

'Yeah, not bad. We're up on last summer anyway.'

'That's good, that's good.' Jack takes a sip from his pint.

'How are you getting on with two helpers now that Ben is here? It must be easier for you?'

'Yeah, Ben has settled in well. Him and Bronte seem to get on okay, so all is pretty cool in my domain right now.'

'Good,' I say, virtually repeating Jack. I sip from my glass now.

'Kate, I don't want to seem my usual awkward self, but we don't need all these niceties, do we? We know each other a bit better than that by now, I think.'

'Yes, you're right,' I say, somewhat relieved, 'but all we ever seem to talk about when we're together is the pictures. I suddenly felt a bit odd so I started making polite conversation with you.'

'Let's not make polite conversation then – let's make rude conversation.'

'How do you mean?' I ask, wondering if this was some sort of vulgar army game Jack was going to suggest.

'I mean, let's ask each other all the questions we've been too

257

polite to ask before now. There are loads of things I'd like to know about you, and I hope you might feel the same about me?'

I nod, partly with relief and partly with interest.

'Great, who's going to go first then?' Jack asks eagerly.

'You go,' I offer, although I'm a little concerned about what he might ask me.

'The only rules are that we have to answer as honestly as we can and we can ask anything. All right?'

'Sure,' I reply, definitely worried now.

'Promise you'll be honest?' Jack says.

'Yes, I promise.'

'Tell me about your life before you came to St Felix,' Jack asks immediately, as if he's been planning this. 'Like why you came here.'

'Okay ... so I'd always wanted to run my own shop. Well, a craft shop actually. I'd always made bits and pieces at home that had been popular with friends and family, and I thought I might be able to sell it properly and make a business of it if I had my own store.'

'Go on?' Jack says when I pause.

'What do you mean *Go on*? That's it.'

'What I've just heard is your very practised version of the story that you tell anyone when they ask. I want to hear the *real* version. Why St Felix – why not somewhere else? Why at that moment in your life? What made you take the leap?'

'Okay ...' I say, a little more hesitant this time. 'I didn't choose St Felix, more it chose me. I was in the hairdresser's one day and someone next to me was talking about how they'd just been to the funeral of their great-aunt, and how she owned this shop in Cornwall and had worked there all her life. Then she began talking about the place and how lovely

258

it was, and when she said the name St Felix I immediately Googled business properties for rent here and that's how I found the shop.'

'Nice,' Jack says approvingly. 'So what were you doing then? For a job, I mean.'

'I worked for a finance company. I had a bit saved up so I thought why not – let's do it.'

Jack looks at me suspiciously. 'Just like that? You uprooted your whole life, and your daughter's life too? Don't take this the wrong way, but you don't strike me as the most spontaneous of people, Kate. Quite the opposite in fact.'

Jack was correct, of course, but I wasn't about to admit that. 'I'm not saying I didn't think a lot about it,' I reply, ignoring his comment, 'but it seemed like the right thing to do. I talked to Molly, of course I did. She was a little reluctant at first, but she soon came around when we visited St Felix. Who wouldn't want to live by the sea?'

'So, that's it, you saw an opportunity and took it. There were no other reasons for your move?'

I sigh. I had promised to be honest.

'I'd just come out of a very *difficult* relationship,' I say carefully. 'It was a good time to get away.'

Jack nods, and I'm grateful yet surprised when he doesn't ask me any more questions. Most people would want to know why it had been difficult. 'Understood,' is all he says.

'Right, is it my turn now?' I ask quickly, keen to move on. 'I feel like you've grilled me plenty.'

'Ask away,' Jack says, lifting his pint. 'I have no secrets.'

I think for a moment. I already knew how Jack had come to be in his wheelchair, and why he'd snapped at me that night in his flat. 'Why don't you want your friends back home to know where you are?' I ask, suddenly remembering the conversation between Jack and Ben when we'd been in here the last time.

Jack looks mystified.

'When we were in here with Molly and Ben, Ben said one of your friends didn't know you were here in Cornwall running a shop. He was surprised to hear it.'

Jack nods slowly as if he's considering his reply.

'You promised to be honest,' I remind him.

'Actually *you* promised to be honest. I never promised anything.'

I glare at him.

'Okay, okay, I'll be honest with you.' He pauses. 'The truth is I don't want them to know.'

'Why?'

'Because I'm ashamed of what I've become.' Jack looks away across the bar at something, anything, in the distance. 'I used to be a strong, fit soldier. I used to travel all over the world defending Queen and country. I risked my life during that time more than once, and I earned the respect of my comrades. Now I'm just a sad guy in a wheelchair who runs an art shop in a funny little seaside town in Cornwall.'

I stare at Jack again, but this time because I can't quite grasp what he's telling me.

'Do you really see yourself like that?' I ask quietly.

He shrugs and reaches for his pint again. 'Pretty much.'

'What about me?'

'How do you mean?'

'I thought I made it clear at your flat that's not how I see you at all.'

'Well, yes, but that's different – you were just being nice, weren't you? Like you always are. I'm talking about everyone else.'

260

'*Hmm.*' I sit back in my chair thoughtfully. 'So I'd be wasting my time sitting here telling you that's not what anyone else sees either?'

'Yep, pretty much.'

'Right, then, I won't, but you are very, very wrong about this, Jack. I can't tell you how wrong.'

'But you can't deny the contrast,' Jack says, taking my bait as I knew he would. 'The decorated brave soldier was the person I used to be, and this,' he gestures in disgust towards his legs and his chair, 'is the thing I am now.'

'Stop that right now,' I tell him sternly.

'What?'

'Feeling sorry for yourself. You were very clear when we first met that pity was the last thing you wanted from me, so you're not allowed the honour of feeling it for yourself.'

Jack glares at me, but I stare back at him with an equally challenging expression.

'You've every right to feel sad. Every right to feel aggrieved at the life you've lost. Any normal person would, but what you're not allowed to do is refer to yourself as a thing. You're still the same person you used to be. Just because your body isn't quite as complete as it once was, it doesn't mean you shouldn't have compassion for yourself, and faith in those who love and care for you.'

Jack's expression has been softening gradually throughout my little speech. Now his face looks back at me with tenderness, rather than anger.

'You're right, of course,' he says quietly. 'About everything. I just can't help it sometimes.'

'That's totally understandable,' I say, taking his hand across the table. 'Anyone who's been through the shock and transformation that you have is going to have their off days – days when they doubt themselves and their worth. If you didn't grieve for what your life used to be there would be something wrong with you, but never for one moment doubt the worth of your existence now. You, Jack Edwards, mean too many things to too many people.'

'Including you?' Jack says, looking into my eyes.

'Especially me,' I reply, squeezing his hand. 'After all, who else am I going to find to watch my secret soap opera with?'

I smile at Jack, and he grins back.

'That's very true. No one else would believe it, would they? I'm still not sure I really do, and I've been invested in every episode.'

We gaze at each other over the table, still holding hands.

'I'm sorry about just now,' Jack says sheepishly. 'You don't need to be burdened with my worries.'

'Neither you nor your worries are a burden. I'm glad you shared all that with me – it somehow makes you more . . . human.'

Jack laughs, 'More human? What did you see me as before then? A superhero in a wheelchair?'

'No, but you do have a certain invincibility about you.'

'Really? Even in this?'

'Definitely. Most of the time I forget you're even in it. Remember when we first met I had no idea until you went to buy a drink.'

'That was funny – your face was a picture.'

'That's what I mean. I just thought you were an awkward, obstinate, pig-headed bloke full of himself and his own importance.'

Jack laughs again. 'That does sound like me – but what do you think now?'

'Pretty much the same really . . .' I smile.

'Hilarious,' Jack says sourly. 'No, really, what do you honestly think?'

'Fishing for compliments again, are we?' I ask lightly, but Jack's face is serious. 'I think you're a highly complex man,' I add, desperately trying to think of the right words. 'Your tough exterior doesn't suggest at all your more sensitive side I know you try to keep hidden.'

'How do you know I have a sensitive side?'

'Because I've seen it – when you're with Ben, or my Barney, or when we're watching Clara and Arty. That's the real you, Jack, not the Jack you want people to think you are.'

'Seems like you know me pretty well already.'

'Nope, I think there's much more to discover.'

'I really want to kiss you right now,' Jack says in a low voice, his eyes not moving from mine.

'I *really* want you to as well . . .'

'Let's get out of here then,' Jack suggests. 'And find somewhere *a lot* quieter.'

I nod, and I'm about to stand up when someone comes over to our table.

'Kate, I thought that was you,' Julian says, beaming at me. He glances at Jack. 'Hi! Jack, isn't it?'

Jack nods.

'Sorry to disturb you both, but I wanted to give you this, Kate.' He hands me a small carrier bag. 'It's your vest top. You left it at mine the other day when you got dressed in a hurry.' He glances at Jack again to make sure he's following this.

I look at Jack too, and I'm in no doubt whatsoever that he has understood Julian's meaning completely.

Thirty

'Jack!' I say, leaping up as he begins to reverse back from the table as if he's going to leave. 'It's not what you think!'

'What do I think, Kate?' Jack asks, a stony expression clouding his face.

I stare at Julian. 'I thought we were supposed to be friends?' I say. 'And yet you do this.'

'I don't understand?' Julian asks in confusion. 'What's going on?' He looks between Jack and me, and then at the bag lying on the table between us all. 'Oh! I see how this looks. No, Jack, nothing inappropriate took place that day . . . nothing at all. You have my word.'

'I bet you'd have liked it to though, wouldn't you?' Jack asks accusingly. 'I'm not stupid. I didn't get what you meant that day, as you know I had other things I was dealing with at the time, but you were desperate for me to know that Kate was at your cottage in a state of undress. I didn't pick up on your crude clues as I thought you were simply fetching coffee.'

'Wait, you bumped into Jack when you went to fetch our hot

chocolate?' I ask, puzzled. 'I didn't know that. Why didn't you say when you came back, Julian?'

Julian shrugs.

'My point exactly,' Jack says, folding his arms in such a way that his biceps become even more prominent.

Julian looks sulkily at Jack. 'You were the one who said I shouldn't mention it to Kate.'

'I didn't know you were going to see her in a matter of minutes, did I?'

'Stop it, you two!' I demand. 'And lower your voices, people have noticed us. Let's try to discuss this quietly like the civilised adults I'm sure we can be. Take a seat, Julian.'

Only a couple of people had actually glanced our way, but I needed to calm this situation down fast. Jack was right, Julian pretty certainly had had other things on his mind that day, but he didn't need to know I thought that too.

Jack unfolds his arms and reaches for his pint again, while Julian sits down on a spare seat opposite mine with his hands clasped loosely together on the table.

'Right,' I say, as calmly as I can. 'Now we've established that *nothing* went on between Julian and me,' I look pointedly at Jack, 'may I ask why you didn't want Julian to say anything about bumping into you that afternoon? It strikes me as a bit odd.'

Julian glances nervously at Jack, while Jack stares challengingly at Julian.

Julian swallows hard.

'Julian?' I ask, thinking he might be the easier of the two to crack. 'What's going on?'

Julian looks at Jack again, but Jack shakes his head.

'Right then,' I say, getting exasperated by all this. 'Jack, you tell me why. Remember,' I add, 'we promised tonight to answer any question we were asked honestly ... Your rules.'

Jack shakes his head again, but this time in defeat. 'The reason I didn't want Julian to say he'd seen me was I was dealing with a bit of bother at the time, and I didn't think it was in your best interests to know about it, that's why.' Jack toys with his now empty pint glass.

'Bother?' I ask staring at him. 'What sort of bother? Was someone hassling you?' I glance at Jack's wheelchair.

'No, not me,' Jack says, looking annoyed. 'Anita.'

'*Anita!*' I cry, then I quickly lower my voice. 'Anita?' I ask again. 'Who would want to do that?'

Jack glances at Julian again. This time Julian nods his encouragement.

Jack sighs heavily. 'It was your ex ... Joel.'

I suck my breath in sharply at his name. 'Joel was *here*?'

Jack nods. 'At the shop. I was passing by on my way back from getting some fish and chips for Ben and me – if you remember his lunch had been rained off that day – when I heard raised voices coming from your shop. I stopped and popped my head around the door to see if everything was okay.'

'And Joel was there?'

Jack nods again. 'Anita, to be fair, was doing a great job of trying to get rid of him. I didn't know why at the time – I just thought he was an awkward customer. She was staying very calm. It was this Joel who was doing all the shouting.'

That sounded about right.

'So what did you do?' I ask quietly.

'Not a lot I could do,' Jack says, sounding almost ashamed. 'Not in this thing. I tried talking to him to calm him down, which seemed to work for a bit, and I almost got him out of the shop, but then he started talking about you again and demanding to see you. Anita had to explain to me who he was and why you wouldn't want to see him, and that's when he lost it.'

'That's where I come in,' Julian says, keen to play his part. 'I'd just got our drinks and saw Jack talking to someone through the door of your shop, and then I too heard a raised voice and asked if I could be of assistance in any way.'

'You did?' I ask, most surprised to hear this.

'Yes,' Julian says, looking perturbed that I should ever doubt he'd willingly enter into conflict on my behalf. 'I may not have Jack's army background, but I am trained in the art of negotiation.'

Julian makes this sound like he's negotiated hostages to safety from armed situations.

'In what way are you trained?' I ask sceptically.

'I was on the university debating team for several terms,' Julian says proudly. 'We had some very heated and lively discussions in our debating chamber.'

Surprisingly, I want to giggle at this, but I notice Jack is not even breaking a smile.

'Julian actually came in very handy,' he says supportively. 'While he was keeping Joel busy talking to him, I made a few quick phone calls and rounded up a bit of muscle.'

'Muscle?' I repeat. 'You used physical violence to get rid of Joel?'

'No, it wasn't needed in the end. When Joel realised a few locals had turned up outside the shop suggesting it might be a good idea for him to leave and never return, he seemed to get the message.'

'But he might still come back,' I say anxiously, 'That won't stop him.'

'No, but what Anita told him will. Like I said to you the other day, she's a very wise lady.'

'What did she say?'

'It's a bit more complex than I can explain now, but the gist was that you and Molly had moved on with your lives and, if he cared that much about you, he'd let you go and allow you to be happy.'

'And he listened to that?'

'He seemed to. It was like he suddenly got it. I'm sure the line of lads outside the shop helped drum in the message that little bit harder though.'

'I'm sure,' I say, trying to take all this in. I couldn't believe that Joel had been here in St Felix and I hadn't known about it.

'I guess thanks are in order,' I say after a few moments. I look at them. They both seem to have visibly relaxed either side of the table now their secret is out. 'Thank you so much for helping Anita out that day – I'm sure she was very grateful to you. However, you should have told me what happened.' I turn to Julian. 'You, Julian, because you're my friend, and friends don't lie to each other.' Julian looks immediately ashamed. 'And you, Jack.' I turn to face him now. 'You should have told me because I think we mean a great deal to each other, and I didn't think we had any secrets.'

'We don't,' Jack says defensively. 'Not from each other anyway. You know how much you mean to me, Kate. I wanted to protect you, that's all.'

'Protect me?' I challenge. 'Cosset me, more like. You both have no idea what that man put me through. If he's been any-where near me again then I have the right to know about it.'

'But—' Jack begins.

'No, save it, Jack.' I wave my hand at him. 'You really don't understand.'

'Well, I think I—'

'Tell me,' I say suddenly, 'what you hate the most about being in your chair, Jack?'

Jack looks confused.

'You hate it when people treat you like a child, when they patronise you and don't speak to you like an equal. That's right, isn't it?'

Jack nods, 'Yes, but that's different to this.'

'How is it different?' I demand. 'How is you two colluding behind my back and keeping secrets from me treating me like an equal? Did you think I wouldn't cope with the truth? Do you think keeping me safe means lying to me?'

'We didn't lie, Kate,' Julian says now. 'We just didn't tell you, that's all.'

'But it's not all,' I cry. 'You don't understand. I need people around me I can trust. After this, how can I ever trust either of you again?'

As I storm towards the door of the pub, I feel tears beginning to well up. *No, Kate,* I order myself. *Don't you dare cry now!*

I glance back at Jack and Julian through the crowded pub and I can see them arguing with each other, most likely about who is going to come after me.

Jack seems to be winning, so I head quickly through the pub door knowing that pushing through the hordes of people around the bar will be far harder for him than it has been for me. If he is the one in pursuit I don't need to worry about getting away. Feeling bad about that thought I pause outside, wondering which way to turn. I know I shouldn't use Jack's disability against him.

It's a pleasant evening in St Felix and people are enjoying gentle strolls along the harbour front, stopping to browse the closed shop windows and taking in the burnt orange glow of the sky as the sun sets across the bay.

Jack, surprisingly, appears through the pub door much faster than I'd anticipated so I suddenly have to move fast. As usual, I'd forgotten that people automatically jump out of the way when someone comes through in a wheelchair – as if they don't want to be accused of not helping the disabled person. I'd thought it was just people being nice and helpful to begin with, and some of the time it likely was, but I'd witnessed it too many times with Jack to pretend it didn't exist.

It doesn't take him long to spot me running away along the harbour and he quickly sets off in pursuit.

'*Kate!*' I hear him call, when I've turned away from the harbour and am heading up a fairly steep cobbled hill. 'Kate, please wait!'

I hesitate. I feel bad that Jack is trying to chase after me in his chair. *But would you feel bad if he was an able-bodied person running after you?* I ask myself. When the answer is *no*, I keep running, telling myself Jack wouldn't want me to treat him any other way.

Eventually, I turn another corner and come to the same steep grassy hill where Jack and I had bumped into each other when I'd been walking Barney, and Jack now slows as we make our way up the central tarmac path. Luckily for him, I also begin to slow down as my lack of fitness catches up with me and I'm left gasping for breath. After a minute or so, Jack's superior level of fitness finally allows him to pull level with me.

'At last!' Jack says, coming alongside me. 'I didn't think I was ever going to catch you.'

'You might as well ... just ... wheel yourself ... back down the hill again,' I reply sulkily, still trying to catch my breath. 'I don't want to talk about this ... You've wasted your time.'

'No way,' Jack says. 'I've not gone to all this effort for you to get away with storming off like that.'

'I think I had every right to *leave* the pub when I did.'

'Explain to me how having two friends – actually, make that three – care enough about you that they want to protect you gives you the right to a childish tantrum?'

'Well, if you hadn't treated me like a child maybe I wouldn't have to behave like one.'

'I'm sorry we didn't tell you about Joel. Anita and I had a long discussion about whether to or not after Julian left us. We thought it was best. You trust Anita's judgement, don't you?'

'Yes, but—'

'I think she was thinking of Molly as much as anything. I understand she was the reason why Joel knew your whereabouts. I think Anita was protecting her too. Molly would have felt terrible if she knew she was the reason Joel showed up.'

Jack was right, of course. Molly would feel awful. Especially now she knows the real reason why Joel and I broke up.

'You still could have told me though,' I reply, not giving in. 'I had the right to know.'

'Yes, I agree. In hindsight perhaps I should have been a little stronger with Anita, but sometimes we make decisions on the spur of the moment that aren't always the right ones.'

We've reached the brow of the hill now. I could take the narrow dirt footpath up to the little chapel that stands at the very top, but Jack wouldn't be able to make it in his chair so this is as far as we're going.

271

'I'm sorry again, Kate,' Jack says, as I stop at the edge of the hill and look out over the sea. 'I only wanted to protect you.'

'Yes, you've said that, but I don't need protecting.'

Jack is silent for a moment as we both look out at the vast ocean in front of us.

'Have you ever stopped to think that maybe I didn't just do this for you, I did it for me too,' Jack says quietly.

'What do you mean?' I ask, turning to him.

'How do you think I felt when I saw Joel in your shop and saw a visibly upset Anita trying to deal with him? The old me would have gone in there and marched him straight out, whether he wanted to go or not. Instead I had to call for back-up to do something I should have been able to do myself.'

I hadn't thought about it like that.

'So perhaps protecting you and Molly from hearing about what had happened might have been a selfish, if stupid, move on my part to make myself feel a little better about once again finding myself lacking.'

'You're not lacking in anything, Jack,' I tell him. 'Really, you're not. I keep trying to tell you.'

'Why were you at Julian's house?' Jack asks suddenly, trying to make it sound like it's a casual question.

This again.

'Don't be coy, Jack,' I tell him, feeling myself getting annoyed again moments after I've calmed down. 'Just come right out and say it. What you mean is: Why were you at Julian's house *undressed*? I thought we explained all that in the pub, but you still don't trust me, do you?'

'There are very few reasons why a woman would get undressed in a man's house in my experience. I may be disabled in the body, but I'm not in my head.'

Jack stares out to sea again, irritatingly avoiding my gaze.

'Don't you dare pull the disabled card twice on me!' I tell him, stomping around in front of his wheelchair so he has to look at me properly. 'Not after all the times you've moaned at me for mentioning it.'

'You're in my way,' he says. 'I can't see the view.'

'Why are you so obsessed with the view today? I'm not moving until you listen. Whatever you choose to think of me, Jack, I do not cheat when I'm in a relationship. I do not sleep around and I *never* lie.'

'Is that last part a dig at me again?' Jack asks.

'The *only* reason I left my vest top in Julian's tumble-drier was because I got wet in the rain after I left your shop that day. I went to look at Freddie's old house – the one we'd seen in the pictures together. I didn't know then that was the house Julian owned in St Felix or that he was staying there. He saw me outside soaking wet and invited me in, and then he offered to dry my clothes. I wore a dressing gown while my clothes were in the drier, we had hot chocolate and we talked about his dad. That is all, and then I left. I must have missed my vest in the drier and just worn my shirt and jeans back to the shop. I did leave in a bit of a hurry.'

'Why did you leave in a hurry?' Jack asks, keen to know the answer.

'If you must know, Julian tried it on – with me, I mean. He didn't try on my vest.' I grimace at my awful joke, but Jack is silent. 'So, yes, you were right, apparently he does have some feelings for me and he chose that afternoon to make them abundantly clear.'

A smug expression appears on Jack's face.

'You can take that look off your face! You're the one still in the wrong here not me.'

'So nothing happened then at the cottage?'

'How many more times? No, of course nothing happened. Jack, it's you I like – can't you see that? Goodness knows why when you behave like you do sometimes, but for all our differences there's something between us. Something special, I hope.'

To my enormous relief Jack smiles up at me. He takes hold of my hand and pulls it towards him so he can kiss the back of it. Then he tugs on it again so I have no choice but to follow my hand with my body.

Suddenly I find my lips on Jack's, and we share the softest of kisses. Nothing like what I'd imagined Jack's kisses might feel like. When I'd kissed him before it had very much been me kissing him, now it was his turn.

'Sit on my lap?' he asks.

Without saying anything I do as he requests, tentatively sitting as gently as I can on him, but Jack is having none of that. Before I know what he's doing he scoops my legs up and turns me sideways so my legs are now dangling over the side of his chair and my head is nestling into his broad chest. As he wraps his strong arms around my body to hold me close to him I feel completely at home, enveloped in his warm embrace.

I tilt my head up towards him so our faces are millimetres apart.

Jack looks into my eyes, 'Now I can kiss you properly.'

'Why don't you?' I ask, eager for the touch of his lips on mine. His upper body feels taut and firm against me. Close contact with Jack is very pleasurable indeed.

'Because I don't want you to miss this,' he says, and he looks past me out over the sea.

I follow his gaze and I'm amazed to see the most beautiful blood-red sunset in front of us.

'It's just like the painting,' I whisper softly as I turn to Jack. 'Arty and Clara's painting.'

'I know,' he whispers back, before he kisses me again. 'Like history is repeating itself . . . but this time it's just for us.'

Thirty-one

'Morning, Kate!' Anita says, as she arrives at the shop the next morning. 'How are you today, dear?'

'Great, thank you, Anita,' I reply happily. 'Really well.'

'Good, I'm glad to hear it.' Anita adds while she hangs up her cardigan and handbag in the back of the shop: 'Only I heard you had a bit of bother last night.'

'Bother? No I don't think so. Who told you that?'

I'd decided not to say anything to Anita about Joel's visit. I didn't want to fall out with her any more than I wanted to fall out with Jack or Julian.

'Rita from The Merry Mermaid told Janice at the chemist, so when I called for my prescription this morning Janice asked me if you were all right?'

I shake my head. The speed at which gossip travels around here is unbelievable!

'Something about you storming out of the pub and Jack chasing after you?' Anita says as she comes back into the shop. 'But obviously she was mistaken?'

I sigh. 'All right, so we did have a small disagreement, but it's all sorted now.' I can't help smiling to myself as I remember last night up on the hill.

Jack and I had sat for ages watching the sunset and each other, just the two of us snuggled together getting to know each other even better. The incredible sunset had eventually turned into a star-filled sky, and we'd watched that with the same wonderment and togetherness, until eventually it had become too cold to sit there any longer, and we'd sadly had to head back into town.

There had been a brief discussion about the possibility of spending the night together, but we'd both agreed that it might be a bit of a worry for our respective children to find either one of us not in our own bed the next morning. Or it would have been even more of a shock if either one of them had found an unexpected visitor in their parent's bedroom.

Regretfully, we'd parted, promising to be in touch the next day.

'By the expression on your face,' Anita says, smiling at me, 'I'd say it had been more than just *sorted*.'

'Let's just say Jack and I have moved our relationship up a gear,' I reply, beaming at Anita.

Anita to her credit simply nods contentedly, and doesn't ask me anything further.

'Morning, campers!' Sebastian calls, as he comes through the door a few minutes later. We had our large delivery coming in this morning so I had both my staff in with me in order to process it quickly with as little disruption to the shop as possible. 'Now then, boss, what have you been up to?' Sebastian asks with a wicked grin. 'You're the talk of the town!'

'Don't tell me, you went into the chemist and Janice asked how I was?' I reply wearily.

Sebastian looks puzzled. 'No, I called in at the bakery, and Ant asked me what was going on with Jack and you. When I said I didn't know what he meant, he told me you'd been spotted up on the hill last night at sunset, kissing and canoodling!'

I roll my eyes. *This town.*

'You know we're the talk of the town?' Jack asks me later when I've gone over to his shop with the latest embroidered felt pieces. They were really coming thick and fast at the moment, and now so many people seemed to know that Jack and I were an item – including my own friends and family – it suddenly wasn't as difficult for us to sneak off and pretend we were having some 'us time'.

'Yes, I've heard all the gossip,' I tell him, as I lift the easel into Jack's sitting room. 'Apparently we were seen last night.'

'Do you mind?' Jack asks as I pull up a chair next to him.

'Do I look as if I do?' I bypass my chair and instead straddle Jack's so I can kiss him. Jack's response to this spontaneous movement is equally as fervent, pulling me back on to his lap like last night.

'Jack,' I eventually say, trying to pull away from him a little, 'we really need to look at the pictures. We don't have long today.'

'I can think of some much better things we could fill that short time with,' Jack murmurs, not letting me go.

'I don't want a *short* time with you,' I whisper. 'I want a really *long* time.'

'I can't guarantee that,' Jack says, grinning at me, 'but I'll do my very best.'

'Right then, the pictures!' I wriggle from his embrace and begin to line up the first of the paintings and embroidery. 'We have two different ones to watch today . . . I wonder why these have suddenly appeared together?'

'Heaven knows,' Jack says, 'Maybe it's a two-part episode of our fifties' soap opera? I long ago stopped questioning it, I just let it happen now.'

'I have to say I'm a bit worried about this first one,' I say as I sit down on my chair next to Jack. 'It looks a bit bleak, doesn't it?'

'That's what I thought. It's a church though, isn't it? Perhaps we're going to see Clara and Arty's wedding?'

'If we are, it doesn't look like a very happy day,' I say, warily regarding the artwork in front of us. Jack is right – his picture is definitely a painting of a church, but it's in drab shades of grey and dark blue, not how an artist would usually depict a joyous wedding day. My matching felt is of the gravestones in front of the church. 'I really hope nothing has gone wrong for them.'

Jack takes hold of my hand, I move the embroidered felt across so it's in exactly the right place, and then we wait anxiously as we travel back to St Felix once more.

St Felix ~ December 1958

Clara, Arty and Maggie stand in a windswept graveyard looking down at a newly filled-in grave. There is no headstone yet, just loose earth denoting that the incumbent of the plot hasn't been there all that long.

They are all wearing sombre colours. Arty, very unusually, is wearing a suit, and Clara and Maggie black formal-looking dresses. Clara has the addition of a tiny black hat, and Maggie's long hair is tied up with a black ribbon.

'You'd have thought that more people would have turned up to the funeral,' Clara says, looking down at the grave. 'There were only us three and a few others. It's very sad.'

'He kept himself to himself,' Arty says, standing next to her. 'He wasn't one for the social side of life really. It was just him and his painting. He said after his wife Irene died he didn't have any other family left.'

'Still, I would have expected more people to pay their respects. It's simply good manners.'

Arty squeezes Clara's gloved hand.

'Are you all right, Maggie?' he asks, putting his arm around her shoulder.

Maggie just nods. She'd been very quiet since Freddie had died. He'd gone peacefully in his sleep, the doctor had said, and had been discovered by a neighbour who wondered why he hadn't opened up the top of his stable door, as he always did every morning come rain or shine to 'let the St Felix air in'.

'What will happen to all his paintings now he's gone?' Maggie asks, voicing a very good question that no one else had even considered yet. 'What if they get thrown out when someone clears his house. Freddie wouldn't like that.'

'We'll make sure that doesn't happen, Maggie,' Arty says reassuringly. 'How about we go over there tomorrow and see what the landlord is going to do with them?'

Maggie nods.

'Time to say goodbye now, Maggie,' Clara says gently. She hadn't realised quite how much this kind old man had meant to Maggie until the news of his death had reached them. Clara and Arty had both lived through the war, during which hearing news of people dying had become commonplace to them, but death and everything that came with it was new to her daughter, and it had hit her hard.

Maggie nods. 'Goodbye, lovely Freddie,' she says sadly. 'Thank you for all the lovely times we shared. I'll never forget you.' She places a white flower on top of the grave.

'We all had a lot to thank Freddie for,' Arty says, looking down at the grave again and then across at Clara. 'If it wasn't for him your mother and I might not be together.'

Clara nods knowingly. She knew Arty meant that after he'd taken Maggie to Freddie's that first time to check all was well, Clara had realised that Arty only had their best interests at heart. She had softened towards him, and their relationship had begun to flourish from that moment on so that a few months ago Clara had accepted Arty's proposal and they were now engaged.

'If only he knew,' Clara says gently.

'I think Freddie knew a lot more than people thought,' Maggie says, stepping back from the grave and taking hold of her mother's hand. 'A lot, lot more.'

'Oh, how sad,' I say, looking away from the images that have begun to swirl again.

'Yes, it was, but he was an old man,' Jack says seriously. 'He'd had a good innings.'

'I guess so, but Maggie was clearly very close to him and it's obviously very upsetting for her . . . ' I pause. 'Shall we move on to the second picture? The colours are a bit brighter. I think it's of Freddie's house, isn't it?'

'Seems like it. Good job we're viewing them in the order they appeared so it's all chronological. We wouldn't have known what was going on otherwise . . . I barely do anyway for that matter.'

'Stop it, you fibber,' I tease, as I lift the second picture on to the easel. 'You're enjoying all this just as much as I am.'

'Having you here does have its benefits,' Jack says, grinning. He takes my hand again as he waits for me to move the felt into its corresponding place on the front of the painting. 'That's one thing I do have to thank these pictures for.'

I squeeze his hand. 'Ready?' I ask, sliding the felt across.

'Ready.'

St Felix ~ December 1958

Maggie and Arty walk together towards Freddie's cottage. Both of them feel apprehensive about visiting again knowing that he won't be there this time.

Arty had accompanied Maggie on her visits on quite a few occasions over the last year, and he'd got to know Freddie well in that time. He was a quiet man, gentle and intelligent, and Arty had enjoyed sitting painting with him and listening to his stories about St Felix and his life there almost as much as Maggie. Arty had brought him some of his own canvases to use with the excuse that he didn't use that size any more. Freddie was a proud man and Arty knew he wouldn't accept anything that looked like charity, so when he'd brought him as many pieces of art equipment as he could he always used the 'unwanted/ unused' excuse. He wasn't sure Freddie always believed him, but he was gracious enough to accept Arty's gifts without a fuss.

He and Maggie arrive outside Freddie's cottage and are surprised to see the doors open, and the sounds of hammering, banging and raised voices coming from inside.

'Good morning!' Arty calls tentatively through the doors.

"'ello, mate can I 'elp you?' asks a man wearing blue overalls and a tweed cap, approaching them across the kitchen floor.

'Yes, perhaps you can. What are you all doing here?'

'Renovations, mate. This place ain't been touched in years. The new owner wants it all ship-shape as fast as possible.'

'New owner? But I thought this house was rented?'

"'Twas, I think, but the landlord has sold it on now. Far as I know he got an offer he couldn't refuse.'

Maggie tugs at Arty's hand.

'And do you know what happened to the paintings that were here?' Arty asks, looking at the bare walls. The place was hardly recognisable as Freddie's house any longer as the builders were pulling down the old kitchen cabinets and there was dust everywhere.

'Don't know nothing about any paintings, mate. Place was all empty when we arrived.'

'Right, thank you. Just one more thing, do you know who the new owner is by any chance?'

The builder shrugs. 'Nope, we've been hired by some company in London. We're Penzance-based as a rule.'

'I see. Well, thank you for your time,' Arty says, pulling on Maggie's hand for them to leave.

'But where are Freddie's paintings?' she cries, staying put. 'Have they been thrown away?'

'No, I'm sure that hasn't happened, Maggie,' Arty says gently. 'Don't worry, we'll find them.'

'You could ask George along at number ten,' the builder suggests, regarding Maggie with concern. 'If there was something important here, maybe he would know?'

'George?' Arty asks.

'He was the landlord here beforehand. Even though he's sold the place he's still overseeing the building works for the new owner. He'll come and check on us occasionally.'

'Right, we'll do that. Thank you again.' Arty pulls on Maggie's hand again and this time she follows him.

'Where are Freddie's paintings, Arty?' Maggie asks again.

'I don't know, Maggie,' Arty replies with determination, 'but we're going to find out.'

They knock on the door of number ten and a man wearing a white vest, braces and slippers opens it.

'Yes?' he asks suspiciously, 'What is it?'

'Good morning,' Arty says confidently, assuming this must be George. 'I believe you used to be the landlord of number three, back along the road?'

'Yes, who wants to know?'

'We were friends with the man who used to live there – Freddie ...' Arty says, suddenly realising he didn't know Freddie's last name.

'You mean Wilfred,' George says. 'That was his proper name. He let children call him Freddie because he reckoned it was friendlier. Weren't you at his funeral?' he asks, looking at them both.

'Yes, we were. So must you have been then?'

'Yeah, I look a bit different in me suit, I do,' George says, running his hand over his receding hair. 'Thought someone should go as I didn't expect many people would show up, and I was right. Why are you asking about Wilfred?'

'We wondered what happened to his paintings when he passed on?' Arty asks. 'I know you've sold the house now, but before the builders arrived did you clear the house at all?'

'It's funny you should ask that,' George says, his brow

284

furrowing, 'because I was wondering the exact same thing. One day old Wilfred was in there painting away and the next he was carted off by the undertaker. When I went to check on the house a few days later to make sure it was still locked up, all his paintings were gone.'

'Gone!' Arty repeats. 'Gone where?'

'I don't know. It was odd, it was. Nothing else seemed to have been taken, not that the old fella had a lot – just the paintings. They weren't worth anything so I didn't bother the police. Maybe someone took a shine to them ... Dunno why though – some of them looked like they'd been done by a child. No offence, lovey,' he says to Maggie.

Maggie just stares up at him.

'When did you get the offer for the house?' Arty asks.

'Few days later. Came out of the blue, it did, but it was too 'andsome an offer to refuse. It's given the wife and me a nice little nest egg, it has.'

'Do you know who bought it?'

'Some company – London-based, I think they was? I don't know much about this sort of stuff so my son helped us out with all the documents and complicated stuff to make sure it was all above board. He's works in a bank, you know,' George says proudly. 'Ever so clever.'

'I'm sure,' Arty says, nodding. 'And you got paid all right. The money all came through?'

'Yep, sitting in me brand new bank account. My son opened it for us.'

'That's wonderful. Good for you,' Arty says, feeling totally dismayed. The chances of finding Freddie's paintings were fading fast.

'Sorry I couldn't be of more help with the paintings though,'

285

George says. He looks down at Maggie again. 'I sees you coming and going a lot into Wilfred's. I know he always appreciated your visits.'

Maggie looks like she might cry at any moment.

'Why they disappeared is anyone's guess ...' George adds, shaking his head. 'Must have been taken at night though, as someone would have seen them in the day. It's a mystery, it is.'

'A mystery that I'm going to solve,' Arty says with determination. 'An artist as good as Freddie, no, Wilfred— What was his surname?'

'Jones,' George says. 'Wilfred Jones, his full name was.'

' ... as good as Wilfred Jones is not going to be forgotten. I'm going to make sure of it.'

The pictures swirl together and begin to fade.

'Oh no, another sad one,' I say, turning to Jack. 'I wonder what happened to the paintings?'

'Stolen, obviously,' Jack answers, still staring at the easel.

'Who would want to steal some old man's paintings though? Everyone described them as childlike – they can't have been all that good ...' My voice fades out as I stare at the pictures in front of us.

'What's wrong?' Jack asks. 'You've gone a bit pale all of a sudden.'

'Childlike,' I repeat. 'Everyone described them as childlike.'

'And so?'

'The last time I saw paintings like that was at the Lyle Gallery – at the Winston James exhibition. The art world uses the terms like "naive" and "innocent" to describe that sort of painting. But there's something more to it apparently that not everyone, including myself, always gets.'

286

'I'm really not following you, Kate.'

I stare at Jack. 'It couldn't be, could it?'

'Couldn't be what?' Jack asks, looking bewildered. 'What *are* you talking about?'

'Wilfred Jones. Winston James,' I say. 'Same initials too.'

Jack stares at me again, about to say something, but then suddenly he understands. 'Wait a minute, are you saying you think that this Winston James stole Freddie's paintings?'

'I can't be sure, but Julian said his father bought Freddie's cottage around that time. It's a huge coincidence, don't you think?'

'But why would he do that? Wasn't he an artist in his own right? Why steal someone else's paintings?'

'I don't know.' My forehead wrinkles as I try to recall the conversations I'd had with Julian about his father. 'I'm not sure he was all that successful back then. Perhaps he saw Freddie's paintings and thought he could make some money with them. Arty seemed to think they were pretty good.'

'If he wasn't successful, how could he possibly afford to buy the cottage?'

'Oh, I don't know!' I snap in frustration. 'But,' I continue, sounding as determined as Arty had just now, 'I'm damn well going to find out. This might be it,' I say to an astonished-looking Jack. 'The reason we've been seeing all this. This could be the reason the St Felix magic has chosen us to help.'

Thirty-two

'I'm so glad you called, Kate,' Julian says, when I meet him for coffee in one of the many cafés in St Felix a couple of days later. 'I desperately want to apologise for the other night. I'm truly sorry for what happened.'

'It's fine, Julian. Water under the bridge and all that. And actually you did me a favour,' I say, trying to remain calm and composed. I had to find out more about Julian's father and his possible connection to the missing paintings.

Jack and I had visited the Winston James exhibition at the Lyle Gallery the previous day, and we'd looked carefully at each and every painting in great detail. They were all in the same simplistic style with the same harsh lines and bold brush strokes, and they all had the initials *WJ* etched into the bottom right-hand corner. What I hadn't noticed previously though was that some of the images had been created on pieces of wood and metal as well as on artist's canvases, just like Freddie's had been.

'WJ,' I'd whispered to Jack as we'd examined the pictures. 'Everyone assumes it's Winston James' initials, but what if they stand for Wilfred Jones instead?'

'It doesn't prove anything though,' Jack had whispered back. 'Lots of people have the same initials.'

'I know, but it's so easy to make assumptions, isn't it? Remember when I received those mystery bunches of flowers? I thought at first they were from you, didn't I? Because the card with them was signed with a J. Then I thought they were from Joel – thank heaven they weren't. When I eventually discovered they were both from Julian I was shocked. It's so easy to see what you want to, Jack. No one ever questioned these paintings were by anyone else, because they didn't need to.'

'Julian sent you more than one bunch of flowers?' Jack had asked with a hint of jealousy. 'You didn't mention that before.'

Jack and I had also taken another look at the painting and embroidery we had of Freddie's house – from when Arty visited for the first time – to see if we could get a better glimpse of his paintings inside. We'd wondered if the magic would work for a second time as we'd only ever watched the pictures come to life once each before, but to our joy it had. It was like seeing a repeat of one of your favourite shows on TV – we knew what was going to happen but we were still keen to watch it again, and as is common when you view something twice, we noticed things we hadn't seen the first time. Sadly, however, it was still incredibly difficult to catch sight of Freddie's paintings properly, but we had our suspicions as they definitely *looked* like they might be the same as some of those hanging in the Lyle Gallery. If they were though how did we go about proving it?

'*I* did *you* a favour?' Julian asks with a puzzled expression while lifting his coffee. 'How so?'

'Let's just say Jack and I got to know each other *a lot* better that night.'

I bite my bottom lip. I hadn't meant to reply quite so obviously. It wasn't nice to taunt Julian even though I was still annoyed with him about the vest incident.

'Ah, I see,' Julian says. He nods matter-of-factly and looks down at the table. 'The best man won in the end, I suppose.'

'I'm not a prize to be fought over,' I tell him sternly. 'I'm afraid, Julian, it was always going to be Jack. Like I tried to tell you, I only want to be your friend.'

'Still?' Julian asks, looking up again. 'I thought I'd ruined that by not telling you about Joel and bringing your undergarment into the pub.'

'You almost did, but like I said, it's all worked out for the best and I'm here now, aren't I?'

'I'm glad you are, Kate, and I'm sorry again. I've behaved like such a fool.'

'It's fine, Julian, really. All forgotten now.'

'No, it's not fine. I need to learn how to behave like a proper decent adult, not some overprivileged public school boy who always gets what he wants. I've been cosseted my whole life, Kate, and the time has come to grow up. You've made me realise that, and until the other day I thought I was doing quite well at it. I was trying hard anyway, and then I blew it when I saw you with Jack at the pub. I'm ashamed to say I was jealous, and my immediate reaction was to bite back and try to hurt the two of you, but when I'd actually done the dreadful deed I felt so bad I quickly tried to put things right.'

I nod. 'I thought it might be something like that, but like I said, it's forgotten now. Everything has worked out fine.' I pause. I need to get this conversation back on track. I'm here to try to find out more about Winston James, but now I am here I'm feeling sorry for Julian again. He really isn't a bad person, just misguided. 'So why do you think you behave like you do?' I ask tentatively, hoping this might lead on to talk of his father again.

'It's so easy for people to say "blame the parents",' Julian says weakly, 'but the truth is I do blame mine.'

'Go on,' I encourage.

'Even though they sent me away to boarding school, and didn't bother to make the effort to see me most holidays, they still managed to spoil me as a child, with money and expensive gifts. Then they kept spoiling me in the same way when I finally left education. I went to university first of course, but that was subsidised with a healthy payout each month – from my mother too this time as she had almost as much money as my father when she inherited from my grandparents. I didn't struggle to make ends meet like some of my fellow students, I had very generous allowances from my rich parents to fritter away.'

'Some might think you very lucky?' I suggest.

'I know I sound like a whiny, pampered child, Kate. Believe me, I can hear it myself, but I'm simply trying to piece together for you and for me why I am the way I am now.'

'Go on,' I encourage.

'After university it was decided I should work in the family business, but I didn't start at the bottom and work my way up so I could properly learn what went on. Oh no, I went straight in at the top, and I wish I could sit here and say that I behaved with some sense of modesty and decorum in that position, but I'm ashamed to say I didn't. I'm sure all the staff hated me, and I'm certain most of them still do.' He lifts his cup again and takes a large gulp of his coffee.

'Perhaps your parents were simply doing what they thought was the best for you?' I try to suggest helpfully. 'Maybe they felt ashamed that they didn't spend more time with you when you were very young, so they tried to show their love the only way they knew how, by showering you with gifts and subsequently money? Some parents do that, don't they? They think they can buy their children's love when all the child really wants is their time and their affection.'

Julian gazes at me across the table. 'Oh, Kate, how very wise,' he says softly. 'I bet you don't do that with your daughter, do you? I bet she gets all your time and more love than she knows what to do with?'

'Well,' I say, 'I'm sure I could have given her more time in the past – it's not easy being a single parent and running your own business – but she knows I love her.'

'I'm certain she does,' Julian says, nodding. 'And I bet you don't spoil her either, do you?'

This was getting us way off track. How had we ended up taking about Molly now? I needed to bring this back to Julian's father, but the more I listened to Julian the harder I found it to dislike him. Yes, he was sometimes trying and difficult, but was that really his fault when you knew about his upbringing?

'No, I definitely don't spoil her,' I reply, 'but then I've never really had the means to be a single parent. Perhaps your parents wanted to spoil you because they could? You said your mother had an inheritance, but what about your father – did he come from a rich family?'

'No, not that I'm aware of. It was my mother's family that had all the wealth, but my paternal grandparents must have supported him in his early days of painting. He didn't make much money from that to begin with, that I do know. It was only when he went to the States that he began to see some success – they really seemed to get his work there.'

'Do you know why he went to America? Surely it wasn't that common in the fifties?'

Julian looks puzzled. 'How did you know it was then that he went there?'

'You told me, remember?' I say hurriedly. 'When we had dinner.'

'Oh yes, so I did. Golly, it seems all I do is pour my heart out to you, Kate.'

'I don't mind,' I assure him. 'I want to help. So, why did he go?'

'I really don't know. I think he wanted to try selling his art somewhere else ... and it worked! He became very successful very quickly. I don't think the Americans had seen anything like my father's work before then.'

I nod taking all this in. 'So when did he buy the cottage you were in the other day? Did he do that with the proceeds of his sales, or did he buy it before he left St Felix?'

Luckily, Julian doesn't seem to think this an odd question. 'Oh no, he didn't buy the cottage until the early sixties when he'd sold a lot of his work and started to make a bit of money. I think it was a B&B before.'

'Must have been a pretty small one? That cottage only had a couple of rooms upstairs.'

'Yes, I suppose it must. I believe there were a few properties down the street that were B&Bs back then. If I remember rightly they were bought one by one by a London firm then run by a single landlady. I suppose her guests simply all breakfasted together of a morning in one of her many properties!' He smiles at his little joke, then shakes his head, 'Anyway none of that matters now.'

'No, it doesn't. I just wondered why your father would buy an old fisherman's cottage when he was living in America?'

'Memories, perhaps?' Julian says. 'Or more likely, knowing my father, he saw a good business opportunity. Wasn't it in the sixties that people began to holiday abroad for the first time? I bet the B&B wasn't doing too well and Dad swooped in and bought it at a bargain price. That sounds like him.'

I just smile. This still wasn't getting me anywhere with Freddie's pictures. It was simply painting a not very flattering picture of Winston James.

'I was in the gallery the other day,' I tell him casually, as I stir my coffee spoon around my now half-empty cup. 'And I was looking at your father's work again.'

'Oh, yes,' Julian says, finishing off his own coffee. 'Were there people fawning all over it, gushing about how wonderful it all is?'

This almost sarcastic tone doesn't sound at all like the Julian I'd originally met – the one who had bigged up his father's paintings at the opening of the exhibition. That Julian had been full of himself and his father's work, but the Julian I was with now with was a much different character, one who wanted to be redeemed of his many failings and removed from those of his father.

'No,' I tell him, 'it was only me taking another look. Forgive me if I'm speaking out of turn here, but the way you describe your father doesn't seem to fit at all with his style of painting. I mean it's so . . . ' I choose my words carefully, ' . . . simple and pure, and you describe your father as a bit of a . . . ' I hesitate, but Julian finishes off my sentence for me.

'A bit of a bastard? Will that do as an adequate description?'

'Well, I wouldn't go that far.'

'He was though,' Julian insists. 'All my father ever thought about was money and how he could make more of it. He never really cared about me or anyone else for that matter. I imagine my mother was simply a trophy wife to him. She was very beautiful in her day – and as I've already mentioned she was from an extremely wealthy family. That's why Father was so interested in her. Like I said, he loved money.'

'I'm sure that's not true.'

'It is, Kate. Whatever I did was never good enough for him. Giving me the position in his company wasn't because he trusted me to do it, it was so he could keep an eye on me, make sure I didn't do anything to embarrass him and his name. I'm surprised he actually left me in charge of the business when he died. I might have been better off if he hadn't. At least I'd have had to stand on my own two feet then.'

'Your mother – is she still alive?' I ask delicately.

Julian shakes his head. 'No, she died five years ago.

'So it's just you? No brothers or sisters?'

Again, Julian shakes his head.

'This might sound like an impertinent question, but did you inherit your mother's wealth?'

Julian stares at me for a second. 'Yes, why?'

'And is it separate from your father's business assets?'

'Totally. I've always kept it that way. Just between you and me, Kate, I'm only employed by the company. I don't even own any shares in it. When my father died, I chose to keep it that way. It seemed simpler to continue taking a generous salary than anything else.'

'Good,' I say, nodding as I think this through. 'That's very good.'

'Why?' Julian looks puzzled. 'What are you suggesting, Kate?'

'Can I suggest you give up your job as soon as possible and think about starting somewhere or some*thing* new.'

'Why on earth would I want to do that?'

'For one, it would rid you of the constant shadow that your father's name casts over both you and everything you do. And two,' I hesitate again, should I really be telling him this? But I had to. It was only fair he was warned. None of this was his fault. 'And two,' I repeat, 'I have a feeling that the name Winston James and any company he's associated with is going to suffer quite badly very soon from . . . let's just say, from some *bad news*. And when that news breaks, I think you'd be well advised to be as far away from it as possible.'

Thirty-three

'And he's going to help us?' Jack asks suspiciously. 'Just like that?'

'Yes. I told you Julian wasn't all bad.'

'But why would he want to help you tarnish his father's name? I'd have thought it would have been the other way around, and he'd be trying to stop you.'

I throw Barney's ball along the sand, and he chases after it while Jack and I watch him. We'd taken Barney for a walk so we could discuss in private what had taken place earlier today with Julian, away from the prying ears of both our shops and their various staff.

'Julian never liked his father, and I think he's got quite strong principles. If he thought for one moment his father had stolen those paintings he'd be the first to hold his hand up and admit it.'

Jack doesn't look so sure.

'Trust me, Jack. Julian will come through on this.'

'And didn't he want to know how we knew all this?' Jack asks. 'You can't have told him *everything*?'

'No, not everything. I didn't mention the paintings and

embroideries, of course. I said I couldn't tell him how I knew or I'd be breaking a confidence. I asked him to trust me.'

'And he did?'

'I think so.'

'I'm not sure I would,' Jack says, reaching down from his chair to throw Barney's ball for him again.

'Cheers!'

'No, I mean without seeing some proof. Of course I'd trust you. I'd trust you with my life, Kate.' He reaches up and takes hold of my hand, and I smile down at him. 'So we just wait then?' Jack asks.

'Yep, we just wait for now, and hope Julian does what he says he's going to.'

The next day I'm standing in the shop gazing out of the window thinking about Clara, Arty, Maggie and now Freddie as well when Molly comes into the shop.

'I've done it,' she says dismally.

'Done what?' I ask, still distracted.

'Broken up with Chesney.'

'Oh, Molly, I'm sorry I didn't realise. How did it go?'

Molly shrugs. 'Not great.'

'Break-ups rarely are. How was he?'

'Angry at first, then sort of . . . dismissive.'

'Dismissive?'

'Yeah, like I was joking or something. I'm not sure he really believed that's what I truly wanted to do.' She half laughs. 'That's how high an opinion he must have of himself.'

I put my arms around her and pull her close.

'I'm sure it won't be the last time you have to break up with a boy. Like I said, it's never easy.'

'I don't think I'll bother with men in the future,' Molly says sighing. 'It's too much like hard work. I'm gonna stick with Ben – did you know he's gay?'

'Yes,' I say smiling. 'I did. He's a lovely boy.'

'Oh yeah, the best, and much more fun than a proper boy-friend! We can hang out together without all the other hassles.'

My phone rings in my pocket. I pull it free and look at the screen. It's Julian.

'Sorry, Molly, I need to take this. Will you be all right?'

''Course!' Molly says. 'Anita left us some Victoria sponge upstairs, so I think I'll let that drown my sorrows for a while!'

'Hi, Julian,' I say quickly into the receiver as Molly heads upstairs to the flat. 'Any joy?'

'I have it,' Julian says.

'So soon?'

'Yep, it wasn't that simple to get, but you'd be surprised how easily people can be persuaded when money comes into the equation.'

I didn't like to think of Julian having to bribe someone to get the information we required, but it was the only way we might ever get to the bottom of this mystery.

'What do you have? A name, a number, an address?' I ask hopefully.

'All of the above,' Julian says proudly. 'Do you really think it will help?'

'Yes,' I reply confidently. 'I really do.'

At lunchtime I meet Jack, and we head around to Julian's cottage.

Jack and Julian greet each other slightly awkwardly, but I have no time for their male insecurities today as I need to get on with what we're actually here for.

'Here you go,' Julian says, handing me a piece of paper. 'All the details of the last owner of number seven Treleven Hill, St Felix.'

Julian had managed to do what we couldn't – he'd been able to procure the name, number and address of the last owner of the house with the blue door. The house that both the sewing machine and the easel had come from, and the house where we'd found Maggie's name scrawled in the cupboard under the stairs.

I look down at the paper. *Susan Cross*, it said, followed by a mobile number and an address near Penzance.

'Shall I phone it?' I ask them both.

'That's the plan,' Jack says. 'Unless you want me to?'

'No, I'll do it,' I say, and I take a deep breath before pressing the digits into my phone.

I half expect this Susan Cross not to answer. I was always wary when an unknown number called me, so I prepare myself to leave a message, but to my surprise someone answers.

'Hello?'

'Oh, hello,' I say, staring wildly at the other two. 'Is that Susan?'

'It is, yes. Who is this, please?' The person I'm speaking to has an odd accent – half British, half American.

'Oh, you don't know me, but my name is Kate … Kate Anderson. I wondered if I could ask you some questions about the house you have for sale?'

There is a slight pause before Susan says in a terse voice, 'All queries about the house should go through the realtor … sorry, the estate agent. How did you get my number?'

'No, it's not about purchasing the house,' I say quickly. 'It's about who used to live there. I wonder if you know anyone called Maggie, Clara or even an Arty perhaps?'

There's silence at the other end of the line, and I wonder if Susan has hung up on me.

'Who are you again?' she asks.

'My name is Kate and I'm looking for anyone who might have known them. I know either they lived at the house or someone in their family did.'

'I have no clue what you're talking about,' Susan says. 'Like I said, if you have a query about the house then please contact our estate agent. The house will be going up for auction very soon, and you are welcome to bid for it then.'

Damn! I glance up at the wall and see one of the Winston James prints. 'What about Freddie?' I say quickly, before she can hang up. 'Do you know anything about him?'

'What did you say?' Susan asks sharply.

'Freddie,' I repeat. 'I think he might have been called Wilfred too?'

There's another long pause, but this time I don't think Susan has hung up. Instead, she says eventually, 'I think we need to talk.'

Thirty-four

'Stop fidgeting,' Jack says, as we wait in the café for Susan the next day. 'You're making me nervous.'

'Sorry, I can't help it. I am nervous. I wonder what this Susan wants to talk to us about?'

'You'll find out soon enough, won't you?'

Susan had agreed to meet us the next day in St Felix. She said she would drive up from Penzance to meet us, but she didn't say anything else that gave us any hope or expectation at all.

'It must be something to do with Freddie,' I continue, tapping my finger on the table. 'She wasn't at all interested in anything I had to say until then.'

'You won't have to wait much longer,' Jack says, looking across at the entrance to the café. 'I think this might be her.'

A middle-aged woman with dark hair tied back in a loose pony tail is staring anxiously around the café's interior.

'Susan?' I say, standing up.

She nods and makes her way over to our table.

'I'm Kate,' I say, holding out my hand to her. 'And this is Jack. Thank you for agreeing to meet with us.'

Susan shakes both our hands, then pulls out a chair and sits down.

'Would you like a drink?' I ask. 'Tea, maybe, or coffee perhaps?'

'No, thank you,' she says. 'I can't stay too long.'

'Right, okay then,' I say, suddenly feeling incredibly nervous again. I don't know why but I felt a huge weight was upon me – the weight of not only our expectations but of Arty and Maggie's too – to solve this mystery.

'So, Susan,' Jack says, taking over when I don't speak. 'The names Kate mentioned to you on the phone yesterday. Do you know any of them?'

Susan nods. 'I know all of them,' she admits to my surprise. 'Well, I say know. I knew some of them.' She takes a deep breath. 'Clara and Arty were my grandparents, and Maggie is my mother.'

I stare at Susan while Jack continues. *Little Maggie from the paintings is still alive? I don't know why but I'd assumed all of them would have passed away by now.*

'I see ...' Jack says, sounding like a detective in a police drama about to solve the crime.

'Why are you asking about them?' Susan asks. 'Is this to do with the house?'

'Some information has come to us,' Jack says enigmatically. 'We can't say how or from whom, but we think it involves your family and possibly the relationship they had with a painter called Freddie, or rather Wilfred Jones, to give him his correct name.'

Susan looks at Jack suspiciously. 'I'm going to be honest with the pair of you,' she says, turning to me as well now, 'in the hope you will be with me in return. The only reason I'm here today is that my mother is ill ... very ill actually. She has dementia.'

'I'm so sorry to hear that,' I say, finding my voice now. 'Really sorry. Poor Maggie.'

Susan looks oddly at me. I don't blame her – after all she doesn't know how we knew her mother. We're just two strangers asking a few peculiar questions.

'Do you know my mother?' Susan asks, mirroring my thoughts, 'because it sounds like you do.'

'I don't know her exactly ...' I glance at Jack, maybe I should just be quiet.

'What Kate means is we've heard lots about her. We know she overcame polio in the fifties, and that she was in a wheel-chair and then learnt to walk again. She must have been a strong woman, your mother. Believe me, I know how difficult it is to lose the use of your legs.'

Susan nods. 'Yes, she did indeed do those things, but how do you—'

'That doesn't matter,' Jack says quickly. 'What's important now is Freddie. You obviously know something about him. Kate said you reacted on the telephone when his name was mentioned?'

'Yes, I did, and that's what I was coming to. Because my mother has dementia she doesn't always make a lot of sense, and she gets lost in her memories of the past quite a bit. But sometimes she can be as sharp as a pin, and you'd think there was nothing wrong with her. It's those times we cherish now.'

We nod sympathetically and wait for Susan to continue.

'I'm going to have to tell you some background information so that what I'm going to say will hopefully make sense – is that all right?'

'Perfectly,' I say, keen to know as much as we can about Maggie.

'My grandparents lived in St Felix for many years. My grandfather was an artist and my grandmother ran a little shop there. A few years after they got married they bought the house we're selling now.' She smiles. 'They had every intention of naming the house but my grandmother always called it "the house with the blue door", and it sort of stuck.'

A warm feeling floods through my body.

'Sadly, my grandmother, who I never knew, died before I was born from pneumonia contracted during a bout of 'flu, I believe.'

My stomach twists at this news. Poor Clara.

'But my grandfather continued to live at the house with my mother for many years. She wasn't his real daughter, but he always cared for her like she was. One day when she was of an age to do so, my mother decided she wanted to trace her real father. I'm sure my grandfather wasn't too happy about it, but my mother was pretty stubborn, and still is, for that matter,' Susan smiles. 'Anyway, all she knew was he was a US serviceman by whom my grandmother had become pregnant at the end of the war when he was stationed near to her home, so you can imagine it wasn't the easiest of searches trying to find him.'

I glance at Jack. At last we knew Clara's story. Maggie was the product of a war-time dalliance with an American soldier.

'So she decided to go to the States to try to find him, which is how I came along. My mother, like my grandmother before her, became pregnant by someone she only knew briefly and never saw again. Our family is good at that.' She smiles again. 'It nearly happened to me too, but I'm pleased to say I eventually married the father of my child.'

I smile now. Their family tale was all too familiar to me.

'Did your mother find her real father eventually?' I ask.

'Amazingly, she did. He was married by then, with another family, but they welcomed Mom and then me too into their family.'

'How lovely,' I say. 'So you and Maggie stayed on in America?'

'Yes, for about ten years. We saw quite a lot of my step-family – we spent Thanksgivings and Christmases with them. They were very generous to us, but then my English grand-father became ill, and my mother decided to move back here to take care of him. After all, he'd looked after her when she needed it, and now it was her turn to repay the favour.'

I think about Arty all alone in that large house for so long, and how much it must have meant to him to have Maggie back with him again.

'So, we moved back here again and we lived in that house for many years. My grandfather Arty passed away eventually, so then it was just Mom and me there until it was suddenly my turn to move on. I was desperate to return to the States again. It was where I felt I'd done a lot of my growing up. I always made regular trips back to the UK to see my mother though, and it was on one of those trips I met my husband-to-be – the father of my daughter Maggie.'

'You called your daughter after your mother? That's nice. Must have been a little confusing with two Maggies in the family.'

'Usually it would be, but my mother became more and more eccentric as she got older. She began only answering to the name Peggy for a while.'

'Another pet name for Margaret!' I say, suddenly getting it. 'That's why no one in St Felix knew a Maggie, because she called herself Peggy when she was here last. My colleague thought she remembered an eccentric old lady called Peggy living in the house with the blue door. She said she liked to keep herself to herself.'

'She did indeed. She became something of a recluse in that big old house, but we began to notice that she was becoming forgetful and we were worried about her. My daughter moved down here to Cornwall to be closer to her – she's an artist too so it was no hardship for her to come down to Cornwall to paint and keep an eye on Mom. She'd been living in London previously. We didn't want my mother to know she was being watched over so we made it seem as natural as we could.'

Something else occurs to me. 'Did your daughter spend a lot of time in the house when she was younger?' I ask.

'Yes, we took holidays down here with my mother.'

'That explains the graffiti in the cupboard! We thought it was your mother, but she seemed a bit old to be playing in a cupboard under the stairs.'

'No, that was my Maggie,' Susan says. 'She was obsessed with Harry Potter at the time – still is a bit, I guess, even though she's almost thirty now. So you *do* know the house then?'

'Yes,' I admit. 'We did visit with the estate agent when it came up for sale.'

'But why?'

'It's an odd thing, but Jack and I met because we'd both bought things that had come from that house. You asked the owner of Noah's Ark antique shop to do a house clearance for you, didn't you?'

Susan nods. 'Yes, it took a number of years but we began to realise that Mom's forgetfulness was becoming more serious. She was forgetting to feed herself and wash, and often she didn't seem to know what year it was, let alone what day. She resisted moving out of the house, of course. She was stubborn, as I said earlier, but we had to make her for her own good. Maggie, my daughter, said she would look after her at her house in Penzance as there was more care assistance available there, so Mom didn't have to go into a retirement home, but how long she can do that I'm not sure. She's getting pretty bad these days. Have either of you ever had anyone close to you suffer from dementia?'

We shake our heads.

'I'm glad. I hope you never do. It's truly awful to witness, but like I said earlier there are some brighter days. I've been staying with Maggie while the house is cleared and sold, so she doesn't have all that to deal with as well as Mom. We didn't want to sell the house, but if Mom does need specialist care then that will help to pay for it as it's incredibly expensive. You said you bought some things from the house?'

'Yes, I believe I have your grandmother's old sewing machine.'

'And I have Arty's old easel,' Jack says.

'You do! Oh how wonderful. I'm glad they went to good homes. My mother always said they were special. It's a real shame we couldn't keep everything, but that house held a lot of stuff and a lot of memories too,' she says wistfully. 'That's why we brought my mother back here not so long ago. She was desperate to see the place again, so we let her – well, her memories – lead us around St Felix. She took us to some strange places.'

'Like where?' I ask, wondering if I already knew the answer to my question.

'She took us to the end of the harbour up by the lighthouse? And then along the coastal path. My mother's mind may be failing her but her body certainly isn't! Then to some holiday flats that I think might once have held Arty's studio judging by what she was saying, and afterwards, and this is really odd, to one of the old fisherman's cottages. She just stood outside looking at it, and then started muttering something really strange. She kept saying something about Freddie and Freddie's paintings. We had no idea what she meant?'

I glance at Jack. He looks as white as I suddenly feel.

'She got quite upset,' Susan continues, 'so we took her for a cup of tea in the outdoor café, up by the Lyle Gallery. She calmed down a bit, so we thought everything was okay, but then she saw a poster for an art exhibition that was on at the gallery and I swear I've never seen my mother move so fast. It was like she was a young girl again.'

'What happened then?' I ask, knowing almost exactly what had taken place. Julian had mentioned an incident at the gallery, and knowing what I knew now I was sure this was going to be it.

'We paid to go in and she headed straight for the temporary exhibition they had on. That's when she went very quiet. She stared at the paintings for a short while and then she began to cry. She broke down completely in the middle of the gallery, sobbing. We tried to console her and explain to some silly woman who came over to see what was happening that she had dementia and didn't really know what she was doing, but she asked us to leave as we were disturbing the other visitors. There were only a couple of people in there, for goodness sake!'

I bet that was Ophelia, I think. Stupid stuck-up—

'And that's when my mother truly lost it,' Susan continues, before I have time to finish my thought. 'She turned from inconsolable to incensed in seconds. She started shouting about how this guy's paintings were stolen and that they weren't by him, that they were by this Freddie again. We could barely control her. Like I say, it's not my mother's body letting her down at

309

all – she's still very strong. Eventually my daughter and I managed to calm down both her and the gallery staff, and we were escorted from the building.'

'Did your mother say anything else?' I ask. 'About Freddie?'

Susan shakes her head. 'She's barely said a word since. She's retreated back into her own world. She hardly communicates with us. It's heartbreaking, and I know it's something to do with this Freddie person, but she won't talk to us about it. When we ask she just clams up, so when you phoned me out of the blue and mentioned his name, I knew I had to come and find out what you knew – to see if we could piece this mystery together between us.'

'I think we can do better than that,' I tell a distressed-looking Susan. 'I think we might be able to solve the mystery *and* put right a wrong that's been kept secret for far too long.'

Thirty-five

'Thanks for driving,' Jack says, as we travel together down towards Penzance in my battered old Land Rover. 'I've not got around to getting myself a permanent car yet, and as you can imagine it has to be a *special* one.' He rolls his eyes as he says the word special.

'That's okay,' I tell him, 'I don't mind. I don't really drive all that much either. This poor thing sits in a locked garage most of the time. Cars aren't really necessary when you spend nearly all your days in a little seaside fishing town like we do.'

'No, that's true. I guess that's why I haven't really needed one yet. Luckily all my stock is delivered to me, and the public transport around here is quite good if you need to travel further afield.'

'How do you get on with that?' I ask, overtaking a slow-moving tractor and trailer. 'Public transport, I mean?'

Jack shrugs. 'Okay, it can be a hassle if you have to ask for ramps and the like on trains and taxis, but a lot of buses have steps that lower automatically these days, so that's a bonus.'

I nod. 'I expect it's the things you don't think about that are the hardest.'

'How do you mean?'

'Like when you turn up somewhere and there's no lift, or you have to go up steps to get in.'

'Yes, that can be annoying, but I rarely go anywhere without checking out how accessible it is first. That's one thing my life is definitely lacking these days – spontaneity. I have to plan everything in advance. Especially trips to somewhere I haven't been before.'

'It must be tough.'

'You get used to it. *You'll* get used to it too if you intend on spending any length of time with me.' He glances across at me, but I pretend to be concentrating on the road.

'Who's looking after your shop today?' I ask. 'Ben again?'

'Ben and Bronte. What about you?'

'Sebastian and Anita are both in. Luckily Sebastian is eager to amass as much money as he can this summer. I've had to call on him a lot just lately when we've been dashing here, there and everywhere.'

'You haven't asked Molly then?'

'On occasion, yes, but she's too young to be left on her own with the shop. Sebastian and Anita need to be there with her, so it's not always feasible when it comes to breaks and stuff.'

'It's good our two kids are getting along,' Jack says. 'I'm really pleased about that.'

'Molly thinks Ben is great. It's like he's the big brother she's never had.'

'Ben is fond of Molly too. I think it might have been a bit awkward to begin with, but once Molly realised he was gay their relationship changed for the better.'

'He's a handsome young man. Hot, like his dad.'

I glance across at Jack.

'It's a while since anyone called me that,' he says, looking ahead at the road with flushed cheeks.

'Just as well, otherwise I might not have had the chance to.'

'I'm serious, Kate. My track record with women hasn't been exactly great since I had my accident. I mean, who would want to go out with me?'

'I assume you're talking about your sometimes uncouth and often forceful manner?' I retort flippantly. 'And not your physical attributes or lack of them?' I glance over at him to see how he's taken this.

'You know what I mean,' Jack says seriously. 'I'm a burden to whoever I'm with.'

'Did you get out of bed the wrong side this morning?' I ask. 'Or have you taken a *poor me* pill? You're feeling very sorry for yourself today.'

'It's you I feel sorry for, hooking up with me. You could do so much better than a cripple.'

'Right, that's it!' I say, and I swerve into the forecourt of a petrol station we're about to pass.

'Whoa!' Jack says, grabbing on to the dashboard as I brake hard in the area for filling tyres with air. 'Why did you do that?'

'Because I'm not going any further until you tell me what's wrong?' I say, turning off the engine.

'What do you mean?'

'You know what I mean. Why the pity party?'

'I was just thinking last night about you and Julian, that's all.'

'What do you mean, me and Julian? There isn't a me and Julian.'

'He obviously likes you still or why would he do everything he's done for us regarding Maggie?'

I sigh. 'If Julian likes me in any way other than as a friend

313

then it's his issue not mine. I've made it very clear to him that's how I feel. I thought you knew that?'

'I do. It's just that he's a fit, able-bodied man – rich, too. You'd be much better off with him than with me. I'm only going to hold you back.'

I grab hold of the steering wheel and bang my head against it a couple of times, but I've forgotten that the horn is in the centre of the wheel so it beeps a couple of times too.

Jack and I both laugh.

'That's more like it,' I say, taking hold of his hand. 'Jack, you know how much I care for you. I've told you, haven't I?'

Jack nods. 'But—'

'No buts,' I say, putting my finger on his lips. 'I care about *you*, Jack! Not about your ability to run a marathon or sprint up a flight of stairs. I don't want your legs. I want you! Why can't you see that?'

Jack takes hold of my other hand and pulls it gently away from his mouth so he's now holding on to both of my hands.

'I don't deserve you,' he whispers. 'I really don't.'

'Yes, you do,' I tell him. 'Even if I am quite the catch!' I lean in to him and we kiss, and as always when I kiss Jack in that moment I forget everything else that's going on around us. On this occasion, however, the fact that we're sitting in the middle of a petrol station doesn't fade out for too long as a car behind us toots its horn.

I pull away from Jack and turn towards the car behind us. 'All right!' I call through the open window. 'Some of us are having a romantic moment here!'

'Get a room then, love!' the driver calls back.

'Oh, I intend to,' I tell him, as I start the engine again. 'Don't you worry!'

314

I pull out into the traffic again, and I glance at Jack. I don't think I've ever seen him smile quite so much as he is right now.

'Hi, again,' I say to Susan, as we stand on her daughter's door-step waiting to go inside.

'Hello, Kate. Hi, Jack,' Susan says, standing back to let us pass. 'Thank you for coming. We're just through here.'

We follow her through the hallway of the Victorian terrace house towards a living room at the back.

'Now, I can't guarantee this is going to help,' Susan says, stopping just short of the entrance. 'Like I've warned you before, Mom can be . . . *difficult* to communicate with on her best days.'

'We can only try,' I say gently.

Susan nods, and we follow her into the room.

Sunlight streams through two tall French windows at the end of a large bright sitting room. It's furnished in a comfortable yet modern style and dotted about with artistic touches. A large sofa and two armchairs bathe in the natural light, and sitting in one of the chairs is a young woman, and in the other a much older one.

I pause as we enter the room. I knew coming here today and meeting the Maggie from our pictures for the first time was going to be slightly odd, but what I hadn't banked on was also seeing someone who looked just like her.

Susan's daughter stands up to greet us. It's truly amazing – she looks exactly how I'd imagined Maggie would when she'd grown up. She has the same eyes, the same pale complexion and the same jet black hair that our Maggie had so often tied into pigtails, but that this Maggie has pinned up into a loose bun.

'Hi, I'm Maggie,' she says, coming over to shake our hands. 'Thank you so much for coming today. This is my grandmother . . . What do you wish to be called today, Granny?' she asks in a clear voice.

The older woman, who doesn't appear to have even noticed us as we enter the room, stares up with confusion at her granddaughter.

'We have visitors, Granny,' young Maggie says again. 'Would you like to be called Peggy or Maggie today? She changes her mind on an almost daily basis,' she explains to us. 'Don't you, Granny?'

The old woman turns towards us now, but she doesn't say anything. She just looks intently at us with the same eyes that her granddaughter has – first at me, and then at Jack.

'You're in a wheelchair,' she says. 'I was in a wheel-chair once.'

'Yes, I know,' Jack says, pushing himself over towards her.

'Your chair is a lot fancier than mine was. I had to be pushed around by my mother, and that wasn't fun for either of us.' She grins at Jack.

'I can imagine,' Jack says. 'It's bad enough having to push myself about.'

This is progress already,' Susan whispers to me. 'She doesn't usually say anything to strangers.'

'My name is Maggie,' this older Maggie says, making her choice for the day and she holds her hand out to Jack. 'What's yours?'

'I'm Jack,' Jack answers, taking her delicate hand in his strong one, 'and this is Kate.' He gestures to me, and I move forwards, but Maggie only has eyes for Jack right now.

'You were a soldier,' Maggie says, as a statement rather than a question.

'Yes, I was. How do you know?'

Maggie points to one of Jack's tattoos peeking out from the sleeve of his T-shirt. 'Military.'

'That's right, it is.'

'My father was in the army,' Maggie says. 'The US Army ... maybe you knew him?'

'No, I don't think so,' Jack says diplomatically, 'I was in the British Army.'

Maggie nods. 'Yes, that would make sense. Were you at Normandy for the landings? My father was at Omaha. He was injured but he survived.'

Jack shakes his head. 'No, that was a bit before my time, I'm afraid.'

Maggie seems to accept this and nods again.

'Mom, these nice people have come to talk to you today about when you used to live in St Felix with your mother and Arty,' Susan says gently. 'Do you remember?'

'Of course I remember, girl. I'm not infirm, even though you all treat me as though I am most of the time.'

Susan turns to me and grimaces. 'Good luck.'

I sit down in the armchair next to Maggie, so she is now in between Jack and me.

'Who are you?' Maggie asks.

'I'm Kate,' I say. 'Pleased to meet you, Maggie.'

I hold out my hand but Maggie turns towards Jack. 'Is this your sweetheart?' she asks.

'Yes,' Jack says smiling at me, and I feel my cheeks flush. 'She is.'

'Pity,' Maggie says. 'Not often a handsome soldier comes to visit me.'

I nod encouragingly at Jack. It was obvious he was going to get further with Maggie than I was.

'Maggie,' Jack says softly. 'We wanted to talk to you about Freddie.'

Maggie's slightly vacant expression suddenly sharpens. 'Did you know him?' she asks immediately.

'Sort of,' Jack says. 'We know that you used to paint with him.'

'I did,' Maggie says in a forlorn voice. 'But then he left me, like everyone leaves me eventually – my father, then Freddie, then my mother, then Arty, then Susan. They all go eventually.'

'Mom, I'm not dead,' Susan protests.

'Might as well be living with the Yanks. My father was a Yank,' she tells Jack again. 'He was in the army, you know?'

'Yes, I know,' Jack says gently. 'We were wondering though whether you and Arty ever found out what happened to Freddie's paintings? They went missing, didn't they?'

Maggie shakes her head sadly. 'No, Arty searched and searched for them, but he never found them.'

'Did he have any idea where they went?' Jack asks. 'Any clues?'

Maggie again shakes her head. 'No, they just disappeared, and with it Freddie's name. No one remembers him now. Only me. He was a great painter, you know, and a lovely, lovely man.'

Maggie looks so desolate now that I'm starting to feel bad we ever came here and disturbed this old lady's memories.

'Did you know him?' she asks Jack again. 'Freddie?'

Jack shakes his head. 'No, sadly not, but we've heard a lot about him and we wanted to help find his lost paintings. We knew you knew him and we hoped that you might be able to help us.'

'Mom, if this is too upsetting for you, then Jack and Kate can go?' Susan asks, looking with concern at her mother.

'No!' Maggie says in a stern voice. 'I don't have much left

that's mine these days, but I do have my memories. You can't take those away from me.'

'No one wants to take your memories away from you, Granny,' her granddaughter says gently. 'No one can or wants to do that.'

'Not now I have them hidden in my room, you can't!' Maggie says cryptically. She nods and folds her arms across her chest.

'You're getting confused again, Granny. Your memories are kept up here.' She points to her head, and then her heart. 'And here.'

I look at Jack. *Exactly like Clara, her great-grandmother, had before her . . .*

'No, you silly girl!' Maggie says crossly. 'I mean my real memories. I have my box.'

Susan looks at the younger Maggie and mouths silently, 'What box?'

Her daughter shrugs and shakes her head.

'You see,' Maggie says, patting Jack on the hand and grinning. 'They think they know everything about me, but they don't.'

'What are you talking about, Mom?' Susan asks. 'What box?'

'If you'd care to go to my room, Susan, you'll find a tin box hidden under my bed. Please bring it back here to me immediately.'

Susan, looking puzzled, does as she's asked, while her mother sits back in her chair with her hands in her lap and patiently waits for her daughter to return.

'Would anyone like some tea?' Maggie's granddaughter asks. 'I meant to ask you when you came in, but completely forgot. I'm so sorry.'

'Tea!' Her grandmother snorts. 'These people haven't come here to drink tea. They're professionals doing an important job.'

I would have quite liked a cup of tea, but now I don't dare say anything.

'I'll put the kettle on anyway, Granny. Professionals or not.' Her granddaughter smiles at us. 'They still get thirsty.'

Maggie shakes her head as the young woman disappears into the kitchen. 'They have no idea,' she says, addressing me for the first time. 'They think I'm completely doolally. I'm not, of course, I'm just a little forgetful sometimes.'

I nod.

'I don't forget the important things though – the things that matter. Did you know my mother?' she asks me. 'You remind me of her.'

'Not really, no ... but I've heard she was a fine lady.'

'She was. Very fine. She liked to sew, you know?'

'Yes, I know.'

'She made clothes at first, then she got more adventurous when the sixties came and began to stitch felts with her machine. She embroidered them on to skirts and dresses, and then eventually started to create her own pictures with them. Arty would paint and she would sew. We were quite the artistic family. Did you know I nearly went to art college? I wasn't too shabby ... But then I had Susan and all that was forgotten about.'

'That happens sometimes when children come along,' I tell her knowingly. 'Your dreams get pushed aside.'

'They do indeed.'

'Is this what you're talking about?' Susan asks, coming back into the room clutching a tin box about the size of a large biscuit tin.

'Yes, that's the one,' Maggie says, taking it from her. 'You didn't know I had this, did you?' she says cunningly to Susan. 'I

320

smuggled it in with the few things I was allowed to keep from *my* house before you sold them all off.'

'*Mom*, now you know that's not how it was,' Susan says, shaking her head. 'Stop exaggerating.'

'That's how it felt,' Maggie says, clutching the box tightly to her chest, 'but you didn't get this one, did you? No, I made sure of that.'

'Right, that's the kettle on,' her granddaughter says, coming back into the room. 'Oh, you found it then? What's inside, Granny?'

Maggie looks conspiratorially around at all of us, as if she's weighing up whether she can trust us with the contents of her precious box. 'Inside here are my memories,' she says quietly. 'When I can't remember, I look in here and it's all there for me so I don't have to try too hard.'

She carefully prises open the lid of the tin, and lifts from it a few photos.

'Arty took lots of photos when I was young,' she says. 'He bought a camera and never stopped using the thing. He took photos of everything – even had his own dark room set up in the big house so he could develop them, he took that many. It drove my mother mad to always find him clicking away with his little Brownie, but his hobby has turned out to be my saviour.'

She turns one of the black and white photos around towards us and I recognise Clara immediately, likely wearing one of her own creations – a flowery dress with a full skirt. She's standing beside a bicycle and there's a picnic basket at her feet.

'I couldn't remember this day at all until I saw this photograph,' Maggie says, 'but it was taken on my sixteenth birthday. The three of us rode along to the next town and had a picnic on the beach there ... It was glorious weather.' She looks through the photos on her lap. 'Here,' she says, holding a photo up to us again. 'This is me. You'd never have known I was in a wheel-chair a few years before.'

We all look at the photo of a pretty girl with long dark hair cascading down her shoulders. She looks incredibly happy as she smiles at the camera.

'I didn't know you had all these photos, Mom,' Susan says, moving towards her. 'How wonderful.'

Maggie holds up her hand. 'No, Susan, you can look later. Now it's time for my soldier friend to look at some photos with me.'

She rifles around in her tin again.

'Here,' she says, pulling out another black and white photo. 'This is Freddie.'

Jack takes the photo from her. 'It is indeed,' he says, 'taken outside his cottage. Can Kate take a look too?'

Maggie nods, so Jack passes me the photo and I see Freddie wearing a similar outfit to one we'd seen him in, standing with his hands in his pockets and looking suspiciously at Arty behind the lens. It was strange – when he'd appeared to us before he'd been in colour and had seemed so real and full of life. Now in black and white Freddie appeared much more removed and from a distant age.

'Another,' Maggie says, handing the next picture to Jack. 'Me painting with Freddie in his cottage.'

Jack examines the photo, then passes it to me. It was almost the same as the scene we'd witnessed together previously – Maggie sat at a table painting next to Freddie.

'This one is Freddie in full flow,' Maggie says. 'He's nearly finished his painting in this one.'

This time we look at a photo of Freddie standing next to a

painting that is propped up on an easel – likely one of Arty's. He has a brush in one hand and oil paint in the other.

'Arty gave him that easel,' Maggie says, 'because he didn't have one of his own.'

Maggie continues to pull out photo after photo of Freddie and herself in his little cottage painting, drawing and, most of all, smiling.

'It haunts me to this day that someone has stolen this kind, lovely man's paintings,' Maggie says, gazing at the photos now laid out on the coffee table in front of her. 'People must know what happened to them. They simply must.'

To my dismay, silent tears begin to roll down her face into the tin box still sitting on her lap.

Her granddaughter shoots forwards with a box of tissues, and Susan rushes to her mother's side.

'I think that's enough memories for today,' she says, looking with concern at Jack and me as she puts a comforting arm around her mother's shoulders. 'Perhaps you should go.'

'No!' Maggie cries, pushing both her daughter and granddaughter away. 'No, I want to know if they can help me find the person who took all Freddie's paintings.'

Jack looks at me and nods.

'Maggie,' I say quietly but firmly, taking in the images in front of us. 'If you lend us these photos for a little while, *and* the Wilfred Jones original I noticed hanging in the hall when we came in, then I think we might not only be able to recover *all* of Freddie's paintings but we'll at last also be able to give him the recognition he truly deserves.'

Thirty-six

One month later ...

I watch the bride and groom spin around on the dancefloor looking lovingly into each other's eyes and I smile.

Weddings are always such a joyful time full of thoughts and expectations for the future, and tonight was no exception.

Amber from the flower shop and Woody our local policeman had been married earlier today in St Felix, and along with their guests that joined them inside our local church, a second congregation had stood outside and waited for the happy couple to emerge so they could wish them well.

Woody was a very popular figure in St Felix – a relaxed friendly chap who enjoyed the simple pleasures of life, and Amber was well known not only in the town but far beyond for the special bouquets of flowers that she created alongside Poppy.

I, along with Molly, Anita and Sebastian, have been invited to their evening reception which is being held in one of the larger local hotels. It's here some of us sit at a table alongside

Jack, who I had brought as my plus one, watching the married couple take their first dance together.

'Cute pair,' Jack says, as we watch Amber and Woody sway from side to side with their arms around each other.

'Yes, they are,' I reply, turning my gaze to Jack instead. 'It sounds like it was a lovely wedding from what I've heard. They had a wonderful day for it.' The weather had behaved itself with the sun shining down on all concerned, allowing their day to be bathed in light as well as love.

Jack takes hold of my hand. 'Thanks for inviting me. Weddings aren't usually my thing, but I've enjoyed being here tonight with your friends – they're a good bunch.'

'They are, aren't they?' I reply, smiling at them. 'I'm very lucky to have all of you in my life.'

Jack squeezes my hand. 'I'm sure we all feel the same way about you.'

I lean across and kiss him.

'*Steady on!*' I hear Sebastian call across the table, but I don't care. Jack and I are in a proper relationship now, and I've never been happier.

'Sorry to interrupt you two love birds,' the familiar voice of Ben says above us, 'but have you seen Molly lately?'

To my enormous relief Ben has been Molly's plus one tonight. I am so pleased that Chesney isn't in the picture any more. Even though I haven't seen or heard much of him over the last few weeks I have the impression he is still hanging around Molly, and I fervently wish he'd just move on and let her go. I'd recently heard some bad things about him, and I was grateful that Molly had broken up with him when she had.

'No, actually, I haven't,' I answer, looking around. 'She said a while ago she was popping out for some air.'

'Don't worry,' Ben says in his usual calm manner, 'I'll go look for her.'

'Do you think I should go too?' I ask Jack as he walks away.

Jack shakes his head. 'No, Ben will find her. Don't worry.'

I sit back in my chair doing exactly the opposite of that, but luckily after a minute or two of imagining all the bad things that might have happened another familiar voice distracts me from my anxious thoughts.

'Kate?'

'Julian! Hi! I didn't know you were invited tonight?'

'I'm not, I popped in because Molly said you were in here.'

'You've seen her?'

Julian looks confused. 'Er ... yes, she was sitting on the wall outside the hotel with some other young people.'

'Oh right,' *Please don't let it be Chesney,* I pray.

'I wondered if I could have a word?' Julian says. 'In private.'

I glance at Jack. 'Go on,' he says amiably. 'It's fine.'

'I'll be back in a few minutes,' I tell him, kissing him on the cheek.

I follow Julian outside to a pretty garden at the back of the hotel. The evening air is cool, which makes a nice change from the warmth and stuffiness of the reception hall.

We find a bench and sit down in the fast fading light of the evening sun.

'What's up?' I ask.

'I'm leaving St Felix,' Julian says. 'Early tomorrow morning, and I wanted to speak with you before I left.'

'You're leaving ... but why? Everything is almost sorted. You can't go now, Julian.'

*

After we'd left Maggie, Susan and her daughter at their home in Penzance, and given them reassurance and guarantees that we weren't simply absconding with Maggie's photos and the Wilfred Jones original, events had started moving pretty quickly. I'd gone to Julian first and told him what Maggie had revealed, and showed him both the photos and the painting. His reactions had been mixed. Shock had come first, then sorrow – there had even been a few tears before the shame at what his father had done had finally kicked in – followed by a steely resolve to put right the wrong.

'There is the possibility that your father didn't actually steal the paintings,' I'd told him to try to soften the blow a little. 'He might simply have come across them somewhere, or bought them from the real thief.'

'Come on, Kate,' Julian had said, 'You don't really believe that? My father was in St Felix at the time – we know that – and then he left for America shortly after. It doesn't take a genius to work out why. He saw an opportunity to use someone who had some talent to try to further his own career, and it worked.'

'But why would he go back years later and buy Freddie's, I mean Wilfred's, old cottage? Surely he wouldn't want to link himself to it?'

'Guilt, perhaps? Maybe the old codger did have some morals after all?'

'Perhaps he did. I mean it, Julian,' I say, when he pulls a face. 'Maybe he felt remorse for what he'd done, bought the cottage and decided to furnish it with prints of Wilfred's pictures. No one else would know why, but he would know that copies of the paintings had been returned to where they were originally created?'

'I appreciate you trying to make me feel better, Kate,' Julian says, 'but really you don't have to. I knew the man, remember?

He was quite capable of doing this and having no remorse whatsoever. Have no illusions otherwise.'

Julian, Jack and I had all then travelled to London to speak first with a solicitor and then an art expert who Julian knew and trusted, and from that moment on things had snowballed.

As Jack and I had hoped Maggie's photos were indeed enough evidence to prove that Winston James was not the creator of the majority of paintings that had been attributed to him. The photos not only showed Wilfred Jones in the process of creating some of his now well-known paintings, but they clearly showed many of his other works hanging behind him on his cottage walls that were in various stages of completion. This and Maggie's original painting, which Freddie had given her and she had treasured all these years, along with her written testimony, were going to be enough to discredit Winston James and allow instead Wilfred Jones's story to be told, so that he would be recognised not only by the global art community but also by the town where he'd lived all his life.

Something I hadn't expected, but which had happened pretty quickly, was media interest in the story, and I had had to rapidly become adept at handling press interviews and being filmed for both local and even national news. Luckily, most of the press weren't really interested in Julian and the company – all they wanted to know about was how I'd managed to play detective and solve this cover-up.

Jack had stayed well and truly in the background, but he'd been invaluable in helping me keep everything on track, as had Julian, who similarly had stayed out of the way, for obvious reasons.

Not surprisingly, there had been police interest, but thankfully after their initial investigations they were satisfied that

Julian had had no knowledge of any theft by his father or of his passing off the work as his own. Julian now had a very good lawyer who was working with him to sort out the mess this had made of his father's company, but he seemed confident that everything would be resolved to everyone's satisfaction.

In addition, Julian had helped us put in place our plans for the new Wilfred Jones Society in St Felix. Wilfred had no living relatives, so no one had stepped forward to claim what was now his Estate.

'And that is exactly why I'm leaving,' Julian says as we sit together in the hotel gardens. 'Everything is finished for me here – there's nothing more for me to do. You and Jack have got this covered, my usefulness has come to an end. In fact, having me around could cause you problems if anyone discovered I was still involved in the new society. All links to my father need to be removed from this new venture to give it the clean start it truly deserves.'

'But you've helped us so much, Julian,' I tell him. 'Don't go now before the new gallery has come to fruition.'

'I'm afraid I must. I'm going to use some of my mother's legacy to take me on a little trip.'

'A trip – to where?'

'Everywhere. I am going to see the world, Kate. You've shown me that even somewhere as small as St Felix contains so many types of people and new experiences to be had. If I can find all that here, imagine what I'll discover around the world! I'd never even thought about what a sheltered life I'd led until I came here and met you. A privileged life, yes, but a sheltered one as a result. You've opened up my eyes, Kate, and I'll always be grateful to you.'

How odd life is, I think, as I hug Julian. If you'd told me a few months ago when I'd first met him that I'd be hugging him and genuinely wishing him well, I'd have laughed in your face. Julian had seemed like a ridiculously foolish man, full of himself and his position, but time and some very strange circumstances had proved otherwise.

'You're sure you can't stay and see the gallery come to life?' I ask again. 'I know it's going to be a while yet before the cottage is ready, but it seems right you should be there. After all, it did belong to you.'

Julian had offered us Freddie's old cottage so it could be turned into the Wilfred Jones Gallery – a place where all his paintings, along with duplicates of Maggie's photos showing the paintings in progress, could be displayed for all to see. It was a little complicated currently because of the ongoing issues with the Winston James Estate, but we had high hopes that the gallery would be able to open in the near future.

Julian shakes his head. 'No, I won't ... but maybe you could email me some photos? I believe they have wi-fi in the remotest of places these days!'

'I'd be happy to, as long as you send me photos of your travels in return.'

'I'd be more than happy to keep in touch with you, Kate. That goes without saying.'

'I'm almost jealous of you,' I tell him. 'Going off and travelling the world while the rest of us are left here in one of the remotest parts of Cornwall. It's hardly the Amazon rainforest, is it?'

'You wouldn't have it any other way,' Julian says, smiling at me. 'You love it here. And St Felix loves you. That's why I've got a surprise for you.'

'Really? What?'

'It wouldn't be a surprise if I told you, would it? Now, don't ask me any more questions, you'll find out in a few days, all right?'

I pull a huffy expression, but then I grin. 'Okay then, you win, I suppose, but now you've got me wondering.'

'You'll like it. I guarantee that,' he says. 'Just promise me you'll accept it.'

'Why wouldn't I accept it?' I ask, puzzled all the more.

'Kate, just promise?'

I nod. 'Sure. I promise.'

'Excellent. Now I must go. Goodbye, my dear Kate, and thank you once again.'

'No, thank you, Julian, for making everything so easy for us.'

'It's been my pleasure,' he says, standing up. 'Really it has. You've freed me from my self-imposed prison, and I can never thank you enough.' We hug again and then I watch Julian walk along a path that leads from the garden out to the hotel car park. He waves one last time and he's gone.

I sigh. I was going to miss Julian and his funny ways. He'd really been so understanding about his father, and had made everything so stress-free with regard to Freddie being finally acknowledged. It was a real shame he wouldn't be here to see the paintings returned to where they truly belonged.

Still pondering what his surprise might be, I'm about to walk back inside the hotel when I hear raised voices from around the corner. I walk in the direction of the noise, but stop when I see what I think are a group of young guests arguing.

'None of my business,' I think, deciding I'll leave them be. It wouldn't be the first wedding to host a family quarrel as part of its celebrations. I'm about to turn away when I notice that the back view of one of the people looks familiar. It's Ben.

I'm about to move forwards again when I hear what he's saying.

'Say that again?' he says to another boy in a calm yet forceful tone.

'Your dad is a useless cripple,' the same boy says in a sneering voice. 'And you are a gay wanker.'

I gasp, and my hand flies automatically to my mouth, but the group is far enough away not to hear me.

Ben just nods his head slowly, then he steps forwards equally as slowly and stands in front of the boy, towering over him. 'I should punch you for that,' he says quietly, 'but then I'd be lowering myself to your standards, which I don't particularly wish to do, so I will politely request that you take that back.'

'Take what back?' the boy, who I can now clearly see is Chesney, jeers mockingly. 'It's the truth, ain't it?'

There's a horrible pause, and I think for a moment that Ben is actually going to punch him. *I* want to punch Chesney, so how Ben is stopping himself I have no idea.

'Come on, Molly,' he says calmly. 'Shall we go back inside?'

To my horror, I suddenly realise that Molly is also one of the people standing in the small group, and I have to stop myself from rushing forwards and immediately getting involved.

'Molly don't wanna go with you, you *queer*!' Chesney taunts. 'Do ya, Molls? She's my girlfriend, ain't ya, babe?'

Molly is silent for what seems like for ever, but what is in fact likely only a few seconds, before she sidles up in front of Chesney and says in a low, and if it wasn't my daughter I was listening to, I'd say seductive voice, '*Chesney?*'

'Yeah, babe,' Chesney says, glancing away from Molly to grin at Ben triumphantly.

'I am no longer *your* girlfriend,' Molly now speaks in a loud and commanding voice so everyone can hear. 'I broke up with you ages ago, which you would know if you weren't so thick, so the *last* thing I want to do is go anywhere with *you*, you homophobic Neanderthal!'

I gasp again, but this time I don't bother to cover my mouth because my hand is tightly gripped around a drainpipe to prevent me from dashing forwards and rescuing my daughter.

Chesney's face darkens, and he steps forward and grabs Molly. 'You little bitch!' he murmurs, 'I'll teach you.'

Ben steps forwards also, but he's too late. In a deft move Molly manages to knock Chesney's hands away, then she elbows him in the stomach so he crumples to the ground.

'Those self-defence lessons at school came in handy! Shame you were never there, Chesney, or you might have learnt something,' she says, straightening her top and brushing her hands over her jeans. Then she walks victoriously over to Ben and links her arm through his.

'Come on, big bro,' she says happily, looking up at him. 'Let's go back to the party.'

Quickly I tuck myself back around the corner so Molly and Ben don't see me as they walk into the hotel together arm in arm.

As I try to get my shallow breathing back under control before I join them again, I feel prouder of my little girl than I ever have.

She's all grown up.

Thirty-seven

Six months later ...

St Felix ~ September 1959

Clara and Arty emerge from the little St Felix church radiating happiness and love.

Clara is a beautiful bride, wearing one of her own creations – a pale pink dress, tightly nipped in at the waist, with a co-ordinating pale pink cropped jacket. She simply oozes happiness as she holds tightly on to the arm of her new husband, who today looks incredibly smart in his brand new suit and tie – a long way from his usual attire of a loose painting smock and paint-splattered trousers.

Maggie emerges behind them wearing a flowery dress in the same shade of pink as her mother, looking every inch the pretty yet proud bridesmaid after witnessing her two favourite people in the world declaring their intention to spend the rest of their lives together.

As they stand there having their photograph taken with

their friends and family, the delighted group couldn't contrast more with the scene taking place in the graveyard at the back of the church.

A man stands in front of a shiny new gravestone looking sombrely down at it. He is well dressed, wearing expensive shiny shoes and a tailored suit that definitely haven't been bought in the local gentlemen's outfitter but rather from somewhere abroad.

'I'm sorry,' he says to the gravestone. 'Truly I am.'

He glances around to see if anyone is watching him, but there's no one about, only the distant hum of people chattering excitedly, and the sound of the church bells ringing out to signal the end of the wedding he'd realised with horror was taking place today.

He couldn't change his plans though. He wasn't here in St Felix for long enough to do that – it was a flying visit, literally. He was travelling back to America tomorrow having managed at great expense to get a seat on one of the new transatlantic flights from London to New York. It was far more expensive than the boat, but so much quicker, and what he didn't have these days was time. His recent success across the Atlantic was making sure of that.

However, he had needed to visit this spot today to pay his respects, and to make sure that the gravestone he'd anonymously paid for had been properly created and laid. He'd been extremely pleased to find that it had been, and that it was everything he had hoped it would be. Even though this slightly extravagant stone would now permanently mark the last resting place of the man who was helping him to fame and fortune, it didn't help to ease his sense of guilt. No monetary gift could ever do that.

'I'm sorry, Freddie,' the man says again, as a tear rolls down his cheek. 'Really, I am. You were, and always will be, the better man. I shouldn't have done what I did. I saw a chance and took it without thinking. I never knew it would take off like it has. I thought perhaps your paintings might get me noticed a bit more and get my own paintings recognised, but I should have known they would only want your work. Your innocent creations, untouched by greed – something I could never hope to achieve. Perhaps one day someone will know the truth. They will know what a genius you were, and what a cowardly, sad individual I am. Until that time I can only offer you my most sincere apologies again, and hope that this memorial and your cottage, which I intend to buy when it comes up for sale and decorate as a shrine to you, goes just a tiny way to making it up to you.' The images fade away as they always do, leaving us with a painting of a church and in front of that a piece of embroidered felt in the shape of a gravestone.

'Well, that was a mixture of emotions,' I say to Jack, as we sit back like we always do to discuss our latest dip into St Felix's always colourful and interesting past. It had been such a long time since the easel and the sewing machine had produced anything for us we'd begun to wonder if we were going to receive any more of their unique creations. 'How lovely to see Clara and Arty on their wedding day, but I don't know how I feel about seeing Winston James at Freddie's grave.'

'How do you know it was Winston?' Jack asks. 'We're just assuming that was him.'

'I've seen a photo of him – I think it was at the gallery with his paintings ... well, Freddie's paintings. Didn't you see it when we went there?'

'Oh yeah, I thought the guy looked familiar, but I couldn't

place him. He was a lot younger there,' he gestures to the painting, 'than in the photo, but you can see the resemblance to Julian.'

'Yes, you can. Poor Julian. I tried to tell him his father might have had some remorse for his actions, but he wouldn't have it. I can't really tell him I was right, can I – how would I know?'

'That was the most difficult thing with all of this,' Jack says, looking at the easel again. 'Trying to cover up how we came to know so much about Freddie, Maggie, Arty and Clara. I think we managed to make our story sound convincing, don't you?'

'I don't think anyone really cared how we knew once we proved we were right. Everyone was just happy that justice had been done and that Freddie's lost paintings had been found.'

'Maggie's face was amazing when we told her, wasn't it?' Jack says wistfully. 'I can still see her look of complete euphoria now.'

'And then suddenly she was at peace. You could see the years simply roll off her. It was obviously something she'd carried with her her whole life. I can't wait for her to see the gallery when it opens – it will be the perfect end to this story.'

'Yes, it will. I still find it odd though,' Jack says, 'that we've found ourselves involved in all this.'

'Perhaps we'll never know why?' I shrug. 'But does it really matter now? We've done a great thing with the help of an antique sewing machine and a battered old easel.'

'Why does yours get to be antique and mine battered and old?' Jack asks, smiling. 'I think they've played their part equally.'

'They have, maybe we should reunite them sometime so they can say hello again.'

'Say hello again,' Jack scoffs. 'You're talking like they're real now.'

'They're hardly normal, are they?'

'That's true. Do you think they'd like to be reunited? I mean permanently . . .'

I look at Jack questioningly. Was he saying what I thought he was?

'Yes, Kate, I'm asking if you'd like to move in together? I know we haven't known each other all that long but—'

'Yes,' I say quickly, before he changes his mind. 'Yes, Jack, I would. Very much.'

Jack's smile broadens even further, and we're about to lean in for a kiss when I turn my head suddenly so Jack ends up kissing my cheek.

'Hey!' I say, staring at the easel. 'How did that happen?'

'What?' Jack asks, following my gaze. 'What the hell!'

The easel that until a moment ago had held a painting of a church now displays a painting of a house standing elegantly on top of a hill, and my gravestone-shaped felt is now a door. A blue door.

'It's the house,' I whisper excitedly, as we both stare at the easel in amazement. 'The house that Clara, Arty and Maggie used to live in. It's the house with the blue door, Jack!'

'Put it together,' Jack instructs, in a much calmer voice than mine. 'The door, I mean. Match it up to the one on the painting.'

I do as he says, carefully matching up the two creations, and as always happens the colours immediately start swirling together to form a new moving image that slowly comes into focus.

As we watch the images a car passes along the road in front of the house, followed by a man riding a bicycle. He's wearing a helmet and tight, brightly-coloured Lycra.

'It's not the fifties!' I hiss at Jack. 'It can't be. It looks like now!'

Jack is silent as we enter this new modern-day world.

A woman carrying a reusable shopping bag and talking on a mobile phone walks through the gate. She has her back to us so we can't see her face, but she's tall and has long dark hair; an elderly golden Labrador poddles slowly behind her.

She ends the call, walks up to the front door and pulls a key from her pocket, but as she's about to put it in the door it swings open and a man greets her with a loving smile. As the woman enters she has to bend down to kiss him because he's in a wheelchair.

'It's us,' I whisper so quietly I can barely hear myself. 'It's us, Jack, and that's Barney following me through the door.'

I feel Jack's hand take mine as we continue to watch ourselves.

The woman, who I can clearly see is me now she's turned around, suddenly smiles at someone coming up the path behind her and we quickly recognise slightly older versions of Molly and Ben messing about as they walk towards the house, playfully pushing and nudging each other like siblings often do. They have a second dog on a lead – this time it's a chocolate Labrador puppy.

Then, just as I'm desperate to see more of what can only be our future selves, the door of the house closes behind them and the picture begins to fade …

'No!' I call out. 'No, I want to see more.' I turn to Jack expecting him to say something similar, but instead I see his broken face and a tear rolling down his cheek.

'You still want me in the future then?' Jack says, more as an observation than a question. 'You don't get tired of being with me.' He wipes the stray tear away.

'Of course I want you! Why would you even think I wouldn't want to be with you? I love you, Jack. You know I do.'

'I love you too, Kate. More than you know.'

As we try to kiss my phone begins to ring in my bag. 'Leave it,' I say, leaning forwards again to Jack. 'It won't be important.'

But as soon as the phone rings off, it starts again.

'Don't worry, they'll leave a message this time if it's important,' I say.

The third time it rings Jack insists I answer. 'You'd better get it, Kate. It sounds urgent.'

Reluctantly I lean over and reach into my bag but as I suspect it's an unknown number. Of all the times to get a junk call.

'Yes!' I snap aggressively into the phone. 'Who is this?'

'Kate,' a distant voice says. 'Kate, is that you?'

'Julian!' I cry, 'Where are you? You sound like you're in the middle of nowhere.'

'Sorry . . . line isn't great here . . . breaking up quite a lot . . . you like your surprise?'

'What surprise?' I ask.

' . . . you get the email?'

'What email?' I say. 'What email, Julian? I'm losing you . . . *Julian, can you hear me?*' I shout into the phone.

'Yes, I'm still . . . just! We'd better make it quick. I might . . . at any moment. You should have got an email, Kate, from . . . solicitor. I'm giving you the house. The one you liked in St Felix . . . house on the hill with the blue door . . . all yours.'

'What do you mean all mine? How?'

' . . . *bought it, Kate!*' Julian is now shouting too. 'Agreed . . .

340

really good price with ... Susan and ... your Maggie ... wanted you to have it ... bought it with Mother's money ... ago ... now I'm giving it to you to live in ... to say thank you.'

'*No, Julian, you can't!*' I cry. 'I can't let you. If you bought it, it's yours.'

'Sorry, Kate ... losing you,' Julian says, sounding fainter by the moment. ' ... solicitor will be in touch ... what Maggie wanted, and you *promised* me, remember?'

The line goes dead.

I stare at Jack. He looks as mystified as I feel right now.

'Julian is giving us the house,' I say slowly, so both Jack and I can try to take this all in. The last few minutes have been complete madness.

'What house?' Jack asks.

'The house in the painting – the one with the blue door. It's ours.'

'How can he do that?'

'I think he said he agreed a good price with Susan and both he and Maggie want us to live there.'

'I was wondering how we were going to afford that house,' Jack says, grinning at me. 'I thought we would have to win the lottery or something!'

I smile and shake my head at him. Trust Jack to bring me back to reality.

I stare at the painting again, and I try moving the door back into place to make the images come to life once more. I wanted to see more of my future with Jack.

However, this time the images remain still.

'I think that's it,' Jack says, watching me. 'I think our time as guardians of these magical images has come to an end.'

'A very happy end,' I tell him, sitting down next to him

341

again and taking his hand, 'for everyone who's been created and crafted by one amazing little sewing machine . . .'

' . . . and one very clever easel,' Jack finishes for me.

'May their owners past and present be united together for ever.'

Acknowledgements

Hello, Dear Reader!

Thank you for choosing this book.

Whether it's your first or your eleventh book of mine, I do hope you've enjoyed it and it will encourage you to read more of my novels in the future.

I always love writing about St Felix and the people who live there, and I love that you enjoy it just as much as I do! I've returned to this magical Cornish town three times now, and I hope that I will be able to tell you lots more stories from there in the future.

But other than thanking you, lovely reader, I'd also like to thank a few other folk who have helped make this book what it is: Hannah Ferguson – my fantastic agent; Maddie West – my wonderful editor; the whole fabulous team at Sphere and Little, Brown including Clara Diaz, Tamsyn Berryman and my new editor Darcy Nicholson; my amazing family – Jim, Rosie, Tom and our two dogs Oscar and Sherlock. I couldn't do it without any of you.

I'd also like to send special posthumous thanks to the

St Ives artist Alfred Wallis, who the character of Freddie was inspired by, and whose real-life story gave me the idea for this book.

To all of you above, I send my love and thanks for all you do.

Ali xx